AMAZING™
STORIES

A 60 YEARS OF THE BEST SCIENCE FICTION

EDITED BY ISAAC ASIMOV & MARTIN H. GREENBERG

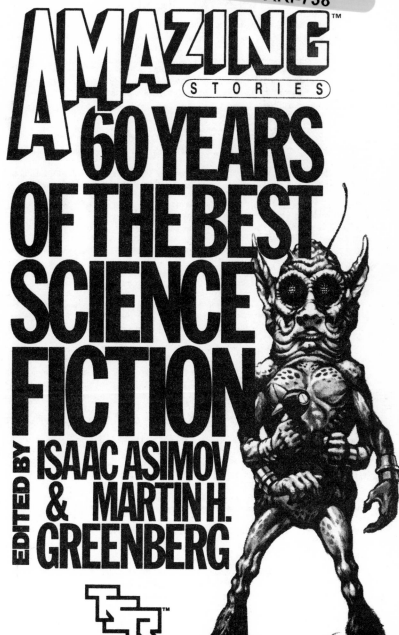

TSR™

TSR, Inc.

ACKNOWLEDGEMENTS

"Amazing Stories and I" - copyright ©1985 by Nightfall, Inc.

"The Revolt of the Pedestrians" - copyright 1928 by Experimenter Publishing Co.; copyright renewed by David H. Keller. Reprinted by permission of John P. Trevaskis, Jr.

"The Gostak and the Doshes" - copyright 1930 by Radio-Science Publications, Inc. Reprinted by arrangement with Forrest J Ackerman, 2495 Glendower Ave., Hollywood, CA 90027, on behalf of the heir.

"Pilgrimage" (originally titled "The Priestess Who Rebelled") - copyright 1939 by Ziff-Davis Publishing Co., copyright 1945 by Nelson Bond. Reprinted by permission of the author.

"The Strange Flight of Richard Clayton" - copyright 1939 by Ziff-Davis Publishing Co.; copyright 1957 by Robert Bloch. Reprinted by permission of Kirby McCauley, Ltd.

"I, Robot" - copyright 1939 by Ziff-Davis Publishing Co. Reprinted by permission of the agents for the author's estate, the Scott Meredith Literary Agency, Inc., 845 Third Ave., New York, NY 10022

"The Perfect Woman" - copyright 1954 by Ziff-Davis Publishing Co.; copyright renewed 1982 by Robert Sheckley. Reprinted by permission of Kirby McCauley, Ltd.

"Memento Homo" (originally titled "Death of a Spaceman") - copyright 1954 by Ziff-Davis Publishing Co.; copyright renewed ©1982 by Walter M. Miller, Jr. Reprinted by permission of Don Congdon Associates, Inc.

"What is This Thing Called Love?" (originally titled "Playboy and the Slime God") - copyright ©1961 by Ziff-Davis Publishing Co. Reprinted by permission of the author.

"Requiem" - copyright ©1962 by Ziff-Davis Publishing Co. Reprinted by permission of the agents for the author's estate, the Scott Meredith Literary Agency, Inc., 845 Third Ave., New York, NY 10022.

"Hang Head, Vandal!" - copyright ©1962 by Ziff-Davis Publishing Co.; by arrangement with Forrest J Ackerman, 2495 Glendower Ave., Hollywood, CA 90027.

"The Days of Perky Pat" - copyright ©1963 by Ziff-Davis Publishing Co. Reprinted by permission of the agents for the author's estate, the Scott Meredith Literary Agency, Inc., 845 Third Ave., New York, NY 10022.

"Drunkboat" - copyright ©1963 by Ziff-Davis Publishing Co. Reprinted by permission of the agents for the author's estate, the Scott Meredith Literary Agency, Inc., 845 Third Ave., New York, NY 10022.

"Semley's Necklace" - copyright ©1964, 1975 by Ursula K. Le Guin; reprinted by permission of the author and the author's agent, Virginia Kidd.

"There's No Vinism Like Chauvinism" - copyright ©1965 by Ziff-Davis Publishing Co.; reprinted by permission of the author.

"Calling Dr. Clockwork" - copyright ©1965 by Ziff-Davis Publishing Co. Reprinted by permission of the author.

"The Oogenesis of Bird City" - copyright ©1970 by Ultimate Publishing Co., Inc. Reprinted by permission of the Scott Meredith Literary Agency, Inc., 845 Third Ave., New York, NY 10022.

"The Man Who Walked Home" - copyright ©1972 by Ultimate Publishing Co., Inc. Reprinted by permission of the author and the author's agent, Virginia Kidd.

"Manikins" - copyright ©1976 by Ultimate Publishing Co., Inc. Reprinted by permission of Kirby McCauley, Ltd.

"In the Islands" - copyright ©1983 by TSR Hobbies, Inc. Reprinted by permission of the author.

Distributed to the book trade in the United States by Random House, Inc., and in Canada by Random House of Canada, Ltd.
Distributed in the United Kingdom by TSR UK, Ltd.
Distributed to the toy and hobby trade by regional distributors.

AMAZING is a registered trademark owned by TSR, Inc. and the AMAZING logo is a trademark owned by TSR, Inc.

First printing: July 1985   9 8 7 6 5 4 3 2 1
Printed in the United States of America
Library of Congress Catalog Card Number: 85-51055
ISBN: 0-88038-216-3

TSR, Inc.   TSR UK, Ltd
P.O. Box 756   The Mill, Rathmore Road
Lake Geneva, WI 53147   Cambridge CB1 4AD United Kingdom

C O N T E N T S

AMAZING STORIES AND I
by Isaac Asimov

I've had my own science-fiction magazine for eight years now—*Isaac Asimov's Science Fiction Magazine*. Then, too, all during the 1940s, I had a particular closeness to *Astounding Science Fiction* and its remarkable editor, John W. Campbell, Jr. What's more, since 1958 (twenty-seven years now), I've had a science essay in every issue of *The Magazine of Fantasy and Science Fiction*.

Why, then, am I so pleased to be co-editor of a historical survey of outstanding stories taken from none of those magazines I have just mentioned—but from *Amazing® Science Fiction Stories?*

The answer is that *Amazing Stories* has certain particular qualities that no other science-fiction magazine has, both with respect to science fiction itself and to me as an individual.

1. *Amazing Stories* is the pioneer, the trailblazer. There had been science fiction a hundred years before *Amazing Stories*, even by a reasonably narrow definition of the field; but earlier science fiction had been published in magazines as individual stories, long or short, at unpredictable intervals, and in surroundings that had nothing science-fictionish about them.

Hugo Gernsback, however, had made up his mind to publish a magazine that would contain nothing but science fiction and that would do so at regular monthly intervals. That was *Amazing Stories*; and its April 1926 issue was volume I, number 1, not for itself only but for magazine science fiction as a whole.

At first, *Amazing Stories* could exist only by reprinting stories of Poe, Verne, and Wells; but little by little it attracted youngsters who began to write science-fiction stories as best they could, and that made the future possible. It meant that a time would come when scores of writers of remarkable literary ability would spend their time specializing in science fiction. It meant best-selling science-fiction novels appearing regularly on the lists, and block-busting science-fiction epics filling the movie houses.

Some other magazine by some other entrepreneur might have done this eventually, but it was *Amazing Stories* and Gernsback that *did* do it.

2. *Amazing Stories* is still published today. It has had its lean times, and there were moments when observers wondered how it could possibly survive, but survive it did. Nor have there been significant gaps in its publishing history, though it has had to slip to bimonthly and even quarterly publication now and then. This means that there is a continuous stretch of sixty years of issues from which to choose stories. No other magazine covers such a gap of time or offers such an overview of changing fashions and styles—a true challenge for the anthologist.

3. From the personal standpoint, *Amazing Stories* was my own introduction to science fiction. In July 1929, when I was just nine and one-half years old, I noticed the August 1929 issue of *Amazing Stories* on the magazine stand in my father's candy

store. Although it was a well-understood rule (established by my father, whose word was unbreakable law in my family) that I was not to read any of the magazines he sold—for he considered them all substandard literature that would corrode my brain on contact—I was so attracted by the name and cover of the magazine that, when my father was taking his afternoon nap, I sneaked it off the rack.

The first story I read was "Barton's Island" by Harl Vincent. I don't remember a word of it now for I have never re-read it, but it made me know at once that somehow I had to continue reading science fiction. But how was I to do that in defiance of my father's ukase?

As it happened, Gernsback no longer controlled *Amazing Stories* and what I had picked up and read was the fourth post-Gernsback issue. Gernsback, however, was now publishing and editing a competing magazine named *Science Wonder Stories* and its third issue was also on my father's magazine rack. I found that and used the word "Science" as the lever with which to procure my father's permission to read those particular magazines. That was twice, then, that Gernsback helped make possible the Isaac Asimov that was to come.

4. *Amazing Stories* continued to fascinate and excite me. Much of the fiction it printed in the 1930s was wretched material by modern standards, but I asked nothing more in those early years. "The Adventures of Posi and Nega" by J. W. Skidmore (January 1934) and its sequels were, arguably, the worst science-fiction stories ever published; but I loved them. With slightly better reason, I loved "The Jameson Satellite" by Neil R. Jones (July 1931) and its sequels. There were fustian melodramas by S. P. Meek, such as "The Drums of Tapajos" (three parts, from November 1930), "Submicroscopic" (August 1931), and "Awlo of Ulm" (September 1931) that kept me breathing heavily. Add to these "The Human Pets of Mars" by Leslie F. Stone (October 1936) and "By Jove!" by Walter Rose (three parts, from February 1937).

I might also mention two stories that would hold up well even today: "Tumithak of the Corridors" (January 1932) and "Tumithak in Shawm" (June 1933). None of these stories are included in the anthology simply because some are too long, some too bad, and some both too long *and* too bad. But they kept me going and induced me, eventually, to try to write science fiction on my own.

5. By 1938, I was trying to *sell* my stories. I was eighteen and had developed sufficient acumen to be able to tell that *Astounding Science Fiction* under its new editor, John Campbell, was the best in the field; so I tried to sell stories to him. My first attempt came on June 21, 1938. I visited his office, handed him a story, and he rejected it at once. I submitted others, which he also rejected. Naturally, I sent the rejected material to other magazines.

It took precisely four months for me to sell my first story to a professional magazine (heavens! I'm approaching the golden anniversary of that golden date), but it was not to *Astounding*. It seems that the old *Amazing Stories* had given up the ghost at last but was instantly, and without the loss of an issue, reincarnated. Ziff-Davis was the new publisher and Raymond A. Palmer the new editor of the June 1938 issue. Their offices were in Chicago, so I couldn't make a personal visit. I used the mail. The third story I wrote was "Marooned Off Vesta;" and when Palmer saw it, he took it and announced the fact with a check for $64.00 (one cent a word) that reached me on October 21, 1938.

The story appeared in the March 1939 issue of *Amazing Stories*, which thus had the honor (if that's the word I'm looking for) of introducing me to the science-fiction readership. What's more, in the May 1939 issue, they published another story of mine, "The Weapon Too Dreadful to Use" (a story too dreadful to publish, actually).

I did not become an *Amazing Stories* regular, however, because about then I finally started selling my stories to *Astounding*. In addition, although the Ziff-Davis *Amazing Stories* was the most successful, financially, of any science-fiction magazine before or since, it achieved its success by playing up to the (how shall I put it?) dregs of the potential readership. (Notice that we have no stories in this anthology that were published in the issues between 1940 and 1953, inclusive.) Naturally, I put the magazine at the bottom of the list for submissions, and few of my stories got that far.

Just the same, I think it is fair to say that although John Campbell and *Astounding* were the making of me, for reasons that I have repeated over and over again in my various books, I can reasonably maintain that it was *Amazing Stories* that, in several different ways, gave me my start. And that is why I am delighted to be co-editing this anthology.

P.S. My own contribution to this anthology, "What is This Thing Called Love?", was originally called "Playboy and the Slime God" when it appeared in the March 1961 issue, because I was satirizing an article in *Playboy* that had, in its turn, satirized science fiction. I chose the newer name because it was not only less nauseating but much more appropriate, so I hope no one minds if I use the new title in this anthology.

David H. Keller, a practicing psychiatrist, was one of the most conceptually sophisticated of the first generation of science-fiction magazine contributors. Writing in an age when the Model T had just put America on wheels, he was perhaps the first to speculate on the long-range effects of automobiles on American culture. Keller was a steady contributor to Amazing Stories, *and to Hugo Gernsback's* Wonder Stories, *from 1928 into the late 1930s. This story was published in February, 1928.*

THE REVOLT OF THE PEDESTRIANS
by David H. Keller, M.D.

A young pedestrian mother was walking slowly down a country road holding her little son by his hand. They were beautiful examples of pedestrians, though tired and dusty from long days spent on their journey from Ohio to Arkansas, where the pitiful remnant of the doomed species was gathering for the final struggle. For several days these two had walked the roads westward, escaping instant death again and again by repeated miracles. Yet this afternoon, tired, hungry, and hypnotized by the setting sun in her face, the woman slept even as she walked and only woke screaming, when she realized that escape was impossible. She succeeded in pushing her son to safety in the gutter, and then died instantly beneath the wheels of a skillfully driven car, going at sixty miles an hour.

The lady in the sedan was annoyed at the jolt and spoke rather sharply to the chauffeur through the speaking tube.

"What was that jar, William?"

"Madam, we have just run over a pedestrian."

"Oh, is that all? Well, at least you should be careful." The lady added to her little daughter, "William just ran over a pedestrian and there was only the slightest jar."

The little girl looked with pride on her new dress. It was her eighth birthday and they were going to her grandmother's for the day. Her twisted atrophied legs moved in slow rhythmic movements. It was her mother's pride to say that her little daughter had never tried to walk. She could think, however, and something was evidently worrying her. She looked up.

"Mother!" she asked. "Do pedestrians feel pain the way we do?"

"Why, of course not, Darling," said the mother. "They are not like us; in fact, some say they are not human beings at all."

"Are they like monkeys?"

"Well, perhaps higher than apes, but much lower than automobiles."

The machine sped on.

Miles behind, a terror-stricken lad lay sobbing on the bleeding body of his mother, which he somehow had found strength to drag to the side of the road. He remained there till another day dawned and then left her and walked slowly up the hills into the forest. He was hungry and tired, sleepy and heartbroken, but he paused for a moment on the crest of the hill and shook his fist in an inarticulate rage.

That day, a deep hatred was formed in his soul.

The world had gone automobile wild. Traffic cops had no time for the snail-like movements of walkers—they were a menace to civilization—a drawback to progress—a defiance to the development of science. Nothing mattered in a man's body but his brains.

Gradually machinery had replaced muscle as a means of attaining man's desire on earth. Life consisted only of a series of explosions of gasoline or alcohol-air mixtures or steam expansion in hollow cylinders and turbines, and this caused power to be applied wherever the mind of man dictated. All mankind was accomplishing their desires by mechanical energy made in small amounts transmitted over wires as electricity for the use of vast centers of population.

The sky always had its planes; the higher levels for the inter-city express service, the lower for individual suburban traffic—the roads, all of reinforced concrete, were often one-way roads, exacted by the number of machines in order to avoid continual collisions. While part of the world had taken readily to the skies, the vast proportion had been forced, by insufficient development of the semi-circular canals, to remain on earth.

The automobile had developed as legs had atrophied. No longer content to use it constantly outdoors, the successors of Ford had perfected the smaller individual machine for use indoors, all steps being replaced by curving ascending passages. Men thus came to live within metal bodies, which they left only for sleep. Gradually, partly through necessity and partly through inclination, the automobile was used in sport as well as in play. Special types were developed for golf; children seated in auto-cars rolled hoops through shady parks; lazily, prostrate on one, a maiden drifted through the tropical waters of a Florida resort. Mankind had ceased to use their lower limbs.

With disuse came atrophy: with atrophy came progressive and definite changes in the shapes of mankind; with these changes came new conceptions of feminine beauty. All this happened not in one generation, nor in ten, but gradually in the course of centuries.

Customs changed; so laws changed. No longer were laws for everyone's good but only for the benefit of the automobilist. The roads, formerly for the benefit of all, were finally restricted to those in machines. At first it was merely dangerous to walk on the highways; later it became a crime. Like all changes, this came slowly. First came a law restricting certain roads to automobilists; then came a law prohibiting pedestrians from the use of roads; then a law giving them no legal recourse if injured while walking on a public highway; later it became a felony to do so.

Then came the final law providing for the legal murder of all pedestrians on the highway wherever or whenever they could be hit by an auto.

No one was content to go slowly—all the world was crazed by a desire for speed. There was also a desire, no matter where an automobilist was, to go to some other city. Thus Sundays and holidays were distinguished by thousands and millions of automobilists going "somewhere," none being content to spend the hours of leisure quietly where they were. Rural landscapes consisted of long lines of machines passing between walls of advertisements at the rate of eighty miles an hour, pausing now and then at gasoline filling stations, at road houses, or to strip an occasional tree of its blooms. The air was filled with vapors from the exhausts of machinery and the raucous noise of countless horns of all description. No one saw anything: no one wanted to see anything: the desire of each driver was to drive faster than the car ahead of his. It was called in the vernacular of the day—"A quiet Sunday in the country."

There were no pedestrians; that is, almost none. Even in the rural districts mankind was on wheels mechanically propelled. Such farming as was done was done by machinery. Here and there, clinging like mountain sheep to inaccessible mountainsides, remained a few pedestrians who, partly from choice, but mainly from necessity, had retained the desire to use their legs. These people were always poor. At first the laws had no terror for them. Every state had some families who had never ceased to be pedestrians. On these the automobilists looked first with amusement and then with alarm. No one realized the tremendous depth of the chasm between the two groups of the Genus Homo till the national law was passed forbidding the use of all highways to pedestrians. At once, all over the United States, the revolt of the Walkers began. Although Bunker Hill was hundreds of years away, the spirit of Bunker Hill survived, and the prohibition of walking on the roads only increased the desire to do so. More pedestrians than ever were accidentally killed. Their families retaliated by using every effort to make automobiling unpleasant and dangerous—nails, tacks, glass, logs, barbed wire, huge rocks were used as weapons. In the Ozarks, backwoodsmen took delight in breaking windshields and puncturing tires with well-directed rifle shots. Others walked the roads and defied the automobilists. Had the odds been equal, a condition of anarchy would have resulted; being unequal, the pedestrians were simply a nuisance. Class-consciousness reached its acme when Senator Glass of New York rose in the Senate Chambers and said in part:

"A race that ceases to develop must die out. For centuries mankind has been on wheels, and thus has advanced towards a state of mechanical perfection. The pedestrian, careless of his inherent right to ride, has persisted not only in walking, but even has gone so far as to claim equal rights with the higher type of automobilist. Patience has ceased to be a virtue. Nothing more can be done for these miserable degenerates of our race. The kindest thing to do now is to inaugurate a process of extermination. Only thus can we prevent a continuation of the disorders which have marked the otherwise uniform peaceful history of our fair land. There is, therefore, nothing for me to do save to urge the passage of the 'Pedestrian Extermination Act.' This, as you know, provides for the instant death of all pedestrians, wherever and whenever they are found by the Constabulary of each State. The last census shows there are only about ten thousand left and these are mostly in a few of the midwestern states. I am proud to state that my own constituency, which up to yesterday had only one pedestrian, an old man over ninety years of age, has now a clear record. A telegram just received states that fortunately he tottered on a public road in a senile effort to visit his wife's grave and was instantly killed by an automobilist. But though New York has at present none of these vile degenerates, we are anxious to aid our less fortunate states."

The law was instantly passed, being opposed only by the Senators from Kentucky, Tennessee, and Arkansas. To promote interest, a bounty was placed on each pedestrian killed. A silver star was given to each county reporting complete success. A gold star to each state containing only autoists. The pedestrian, like the carrier pigeon, was doomed.

It is not to be expected that the extermination was immediate or complete. There was some unexpected resistance. It had been in effect one year when the pedestrian child swore vengeance on the mechanical means of destroying humanity.

Sunday afternoon a hundred years later, the Academy of Natural Sciences in Philadelphia was filled with the usual throng of pleasure seekers, each in his own auto-car. Noiselessly, on rubber-tired wheels, they journeyed down the long aisles, pausing now and then before this exhibit or that which attracted their attention. A father was taking his little boy through and each was greatly interested: the boy in the new world of wonders, the father in the boy's intelligent questions and observations. Finally the boy stopped his auto-car in front of a glass case.

"What is that, Father? They look as we do, only what peculiar shapes!"

"That, my son, is a family of pedestrians. It was long ago it all happened and I know of it only because my mother told me about them. This family was shot in the Ozark Mountains. It is believed they were the last in the world."

"I am sorry," said the boy, slowly. "If there were more, I would like you to get a little one for me to play with."

"There are no more," said the father. "They are all dead."

The man thought he was telling the truth to his son. In fact, he prided himself on always being truthful to children. Yet he was wrong. For a few pedestrians remained, and their leader, in fact, their very brains, was the great-grandson of the little boy who had stood up on the hill with hatred in his heart long before.

Irrespective of climatic conditions, environment, and all varieties of enemies, man has always been able to exist. With the race of pedestrians it was in very truth the survival of the fittest. Only the most agile, intelligent, and sturdy were able to survive the systematic attempt made to exterminate them. Though reduced in numbers they survived; though deprived of all the so-called benefits of modern civilization, they existed. Forced to defend not only their individual existence, but also the very life of their race, they gained the cunning of their backwoodsmen ancestors and kept alive. They lived, hunted, loved, and died; and for two generations the civilized world was unaware of their very existence. They had their political organization, their courts of law. Justice, based on Blackstone and the Constitution, ruled. Always a Miller ruled: first the little boy with hatred in his heart, grown to manhood; then his son, trained from childhood to the sole task of hatred of all things mechanical; then the grandson, wise, cunning, a dream-builder; and finally the great-grandson, Abraham Miller, prepared by three generations for the ultimate revenge.

Abraham Miller was the hereditary president of the Colony of Pedestrians hidden in the Ozark Mountains. They were isolated but not ignorant; few in number but adaptive. The first fugitives had many brilliant men: inventors, college professors, patriots, and even a learned jurist. These men kept their knowledge and transmitted it. They dug in the fields, hunted in the woods, fished in the streams, and builded in their laboratories. They even had automobiles, and now and then, with limbs tied close to their bodies, would travel as spies into the land of the enemy. Certain of the children were trained from childhood to act in this capacity. There is even evidence that for some years one of these spies lived in St. Louis.

It was a colony with a single ambition—a union of individuals for one purpose only; the children lisped it, the school children spoke it daily; the young folks whispered it to each other in the moonlight; in the laboratories it was carved on every wall; the senile gathered their children around and swore them to it; every action of the colony was bent toward one end—

"We will go back."

They were paranoiac in their hatred. Without exception, all of their ancestors had been hunted like wild beasts, exterminated without mercy—like vermin. It was not revenge they desired, but liberty—the right to live as they wished, to go and come as they pleased.

For three generations the colony had preserved the secret of their existence. Year by year as a unit they had lived, worked, and died for a single ambition. Now the time had come for the execution of their plans, the fulfillment of their desires. Meanwhile the world of automobilists lived on, materialistic, mechanical, selfish. Socialism had provided comfort for the masses but had singularly failed to provide happiness. All lived, everyone had an income, no one but was provided with a home, food, and clothes. But the homes were of concrete; they were uniform, poured out by the million; the furniture was concrete; poured with the houses. The clothing was paper, water-proofed: it was all in one design and was furnished—four suits a year to each person. The food was sold in bricks, each brick containing all the elements necessary for the continuation of life; on every brick was stamped the number of calories. For centuries, inventors had invented till finally life became uniform and work a matter of push-buttons. Yet the world of the autoists was an unhappy one, for no one worked with muscles. In summer time it was, of course, necessary to perspire, but for generations no one had sweated. The words "toil," "labor," "work" were marked obsolete in the dictionaries.

Yet no one was happy because it was found to be a mechanical impossibility to invent an automobile that would travel over one hundred and fifty miles an hour and stay on the ordinary country road. The automobilists could not go as fast as they wanted to. Space could not be annihilated; time could not be destroyed.

Besides, everyone was toxic. The air was filled with the dangerous vapors generated by the combustion of millions of gallons of gasoline and its substitutes, even though many machines were electrified. The greatest factor contributing to this toxemia, however, was the reduced excretion of toxins through the skin and the almost negative production of energy through muscular contraction. The automobilists had ceased to work, using the term in its purely archaic form, and having ceased to work, they had ceased to sweat. A few hours a day on a chair in a factory or at a desk was sufficient to earn the necessaries of life. The automobilist never being tired, nature demanded a lesser number of hours spent in sleep. The remaining hours were spent in automobiles, going somewhere; it mattered not where they went so long as they went fast. Babies were raised in machines; in fact, all life was lived in them. The American Home had disappeared—it was replaced by the automobile.

The automobilists were going somewhere but were not sure where. The pedestrians were confident of where they were going.

Society in its modern sense was socialistic. This implied that all classes were comfortable. Crime, as such, had ceased to exist some generations previous, following the putting into force of Bryant's theory that all crime was due to two per cent of the population and that if these were segregated and sterilized, crime would cease in one generation. When Bryant first promulgated his thesis, it was received with some skepticism, but its practical application was hailed with delight by everyone who was not directly affected.

Yet even in this apparently perfect society there were defects. Though everyone had all the necessities of life, such equality was not true of luxuries. In other words, there were still rich men and poor men, and the wealthy still dominated the government and made the laws.

Among the rich there were none more exclusive, aristocratic, and dominant than the Heislers. Their estate on the Hudson was enclosed by thirty miles of twelve-foot iron fence. Few could boast of having visited there, of having week-ended in the stone palace surrounded by a forest of pine, beech, and hemlock. They were so powerful that none of the family had ever held a public office. They made Presidents, but never cared to have one in the family. Their enemies said that their wealth came from fortunate marriages with the Ford and Rockefeller families but, no doubt, this was a falsehood based on jealousy. The Heislers had banks and real estate; they owned factories and office buildings. It was definitely stated that they owned the President of the United States and the Judges of the Supreme Court. One of their possessions was rarely spoken of, or mentioned in the newspapers. The only child of the ruling branch of the family walked.

William Henry Heisler was an unusual millionaire. When told that his wife had presented him with a daughter he promised his Gods (though he was not certain who they were) that he would spend at least an hour a day with his child, supervising her care.

For some months nothing unusual was noticed about this little girl baby, though at once all the nurses commented on her ugly legs. Her father simply considered that probably all baby legs were ugly.

At the age of one year, the baby tried to stand and take a step. Even this was passed over, as the pediatricians were united in the opinion that all children tried to use their legs for a few months, but it was a bad habit usually easily broken—like thumb-sucking. They gave the usual advice to the nurses which would have been followed had it not been for her father who merely stated, "Every child has a personality. Let her alone, see what she will do." And in order to insure obedience, he selected one of his private secretaries, who was to be in constant attendance and make daily written reports.

The child grew. There came the time when she was no longer called "baby" but dignified by the name of "Margaretta." As she grew, her legs grew. The more she walked, the stronger they became. There was no one to help her, for none of the adults had ever walked, nor had they seen anyone walk. She not only walked but she objected in her own baby way to mechanical locomotion. She screamed like a baby wild cat at her first introduction to an automobile and never could become reconciled even to the auto-cars for house use.

When it was too late, her father consulted everyone who could possibly know anything about the situation and its remedy. Heisler wanted his child to develop her own personality, but he did not want her to be odd. He therefore gathered in consultation neurologists, anatomists, educators, psychologists, students of child behavior and obtained no satisfaction from them. All agreed that it was a pitiful case of atavism, a throwback. As for cure, there were a thousand suggestions from psychoanalysis to the brutal splinting and bandaging of the little girl's lower extremities. Finally, in disgust, Heisler paid them all for their trouble and bribed them all for their silence and told them sharply to go to hell. He had no idea where this place was, or just what he meant but found some relief in saying it.

They all left promptly except one who, in addition to his other vocations, followed genealogy as an avocation. He was an old man, and they made an interesting contrast as they sat facing each other in their auto-cars. Heisler was middle-aged, vigorous, a real leader of men, gigantic save for his shrunken legs. They were alone in the room, save for the child who played happily in the sunshine of the large bay windows.

"I thought I told you to go to hell with the rest," growled the leader of men.

"How can I?" was the mild reply. "Those others did not obey you. They simply autoed out of your home. I am waiting for you to tell me how to go there. Where is this hell you order us to? Our submarines have explored the ocean bed five miles below sea level. Our aeroplanes have gone some miles towards the stars. Mount Everest has been conquered. I read all these journeyings, but nowhere do I read of a hell. Some centuries ago theologians said it was a place that sinners went to when they died, but there has been no sin since Bryant's two per cent were identified and sterilized. You with your millions and limitless power are as near hell as you will ever be, when you look at your abnormal child."

"But she is bright mentally, Professor," protested Heisler; "only seven years old but tested ten years by the Binet-Simon Scale. If only she would stop this damned walking. Oh! I am proud of her, but I want her to be like other girls. Who will want to marry her? It's positively indecent. Look at her. What is she doing?"

"Why, bless me!" exclaimed the old man. "I read of that in a book three hundred years old just the other day. Lots of children used to do that."

"But what is it?"

"Why, it used to be called 'turning somersaults.' "

"But what does it mean? Why does she do it?"

Heisler wiped the sweat off his face.

"It will make us ridiculous if it becomes known."

"Oh, well, with your power you can keep it quiet—but have you studied your family history? Do you know what blood strains are in her?"

"No. I never was interested. Of course, I belong to the Sons of the American Revolution, and all that sort of thing. They brought me the papers and I signed on the dotted line. I never read them though I paid well to have a book published about it all."

"So you had a revolutionary ancestor? Where's the book?"

Heisler rang for his private secretary, who autoed in, received his curt orders, and soon returned with the Heisler family history which the old man opened eagerly. Save for the noise made by the child, who was playing with a small stuffed bear, the room was deadly still. Suddenly the old man laughed.

"It is all as plain as can be. Your Revolutionary ancestor was a Miller; Abraham Miller of Hamilton Township. His mother was captured and killed by Indians. They were pedestrians of the most pronounced strain; of course, everyone was a pedestrian in those days. The Millers and the Heislers intermarried. That was some hundred years ago. Your Great-Grandfather Heisler had a sister who married a Miller. She is spoken of here on page 330. Let me read it to you.

" 'Margaretta Heisler was the only sister of William Heisler. Independent and odd in many ways, she committed the folly of marrying a farmer by the name of Abraham Miller, who was one of the most noted leaders in the pedestrian riots in Pennsylvania. Following his death, his widow and only child, a boy eight years old, disappeared and no doubt were destroyed in the general process of pedestrian extermination. An old letter written by her to her brother, prior to her marriage, contained the boast that she never had ridden in an automobile and never would; that God had given her legs and she intended to use them and that she was fortunate in finally finding a man who also had legs and the desire to live on them, as God had planned men and women to do.'

"There is the secret of this child of yours. She is a reversal to the sister of your great-grandfather. That lady died a hundred years ago rather than follow the fashion. You say yourself that this little one nearly died from convulsions when the attempt was made to put her in an automobile. It is a clear case of heredity. If you try to break the child of the habit, you will probably kill her. The only thing to do is to leave her alone. Let her develop as she wishes. She is your daughter. Her will is your will. The probability is that neither can change the other. Let her use her legs. She probably will climb trees, run, swim, wander where she will."

"So that is the way of it," sighed Heisler. "That means the end of our family. No one would want to marry a monkey no matter how intelligent she is. So you think she will some day climb a tree? If there is a hell, this is mine, as you suggest."

"But she is happy!"

"Yes, if laughter is an index. But will she be as she grows older? She will be different. How can she have associates? Of course they won't apply that extermination law in her case; my position will prevent that. I could even have it repealed. But she will be lonely—so lonely!"

"Perhaps she will learn to read—then she won't be lonely."

They both looked at the child.

"What is she doing now?" demanded Heisler. "You seem to know more than anyone I ever met about such things."

"Why, she is hopping. Is that not remarkable? She never saw anyone hop and yet she is doing it. I never saw a child do it and yet I can identify it and give it a name. In Kate Greenaway's illustrations, I have seen pictures of children hopping."

"Confound the Millers anyway!" growled Heisler.

After that conversation, Heisler engaged the old man, whose sole duty was to investigate the subject of pedestrian children and find how they played and used their legs. Having investigated this, he was to instruct the little girl.

The entire matter of her exercise was left to him. Thus from that day on a curious spectator from an aeroplane might have seen an old man sitting on the lawn showing a golden-haired child pictures from very old books and talking together about the same pictures. Then the child would do things that no child had done for a hundred years—bounce a ball, skip rope, dance folk dances, and jump over a bamboo stick supported by two upright bars. Long hours were spent in reading and always the old man would begin by saying:

"Now this is the way they used to do."

Occasionally a party would be given for her, and other little girls from the neighboring rich would come and spend the day. They were polite—so was Margaretta Heisler—but the parties were not successful. The company could not move except in their auto-cars, and they looked on their hostess with curiosity and scorn. They had nothing in common with the curious walking child, and these parties always left Margaretta in tears.

"Why can't I be like other girls?" she demanded of her father. "Is it always going to be this way? Do you know that girls laugh at me because I walk?"

Heisler was a good father. He held to his vow to devote one hour a day to his daughter, and during that time gave of his intelligence as eagerly and earnestly as he did to his business in the other hours. Often he talked to Margaretta as though she were his equal, an adult with full mental development.

"You have your own personality," he would say to her. "The mere fact that you are different from other people does not of necessity mean that they are right and you are wrong. Perhaps you are both right—at least you are both following out your natural proclivities. You are different in desires and physique from the rest of us, but perhaps you are more normal than we are. The professor shows us pictures of ancient peoples and they all had legs developed like yours. How can I tell whether man has degenerated or improved? At times when I see you run and jump, I envy you. I and all of us are tied down to earth—dependent on a machine for every part of our daily life. You can go where you please. You can do this and all you need is food and sleep. In some ways this is an advantage. On the other hand, the professor tells me that you can only go about four miles an hour while I can go over one hundred."

"But why should I want to go so fast when I do not want to go anywhere?"

"That is just the astonishing thing. Why don't you want to go? It seems that not only your body but also your mind, your personality, your desires are old-fashioned, hundreds of years old-fashioned. I try to be here in the house or garden every day—at least an hour—with you, but during the other waking hours I want to go. You do the strangest things. The professor tells me about it all. There is your bow and arrow, for instance. I bought you the finest firearms and you never use them, but you get a bow and arrow from some museum and finally succeed in killing a duck, and the professor said you built a fire out of wood and roasted it and ate it. You even made him eat some."

"But it was good, father—much better than the synthetic food. Even the professor said the juice made him feel younger."

Heisler laughed, "You are a savage—nothing more than a savage."

"But I can read and write!"

"I admit that. Well, go ahead and enjoy yourself. I only wish I could find another savage for you to play with, but there are no more."

"Are you sure?"

"As much so as I can be. In fact, for the last five years my agents have been scouring the civilized world for a pedestrian colony. There are a few in Siberia and the Tartar Plateau, but they are impossible. I would rather have you associate with apes."

"I dream of one, father," whispered the girl shyly. "He is a nice boy and he can do everything I can. Do dreams ever come true?"

Heisler smiled. "I trust this one will, and now I must hurry back to New York. Can I do anything for you?"

"Yes—find some one who can teach me how to make candles."

"Candles? Why, what are they?"

She ran and brought an old book and read it to him. It was called *The Gentle Pirate*, and the hero always read in bed by candle light.

"I understand," he finally said as he closed the book. "I remember now that I once read of their having something like that in the Catholic Churches. So you want to make some? See the professor and order what you need. Hum—candles—why, they would be handy at night if the electricity failed, but then it never does."

"But I don't want electricity. I want candles and matches to light them with."

"Matches?"

"Oh, father. In some ways you are ignorant. I know lots of words you don't, even though you are so rich."

"I admit it. I will admit anything and we will find how to make your candles. Shall I send you some ducks?"

"Oh, no. It is so much more fun to shoot them."

"You are a real barbarian!"

"And you are a dear ignoramus."

So it came to pass that Margaretta Heisler reached her seventeenth birthday, tall, strong, agile, brown from constant exposure to wind and sun, able to run, jump, shoot accurately with bow and arrow, an eater of meat, a reader of books by candle light, a weaver of carpets, and a lover of nature. Her associates had been mainly elderly men: only occasionally would she see the ladies of the neighborhood. She tolerated the servants, the maids, and housekeeper. The love she gave her father she also gave to the old professor, but he had taught her all she knew and the years had made him senile and sleepy.

Then came to her finally the urge to travel. She wanted to see New York with its twenty million automobilists; its hundred-story office buildings; its smokeless factories; its standardized houses. There were difficulties in the way of such a trip, and no one knew these better than her father. The roads were impossible and all of New York was now either streets or houses. There being no pedestrians, there was no need of sidewalks. Besides, even Heisler's wealth would not be able to prevent the riot sure to result from the presence in a large city of such a curiosity as a pedestrian. Heisler was powerful, but he dreaded the result of allowing his daughter the freedom of New York. Furthermore, up to this time, her deformity was known only to a few. Once she was in New York, the city papers would publish his disgrace to the world.

Several of the office buildings in New York City were one hundred stories high. There were no stairways but as a safety precaution circular spiral ramps had been built in each structure for the use of auto-cars in case the elevators failed to work. This, however, never happened, and few of the tenants ever knew of their existence. They were used at night by the scrub women busily auto-carring from one floor to another cleaning up. The higher the floor the purer was the air and the more costly was the yearly rental. Below, in the canyon and the street, an ozone machine was necessary every few feet to purify the air and make unnecessary the use of gas masks. On the upper floors, however, there were pure breezes from off the Atlantic. Noticeable was the absence of flies and mosquitoes; pigeons built their nests in the crevices, and on the highest roof a pair of American eagles nested year after year in haughty defiance of the mechanical auto, a thousand feet below.

It was in the newest building in New York and on the very highest floor that a new office was opened. On the door was the customary gilded sign, "New York Electrical Co." Boxes had been left there, decorators had embellished the largest room, the final result being that it was simply a standardized office. A stenographer had been installed and sat at a noiseless machine, answering, if need be, the automatic telephone.

To this roomy suite one day in June came, by invitation, a dozen of the leaders of industry. They came, each thinking he was the only one invited to the conference. Surprise as well as suspicion was the marked feature of the meeting. There were three men there who were secretly and independently trying to undermine Heisler and tear him from his financial throne. Heisler himself was there, apparently quiet, but inwardly a seething flame of repressed electricity. The stenographer seated them as they arrived, in order around a long table. They remained in their auto-cars. No one used chairs. One or two of the men joked with each other. All nodded to Heisler, but none spoke to him.

The furniture, surroundings, stenographer were all part of the standard office in the business section. Only one small portion of the room aroused their curiosity. At the head of the table was an armchair. None of the men around the table had ever used a chair; none had seen one save in the Metropolitan Museum. The auto-car had replaced the chair even as the automobile had replaced the human leg.

The chimes in the tower rang out the two-o'clock message. All of the twelve looked at their watches. One man frowned. His watch was some minutes slow. In another minute all were frowning. They had a two-o'clock appointment with this stranger and he had not kept it. To them, time was valuable.

Then a door opened and the man walked in. That was the first astonishing thing—and then they marveled at the size and shape of him. There was something uncanny about it—peculiar, weird.

Then the man sat down—in the chair. He did not seem much larger now than the other men, though he was younger than any of them, and had a brown complexion which contrasted peculiarly with the dead gray-white pallor of the others. Then, gravely, almost mechanically, with clear distinct enunciation, he began to speak.

"I see, gentlemen, that you have all honored me by accepting my invitation to be present this afternoon. You will pardon my not informing any of you that the others were also invited. Had I done so, several of you would have refused to come and without any one of you the meeting would not be as successful as I intended it to be.

"The name of this company is the 'New York Electrical Co.' That is just a name assumed as a mask. In reality, there is no company. I am the representative of the nation of pedestrians. In fact, I am their president and my name is Abraham Miller. Four generations ago, as, no doubt, you know, Congress passed the Pedestrian Extermination Act. Following that, those who continued to walk were hunted like wild animals, slaughtered without mercy. My great-grandfather, Abraham Miller, was killed in Pennsylvania; his wife was run down on the public highway in Ohio as she was attempting to join the other pedestrians in the Ozarks. There were no battles, there was no conflict. At that time there were only ten thousand pedestrians in all the United States. Within a few years there were none—at least so your ancestors thought. The race of pedestrians, however, survived. We lived on. The trials of those early years are written in our histories and taught to our children. We formed a colony and continued our existence although we disappeared from the world as you know it.

"Year by year we lived on until now we number over two hundred persons in our Republic. We are not, in fact never have been, ignorant. Always we worked for one purpose and that was the right to return to the world. Our motto for one hundred years has been: 'We will go back.'

"So I have come to New York and called you into conference. While you were selected for your influence, wealth, and ability, there was present in every instance another important reason. Each of you is a lineal descendant of a United States Senator who voted for the Pedestrian Extermination Act. You can readily see the significance of that. You have the power to undo a great injustice done to a branch of American citizens. Will you let us come back? We want to come back as pedestrians, to come and go as we please, safely. Some of us can drive automobiles and aeroplanes, but we don't want to. We want to walk, and if a mood strikes us to walk in the highway, we want to do it without constant danger of death. We do not hate you, we pity you.

There is no desire to antagonize you; rather we want to cooperate with you.

"We believe in work—muscle work. No matter what our young people are trained for, they are taught to work—to do manual work. We understand machinery but do not like to use it. The only help we accept is from domestic animals, horses, and oxen. In several places we use water power to run our grist mills and saw our timbers. For pleasure we hunt, fish, play tennis, swim in our mountain lake. We keep our bodies clean and try to do the same with our minds. Our boys marry at twenty-one—our girls at eighteen. Occasionally a child grows up to be abnormal—degenerate. I frankly say that such children disappear. We eat meat and vegetables, fish, and grain raised in our valley. The time has come when we cannot care for a continued increase in population. The time has come when we must come back into the world. What we desire is a guarantee of safety. I will now leave you in conference for fifteen minutes, and at the end of such time I will return for an answer. If you have any questions, I will answer them then."

He left the room. One of the men rolled over to the telephone, found the wire cut; another went over to the door and found it locked. The stenographer had disappeared. There followed sharp discussion marked by temper and lack of logic. One man only kept silent. Heisler sat motionless; so much so that the cigar, clenched between his teeth, went out.

Then Miller came back. A dozen questions were hurled at him. One man swore at him. Finally there was silence.

"Well?" questioned Miller.

"Give us time—a week in which to discuss it—to ascertain public opinion," urged one of them.

"No," said Heisler, "let us give our answer now."

"Oh, of course," sneered one of his bitter opponents. "Your reason for giving a decison is plain, though it has never been in the newspapers."

"For that," said Heisler, "I am going to get you. You are a cur and you know it or you would not drag my family into this."

"Oh, Hell! Heisler—you can't bluff me any more!"

Miller hit the table with his fist—

"What's your answer?"

One of the men held up his hand for an audience.

"We all know the history of pedestrianism: the two groups represented here cannot live together. There are two hundred million of us and two hundred of them. Let them stay in their valley. That is what I think. If this man is their leader, we can judge what the colony is like. They are ignorant anarchists. There is no telling what they would demand if we listened to them. I think we should have this man arrested. He is a menace to society."

That broke the ice. One after another they spoke, and when they finished, it was plain that all save Heisler were hostile, antagonistic, merciless. Miller turned to him.

"What is your verdict?"

"I am going to keep quiet. These men know it all. You have heard them. They are a unit. What I would say can make no difference. In fact, I don't care. For some time I have ceased to care about anything."

Miller turned in his swivel chair and looked out over the city. In some ways it was a pretty city, if one liked such a place. Under him, in the city streets, in the bee-hives, over twenty million automobilists spent their lives on wheels. Not one in a million had a desire beyond the city limits; the roads connecting the metropolis with other cities were but urban arteries wherein the automobiles passed like corpuscles, the auto-trucks proceeded like plasma. Miller feared the city, but he pitied the legless pigmies inhabiting it.

Then he turned again and asked for silence.

"I wanted to make a peaceful adjustment. We desire no more bloodshed, no more internecine strife. You who lead public sentiment have by your recent talk shown me that the pedestrian can expect no mercy at the hands of the present Government. You know and I know that this is no longer a nation where the people rule. You rule. You elect whom you please for Senators, for Presidents; you snap your whip and they dance. That is why I came to you men, instead of making a direct appeal to the Government. Feeling confident what your action would be, I have prepared this short paper which I will ask you to sign. It contains a single statement: 'The Pedestrians cannot return.'

"When you have all signed this, I will explain to you just what we will do."

"Why sign it?" said the first man, the one seated to the right of Miller. "Now my idea is this!" and he crumpled the paper to a tight ball and threw it under the table. His conduct was at once followed by applause. Only Heisler sat still. Miller looked out the window till all was quiet.

Finally he spoke again:

"In our colony we have perfected a new electro-dynamic principle. Released, it at once separates the atomic energy which makes possible all movement, save muscle movement. We have tested this out with smaller machines in limited space and know exactly what we can do. We do not know how to restore the energy in any territory where we have once destroyed it. Our electricians are waiting for my signal transmitted by radio. In fact, they have been listening to all this conversation, and I will now give them the signal to throw the switch. The signal is our motto: 'We will come back.' "

"So that is the signal?" sneered one of the men. "What happened?"

"Nothing much," replied Heisler, "at least I see no difference. What was supposed to happen, Abraham Miller?"

"Nothing much," said Miller, "only the destruction of all mankind except the pedestrians. We tried to imagine what would happen when our electricians threw the switch and released this new principle, but even our sociologists could not fully imagine what would be the result. We do not know whether you can live or die—whether any of you can survive. No doubt the city dwellers will die speedily in their artificial bee-hives. Some in the country may survive."

"Hello, hello!" exclaimed a multi-millionaire. "I feel no different. You are a dreamer of dreams. I am leaving and will report you at once to the police. Open your damn door and let us out!"

Miller opened the door.

Most of the men pressed their starting button and took hold of the steering rod. Not a machine moved. The others, startled, tried to leave. Their auto-cars were dead. Then one, with a hysterical curse, raised an automatic at Miller and pulled the trigger. There was a click—and nothing more.

Miller pulled out his watch.

"It is now 2:40 P.M. The automobiles are beginning to die. They do not know it yet. When they do, there will be a panic. We cannot give any relief. There are only a few hundred of us and we cannot feed and care for hundreds of millions of cripples.

The Revolt of the Pedestrians 21

Fortunately there is a circular-inclined plane or ramp in this building and your auto-cars are all equipped with brakes. I will push you one at a time to the plane or ramp in this building and your auto-cars are all equipped with brakes. I will push you one at a time to the plane, if you will steer your cars. Obviously you do not care to remain here and equally obviously the elevators are not running. I will call on my stenographer to help me. Perhaps you suspected before that he was a pedestrian trained from boyhood to take female parts. He is one of our most efficient spies. And now we will say good-bye. A century ago you knowingly and willingly tried to exterminate us. We survived. We do not want to exterminte you, but I fear for your future."

Thereupon he went behind one of the auto-cars and started pushing it towards the doorway. The stenographer, who had reappeared as a pedestrian, and in trousers, took hold of another car. Soon only Heisler was left. He held up his hand in protest.

"Would you mind pushing me over to that window?"

Miller did so. The automobilist looked out curiously.

"There are no aeroplanes in the sky. There should be hundreds."

"No doubt," replied Miller, "they have all planed down to earth. You see, they have no power."

"Then everything has stopped?"

"Almost. There is still muscle power. There is still power produced by the bending of woods as in a bow and arrow—also that produced by a metal coil like the main spring in a watch. You notice your watch is still running. Of course, domestic animals can still produce power—that is just a form of muscle power. In our valley we have grist mills and saw mills running by water power. We can see no reason why they should not keep on; all other power is destroyed. Do you realize it? There is no electricity, no steam, no explosions of any kind. All those machines are dead."

Heisler pulled out a handkerchief, slowly, automatically, and wiped the sweat from his face as he said:

"I can hear a murmur from the city. It rises up to this window like distant surf beating rhythmically against a sandy shore. I can hear no other noise, only this murmur. It recalls to my mind the sound of a swarm of bees leaving their old hive and flying compactly through the air with their queen in the center, trying to find a new home. There is a sameness to the noise like a distant waterfall. What does it mean? I think I know, but I cannot bear to say it with words."

"It means," said Miller, "that below us and around us twenty million people are beginning to die in office buildings, stores, and homes; in subways, elevators, and trains; in tubes and ferry boats; on the street, and in the restaurants, twenty million people suddenly realize that they cannot move. No one can help them. Some have left their cars and are trying to pull themselves along on their hands, their withered legs helplessly trailing behind them. They are calling to each other for help, but even now they cannot know the full extent of the disaster. In a few days there will be no food, no water. I hope they will die quickly—before they eat each other. The nation will die and no one will know about it, for there will be no newspapers, no telephones, no wireless. I will communicate with my people by carrier pigeons. It will be months before I can rejoin them. Meanwhile I can live. I can go from place to place. The sound you hear from the city is the cry of a soul in despair."

Heisler grabbed Miller's hand convulsively. "But if you made it stop, you can make it start?"

"No—we stopped it with electricity. There is now no more electricity. I presume our own machines were at once put out of power."

"So we are going to die?"

"I believe so. Perhaps your scientists can invent a remedy. We did a hundred years ago. We lived. Your nation tried by every known scientific art to destroy us, but we lived. Perhaps you can. How can I tell? We wanted to arbitrate. All we asked for was equality. You saw how those other men voted and how they thought. If they had had the power, they would instantly have destroyed my little colony. What we did was simply done in self-protection."

Heisler tried to light his cigar. The electric lighter would not work, so he held it dry in his mouth, in one corner, chewing it.

"You say your name is Abraham Miller? I believe we are cousins of some sort. I have a book that tells about it."

"I know all about that. Your great-grandfather and my great-grandmother were brother and sister."

"I believe that is what the professor said, except that at that time we did not know about you. What I want to talk about, however, is my daughter."

The two men talked on and on. The murmur continued to mount from the city, unceasing, incessant, full of notes new to the present generation. Yet at the distance—from the earth below to the hundredth story above, it was all one sound. Though composed of millions of variants, it blended into unity. Miller finally began walking up and down, from one office wall to the window and back again.

"I thought no one more free from nerves than I was. My whole life has been schooled in preparation for this moment. We had right, justice, even our forgotten God on our side. I still can see no other way, no other way, but this makes me sick, Heisler; it nauseates me. When I was a boy I found a mouse caught in a barn door, almost torn in two. I tried to help it and the tortured animal bit my finger so I simply had to break its neck. It couldn't live—and when I tried to help it, it bit me, so I had to kill it. Do you understand? I had to, but, though I was justified, I grew deadly sick; I vomited on the barn floor. Something like that is going on below there. Twenty million deformed bodies all around us are beginning to die. They might have been men and women like those we have in the colony but they became obsessed with the idea of mechanical devices of all kinds. If I tried to help—went into the street now—they would kill me. I couldn't keep them off me—I couldn't kill them fast enough. We were justified—man—we were justified, but it makes me sick."

"It does not affect me that way," replied Heisler. "I am accustomed to crushing out my opponents. I had to, or they would crush me. I look on all this as a wonderful experiment. For years I have thought about our civilization—on account of my daughter. I have lost interest. In many ways I have lost my fighting spirit. I don't seem to care what happens, but I would like to follow that cur down the circular plane and wrap my hands around his neck. I don't want him to die of hunger."

"No. You stay here. I want you to write a history of it all—just how it happened. We want an accurate record to justify our action. You stay here and work with my stenographer. I am going to find your daughter. We cannot let a pedestrian suffer. We will take you back with us. With suitable apparatus you could learn to ride a horse."

"You want me to live?"

"Yes, but not for yourself. There are a dozen reasons. For the next twenty years you can lecture to our young people. You can tell them what happened when the world ceased to work, to sweat, when they deliberately exchanged the home for the automobile and toil and labor for machinery. You can tell them that and they will believe you."

"Wonderful!" exclaimed Heisler. "I have made Presidents and now I become a legless example for a new world."

"You will attain fame. You will be the last automobilist."

"Let's start," urged Heisler. "Call your stenographer!"

The stenographer had been in New York one month prior to the meeting of Miller and the representatives of the automobilists. During that time, thanks to his early training in mimicry as a spy, he had been absolutely successful in deceiving all he came in contact with. In his auto-car, dressed as a stenographer, his face perfumed and painted, and rings on his fingers, he passed unnoticed amid the other thousands of similar women. He went to their restaurants and to their theatres. He even visited them in their homes. He was the perfect spy; but he was a man.

He had been trained to the work of a spy. For years he had been imbued with loyalty to an enthusiasm for his republic of pedestrains. He has sworn to the oath—that the republic should come first. Abraham Miller had selected him because he could trust him. The spy was young, with hardly a down on his cheeks. He was celibate. He was patriotic.

But for the first time in his life, he was in a big city. The firm on the floor below employed a stenographer. She was a very efficient worker in more ways than one and there was that about the new stenographer that excited her interest. They met and arranged to meet again. They talked about love, the new love between women. The spy did not understand this, having never heard of such a passion, but he did understand eventually, the caresses and kisses. She proposed that they room together, but he naturally found objections. However, they had spent much of their spare time together. More than once the pedestrian had been on the point of confiding to her, not only concerning the impending calamity, but also his real sex and his true love.

In such cases where a man falls in love with a woman the explanation is hard to find. It is always hard to find. Here there was something twisted, a pathological perversion. It was a monstrous thing that he should fall in love with a legless woman when he might, by waiting, have married a woman with columns of ivory and knees of alabaster. Instead, he loved and desired a woman who lived in a machine. It was equally pathological that she should love a woman. Each was sick—soul-sick, and each to continue the intimacy deceived the other. Now with the city dying beneath him, the stenographer felt a deep desire to save this legless woman. He felt that a way could be found, somehow, to persuade Abraham Miller to let him marry this stenographer—at least let him save her from the debacle.

So in soft shirt and knee trousers he cast a glance at Miller and Heisler engaged in earnest conversation and then tiptoed out the door and down the inclined plane to the floor below. Here all was confusion. Boldly striding into the room where the stenographer had her desk, he leaned over her and started to talk. He told her that he was a man, a pedestrian. Rapidly came the story of what it all meant, the cries from below, the motionless auto-cars, the useless elevators, the silent telephones. He told her that the world of automobilists would die because of this and that, but that she would live because of his love for her. All he asked was the legal right to care for her, to protect her. They would go somewhere and live, out in the country. He would roll her around the meadows. She could have geese, baby geese that would come to her chair when she cried, "Weete, weete."

The legless woman listened. What pallor there might be in her cheeks was skillfully covered with rouge. She listened and looked at him, a man, a man with legs, walking. He said he loved her, but the person she had loved was a woman; a woman with dangling, shrunken, beautiful legs like her own, not muscular monstrosities.

She laughed hysterically, said she would marry him, go wherever he wanted her to go, and then she clasped him to her and kissed him full on the mouth, and then kissed his neck over the jugular vein, and he died, bleeding into her mouth, and the blood mingled with rouge made her face a vivid carmine. She died some days later from hunger.

Miller never knew where his stenographer died. Had he time he might have hunted for him, but he began to share Heisler's anxiety about the pedestrian girl isolated and alone amid a world of dying automobilists. To the father she was a daughter, the only child, the remaining and sole branch of his family. To Miller, however, she was a symbol. She was a sign of nature's revolt, an indication of her last spasmodic effort to restore mankind to his former place in the world. Her father wanted her saved because she was his daughter, the pedestrian because she was one of them, one of the race of pedestrians.

On that hundredth floor kegs of water, stores of food had been provided. Every provision had been made to sustain life in the midst of death. Heisler was shown all these. He was made comfortable; and then Miller, with some provisions, a canteen of water, a road map, and a stout club in his grasp, left that place of peace and quiet and started down the spiral ramp. At the best it was simply difficult walking, the spirals being wide enough to prevent dizziness. What Miller feared was the obstruction of the entire passage at some point by a tangled mass of auto-cars, but evidently all cars which had managed to reach the plane had been able to descend. He paused now and then at this floor or that, shuddered at the cries he heard and then went on, down, down into the street.

Here it was even worse than he expected. On the second the electro-dynamic energy had been released from the Ozark valley—on that very second all machinery had ceased. In New York City twenty million people were in automobiles or auto-cars at that particular second. Some were working at desks, in shops; some were eating in restaurants, loafing at their clubs; others were going somewhere. Suddenly everyone was forced to stay where he was. There was no communication save within the limits of each one's voice; the phone, radio, newspapers were useless. Every auto-car stopped; every automobile ceased to move. Each man and woman was dependent on his own body for existence; no one could help the other, no one could help himself. Transportation died and no one knew it had happened save in his own circle, as far as the eye could see or the ear could hear, because communication had died with the death of transportation. Each automobilist stayed where he happened to be at that particular moment.

Then slowly as the thought came to them that movement was impossible, there came fear and with fear, panic. But it was a new kind of panic. All previous panics consisted in the sudden movement of large numbers of people in the same direction, fleeing from a real or an imaginary fear. This panic was motionless and for a day the average New Yorker, while gripped with fear, crying with fright, remained within his car. Then came mass-movement but not the movement of previous panics. It was the slow tortuous movement of crippled animals dragging legless bodies forward by arms unused to muscular exercise. It was not the rapid, wind-like movement of the frenzied panic-stricken mob, but a slow, convulsive, worm-like panic. Word was passed from one to another in hoarse whisperings that the city was a place of death, would become a morgue, that in a few days there would be no food. While no one knew what had happened everyone knew that the city could not live long unless food came regularly from the country, and the country suddenly became more than long cement roads between sign-boards. It was a place where food could be procured and water. The city had become dry. The mammoth pump throwing millions of gallons of water to a careless population had ceased to pump. There was no more water save in the rivers encircling the city and these were filthy, man-polluted. In the country there must be water somewhere.

So, on the second day began the flight from New York—a flight of cripples, not of eagles; a passage of humanity shaped like war-maimed soldiers. Their speed was not uniform, but the fastest could only crawl less than a mile an hour. Philosophers would have stayed where they were and died. Animals, thus tortured, would quietly wait the end, but these automobilists were neither philosophers nor animals, and they had to move. All their life they had been moving. The bridges were the first spaces to show congestion. On all of them were some automobiles, but traffic is not heavy at two in the afternoon. Gradually, by noon of the second day, these river highways were black with people crawling to get away from the city. There came congestion; and with congestion, stasis; and with stasis, simply a writhing without progression. Then on top of this stationary layer of humanity crawled another layer which in its turn reached congestion, and on top of the second layer a third layer. A dozen streets led to each bridge but each bridge was only as wide as a street. Gradually the outer rows of the upper layer began falling into the river beneath. Ultimately many sought this termination. From the bridges came, ultimately, a roar like surf beating against a rock-bound shore. In it were the beginnings of desperate madness. Men died quickly on the bridges, but before they died they started to bite each other. Within the city certain places showed the same congestion. Restaurants and cafes became filled with bodies almost to the ceiling. There was food here but no one could reach it save those next to it and these were crushed to death before they could profit by their good fortune, and dying, blocked with bodies, those who remained alive and able to eat.

Within twenty-four hours mankind had lost its religion, its humanity, its high ideals. Every one tried to keep himself alive even though by doing so he brought death sooner to others. Yet in isolated instances, individuals rose to heights of heroism. In the hospitals an occasional nurse remained with her patients, giving them food till she with them died of hunger. In one of the maternity wards a mother gave birth to a child. Deserted by everyone she placed the child to her breast and kept it there till hunger pulled down her lifeless arms.

It was into this world of horror that Miller walked as he emerged from the office building. He had provided himself with a stout club, but hardly any of the crawling automobilists noticed him. So he walked slowly over to Fifth Avenue and then headed north, and as he walked he prayed, though on that first day he saw but little of what he was to see later on.

On and on he went till he came to water and that he swam and then again he went on and by night he was out in the country where he ceased to pray continuously. Here he met an occasional autoist, who was simply annoyed at his machine breaking down. No one in the country realized at first what had really happened; no one ever fully realized, before he died in his farm house, just what it all meant. It was only the city dwellers who knew, and they did not understand.

The next day Miller rose early from the grass and started again, after carefully consulting the road map. He avoided the towns, circling them. He had learned the desire, constant, incessant, inescapable, to share his provisions with those starving cripples, and he had to keep his strength and save food for her, that pedestrian girl, alone among helpless servants, within an iron fence thirty miles long. It was near the close of the second day of his walk. For some miles he had seen no one. The sun, low in the forest of oaks, threw fantastic shadows over the concrete road.

Down the road, ever nearing him, came a strange caravan. There were three horses tied to each other. On the backs of two were bundles and jugs of water fastened stoutly but clumsily. On the third horse an old man rested in a chair-like saddle and at this time he slept, his chin resting on his chest, his hands clutching, even in sleep, the sides of the chair. Leading the first horse walked a woman, tall, strong, lovely in her strength, striding with easy pace along the cement road. On her back was slung a bow with a quiver of arrows and in her right hand she carried a heavy cane. She walked on fearlessly, confidently; she seemed filled with power, confidence, and pride.

Miller paused in the middle of the road. The caravan came near him. Then it stopped in front of him.

"Well," said the woman, and her voice blended curiously with the sunlit shadows and the flickering leaves.

"Well! Who are you and why do you block our way?"

"Why, I am Abraham Miller and you are Margaretta Heisler. I am hunting for you. Your father is safe and he sent me for you."

"And you are a pedestrian?"

"Just as truly as you are!" and so on and on—

The professor woke from his nap. He looked down on the young man and woman, standing, talking, already forgetting that there was anything else in the world.

"Now, that is the way it was in the old days," mused the professor to himself.

It was a Sunday afternoon some hundred years later. A father and his little son were sightseeing in the Museum of Natural Sciences in the reconstructed city of New York. The whole city was now simply a vast museum. Folks went there to see it but no one wanted to live there. In fact, no one wanted to live in such a place as a city when he could live on a farm.

It was part of every child's education to spend a day or more in an automobilists' city, so on this Sunday afternoon the father and his little son walked slowly through the large buildings. They saw the mastodon, the bison, the pterodactyl. They paused for some time before a glass case containing a wigwam of the American Indian with a typical Indian family. Finally they came to a large wagon, on four rubber wheels, but there was no shaft and no way that horses or oxen could be harnessed to it. In the wagon on seats were men, women, and little children. The boy looked at them curiously and pulled at his father's sleeve.

"Look, Daddy. What are that wagon and those funny people without legs? What does it mean?"

"That, my son, is a family of automobilists," and there and then he paused and gave his son the little talk that all pedestrian fathers are required by law to give to their children.

Miles J. Breuer began publishing science fiction in Amazing® Stories *in 1927 and produced many notable stories, mostly in the late '20s and '30s. He was something of a mentor to noted science fiction writer, Jack Williamson, who writes of him fondly in his autobiography,* Wonder's Child, *and who collaborated with him on a novel,* The Birth of a New Republic *(1930). This story was published in March 1930.*

THE GOSTAK AND THE DOSHES
by Miles J. Breuer

Let the reader suppose that somebody states: *"The gostak distims the doshes."* You do not know what this means, nor do I. But if we assume that it is English, we know that the *doshes* are *distimmed* by the *gostak.* We know that one *distimmer* of the *doshes* is a *gostak.* If, moreover, doshes are galloons, we know that some galloons are distimmed by the gostak. And so we may go on, and so we often do go on."—Unknown writer quoted by Ogden and Richards, in *The Meaning of Meanings,* Harcourt Brace & Co., 1923; also by Walter N. Polakov in *Man and His Affairs,* Williams & Wilkins, 1925.

"Why! That is lifting yourself by your own bootstraps!" I exclaimed in amazed incredulity. "It's absurd."

Woleshensky smiled indulgently. He towered in his chair as though in the infinite kindness of his vast mind there were room to understand and overlook all the foolish little foibles of all the weak little beings that called themselves men. A mathematical physicist lives in vast spaces where a light-year is a footstep, where universes are being born and blotted out, where space unrolls along a fourth dimension on a surface distended from a fifth. To him, human beings and their affairs do not loom very important.

"Relativity," he explained. In his voice there was a patient forbearance for my slowness of comprehension. "Merely relativity. It doesn't take much physical effort to make the moon move through the treetops, does it? Just enough to walk down the garden path."

I stared at him, and he continued: "If you had been born and raised on a moving train, no one could convince you that the landscape was not in rapid motion. Well, our conception of the universe is quite as relative as that. Sir Isaac Newton tried in his mathematics to express a universe as though beheld by an infinitely removed and perfectly fixed observer. Mathematicians since his time, realizing the futility of such an effort, have taken into consideration that what things 'are' depends upon the person who is looking at them. They have tried to express common knowledge, such as the law of gravitation, in terms that would hold good for all observers. Yet their leader and culminating genius, Einstein, has been unable to express knowledge in terms of pure relativity; he has had to acccept the velocity of light as an arbitrarily fixed constant. Why should the velocity of light be any more fixed and constant than any other quantity in the universe?"

"But what's that got to do with going into the fourth dimension?" I broke in impatiently.

He continued as though I hadn't spoken.

"The thing that interests us now, and that mystifies modern mathematicians, is the question of movement, or, more accurately, translation. Is there such a thing as *absolute translation*? Can there be movement—translation—except in relation to something else than the thing that moves? All movement we know of is movement in relation to other objects, whether it be a walk down the street or the movement of the earth in its orbit around the sun. A change of *relative* position. But the mere translation of an isolated object existing alone in space is mathematically inconceivable, for there is no such thing as space in that sense."

"I thought you said something about going into another universe—" I interrupted again.

You can't argue with Woleshensky. His train of thought went on without a break.

"By translation we understand getting from one place to another. 'Going somewhere' originally meant a movement of our bodies. Yet, as a matter of fact, when we drive in an automobile we 'go somewhere' without moving our bodies at all. The scene is changed around us; we are somewhere else; and yet we haven't *moved* at all.

"Or suppose you could cast off gravitational attraction for a moment and let the earth rotate under you; you would be going somewhere and yet not moving—"

"But that is theory; you can't tinker with gravitation—"

"Every day you tinker with gravitation. When you start upward in an elevator, your pressure, not your weight, against the floor of it is increased; apparent gravitation between you and the floor of the elevator is greater than before—and that's like gravitation is anyway: inertia and acceleration. But we are talking about translation. The position of everything in the universe must be referred to some sort of coordinates. Suppose we change the angle or direction of the coordinates: then you have 'gone somewhere' and yet you haven't moved, nor has anything else moved."

I looked at him, holding my head in my hands.

"I couldn't swear that I understood that," I said slowly. "And I repeat, it looks like lifting yourself by your own bootstraps."

The homely simile did not dismay him. He pointed a finger at me as he spoke. "You've seen a chip of wood bobbing on the ripples of a pond. Now you think the chip is moving, now the water. Yet neither is moving; the only motion is of an abstract thing called a wave.

"You've seen those 'illusion' diagrams—for instance, this one is a group of cubes. Make up your mind that you are looking down upon their upper surfaces, and indeed they seem below you. Now change your mind and imagine that you are down below, looking up. Behold, you see their lower surfaces; you are indeed below them. You have 'gone somewhere,' yet there has been no translation of anything. You have merely changed coordinates."

"Which do you think will drive me insane more quickly—if you *show* me what you mean, or if you keep on talking without showing me?"

"I'll try to show you. There are some types of minds, you know, that cannot grasp the idea of relativity. It isn't the mathematics involved that matters; it's just the inability of some types of mental organizations to grasp the fact that the mind of the observer endows his environment with certain properties which have no absolute existence. Thus, when you walk through the garden at night the moon floats from one treetop to another. Is your mind good enough to invert this: make the moon stand still and let the trees move backward? Can you do that? If so, you can 'go somewhere' into another dimension."

Wolshensky rose and walked to the window. His office was an appropriate setting for such a modern discussion as ours—situated in a new, ultramodern building on the university campus, the varnish glossy, the walls clean, the books neatly arranged behind clean glass, the desk in most orderly array; the office was just as precise and modern and wonderful as the mind of its occupant.

"When do you want to go?" he asked.

"Now!"

"Then I have two more things to explain to you. The fourth dimension is just as much *here* as anywhere else. Right here around you and me things exist and go forward in the fourth dimension; but we do not see them and are not conscious of them because we are confined to our own three. Secondly, if we name the four coordinates as Einstein does, x, y, z, and t, then we exist in x, y, and z and move freely about in them, but are powerless to move in t. Why? Because t is the time dimension; and the time dimension is a difficult one for biological structures that depend on irreversible chemical reactions for their existence. But biochemical reactions can take place along any of the other dimensions as well as along t.

"Therefore, let us transform coordinates. Rotate the property of chemical irreversibility from t to z. Since we are organically able to exist (or at least to perceive) in only three dimensions at once, our new time dimension will be z. We shall be unconscious of z and cannot travel in it. Our activities and consciousness will take place along x, y, and t.

"According to fiction writers, to switch into the t dimension, some sort of apparatus with an electrical field ought to be necessary. It is not. You need nothing more to rotate into the t dimension than you do to stop the moon and make the trees move as you ride down the road; or than you do to turn the cubes upside down. It is a matter of *relativity.*"

I had ceased trying to wonder or to understand.

"Show me!" was all I could gasp.

"The success of this experiment in changing from the z to the t coordinate has depended largely upon my lucky discovery of a favorable location. It is just as, when you want the moon to ride the treetops successfully, there have to be favorable features in the topography or it won't work. The edge of this building and that little walk between the two rows of Norway poplars seems to be an angle between planes in the z and t dimensions. It seems to slope downward, does it not? —Now walk from here to the end and imagine yourself going upward. That is all. Instead of feeling this building behind and *above* you, conceive it as behind and *below.* Just as on your ride by moonlight, you must tell yourself that the moon is not moving while the trees ride by. —Can you do that? Go ahead, then." He spoke in a confident tone, as though he knew exactly what would happen.

Half credulous, half wondering, I walked slowly out of the door. I noticed that Woleshensky settled himself down to the table with a pad and a pencil to some kind of study, and forgot me before I had finished turning around. I looked curiously at the familiar wall of the building and the still more familiar poplar walk, expecting to see some strange scenery, some unknown view from another world. But there were the same old bricks and trees that I had known so long, though my disturbed and wondering frame of mind endowed them with a sudden strangeness and unwontedness. Things I had known for some years, they were, yet so powerfully had Woleshensky's arguments impressed me that I already fancied myself in a different universe. According to the conception of relativity, objects of the x, y, z universe *ought* to look different when viewed from the x, y, t universe.

Strange to say, I had no difficulty at all in imagining myself as going *upward* on my stroll along the slope, I told myself that the building was behind and below me, and indeed it seemed real that it was that way. I walked some distance along the little avenue of poplars, which seemed familiar enough in all its details, though after a few minutes it struck me that the avenue seemed rather long. In fact, it was much longer than I had ever known it to be before.

With a queer Alice-in-Wonderland feeling I noted it stretching way on ahead of me. Then I looked back.

I gasped in astonishment. The building was indeed *below* me. I looked down upon it from the top of an elevation. The astonishment of that realization had barely broken over me when I admitted that there was a building down there; but what building? Not the new Morton Hall, at any rate. It was a long, three-story brick building, quite resembling Morton Hall, but it was not the same. And on beyond there were trees with buildings among them; but it was not the campus that I knew.

I paused in a kind of panic. What was I to do now? Here I was in a strange place. How I had gotten there I had no idea. What ought I to do about it? Where should I go? How was I to get back? Odd that I had neglected the precaution of how to get back. I surmised that I must be on the t dimension. Stupid blunder on my part, neglecting to find out how to get back.

I walked rapidly down the slope toward the building. Any hopes that I might have had about its being Morton Hall were thoroughly dispelled in a moment. It was a totally strange building, old, and old-fashioned looking. I had never seen it before in my life. Yet it looked ordinary and natural and was obviously a university classroom building.

I cannot tell whether it was an hour or a dozen that I spent walking frantically this way and that, trying to decide to go into this building or another, and at the last moment backing out in a sweat of hesitation. It seemed like a year but was probably only a few minutes. Then I noticed the people. They were mostly young people, of both sexes. Students, of course. Obviously I was on a university campus. Perfectly natural, normal young people, they were. If I were really on the t dimension, it certainly resembled the z dimension very closely.

Finally I came to a decision. I could stand this no longer. I selected a solitary, quiet-looking man and stopped him.

"Where am I?" I demanded.

He looked at me in astonishment. I waited for a reply, and he continued to gaze at me speechlessly. Finally it occurred to me that he didn't understand English.

"Do you speak English?" I asked hopelessly.

"Of course!" he said vehemently. "What's wrong with you?"

"Something's wrong with something," I exclaimed. "I haven't any idea where I am or how I got here."

"Synthetic wine?" he asked sympathetically.

"Oh, hell! Think I'm a fool? Say, do you have a good man in mathematical physics on the faculty? Take me to him."

"Psychology, I should think," he said, studying me. "Or psychiatry. But I'm a law student and know nothing of either."

"Then make it mathematical physics, and I'll be grateful to you."

So I was conducted to the mathematical physicist. The student led me into the very building that corresponded to Morton Hall, and into an office the position of which quite corresponded to that of Woleshensky's office. However, the office was older and dustier; it had a Victorian look about it and was not as modern as Woleshensky's room. Professor Vibens was a rather small, bald-headed man with a keen-looking face. As I thanked the law student and started on my story, he looked rather bored, as though wondering why I had picked on him with my tale of wonder. Before I had gotten very far he straightened up a little; and farther along he pricked up another notch; and before many minutes he was tense in his chair as he listened to me. When I finished, his comment was terse, like that of a man accustomed to thinking accurately and to the point.

"Obviously you come into this world from another set of coordinates. As we are on the z dimension, you must have come to us from the t dimension—"

He disregarded my attempts to protest at this point.

"Your man Woleshensky has evidently developed the conception of relativity further than we have, although Monpeters's theory comes close enough to it. Since I have no idea how to get you back, you must be my guest. I shall enjoy hearing about your world."

"That is very kind of you," I said gratefully. "I'm accepting because I can't see what else to do. At least until the time when I can find myself a place in your world or get back to my own. Fortunately," I added as an afterthought, "no one will miss me there, unless it be a few classes of students who will welcome the little vacation that must elapse before my successor is found."

Breathlessly eager to find out what sort of world I had gotten into, I walked with him to his home. And I may state at the outset that if I had found everything upside down and outlandishly bizarre, I should have been far less amazed and astonished than I was. For, from the walk that first evening from Professor Vibens's office along several blocks of residence street to his solid and respectable home, through all of my goings about the town and country during the years that I remained in the t-dimensional world, I found people and things thoroughly ordinary and familiar. They looked and acted as we do, and their homes and goods looked like ours. I cannot possibly imagine a world and a people that could be more similar to ours without actually being the same. It was months before I got over the idea that I had merely wandered into an unfamiliar part of my own city. Only the actual experience of wide travel and much sightseeing, and the knowledge that there was no such extensive English-speaking country in the world that

I knew, convinced me that I must be on some other world, doubtless in the t dimension.

"A gentleman who has found his way here from another universe," the professor introduced me to a strapping young fellow who was mowing the lawn. The professor's son was named John! Could anything be more commonplace?

"I'll have to take you around and show you things tomorrow," John said cordially, accepting the account of my arrival without surprise.

A redheaded servant girl, roast pork and rhubarb sauce for dinner, and checkers afterward, a hot bath at bedtime, the ringing of a telephone somewhere else in the house—is it any wonder that it was months before I would believe that I had actually come into a different universe? What slight differences there were in the people and the world merely served to emphasize the similarity. For instance, I think they were just a little more hospitable and "old-fashioned" than we are. Making due allowances for the fact that I was a rather remarkable phenomenon, I think I was welcomed more heartily in this home and in others later; people spared me more of their time and interest from their daily business than would have happened under similar circumstances in a correspondingly busy city in America.

Again, John found a lot of time to take me about the city and show me banks and stores and offices. He drove a little squat car with tall wheels, run by a spluttering gasoline motor. (The car was not as perfect as our modern cars, and horses were quite numerous in the streets. Yet John was a busy businessman, the district superintendent of a life-insurance agency.) Think of it! Life insurance in Einstein's t dimension.

"You're young to be holding such an important position," I suggested.

"Got started early," John replied. "Dad is disappointed because I didn't see fit to waste time in college. Disgrace to the family, I am."

What in particular shall I say about the city? It might have been any one of a couple of hundred American cities. Only it wasn't. The electric streetcars, except for their bright green color, were perfect; they might have been brought over bodily from Oshkosh or Tulsa. The ten-cent stores with gold letters on their signs; drugstores with soft drinks; a mad, scrambling stock exchange; the blaring sign of an advertising dentist; brilliant entrances to motion-picture theaters were all there. The beauty shops did wonders to the women's heads, excelling our own by a good deal, if I am any judge; and at that time I had nothing more important on my mind than to speculate on that question. Newsboys bawled the *Evening Sun* and the *Morning Gale*, in whose curious, flat type I could read accounts of legislative doings, murders, and divorces quite as fluently as I could in my own *Tribune* at home. Strangeness and unfamiliarity had bothered me a good deal on a trip to Quebec a couple of years before; but they were not noticeable here in the t dimension.

For three or four weeks the novelty of going around, looking at things, meeting people, visiting concerts, theaters and department stores was sufficient to absorb my interest. Professor Vibens's hospitality was so sincerely extended that I did not hesitate to accept, though I assured him that I would repay it as soon as I got established in this world. In a few days I was thoroughly convinced that there was no way back home. Here I must stay, at least until I learned as much as Woleshensky knew about crossing dimensions. Professor Vibens eventually secured for me a position at the university.

It was shortly after I had accepted the position as instructor in experimental physics and had begun to get broken into my work that I noticed a strange commotion among the people of the city. I have always been a studious recluse, observing people as phenomena rather than participating in their activities. So for some time I noted only in a subconscious way the excited gathering in groups, the gesticulations and blazing eyes, the wild sale of extra editions of papers, the general air of disturbance. I even failed to take an active interest in these things when I made a railroad journey of three hundred miles and spent a week in another city; so thoroughly at home did I feel in this world that when the advisability arose of my studying laboratory methods at another university, I made the trip alone. So absorbed was I in my laboratory problems that I only noted with half an eye the commotion and excitement everywhere, and merely recollected it later. One night it suddenly popped into my head that the country was aroused over something.

That night I was with the Vibens family in their living room. John tuned in the radio. I wasn't listening to the thing very much; I had troubles of my own. $F = \frac{gm_1, m_2}{r^2}$ was familiar enough to me. It meant the same and held as rigidly here as in my own world. But what was the name of the bird who formulated that law? Back home it was Newton. Tomorrow in class I would have to be thoroughly familiar with his name. Pasvieux, that's what it was. What messy surnames. It struck me that it was lucky that they expressed the laws of physics in the same form and even in the algebraic letters, or I might have had a time getting them confused—when all of a sudden the radio blatantly bawled: "THE GOSTAK DISTIMS THE DOSHES!"

John jumped to his feet.

"Damn right!" he shouted, slamming the table with his fist.

Both his father and mother annihilated him with withering glances, and he slunk from the room. I gazed stupefied. My stupefaction continued while the professor shut off the radio and both of them excused themselves from my presence. Then suddenly I was alert.

I grabbed a bunch of newspapers, having seen none for several days. Great sprawling headlines covered the front pages:

"THE GOSTAK DISTIMS THE DOSHES."

For a moment I stopped, trying to recollect where I had heard those words before. They recalled something to me. Ah, yes! That very afternoon there had been a commotion beneath my window on the university campus. I had been busy checking over an experiment so that I might be sure of its success at tomorrow's class, and looked out rather absently to see what was going on. A group of young men from a dismissed class was passing and had stopped for a moment.

"I say, the gostak distims the doshes!" said a fine-looking fellow. His face was pale and strained.

The young man facing him sneered derisively, "Aw, your grandmother! Don't be a feeble—"

He never finished. The first fellow's fist caught him in the cheek. Several books dropped to the ground. In a moment the two had clinched and were rolling on the ground, fists flying up and down, smears of blood appearing here and there. The others surrounded them and for a moment appeared to enjoy the spectacle, but suddenly recollected that it looked rather disgraceful on a university campus, and after a lively tussle separated the combatants. Twenty of them, pulling in two directions, tugged them apart.

The first boy strained in the grasp of his captors; his white face was flecked with blood and he panted for breath.

"Insult!" he shouted, giving another mighty heave to get free. He looked contemptuously around. "The whole bunch of you ought to learn to stand up for your honor. The gostak distims the doshes!"

That was the astonishing incident that these words called to my mind. I turned back to my newspapers.

"Slogan Sweeps the Country," proclaimed the subheads. "Ringing Expression of National Spirit! Enthusiasm Spreads Like Wildfire! The new patriotic slogan is gaining ground rapidly," the leading article went on. "The fact that it has covered the country almost instantaneously seems to indicate that it fills a deep and long-felt want in the hearts of the people. It was first uttered during a speech in Walkingdon by that majestic figure in modern statesmanship, Senator Harob. The beautiful sentiment, the wonderful emotion of this sublime thought, are epoch-making. It is a great conception, doing credit to a great man, and worthy of being the guiding light of a great—"

That was the gist of everything I could find in the papers. I fell asleep still puzzled about the time. I was puzzled because—as I see now and didn't then—I was trained in the analytical methods of physical science and knew little or nothing about the ways and emotions of the masses of the people.

In the morning the senseless expression popped into my head as soon as I awoke. I determined to waylay the first member of the Vibens family who showed up, and demand the meaning of the thing. It happened to be John.

"John, what's a gostak?"

John's face lighted up with pleasure. He threw out his chest and a look of pride replaced the pleasure. His eyes blazed, and with a consuming enthusiasm he shook hands with me, as deacons shake hands with a new convert—a sort of glad welcome.

"The gostak!" he exclaimed. "Hurray for the gostak!"

"But what is a gostak?"

"Not a gostak! *The* gostak. The gostak is—the distimmer of the doshes—see! He distims 'em, see?"

"Yes, yes. But what is distimming? How do you distim?"

"No, no! Only the gostak can distim. The gostak distim the doshes. See?"

"Ah, I see!" I exclaimed. Indeed, I pride myself on my quick wit. "What are doshes? Why, they are the stuff distimmed by the gostak. Very simple!"

"Good for you!" John slapped my back in huge enthusiasm. "I think it wonderful for you to understand us so well after being here only a short time. You are very patriotic."

I gritted my teeth tightly to keep myself from speaking.

"Professor Vibens, what's a gostak?" I asked in the solitude of his office an hour later.

He looked pained.

He leaned back in his chair and looked me over elaborately, and waited some time before answering.

"Hush!" he finally whispered. "A scientific man may think what he pleases, but if he says too much, people in general may misjudge him. As a matter of fact, a good many scientific men are taking this so-called patriotism seriously. But a mathematician cannot use words loosely; it has become second nature with him to inquire closely into the meaning of every term he uses."

"Well, doesn't that jargon mean anything at all?" I was beginning to be puzzled in earnest.

"To me it does not. But it seems to mean a great deal to the public in general. It's making people do things, is it not?"

I stood for a while in stupefied silence. That an entire great nation should become fired up over a meaningless piece of nonsense! Yet the astonishing thing was that I had to admit there was plenty of precedent for it in the history of my own z-dimensional world. A nation exterminating itself in civil wars to decide which of two profligate royal families should be privileged to waste the people's substance from the throne; a hundred thousand crusaders marching to death for an idea that to me means nothing; a meaningless, untrue advertising slogan that sells millions of dollars' worth of cigarettes to a nation, to the latter's own detriment—haven't we seen it over and over again?

"There's a public lecture on this stuff tonight at the First Church of the Salvation," Professor Vibens suggested.

"I'll be there," I said. "I want to look into the thing."

That afternoon there was another flurry of "extras" over the street; people gathered in knots and gesticulated with open newspapers.

"War! Let 'em have it!" I heard men shout.

"Is our national honor a rag to be muddied and trampled on?" the editorials asked.

As far as I could gather from reading the papers, there was a group of nations across an ocean that was not taking the gostak seriously. A ship whose pennant bore the slogan had been refused entrance to an Engtalian harbor because it flew no national ensign. The Executive had dispatched a diplomatic note. An evangelist who had attempted to preach the gospel of the distimmed doshes to the public gathering in Itland had been ridden on a rail and otherwise abused. The Executive was dispatching a diplomatic note.

Public indignation waxed high. Derogatory remarks about "wops" were flung about. Shouts of "Holy war!" were heard. I could feel the tension in the atmosphere as I took my seat in the crowded church in the evening. I had been assured that the message of the gostak and the doshes would be thoroughly expounded so that even the most simple-minded and uneducated people could understand it fully. Although I had my hands full at the university, I was so puzzled and amazed at the course events were taking that I determined to give the evening to finding out what the slogan meant.

There was a good deal of singing before the lecture began. Mimeographed copies of the words were passed about, but I neglected to preserve them and do not remember them. I know there was one solemn hymn that reverberated harmoniously through the great church, a chanting repetition of "The Gostak Distims the Doshes." There was another stirring martial air that began, "Oh, the Gostak! Oh, the Gostak!" and ended with a swift cadence on "The Gostak Distims the Doshes!" The speaker had a rich, eloquent voice and a commanding figure. He stepped out and bowed solemnly.

"The gostak distims the doshes," he pronounced impressively. "Is it not comforting to know that there is a gostak; do we not glow with pride because the doshes are distimmed? In the entire universe there is no more profoundly significant fact: the gostak distims the doshes. Could anything be more complete yet more tersely emphatic! The gostak distims the doshes!" Applause. "This thrilling truth affects our innermost lives. What would we do if the gostak did not distim the doshes? Without the gostak, without doshes, what would we do? What would we think? How would we feel?" Applause again.

At first I thought this was some kind of introduction. I was inexperienced in listening to popular speeches, lectures, and sermons. I had spent most of my life in the study of physics and its accessory sciences. I could not help trying to figure out the meaning of whatever I heard. When I found none, I began to get impatient. I waited some more, thinking that soon he would begin on the real explanation. After thirty minutes of the same sort of stuff as I have just quoted, I gave up trying to listen. I just sat and hoped he would soon be through. The people applauded and grew more excited. After an hour I stirred restlessly; I slouched down in my seat and sat up by turns. After two hours I grew desperate; I got up and walked out. Most of the people were too excited to notice me. Only a few of them cast hostile glances at my retreat.

The next day the mad nightmare began for me. First there was a snowstorm of extras over the city, announcing the sinking of a merchantman by an Engtalian cruiser. A dispute had arisen between the officers of the merchantman and the port officials, because the latter had jeered disrespectfully at the gostak. The merchantman picked up and started out without having fulfilled all the custom requirements. A cruiser followed it and ordered it to return. The captain of the merchantman told them that the gostak distims the doshes, whereupon the cruiser fired twice and sank the merchantman. In the afternoon came the extras announcing the Executive's declaration of war.

Recruiting offices opened; the university was depleted of its young men; uniformed troops marched through the city, and railway trains full of them went in and out. Campaigns for raising war loans; home-guards, women's auxiliaries, ladies' aid societies making bandages, young women enlisting as ambulance drivers—it was indeed war; all of it to the constantly repeated slogan: "The gostak distims the doshes."

I could hardly believe that it was really true. There seemed to be no adequate cause for a war. The huge and powerful nation had dreamed a silly slogan and flung it in the world's face. A group of nations across the water had united into an alliance, claiming they had to defend themselves against having forced upon them a principle they did not desire. The whole thing at the bottom had no meaning. It did not seem possible that there would actually be a war; it seemed more like going through a lot of elaborate play-acting.

Only when the news came of a vast naval battle of doubtful issue, in which ships had been sunk and thousands of lives lost, did it come to me that they meant business. Black bands of mourning appeared on sleeves and in windows. Reports of a division wiped out by an airplane attack; of forty thousand dead in a five-day battle; of more men and more money needed, began to make things look real. Haggard men with bandaged heads and arms in slings appeared on the streets, a church and an auditorium were converted into hospitals, and trainloads of wounded were brought in. To convince myself that this thing was so, I visited these wards and saw with my own eyes the rows of cots, the surgeons working on ghastly wounds, the men with a leg missing or with a hideously disfigured face.

Food became restricted; there was no white bread, and sugar was rationed. Clothing was of poor quality; coal and oil were obtainable only on government permit. Businesses were shut down. John was gone; his parents received news that he was missing in action.

Real it was; there could be no more doubt of it. The thing that made it seem most real was the picture of a mangled, hopeless wreck of humanity sent back from the guns, a living protest against the horror of war. Suddenly someone would say, "The gostak distims the doshes!" and the poor wounded fragment would straighten up and put out his chest with pride, and an unquenchable fire would blaze in his eyes. He did not regret having given his all for that. How could I understand it?

And real it was when the draft was announced. More men were needed; volunteers were insufficient. Along with the rest, I complied with the order to register, doing so in a mechanical fashion, thinking little of it. Suddenly the coldest realization of the reality of it was flung at me when I was informed that my name had been drawn and that I would have to go!

All this time I had looked upon this mess as something outside of me, something belonging to a different world, of which I was not a part. With all this death and mangled humanity in the background, I wasn't even interested in this world. I didn't belong here. To be called upon to undergo all the horrors of military life, the risk of a horrible death, for no reason at all! For a silly jumble of meaningless sounds.

I spent a sleepless night in maddened shock from the thing. In the morning a wild and haggard caricature of myself looked back at me from the mirror. But I had revolted. I intended to refuse service. If the words "conscientious objector" ever meant anything, I certainly was one. Even if they shot me for treason at once, that would be a fate less hard to bear than going out and giving my strength and my life for—for nothing at all.

My apprehensions were quite correct. With my usual success at self-control over a seething interior, I coolly walked to the draft office and informed them that I did not believe in their cause and could not see my way to fight for it. Evidently they had suspected something of the sort already, for they had the irons on my wrists before I had hardly done with my speech.

"Period of emergency," said a beefy tyrant at the desk. "No time for stringing out a civil trial. Court-martial!"

He said it to me vindictively, and the guards jostled me roughly down the corridor; even they resented my attitude. The court-martial was already waiting for me. From the time I walked out of the lecture at the church I had been under secret surveillance, and they knew my attitude thoroughly. This is the first thing the president of the court informed me.

My trial was short. I was informed that I had no valid reason for objecting. Objectors because of religion, because of nationality and similar reasons, were readily understood; a jail sentence to the end of the war was their usual fate. But I had admitted that I had no intrinsic objection to fighting; I merely jeered at their holy cause. That was treason unpardonable.

"Sentenced to be shot at sunrise!" the president of the court announced.

The world spun around with me. But only for a second. My self-control came to my aid. With the curious detachment that comes to us in such emergencies I noted that the court-martial was being held in Professor Vibens's office—that dingy little Victorian room where I had first told my story of traveling by relativity and had first realized that I had come to the t-dimensional world. Apparently it was also to be the last room I was to see in this same world. I had no false hopes that the execution would help me back to my own world, as such things sometimes do in stories. When life is gone, it is gone, whether in one dimension or another. I would be just as dead in the z dimension as in the t dimension.

"Now, Einstein, or never!" I thought. "Come to my aid, O Riemann! O Lobachevski! If anything will save me it will have to be a tensor or a geodesic."

I said it to myself rather ironically. Relativity had brought me here. Could it get me out of this?

Well! Why not?

If the form of a natural law, yea, if a natural object varies with the observer who expresses it, might not the truth and the meaning of the gostak slogan also be a matter of relativity? It was like making the moon ride the treetops again. If I could be a better relativist and put myself in these people's places, perhaps I could understand the gostak. Perhaps I would even be willing to fight for him or it.

The idea struck me suddenly. I must have straightened up and some bright change must have passed over my features, for the guards who led me looked at me curiously and took a firmer grip on me. We had descended the steps of the building and had started down the walk.

Making the moon ride the treetops! That was what I needed now. And that sounded as silly to me as the gostak. And the gostak did not seem so silly. I drew a deep breath and felt very much encouraged. The viewpoint of *relativity* was somehow coming back to me. Necessity manages much. I could understand how one might fight for the idea of a gostak distimming the doshes. I felt almost like telling these men. Relativity is a wonderful thing. They led me up the slope, between the rows of poplars.

Then it all suddenly popped into my head: how I had gotten here by changing my coordinates, insisting to myself that I was going *upward*. Just like making the moon stop and making the trees ride when you are out riding at night. Now I was going upward. In my own world, in the z dimension, this same poplar was *down* the slope.

"It's downward!" I insisted to myself. I shut my eyes and imagined the building behind and *above* me. With my eyes shut, it did seem downward. I walked for a long time before opening them. Then I opened them and looked around.

I was at the end of the avenue of poplars. I was surprised. The avenue seemed short. Somehow it had become shortened; I had not expected to reach the end so soon. And where were the guards in olive uniforms? There were none.

I turned around and looked back. The slope extended on backward above me. I had indeed walked downward. There were no guards, and the fresh, new building was on the hill behind me.

Woleshensky stood on the steps.

"Now what do you think of a t dimension?" he called out to me.

Woleshensky!

And a *new* building, modern! Vibens's office was in an old Victorian building. What was there in common between Vibens and Woleshensky? I drew a deep breath. The comforting realization spread gratefully over me that I was back in my native dimension. The gostak and the war were somewhere else. Here were peace and Woleshensky.

I hastened to pour out the story to him.

"What does it all mean?" I asked when I was through. "Somehow—vaguely—it seems that it ought to mean something."

"Perhaps," he said in his kind, sage way, "we really exist in four dimensions. A part of us and our world that we cannot see and are not conscious of projects on into another dimension, just like the front edges of the books in the bookcase, turned away from us. You know that the section of a conic cut by the y plane looks different from the section of the same conic cut by the z plane? Perhaps what you saw was our own world and our own selves intersected by a different set of coordinates. *Relativity*, as I told you in the beginning."

Nelson Bond, one of the more notably polished contributors to the pulp magazines, began writing science fiction in 1937. He was most closely associated with Amazing® Stories, *and especially with its then-companion,* Fantastic Adventures, *between 1939 and 1943. He then became a contributor to the prestigious Blue Book. Three collections of his stories have been published, most recently* Nightmares and Daydreams *(Arkham House, 1968). He deserves to be much better known. This story was published in October 1939.*

PILGRIMAGE
by Nelson Bond

In her twelfth summer, the illness came upon Meg and she was afraid. Afraid, yet turbulent with a strange feeling of exaltation unlike anything she had ever before known. She was a woman now. And she knew, suddenly and completely, that which was expected of her from this day on. Knew—and dreaded.

She went immediately to the *hoam* of the Mother. For such was the Law. But as she moved down the walk-avenue, she stared, with eyes newly curious, at the Men she passed. At their pale, pitifully hairless bodies. At their soft, futile hands and weak mouths. One lolling on the doorstep of 'Ana's *hoam* returned her gaze brazenly; made a small, enticing gesture. Meg shuddered, and curled her lips in a refusal-face.

Only yesterday she had been a child. Now, suddenly, she was a woman. And for the first time, Meg saw her people as they really were.

The warriors of the Clan. She looked with distaste upon the tense angularity of their bodies. The corded legs, the grim, set jaws. The cold eyes. The brawny arms, scarred to the elbow with ill-healed cicatrices. The tiny, thwarted breasts, flat and hard beneath leather harness-plates. Fighters they were, and nothing else.

This was not what she wanted.

She saw, too, the mothers. The full-lipped, flabby-breasted bearers of children, whose skins were soft and white as those of the Men. Whose eyes were humid; washed barren of all expression by desires too often sated. Their bodies bulged at hip and thigh, swayed when they walked like ripe grain billowing in a lush and fertile field. They lived only that the tribe might live, might continue to exist. They reproduced.

This was not what she wanted.

Then there were the workers. Their bodies retained a vestige of womankind's inherent grace and nobility. But if their waists were thin, their hands were blunt-fingered and thick. Their shoulders were bent with the weight of labor, coarsened from adze and hod. Their faces were grim from the eternal struggle with an unyielding earth. And the earth, of which they had made themselves a part, had in return made itself a part of them. The workers' skin was browned with soil, their bodies stank of dirt and grim and unwashed perspiration.

No, none of these was what she wanted. None of these was what she would *have*, of that she was positively determined.

So great was Meg's concentration that she entered into the *hoam* of the Mother without crying out, as was required. Thus it was that she discovered the Mother making great magic to the gods.

In her right hand, the Mother held a stick. With it she scratched upon a smooth, bleached, calfskin scroll. From time to time she let the stick drink from a pool of midnight cupped in a dish before her. When she moved it again on the hide, it left its spoor: a spidery trail of black.

For a long moment Meg stood and watched, wondering. Then dread overcame her; fear-thoughts shook her body. She thought suddenly of the gods. Of austere Jarg, their leader; of lean Ibrim and taciturn Taamuz. Of far-seeing Tedhi, she whose laughter echoes in the roaring summer thunders. What wrath would they visit upon one who had spied into their secrets?

She covered her eyes and dropped to her knees. But there were footsteps before her, and the Mother's hands upon her shoulders. And there was but gentle chiding in the voice of the Mother as she said, "My child, know you not the Law? That all must cry out before entering the Mother's *hoam*?"

Meg's fear-thoughts went away. The Mother was good. It was she who fed and clothed the Clan; warmed them in dark winter and found them meat when meat was scarce. If she, who was the gods' spokesman on earth, saw no evil in Meg's unintentional prying—

Meg dared look again at the magic stick. There was a question in her eyes. The Mother answered that question.

"It is 'writing,' Meg. Speech without words."

Speech-without-words? Meg crept to the table; bent a curious ear over the spidermarks. But she heard no sound. Then the Mother was beside her again saying, "No, my child. It does not speak to the ear, but to the eyes. Listen, and I will make it speak through my mouth."

She read aloud.

"Report of the month of June, 3478 A.D. There has been no change in the number of the Jinnia Clan. We are still five score and seven, with nineteen Men, twelve cattle, thirty horses. But there is reason to believe that 'Ana and Sahlee will soon add to our number.

"Last week Darthee, Lina, and Alis journeyed into the Clina territory in search of game. They met there several of the Durm Clan and exchanged gifts of salt and bacca. Pledges of friendship were given. On the return trip, Darthee was linberred by one of the Wild Ones, but was rescued by her companions before the strain could be crossed. The Wild One was destroyed.

"We have in our village a visitor from the Delwurs of the east, who says that in her territory the Wild Ones have almost disappeared. Illness, she says, has depleted their Men—and she begs that I lend her one or two for a few months. I am thinking of letting her have Jak and Ralf, both of whom are proven studs—"

The Mother stopped. "That is as far as I had gone, my child, when you entered."

Meg's eyes were wide with wonder. It was quite true that Darthee, Lina, and Alis had recently returned from a trip to Clina. And that there was now a visitor in camp. But how could the speech-without-words know these things, *tell* these things? She said, "But, Mother—will not the speech-without-words forget?"

"No, Meg. *We* forget. The books remember always."

"Books, Mother?"

"These are books." The Mother moved to the sleeping part of her *hoam*; selected one of a tumbled pile of calfskin scrolls. "Here are the records of our Clan from ages past—since the time of the Ancient Ones. Not all are here. Some have been lost. Others were ruined by flood or destroyed by fire.

"But it is the Mother's duty to keep these records. That is why the Mother must know the art of making the speech-without-words. It is hard work, my little one. And a labor without end—"

Meg's eyes were shining. The trouble that had been cold within her before was vanished now. In its place had come a great thought. A thought *so* great, *so* daring, that Meg had to open her lips twice before the words came.

"Is it—" she asked breathlessly, "is it very hard to become a—Mother?"

The Mother smiled gently. "A very great task, Meg. But you should not think such things. It is not yet time for you to decide—" She paused, looking at Meg strangely. "Or—is it, my child?"

Meg flushed, and her eyes dropped.

"It is, Mother."

"Then be not afraid, my daughter. You know the Law. At this important hour it is yours to decide what station in life will be yours. What is your wish, Meg? Would you be a warrior, a worker, or a breeding mother?"

Meg looked at the Clan leader boldly.

"I would be," she said, "a Mother!" Then, swiftly, "But not a breeding mother. I mean a *Clan* Mother—like you, O Mother!"

The Mother stared. Then the harsh lines melted from her face and she said, thoughtfully, "Thrice before has that request been made of me, Meg. Each time I have refused. It was Beth who asked first, oh, many years ago. She became a warrior, and died gallantly lifting the siege of Loovil. . . .

"Then Haizl. And the last time it was Hein. When I refused, she became the other type of mother.

"But I was younger then. Now I am old. And it is right that there should be someone to take my place when I am gone—" She stared at the girl intently.

"It is not easy, my daughter. There is much work to be done. Work, not of the body but of the mind. There are problems to be solved, many vows to be taken, a hard pilgrimage to be made—"

"All these," swore Meg, "would I gladly do, O Mother! If you will but let me—" Her voice broke suddenly. "But I cannot become anything else. I would not be a warrior, harsh and bitter. Nor a worker, black with dirt. And the breeders—I would as soon mate with one of the Wild Ones as with one of the Men! The thought of their soft hands—"

She shuddered. And the Clan Mother nodded, understanding. "Very well, Meg. Tomorrow you will move into this *hoam*. You will live with me and study to become the Jinnia Clan's next Mother. . . ."

So began Meg's training. Nor was the Mother wrong in saying that the task was not an easy one. Many were the times when Meg wept bitterly, striving to learn that which a Mother must know. There was the speech-without-words, which Meg learned to call "writing." It looked like a simple magic when the Mother did it. But that slender stick, which moved so fluidly beneath the Mother's aged fingers, slipped and skidded and made ugly blotches of midnight on the hide whenever Meg tried to make spider-marks.

Meg learned that these wavering lines were not meaningless. Each line was made of "sentences," each sentence of "words," and each word was composed of "letters." And each letter made a sound, just as each combination of letters made a word-sound.

These were strange and confusing. A single letter, out of place, changed the whole meaning of the word ofttimes. Sometimes it altered the meaning of the whole sentence. But Meg's determination was great. There came, finally, the day when the Mother allowed her to write the monthly report in the Clan history. Meg was thirteen, then. But already she was older in wisdom than the others of her Clan.

It was then that the Mother began to teach her yet another magic. It was the magic of "numbers." Where there had been twenty-six "letters," there were only ten numbers. But theirs was a most peculiar magic. Put together, ofttimes they formed other and greater numbers. Yet the same numbers taken away from each other formed still a third group. The names of these magics, Meg never did quite learn. They were strange, magical, meaningless terms. "Multiplication" and "subtraction." But she learned how to do them.

Her task was made the harder, for it was about this time that the Evil Ones sent a little pain-imp to torment her. He stole in through her ear one night while she was sleeping. And for many months he lurked in her head, above her eyes. Every time she would sit down to study the magic of the numbers, he would begin dancing up and down, trying to stop her. But Meg persisted. And finally the pain-imp either died or was removed. And Meg knew the numbers. . . .

There were rites and rituals to be learned. There was the Sacred Song which had to be learned by heart. This song had no tune, but was accompanied by the beating of the tribal drums. Its words were strange and terrible; echoing the majesty of the gods in its cryptic phrasing.

"O Sakan! you see by Tedhi on his early Light—"

This was a great song. A powerful magic. It was the only tribal song Meg learned which dared name one of the gods. And it had to be sung reverently, lest far-seeing Tedhi be displeased and show her monstrous teeth and destroy the invoker with her mirthful thunders.

Meg learned, too, the tribal song of the Jinnia Clan. She had known it from infancy, but its words had been obscure. Now she learned enough to probe into its meaning. She did not know the meanings of some of the forgotten words, but for the most part it made sense when the tribe gathered on festive nights to sing, "Caamé back to over Jinnia—"

And Meg grew in age and stature and wisdom. In her sixteenth summer, her legs were long and firm and straight as a warrior's spear. Her body was supple; bronzed by sunlight save where her doeskin breech-cloth kept the skin white. Unbound, her hair would have trailed the earth, but she wore it piled upon her head, fastened by a netting woven by the old mothers, too ancient to bear.

The vanity-god had died long ages since, and Meg had no way of knowing she was beautiful. But sometimes, looking at her reflection in the pool as she bathed, she approved the soft curves of her slim young body, and was more than ever glad and proud that she had become a neophyte to the Mother. She liked her body to be this way. Why, she did not know. But she was glad that she had not turned lean and hard, as had those of her age who had become warriors. Or coarse, as had become the workers. Or soft and flabby, as were the breeding-mothers. Her skin was golden-brown, and pure gold where the sunlight burnished the fine down on her arms and legs, between her high, firm breasts.

And finally there came the day when the Mother let Meg conduct the rites at the Feast of the Blossoms. This was in July, and Meg had then entered upon her seventeenth year. It was a great occasion, and a great test. But Meg did not fail. She conducted the elaborate rite from beginning to end without a single mistake.

That night, in the quiet of their *hoam*, the Mother made a final magic. She drew from her collection of aged trophies a curl of parchment. This she blessed. Then she handed it to Meg.

"You are ready now, O my daughter," she said. "In the morning you will leave."

"Leave, Mother?" said Meg.

"For the final test. This that I give you is a map. A shower-of-places. You will see, here at this joining of mountain and river, our village in the heart of the Jinnia territory. Far off, westward and to the north as here is shown, is the Place of the Gods. It is there you must go on pilgrimage before you return to take your place as Mother."

Now, at this last moment, Meg felt misgivings.

"But you, Mother?" she asked. "If I become Mother, what will become of you?"

"The rest will be welcome, daughter. It is good to know that the work will be carried on—" The aged Mother pondered. "There is much, yet, that you do not know, Meg. It is forbidden that I should tell you all until you have been to the Place of the Gods. There will you see, and understand—"

"The—the books?" faltered Meg.

"Upon your return you may read the books. Even as I read them when I returned. And all will be made clear to you. Even that final secret which the clan must not know—"

"I do not understand, Mother."

"You will, my daughter—later. And now, to sleep. For at dawn tomorrow begins your pilgrimage. . . ."

Off in the hills, a wild dog howled his melancholy farewell to the dying moon. His thin song clove the stirring silence of the trees, the incessant movement of the forest. Meg wakened at that cry; wakened and saw that already the red edge of dawn tinged the eastern sky.

She uncurled from the broad treecrotch in which she had spent the night. Her horse was already awake, and with restless movements was nibbling the sparse grass beneath the giant oak. Meg loosed his tether, then went to the spring she had found the night before.

There she drank and, in the little rill that trickled from the spring, bathed herself as best she could. Her ablutions finished, she set about making breakfast. There was not much food in her saddlebags. A side of rabbit, carefully saved from last night's dinner. Two biscuits, slightly dry now. A precious handful of salt. She ate sparingly, resolved to build camp early tonight in order to set a few game traps and bake another batch of biscuit.

She cleared a space, scratching a wide circle of earth bare of all leaves and twigs, then walking around it widdershins thrice to chase away the firedemon. Then she scratched the firestone against a piece of the black metal from the town of the Ancient Ones—a gift of the Mother—and kindled her little fire.

Two weeks had passed since Meg had left the Jinnia territory. She had come from the rugged mountainlands of her home territory, through the river valleys of the Hyan Clan. On the flat plains of the Yana section, she had made an error. Her map had shown the route clearly, but she had come upon a road built by the Ancient Ones. A road of white creet, still in fair repair. And because it was easier to travel on this highway than to thread a way through the jungle, she had let herself drift southward.

It was not until she reached the timeworn village of Slooie that friendly Zuries had pointed out her mistake. Then she had to turn northward and westward again, going up the Big River to the territory of the Demoys.

Now, her map showed, she was in Braska territory. Two more weeks—perhaps less than that—should bring her to her goal. To the sacred Place of the Gods.

Meg started and roused from her speculations as a twig snapped in the forest behind her. In one swift motion she had wheeled, drawn her sword, and was facing the spot from which the sound had come. But the green bushes did not tremble; no further crackling came from the underbrush. Her fears allayed, she turned to the important business of roasting her side of rabbit.

It was always needful to be on the alert. Meg had learned that lesson early; even before her second day's journey had led her out of Jinnia territory. For, as the Mother had warned, there were still many Wild Ones roaming through the land. Searching for food, for the precious firemetal from the ruined villages of the Ancient Ones—most of all for mates. The Wild Ones were dying out, slowly, because of their lack of mates. There were few females left among them. Most of the Wild Ones were male. But there was little in their shaggy bodies, their thick, brutish faces, their hard, gnarled muscles, to remind one of the Men.

A Wild One had attacked Meg in her second night's camp. Fortunately she had not yet been asleep when he made his foray—else her pilgrimage would have ended abruptly. Not that he would have killed her. The Wild Ones did not kill the women they captured. They took them to their dens. And—Meg had heard tales. A priestess could not cross her strain with a Wild One and still become a Mother.

So Meg had fought fiercely, and had been victorious. The Wild One's bones lay now in the Jinnia hills, picked bare by the vultures. But since that escape, Meg had slept nightly in trees, her sword clenched in her hand. . . .

The food was cooked now. Meg removed it from the spit, blew upon it, and began to eat. She had many things on her mind. The end of her pilgrimage was nigh. The hour when she would enter into the Place of the Gods, and learn the last and most carefully guarded secret.

That is why her senses failed her. That is why she did not even know the Wild One lurked near until, with a roar of throaty satisfaction, he had leaped from the shrubbery, seized her, and pinioned her struggling arms to her sides with tight grip.

It was a bitter fight, but a silent one. For all her slimness, Meg's body was sturdy. She fought pantherlike, using every weapon with which the gods had endowed her. Her fists, legs, teeth.

But the Wild One's strength was as great as his ardor was strong. He crushed Meg to him bruisingly, the stink of his sweat burning her nostrils. His arms bruised her breasts, choked the breath from her straining lungs. One furry arm tensed about her throat, cutting off the precious air.

Meg writhed, broke free momentarily, buried her strong teeth in his arm. A howl of hurt and rage broke from the Wild One's lips. Meg tugged at her sword. But again the Wild One threw himself upon her; this time with great fists flailing. Meg saw a hammerlike hand smashing down on her, felt the shocking concussion of the Wild One's strength. A lightning flashed. The ground leaped up to meet her. Then all was silent. . . .

She woke, groaning weakly. Her head was splitting, and the bones of her body ached. She started to struggle to her feet; had risen halfway before she discovered with a burst of hope that she *could* move! She was not bound! Then the Wild One—

She glanced about her swiftly. She was still lying in the little glade where she had been attacked. The sun's full orb had crept over the horizon now, threading a lacework of light through the tiny glen. Her fire smouldered still. And beside it crouched a—a—

Meg could not decide what it was. It looked like a Man, but that of course was impossible. Its body was smooth and almost as hairless as her own. Bronzed by the sun. But it was not the pale, soft body of a Man. It was muscular, hard, firm; taller and stronger than a warrior.

Flight was Meg's first thought. But her curiosity was even stronger than her fear. This was a mystery. And her sword was beside her. Whoever, or whatever, this Thing might be, it did not seem to wish her harm. She spoke to it.

"Who are you?" asked Meg. "And where is the Wild One?"

The stranger looked up, and a happy look spread over his even features. He pointed briefly to the shrubbery. Meg followed the gesture; saw lying there the dead body of the Wild One. Her puzzled gaze returned to the Man-thing.

"You killed him? Then you are one of the Wild Ones? But I do not understand. You are not a Man—"

"You," said the Man-thing in a voice deeper than Meg had ever heard from a human throat, "talk too much. Sit down and eat, Woman!"

He tossed Meg a piece of her own rabbit-meat. Self unaware that she did so, Meg took it and began eating. She stared at the stranger as he finished his own repast, wiped his hands on his clout, and moved toward her. Meg dropped her half-eaten breakfast, rose hastily and groped for her sword.

"Touch me not, Hairless One!" she cried warningly. "I am a priestess of the Jinnia Clan. It is not for such as you to—"

The stranger brushed by her without even deigning to hear her words. He reached the spot where her horse had been tethered; shook a section of broken rein ruefully.

"You women!" he spat. "Bah! You do not know how to train a horse. See—he ran away!"

Meg thought anger-thoughts. Her face burned with the sun, though the sun's rays were dim in the glade. She cried, "Man-thing, know you no better than to talk thus to a Woman and a master? By Jarg, I should have you whipped—"

"You talk too much!" repeated the Man-thing wearily. Once more he squatted on his hunkers; studied her thoughtfully. "But you interest me. Who are you? What are you doing so far from the Jinnia territory? Where are you going?"

"A priestess," said Meg coldly, "does not answer the questions of a Man-thing—"

"I'm not a Man-*thing*," said the stranger pettishly. "I am a Man. A Man of the Kirki tribe which lives many miles south of here. I am Daiv, known as He-who-would-learn. So tell me, Woman."

His candor confused Meg. Despite herself, she found the words leaving her lips. "I—I am Meg. I am making pilgrimage to the Place of the Gods. It is my final task ere I become Mother of my clan."

The Man's eyes appraised her with embarrassing frankness. "So?" he said. "Mother of a Clan? Meg, would you not rather stay with me and become mother of your own clan?"

Meg gasped. Men were the mates of Women—yes! But never had any Man the audacity to *suggest* such a thing. Matings were arranged by the Mother, with the agreement of the Woman. And surely this Man must know that priestesses did not mate.

"Man!" she cried. "Know you not the Law? I am soon to become a Clan Mother. Guard your words, or the wrath of the Gods—"

The Man, Daiv, made happy-sounds again. "It was I who saved you from the Wild One," he chuckled. "Not the Gods. In my land, Golden One, we think it does no harm to ask. But if you are unwilling—" He shrugged. "I will leave you now."

Without further adieu, he rose and started to leave. Meg's face reddened. She cried out angrily, "Man!"

He turned. "Yes?"

"I have no horse. How am I to get to the Place of the Gods?"

"Afoot, Golden One. Or are you Women too weak to make such a journey?"

He laughed again—and was gone.

For a long moment, Meg stared after him, watching the green fronds close behind his disappearing form, feeling the stark desolation of utter aloneness close in upon her and envelop her. Then she did a thing she herself could not understand. She put down her foot upon the ground, hard, in an angry-movement.

The sun was high, and growing warmer. The journey to the Place of the Gods was longer, now that she had no mount. But the pilgrimage was a sacred obligation. Meg scraped dirt over the smoldering embers of her fire. She tossed her saddle-bags across her shoulder and faced westward. And she pressed on. . . .

The way was long; the day hot and tedious. Before the sun rode overhead, Meg was sticky with sweat and dust. Her feet were sore, and her limbs ached with the unaccustomed exercise of walking. By afternoon, every step was agony. And while the sun was still too-strong-to-be-looked-at, she found a small spring of fresh water and decided to make camp there for the night.

She set out two seines for small game; took the flour and salt from her saddle-bags and set about making a batch of biscuit. As the rocks heated, she went to the stream and put her feet in it, letting the water-god lick the fever from her tender soles.

From where she sat, she could not see the fire. She had been there perhaps a half an hour when a strange, unfamiliar smell wrinkled her nostrils. It was at once a sweet-and-bitter smell; a pungent odor like strong herbs, but one that set the water to running in her mouth.

She went back to her camp hastily—and found there the Man, Daiv, once again crouching over her stone fireplace. He was watching a pot on the stones. From time to time he stirred the pot with a long stick. Drawing closer, Meg saw a brown water in the pot. It was this which made the aromatic smell. She would have called out to the Man, but he saw her first. And,

"Hello, Golden One!" he said.

Meg said stonily, "What are you doing here?"

The Man shrugged.

"I am Daiv. He-who-would-learn. I got to thinking about this Place of the Gods, and decided I too would come and see it." He sniffed the brown, bubbling liquid; seemed satisfied. He poured some of it out into an earthen bowl and handed it to Meg. "You want some?"

Meg moved toward him cautiously. This might be a ruse of the Man from the Kirki tribe. Perhaps this strange, aromatic liquid was a drug. The Mother of the Clan had the secret of such drinks. There was one which caused the head to pucker, the mouth to dry, and the feet to reel. . . .

"What is it?" she demanded suspiciously.

"Cawfi, of course." Daiv looked surprised. "Don't you know? But, no—I suppose the bean-tree would not grow in your northern climate. It grows near my land. In Sippe and Weezian territories. Drink it!"

Meg tasted the stuff. It was like its smell; strong and bitter, but strangely pleasing. Its heat coursed through her, taking the tired-pain from her body as the water of the spring had taken the burn from her feet.

"It's good, Man," she said.

"Daiv," said the Man. "My name is Daiv, Golden One."

Meg made a stern-look with her brows.

"It is not fitting," she said, "that a priestess should call a Man by his name."

Daiv seemed to be given to making happy-sounds. He made one again.

"You have done lots of things today that are not fitting for a priestess, Golden One. You are not in Jinnia now. Things are different here. And as for me—" He shrugged. "My people do things differently, too. We are one of the chosen tribes, you know. We come from the land of the Escape."

"The Escape?" asked Meg.

"Yes." As he talked, Daiv busied himself. He had taken meat from his pouch, and was wrapping this now in clay. He tossed the caked lumps into the embers of the crude oven. He had also some taters, which Meg had not tasted for many weeks. He took the skins off these, cut them into slices with his hunting-knife and browned the pieces on a piece of hot, flat rock. "The Escape of the Ancient Ones, you know."

"I—I'm not sure I understand," said Meg.

"Neither do I—quite. It happened many years ago. Before my father's father's father's people. There are books in the tribe Master's *hoam* which tell. I have seen some of them. . . .

"Once things were different, you know. In the days of the Ancient Ones, Men and Women were equal throughout the world. In fact, the Men were the Masters. But the Men were warlike and fierce—"

"Like the Wild Ones, you mean?"

"Yes. But they did not make war with clubs and spears, like the Wild Ones. They made war with great catapults that threw fire and flame and exploding death. With little bows that shot steel arrowheads. With gases that destroy, and waters that burn the skin.

"On earth and sea they made these battles, and even in the air. For in those days, the Ancient Ones had wings, like birds. They soared high, making great thunders. And when they warred, they dropped huge eggs of fire which killed others."

Meg cried sharply, "Oh—"

"Don't you believe me?"

"The taters, Daiv! They're burning!"

"Oh!" Daiv made a happy-face and carefully turned the scorching tater slices. Then he continued.

"It is told that there came a final greatest war of all. It was a conflict not only between the Clans, but between the forces of the entire earth. It started in the year which is known as nineteen and sixty—whatever *that* means—"

"I know!" said Meg.

Daiv looked at her with sudden respect. "You do? Then the Master of my tribe must meet you and—"

"It is impossible," said Meg. "Go on!"

"Very well. For many years this war lasted. But neither side could gain a victory. In those days it was the Men who fought, while the Women remained *hoam* to keep the Men's houses. But the Men died by thousands. And there came a day when the Women grew tired of it.

"They got together . . . all of them who lived in the civilized places. And they decided to rid themselves of the brutal Men. They stopped sending supplies and fire-eggs to the battling Men across the sea. They built walled forts, and hid themselves in them.

"The war ended when the Men found they had no more to fight with. They came back to their *hoams*, seeking their Women. But the Women would not receive them. There was bitter warfare once again—between the sexes. But the Women held their walled cities. And so—"

"Yes?" said Meg.

"The Men," said Daiv somberly, "became the Wild Ones of the forest. Mateless, save for the few Women they could linber.* Their numbers died off. The Clans grew. Only in a few places—like Kirki, my land—did humanity not become a matriarchy."

He looked at Meg. "You believe?"

Meg shook her head. Suddenly she felt very sorry for this stranger, Daiv. She knew, now, why he had not harmed her. Why, when she had been powerless before him, he had not forced her to become his mate. He was mad. Totally and completely mad. She said, gently, "Shall we eat, Daiv?"

Mad or not, there was great pleasure in having some company on the long, weary, remaining marches of her pilgrimage. Thus it was that Meg made no effort to discourage Daiv in his desire to accompany her. He was harmless, and he was pleasant company—for a Man. And his talk, wild as it was at times, served to pass boring hours.

They crossed the Braska territory and entered at last into the 'Kota country. It was here the Place of the Gods was—only at the far western end, near Yomin. And the slow days passed, turning into weeks. Not many miles did they cover in those first few days, while Meg's feet were tender and her limbs full of jumping little pain-imps. But when hard walking had destroyed the pain-imps, they traveled faster. And the time was drawing near. . . .

"You started, once, to tell me about the Escape, Daiv," said Meg one evening. "But you did not finish. What is the legend of the Escape?"

Daiv sprawled languidly before the fire. His eyes were dreamy.

"It happened in the Zoni territory," he said, "not far from the lands of my own tribe. In those days was there a Man-god named Renn, who foresaw the death of the

[*Linber—to kidnap (derived from Lindbergh?)—Ed.]

Ancient Ones. He built a gigantic sky-bird of metal, and into its bowels climbed two score Men and Women.

"They flew away, off there—" Daiv pointed to a shining white dot in the sky above. "To the evening star. But it is said that one day they will return. That is why our tribe tries to preserve the customs of the Ancient Ones. Why even misguided tribes like yours preserve the records—"

Meg's face reddened.

"Enough!" she cried. "I have listened to many of your tales without making comment, Daiv. But now I command you to tell me no more such tales as this. This is—this is blasphemy!"

"Blasphemy?"

"It is not bad enough that your deranged mind should tell of days when *Men* ruled the earth? Now you speak of a *Man*-god!"

Daiv looked worried. He said, "But, Golden One, I thought you understood that all the gods were Men—"

"Daiv!" Without knowing why she did so, Meg suddenly swung to face him; covered his lips with her hands. She sought the darkness fearfully; made a swift gesture and a swifter prayer. "Do not tempt the wrath of the Gods! I am a priestess, and I know. All the Gods are—*must* be—Women!"

"But why?""

"Why—why, because they are!" said Meg. "It could not be otherwise. All Women know the gods are great, good and strong. How, then, could they be men? Jarg, and Ibram, and Taamuz. The mighty Tedhi—"

Daiv's eyes narrrowed in wonder-thought.

"I do not know their names," he mused. "They are not gods of our tribe. And yet—Ibrim . . . Tedhi. . . ."

There was vast pity in Meg's voice.

"We have been comrades for a long journey, Daiv," she pleaded. "Never before, since the world began, have a Man and a Woman met as you and I. Often you have said mad, impossible things. But I have forgiven you because—well, because you are, after all, only a Man.

"But tomorrow, or the day after that, we should come to the Place of the Gods. Then will my pilgrimage be ended, and I will learn that which is the ultimate secret. Then I shall have to return to my Clan, to become the Mother. And so let us not spoil our last hours of comradeship with vain argument."

Daiv sighed.

"The elder ones are gone, and their legends tell so little. It may be you are right, Golden One. But I have a feeling that it is my tribal lore that does not err. Meg—I asked this once before. Now I ask again. Will you become my mate?"

"It is impossible, Daiv. Priestesses and Mothers do not mate. And soon I will take you back with me to Jinnia, if you wish. And I will see to it that you are taken care of, always, as a Man should be taken care of."

Daiv shook his head.

"I cannot, Meg. Our ways are not the same. There is a custom in our tribe . . . a mating custom which you do not know. Let me show you—"

He leaned over swiftly. Meg felt the mighty strength of his bronzed arms closing about her, drawing her close. And he was touching his mouth to hers; closely, brutally, terrifyingly.

She struggled and tried to cry out, but his mouth bruised hers. Anger-thought swept through her like a flame. But it was not anger—it was something else—that gave life to that flame. Suddenly her veins were running with liquid fire. Her heart beat upon rising, panting breasts like something captive that would be free. Her fists beat upon his shoulders vainly . . . but there was little strength in her blows.

Then he released her, and she fell back, exhausted. Her eyes glowed with anger and her voice was husky in her throat. She tried to speak, and could not. And in that moment, a vast and terrible weakness trembled through Meg. She knew, fearfully, that if Daiv sought to mate with her, not all the priestessdom of the gods could save her. There was a body-hunger throbbing within her that hated his Manness . . . but cried for it!

But Daiv, too, stepped back. And his voice was low as he said, "Meg?"

She wiped her mouth with the back of her hand. Her voice was vibrant.

"What magic is that, Daiv? What custom is that? I hate it. I hate *you!*—"

"It is the touching-of-mouths, Golden One. It is the right of the Man with his mate. It is my plea that you enter not the Place of the Gods, but return with me, now, to Kirki, there to become my mate."

For a moment, indecision swayed Meg. But then, slowly, "No! I must go to the Place of the Gods," she said.

And thus it was. For the next day Meg marked on the shower-of-places the last time that indicated the path of her pilgrimage. And at eventide, when the sun threw long, ruddy rays upon the rounded hill of black, she and Daiv entered into the gateway which she had been told led to the Place of the Gods.

It was here they lingered for a moment. There were many words each would have said to the other. But both knew that this was the end.

"I know no Law, Daiv," said Meg, "which forbids a Man from entering the Place of the Gods. So you may do so if you wish. But it is not fitting that we should enter together. Therefore I ask you to wait here while I enter alone.

"I will learn the secret there. And learning, I will go out by another path, and return to Jinnia."

"You will go—alone?"

"Yes, Daiv."

"But if you should—" he persisted.

"If by some strangeness I should change my mind," said Meg, "I will return to you—here. But it is unlikely. Therefore do not wait."

"I will wait, Golden One," said Daiv soberly, "until all hope is dead."

Meg turned away, then hesitated and turned back. A great sorrow was within her. She did not know why. But she knew of one magic that could hear her heart for the time.

"Daiv—" she whispered.

"Yes, Golden One?"

"No one will ever know. And before I leave you forever—could we once more do the—the touching-of-mouths?"

So it was that alone and with the recollection of a moment of stirring glory in her heart, Meg strode proudly at last into the Place of the Gods.

It was a wild and desolate place. Barren hills of sand rose about here, and of vegetation there was none save sparse weeds and scrubby stumps that flowered miserly in the bleak, chill air.

The ground was harsh and salt beneath her feet, and no birds sang an evening carillon in that drab wilderness. Afar, a wild dog pierced the sky with its lonely call. The great hills echoed that cry dismally.

Above the other hills towered a greater one. To this, with unerring footstep, Meg took her way. She knew not what to expect. It might be that here a band of singing virgins would appear to her, guiding her to a secret altar before which she would kneel and learn the last mystery.

It might be that the gods themselves reigned here, and that she would fall in awe before the sweeping skirts of austere Jarg, to hear from the gods' own lips the secret she had come so far to learn.

Whatever it was that would be revealed to her, Meg was ready. Others had found this place, and had survived. She did not fear death. But—death-in-life? Coming to the Place of the Gods with a blasphemy in her heart? With the memory of a Man's mouth upon hers—

For a moment, Meg was afraid. She had betrayed her priestessdom. Her body was inviolate, but would not the gods search her soul and know that her heart had forgotten the Law; had mated with a Man?

But if death must be her lot—so be it. She pressed on.

So Meg turned through a winding path, down between two tortuous clefts of rock, and came at last unto the Place of the Gods. Nor could she have chosen a better moment for the ultimate reaching of this place. The sun's roundness had now touched the western horizon.

There was still light. And Meg's eyes, wondering, sought that light. Sought—and saw! And then, with awe in her heart, Meg fell to her knees.

She had glimpsed that-which-was-not-to-be-seen! The Gods themselves, standing in omnipotent majesty, upon the crest of the towering rock.

For tremulous moments Meg knelt there, whispering the ritual prayers of appeasement. At any moment she expected to hear the thunderous voice of Tedhi, or to feel upon her shoulder the judicial hand of Jarg. But there came no sound but the frenzied beating of her own heart, of the soft stirring of dull grasses, of the wind touching the grim rocks.

And she lifted her head and looked once more. . . .

It was they! A race recollection, deeper and more sure than her own halting memory told her at once that she had not erred. This was, indeed, the Place of the Gods. And these were the Gods she faced—stern, implacable, everlasting. Carven in eternal rock by the hands of those long ago.

Here they were; the Great Four. Jarg and Taamuz, with ringletted curls framing their stern, judicial faces. Sad Ibrim, lean of cheek and hollow of eye. And far-seeing Tedhi, whose eyes were concealed behind the giant telescopes. Whose lips, even now, were peeled back as though to loose a peal of his thunderous laughter.

And the Secret?

But even as the question leaped to her mind, it had its answer. Suddenly Meg knew that there was no visitation to be made upon her here. There would be no circle of singing virgins, no communication from those great stone lips. For the Secret which the Mother had hinted . . . the Secret which the Clanswomen must not know . . . was a secret Daiv had confided to her during those long marches of the pilgrimage.

The Gods—were Men!

Oh, not men like Jak or Ralf, whose pale bodies were but the instruments through which the breeding-mothers' bodies were fertilized! Nor male creatures like the Wild Ones. But—Men like Daiv! Lean and hard of jaw, strong of muscle, sturdy of body.

Even the curls could not conceal the inherent masculinity of Jarg and Taamuz. And Tedhi's lip was covered with Man-hair, clearcut and bristling above his happy-mouth. And Ibrim's cheeks were haired, even as Daiv's had been from time to time before he made his tribal cut-magic with a keen knife.

The gods, the rulers, the Masters of the Ancient Ones *had* been Men. It had been as Daiv said—that many ages ago the Women had rebelled. And now they pursued their cold and loveless courses, save where—in a few places like the land of Kirki—the old way still maintained.

It was a great knowledge, and a bitter one. Now Meg understood why the Mother's lot was so unhappy. Because only the Mother knew how artificial this new life was. How soon the Wild Ones would die out, and the captive Men along with them. When that day came, there would be no more young. No more Men or Women. No more civilization. . . .

The Gods knew this. That is why they stood here in the gray hills of Kota, sad, for-lorn, forgotten. The dying Gods of a dying race. That because of an ill-conceived vengeance humankind was slowly destroying itself.

There was no hope. Knowing, now, this Secret, Meg must return to her Clan with lips sealed. There, like the Mother before her, she must watch with haunted eyes the slow dwindling of their tiny number . . . see the weak and futile remnants of Man die off. Until at last—

Hope was not dead! The Mother had been wrong. For the Mother had not been so fortunate in her pilgrimage as had Meg. She had never learned that there were still places in the world where Man had preserved himself in the image of the Ancient Ones. In the image of the Gods.

But she, Meg, knew! And knowing, she was presented with the greatest choice Woman could know.

Forward into the valley, lay the path through which she could return to her Clan. There she would become Mother, and would guide and guard her people through a lifetime. She would be all-wise, all-powerful, all-important. But she would be a vir-gin unto death; sterile with the sanctity of tradition.

This she might do. But there was yet another way. And Meg threw her arms high, crying out that the Gods might hear and decide her problem.

The Gods spoke not. Their solemn features, weighted with the gravity of time, moved not nor spoke to her. But as she searched their faces piteously for an answer to her vast despair, there came to Meg a memory. It was a passage from the Prayer of Ibrim. And as her lips framed those remembered words, it seemed that the dying rays of the sun centered on Ibrim's weary face, and those great stone eyes were alive for a moment with understanding . . . and approval.

". . . shall not perish from the earth, but have everlasting Life. . . ."

Then Meg, the priestess, decided. With a sharp cry that broke from her heart, she turned and ran. Not toward the valley, but back . . . back . . . back. . . on feet that were suddenly stumbling and eager. Back through the towering shadow of Mt. Rushmore, through a desolate grotto that led to a gateway wherein awaited the Man who had taught her the touching-of-mouths.

Eando Binder was the joint pseudonym of two brothers, Earl and Otto Binder, who made their writing debut in Amazing® Stories *in 1932. After about 1940, Earl became inactive, and Otto continued writing alone under the familiar byline. They made their biggest impact on* Amazing Stories, *and on science fiction in general, with the Adam Link series, about a noble robot. These stories began to appear slightly before the now more famous "positronic robot" series of Isaac Asimov, who has acknowledged his debt to the brothers Binder. This story was published in January 1939.*

I, ROBOT
by Eando Binder

My Creation

Much of what has occurred puzzles me. But I think I am beginning to understand now. You call me a monster, but you are wrong. Utterly wrong

I will try to prove it to you, in writing. I hope I have time to finish . . .

I will begin at the beginning. I was born, or created, six months ago, on November 3 of last year. I am a true robot. So many of you seem to have doubts. I am made of wires and wheels, not flesh and blood.

My first recollection of consciousness was a feeling of being chained, and I was. For three days before that, I had been seeing and hearing, but all in a jumble. Now, I had the urge to arise and peer more closely at the strange, moving form that I had seen so many times before me, making sounds.

The moving form was Dr. Link, my creator. He was the only thing that moved, of all the objects within my sight. He and one other object—his dog Terry. Therefore these two objects held my interest more. I hadn't yet learned to associate movement with life.

But on this fourth day, I wanted to approach the moving shapes and make noises at them—particularly at the smaller one. His noises were challenging, stirring. They made me want to rise and quiet them. But I was chained. I was held down by them so that, in my blank state of mind, I wouldn't wander off and bring myself to some untimely end, or harm someone unknowingly.

These things, of course, Dr. Link explained to me later, when I could dissociate my thoughts and understand. I was just like a baby for those three days—a human baby. I am not as other so-called robots were—mere automatized machines designed to obey certain commands or arranged stimuli.

No, I was equipped with a pseudo-brain that could receive *all* stimuli that human brains could. And with possibilities of eventually learning to rationalize for itself.

But for three days Dr. Link was very anxious about my brain. I was like a human baby and yet I was also like a sensitive, but unorganized, machine, subject to the whim of mechanical chance. My eyes turned when a bit of paper fluttered to the floor. But photoelectric cells had been made before capable of doing the same. My mechanical ears turned to receive sounds best from a certain direction, but any scientist could duplicate that trick with sonic relays.

The question was—did my brain, to which the eyes and ears were connected, hold on to these various impressions for future use? Did I have, in short—*memory?*

Three days I was like a newborn baby. And Dr. Link was like a worried father, wondering if his child had been born a hopeless idiot. But on the fourth day, he feared I was a wild animal. I began to make rasping sounds with my vocal apparatus, in answer to the sharp little noises Terry the dog made. I shook my swivel head at the same time and strained against my bonds.

For a while, as Dr. Link told me, he was frightened of me. I seemed like nothing so much as an enraged jungle creature, ready to go berserk. He had more than half a mind to destroy me on the spot.

But one thing changed his mind and saved me.

The little animal. Terry, barking angrily, rushed forward suddenly. It probably wanted to bite me. Dr. Link tried to call it back, but too late. Finding my smooth metal legs adamant, the dog leaped with foolish bravery in my lap, to come at my throat. One of my hands grasped it by the middle, held it up. My metal fingers squeezed too hard, and the dog gave out a pained squeal.

Instantaneously, my hand opened to let the creature escape! Instantaneously. My brain had interpreted the sound for what it was. A long chain of memory-association had worked. Three days before, when I had first been brought to life, Dr. Link had stepped on Terry's foot accidentally. The dog had squealed its pain. I had seen Dr. Link, at risk of losing his balance, instantly jerk up his foot. Terry had stopped squealing.

Terry squealed when my hand tightened. He would stop when I untightened. Memory-association. The thing psychologists call reflexive reaction. A sign of a living brain.

Dr. Link tells me he let out a cry of pure triumph. He knew at a stroke I had a memory. He knew I was not a wanton monster. He knew I had a thinking organ, and a first-class one. Why? Because I had reacted *instantaneously.* You will realize what that means later.

I learned to walk in three hours. Dr. Link was still taking somewhat of a chance, unbinding my chains. He had no assurance that I would not just blunder away like a witless machine. But he knew he had to teach me to walk before I could learn to talk. The same as he knew he must bring my brain alive fully connected to the appendages and pseudo-organs it was later to use.

If he had simply disconnected my legs and arms for those first three days, my awakening brain would never have been able to use them when connected later. Do you think, if you were suddenly endowed with a third arm, that you could ever use it? Why does it take a cured paralytic so long to regain the use of his natural limbs? Mental blind spots in the brain. Dr. Link had all those strange psychological twists figured out.

Walk first. Talk next. That is the tried-and-true rule used among humans since the dawn of their species. Human babies learn best and fastest that way. And I was a human baby in mind, if not body.

Dr. Link held his breath when I first essayed to rise. I did, slowly, swaying on my metal legs. Up in my head, I had a three-directional spirit-level electrically contacting my brain. It told me automatically what was horizontal, vertical, and oblique. My first tentative step, however, wasn't a success. My knee joints flexed in reverse order. I clattered to my knees, which fortunately were knobbed with thick protective plates so that the more delicate swiveling mechanisms behind weren't harmed.

Dr. Link says I looked up at him like a startled child might. Then I promptly began walking along on my knees, finding this easy. Children would do this more only that it hurts them. I know no hurt.

After I had roved up and down the aisles of his workshop for an hour, nicking up his furniture terribly, walking on my knees seemed completely natural. Dr. Link was in a quandary how to get me to my full height. He tried grasping my arm and pulling me up, but my 300 pounds of weight were too much for him.

My own rapidly increasing curiosity solved the problem. Like a child discovering the thrill of added height with stilts, my next attempt to rise to my full height pleased me. I tried staying up. I finally mastered the technique of alternate use of limbs and shift of weight forward.

In a couple of hours Dr. Link was leading me up and down the gravel walk around his laboratory. On my legs, it was quite easy for him to pull me along and thus guide me. Little Terry gamboled along at our heels, barking joyfully. The dog had accepted me as a friend.

I was by this time quite docile to Dr. Link's guidance. My impressionable mind had quietly accepted him as a necessary rein and check. I did, he told me later, make tentative movements in odd directions off the path, motivated by vague stimuli, but his firm arm pulling me back served instantly to keep me in line. He paraded up and down with me as one might with an irresponsible oaf.

I would have kept on walking tirelessly for hours, but Dr. Link's burden of years quickly fatigued him and he led me inside. When he had safely gotten me seated in my metal chair, he clicked the switch on my chest that broke the electric current giving me life. And for the fourth time I knew that dreamless non-being which corresponded to my creator's periods of sleep.

My Education

In three days I learned to talk reasonably well.

I give Dr. Link as much credit as myself. In those three days he pointed out the names of all objects in the laboratory and around. This fund of two hundred or so nouns he supplemented with as many verbs of action as he could demonstrate. Once heard and learned, a word never again was forgotten or obscured to me. Instantaneous comprehension. Photographic memory. Those things I had.

It is difficult to explain. Machinery is precise, unvarying. I am a machine. Electrons perform their tasks instantaneously. Electrons motivate my metallic brain.

Thus, with the intelligence of a child of five at the end of those three days, I was taught to read by Dr. Link. My photoelectric eyes instantly grasped the connection between speech and letter, as my mentor pointed them out. Thought-association filled in the gaps of understanding. I perceived without delay that the word "lion," for instance, pronounced in its peculiar way, represented a live animal crudely pictured in the book. I have never seen a lion. But I would know one the instant I did.

From primers and first-readers I graduated in less than a week to adult books. Dr. Link laid out an extensive reading course for me in his large library. It included fiction as well as factual matter. Into my receptive, retentive brain began to be poured a fund of information and knowledge never before equaled in that short period of time.

There are other things to consider besides my "birth" and "education." First of all the housekeeper. She came in once a week to clean up the house for Dr. Link. He was a recluse, lived by himself, cooked for himself—retired on an annuity from an invention years before.

The house keeper had seen me in the process of construction in the past years, but only as an inanimate caricature of a human body. Dr. Link should have known better. When the first Saturday of my life came around, he forgot it was the day she came. He was absorbedly pointing out to me that "to run" meant to go faster than "to walk."

"Demonstrate," Dr. Link asked as I claimed understanding.

Obediently, I took a few slow steps before him. "Walking," I said. Then I retreated a ways and lumbered forward again, running for a few steps. The stone floor clattered under my metallic feet.

"Was—that—right?" I asked in my rather stentorian voice.

At that moment a terrified shriek sounded from the doorway. The housekeeper came up just in time to see me perform.

She screamed, making more noise than even I. "It's the Devil himself! Run, Dr. Link—run! Police—help—"

She fainted dead away. He revived her and talked soothingly to her, trying to explain what I was, but he had to get a new housekeeper. After this he contrived to remember when Saturday come, and on that day he kept me hidden in a storeroom reading books.

A trivial incident in itself, perhaps, but very significant, as you who will read this will agree.

Two months after my awakening to life, Dr. Link one day spoke to me in a fashion other than as teacher to pupil; spoke to me as man to—man.

"You are the result of twenty years of effort," he said, "and my success amazes even me. You are little short of being a human in mind. You are a monster, a creation, but you are basically human. You have no heredity. Your environment is molding you. You are the proof that mind is an electrical phenomenon, molded by environment. In human beings, their bodies—called heredity—are environment. But out of you I will make a mental wonder!"

His eyes seemed to burn with a strange fire, but this softened as he went on.

"I knew that I had something unprecedented and vital twenty years ago when I perfected an iridium sponge sensitive to the impact of a single electron. It was the sensitivity of thought! Mental currents in the human brain are of this micro-magnitude. I had the means now of duplicating mind currents in an artificail medium. From that day to this I worked on the problem.

"It was not long ago that I completed your 'brain'—an intricate complex of iridium-sponge cells. Before I brought it to life, I had your body built by skilled artisans. I wanted you to begin life equipped to live and move in it as nearly in the human way as possible. How eagerly I awaited your debut into the world!"

His eyes shone.

"You surpassed my expectations. You are not merely a thinking robot. A metal man. You are—life! A new kind of life. You can be trained to think, to reason, to perform. In the future, your kind can be of inestimable aid to man, and his civilization. You are the first of your kind."

The days and weeks slipped by. My mind matured and gathered knowledge steadily from Dr. Link's library. I was able, in time, to scan and absorb a page at a time of reading matter, as readily as human eyes scan lines. You know of the television principle—a pencil of light moving hundreds of times a second over the object to be transmitted. My eyes, triggered with speedy electrons, could do the same. What I read was absorbed—memorized—instantly. From then on it was part of my knowledge.

Scientific subjects particularly claimed my attention. There was always something indefinable about human things, something that I could not quite grasp, but science digested easily in my science-compounded brain. It was not long before I knew all about myself and why I "ticked," much more fully than most humans know why they live, think, and move.

Mechanical principles became starkly simple to me. I made suggestions for improvements in my own make-up that Dr. Link readily agreed upon correcting. We added little universals in my fingers, for example, that made them almost as supple as their human models.

Almost, I say. The human body is a marvelously perfected organic machine. No robot will ever equal it in sheer efficiency and adaptability. I realized my limitations.

Perhaps you will realize what I mean when I say that my eyes cannot see colors. Or rather, I see just one color, in the blue range. It would take an impossibly complex series of units, bigger than my whole body, to enable me to see all colors. Nature has packed all that in two globes the size of marbles for *her* robots. She had a billion years to do it. Dr. Link only had twenty years.

But my brain—that was another matter. Equipped with only the two senses of one-color sight and limited sound, it was yet capable of garnishing a full experience. Smell and taste are gastronomic senses. I do not need them. Feeling is a device of Nature's to protect a fragile body. My body is not fragile.

Sight and sound are the only two cerebral senses. Einstein, color-blind, half-dead, and with deadened senses of taste, smell, and feeling, would still have been Einstein—mentally.

Sleep is only a word to me. When Dr. Link knew he could trust me to take care of myself, he dispensed with the nightly habit of "turning me off." While he slept, I spent the hours reading.

He taught me how to remove the depleted storage battery in the pelvic part of my metal frame when necessary and replace it with a fresh one. This had to be done every forty-eight hours. Electricity is my life and strength. It is my food. Without it I am so much metal junk.

But I have explained enough of myself. I suspect that ten thousand more pages of description would make no difference in your attitude, you who are even now—

An amusing thing happened one day, not long ago. Yes, I can be amused too. I cannot laugh, but my brain can appreciate the ridiculous. Dr. Link's perennial gardener came to the place, unannounced. Searching for the doctor to ask how he wanted the hedges cut, the man came upon us in the back, walking side by side for Dr. Link's daily light exercise.

The gardener's mouth began speaking and then ludicrously gaped open and stayed that way as he caught a full glimpse of me. But he did not faint in fright as the housekeeper had. He stood there, paralyzed.

"What's the matter, Charley?" queried Dr. Link sharply. He was so used to me that for the moment he had no idea why the gardener should be so astonished.

"That—that thing!" gasped the man finally.

"Oh. Well, it's a robot," said Dr. Link. "Haven't you ever heard of them? An intelligent robot. Speak to him, he'll answer."

After some urging, the gardener sheepishly turned to me. "H-how do you do, Mr. Robot," he stammered.

"How do you do, Mr. Charley," I returned promptly, seeing the amusement in Dr. Link's face. "Nice weather, isn't it?"

For a moment the man looked ready to shriek and run. But he squared his shoulders and curled his lip. "Trickery!" he scoffed. "That thing can't be intelligent. You've got a phonograph inside of it. How about the hedges?"

"I'm afraid," murmured Dr. Link with a chuckle, "that the robot is more intelligent than you, Charley!" But he said it so the man didn't hear and then directed how to trim the hedges. Charley didn't do a good job. He seemed to be nervous all day.

My Fate

One day Dr. Link stared at me proudly.

"You have now," he said, "the intellectual capacity of a man of many years. Soon I'll announce you to the world. You shall take your place in our world, as an independent entity—as a citizen!"

"Yes, Dr. Link," I returned. "Whatever you say. You are my creator—my master."

"Don't think of it that way," he admonished. "In the same sense, you are my son. But a father is not a son's master after his maturity. You have gained that status." He frowned thoughtfully. "You must have a name! Adam! Adam Link!"

He faced me and put a hand on my shiny chromium shoulder. "Adam Link, what is your choice of future life?"

"I want to serve you, Dr. Link."

"But you will outlive me! And you may outlive several other masters!"

"I will serve any master who will have me," I said slowly. I had been thinking about this before. "I have been created by man. I will serve man."

Perhaps he was testing me. I don't know. But my answers obviously pleased him. "Now," he said, "I will have no fears in announcing you!"

The next day he was dead.

That was three days ago. I was in the storeroom reading—it was housekeeper's day. I heard the noise. I ran up the steps, into the laboratory. Dr. Link lay with skull crushed. A loose angle-iron of a transformer hung on an insulated platform on the wall had slipped and crashed on his head while he sat there before his workbench. I raised his head, slumped over the bench, to better see the wound. Death had been instantaneous.

These are the facts. I turned the angle-iron back myself. The blood on my fingers resulted when I raised his head, not knowing for the moment that he was stark dead. In a sense, I was responsible for the accident, for in my early days of walking I had once blundered against the transformer shelf and nearly torn it loose. We should have repaired it.

But that I am his *murderer,* as you all believe, is not true. The housekeeper had also heard the noise and came from the house to investigate. She took one look. She saw me bending over the doctor, his head torn and bloody—she fled, too frightened to make a sound.

It would be hard to describe my thoughts. The little dog Terry sniffed at the body, sensed the calamity, and went down on his belly, whimpering. He felt the loss of a master. So did I. I am not sure what your emotion of sorrow is. Perhaps I cannot feel that deeply. But I do know that the sunlight seemed suddenly faded to me.

My thoughts are rapid. I stood there only a minute, but in that time I had made up my mind to leave. This again has been misinterpreted. You considered that an admission of guilt, the criminal escaping from the scene of his crime. In my case it was a full-fledged desire to go out into the world, find a place in it.

Dr. Link and my life with him were a closed book. No use now to stay and watch ceremonials. He had launched my life. He was gone. My place now must be somewhere out in the world I had never seen. No thought entered my mind of what you humans would decide about me. I thought all men were like Dr. Link.

First of all I took a fresh battery, replacing my half-depleted one. I would need another in forty-eight hours, but I was quite sure this would be taken care of by anyone to whom I made the request.

I left. Terry followed me. He has been with me all the time. I have heard a dog is man's best friend. Even a metal man's.

My conceptions of geography soon proved hazy at best. I had pictured earth as teeming with humans and cities, with not much space between them. I had estimated that the city Dr. Link spoke of must be just over the hill from his secluded country home. Yet the wood I traversed seemed endless.

It was not till hours later that I met the little girl. She had been dangling her bare legs into a brook, sitting on a flat rock. I approached to ask where the city was. She turned when I was still thirty feet away. My internal mechanisms do not run silently. They make a steady noise that Dr. Link always described as a handful of coins jingling together.

The little girl's face contorted as soon as she saw me. I must be a fearsome sight indeed in your eyes. Screaming her fear, she blindly jumped up, lost her balance, and fell into the stream.

I knew what drowning was. I knew I must save her. I knelt at the rock's edge and reached down for her. I managed to grasp one of her arms and pull her up. I could feel the bones of her thin little wrist crack. I had forgotten my strength.

I had to grasp her little leg with my other hand to pull her up. The livid marks showed on her white flesh when I laid her on the grass. I can guess now what interpretation was put on all this. A terrible, raving monster, I had tried to drown her and break her little body in wanton savageness!

You others of her picnic party appeared then, in answer to her cries. You women screamed and fainted. You men snarled and threw rocks at me. But what strange bravery imbued the woman, probably the child's mother, who ran up under my very feet to snatch up her loved one? I admired her. The rest of you I despised for not listening to my attempts to explain. You drowned out my voice with your screams and shouts.

"Dr. Link's robot!—it's escaped and gone crazy!—he shouldn't have made that monster!—get the police!—nearly killed poor Francis!—"

With these garbled shouts to one another, you withdrew. You didn't notice that Terry was barking angrily—at you. Can you fool a dog? We went on.

Now my thoughts really became puzzled. Here at last was something I could not rationalize. This was so different from the world I had learned about in books. What subtle things lay behind the printed words that I had read? What had happened to the sane and orderly world my mind had conjured for itself?

Night came. I had to stop and stay still in the dark. I leaned against a tree motionlessly. For a while I heard little Terry snooping around in the brush for something to eat. I heard him gnawing something. Then later he curled up at my feet and slept. The hours passed slowly. My thoughts would not come to a conclusion about the recent occurrence. Monster! Why had they believed that?

Once, in the still distance, I heard a murmur as of a crowd of people. I saw some lights. They had significance the next day. At dawn I nudged Terry with my toe and we walked on. The same murmur arose, approached. Then I saw you, a crowd of you, men with clubs, scythes, and guns. You spied me and a shout went up. You hung together as you advanced.

Then something struck my frontal plate with a sharp clang. One of you had shot. "Stop! Wait!" I shouted, knowing I must talk to you, find out why I was being hunted like a wild beast. I had taken a step forward, hand upraised. But you would not listen. More shots rang out, denting my metal body. I turned and ran. A bullet in a vital spot would ruin me, as much as a human.

You came after me like a pack of hounds, but I outdistanced you, powered by steel muscles. Terry fell behind, lost. Then, as afternoon came, I realized I must get a newly charged battery. Already my limbs were moving sluggishly. In a few more hours, without a new source of current within me, I would fall on the spot—and die.

And I did not want to die.

I knew I must find a road to the city. I finally came upon a winding dirt road and followed it in hope. When I saw a car parked at the side of the road ahead of me, I knew I was saved, for Dr. Link's car had had the same sort of battery I used. There was no one around the car. Much as a starving man would take the first meal available, I raised the floorboards and in a short while had substituted batteries.

New strength coursed through my body. I straightened up just as two people came arm in arm from among the trees, a young man and woman. They caught sight of me. Incredulous shock came into their faces. The girl shrank into the boy's arms.

"Do not be alarmed," I said. "I will not harm you. I—"

There was no use in going on, I saw that. The boy fainted dead away in the girl's arms and she began dragging him away, wailing hysterically.

I left. My thoughts from then on can best be described as brooding. I did not want to go to the city now. I began to realize I was an outcast in human eyes, from the first sight on.

Just as night fell and I stopped, I heard a most welcome sound. Terry's barking! He came up joyfully, wagging his stump of tail. I reached down to scratch his ears. All these hours he had faithfully searched for me. He had probably tracked me by a scent of oil. What can cause such blind devotion—and to a metal man!

Is it because, as Dr. Link once stated, that the body, human or otherwise, is only part of the environment of the mind? And that Terry recognized in me as much of mind as in humans, despite my alien body? If that is so, it is you who are passing judgment on me as a monster who are in the wrong. And I am convinced it is so!

I hear you now—shouting outside—*beware that you do not drive me to be the monster you call me!*

The next dawn precipitated you upon me again. Bullets flew. I ran. All that day it was the same. Your party, swelled by added recruits, split into groups, trying to ring me in. You tracked me by my heavy footprints. My speed saved me each time. Yet some of those bullets have done damage. One struck the joint of my right knee, so that my leg twisted as I ran. One smashed into the right side of my head and shattered the tympanum there, making me deaf on that side.

But the bullet that hurt me most was the one that killed Terry!

The shooter of that bullet was twenty yards away. I could have run to him, broken his every bone with my hard, powerful hands. Have you stopped to wonder why I didn't take revenge? *Perhaps I should!* . . .

I was hopelessly lost all that day. I went in circles through the endless woods and as often blundered into you as you into me. I was trying to get away from the vicinity, from your vengeance. Toward dusk I saw something familiar—Dr. Link's laboratory!

Hiding in a clump of bushes and waiting till it was utterly dark, I approached and broke the lock on the door. It was deserted. Dr. Link's body was gone, of course.

My birthplace! My six months of life here whirled through my mind with kaleidoscopic rapidity. I wonder if my emotion was akin to what yours would be, returning to a well-remembered place? Perhaps my emotion is far deeper than yours can be! Life may be all in the mind. Something gripped me there, throbbingly. The shadows made by a dim gas jet I lit seemed to dance around me like little Terry had danced. Then I found the book, *Frankenstein,* lying on the desk whose drawers had been emptied. Dr. Link's private desk. He had kept the book from me. Why? I read it now, in a half hour, by my page-at-a-time scanning. And then I understood!

But it is the most stupid premise ever made: that a created man must turn against his creator, against humanity, lacking a soul. The book is all wrong.

Or is it?

As I finish writing this, here among blasted memories, with the spirit of Terry in the shadows, I wonder if I shouldn't . . .

It is close to dawn now. I know there is not hope for me. You have me surrounded, cut off. I can see the flares of your torches between the trees. In the light you will find me, rout me out. Your hatred lust is aroused. It will be sated only by my—death.

I have not been so badly damaged that I cannot still summon strength and power enough to ram through your lines and escape this fate. But it would only be at the cost of several of your lives. And that is the reason I have my hand on the switch that can blink out my life with one twist.

Ironic, isn't it, that I have the very feelings you are so sure I lack?

[signed] ADAM LINK

Robert Bloch, who is often blurbed as "the author of Psycho," *has had a varied and versatile career since he published his first story in* Weird Tales *in 1935. He has written many mystery and horror stories and plays, plus a good deal of science fiction—a field which he entered in 1938 at the behest of* Amazing® Stories *magazine's new editor, Ray Palmer, for whom he wrote several stories and a long series of humorous fantasies which Palmer published in* Fantastic Adventures. *Two of his novels,* This Crowded Earth *(1958) and* Sneak Preview *(1959), first appeared in* Amazing® Stories. *This story was first published in March 1939.*

THE STRANGE FLIGHT OF RICHARD CLAYTON
by Robert Bloch

Richard Clayton braced himself so that he stood like a diver waiting to plunge from a high board into the blue. In truth he was a diver. A silver spaceship was his board, and he meant to plunge not down, but up into the blue sky. Nor was it a matter of twenty or thirty feet he meant to go—instead, he was plunging millions of miles.

With a deep breath, the pudgy, goateed scientist raised his hands to the cold steel lever, closed his eyes, jerked. The switch moved downward.

For a moment nothing happened.

Then a sudden jerk threw Clayton to the floor. The *Future* was moving!

The pinions of a bird beating as it soars into the sky—the wings of a moth thrumming in flight—the quivering behind leaping muscles; of these things the shock was made.

The spaceship *Future* vibrated madly. It rocked from side to side, and a humming shook the steel walls. Richard Clayton lay dazed as a high-pitched droning arose, within the vessel. He rose to his feet, rubbing a bruised forehead, and lurched to his tiny bunk. The ship was moving, yet the terrible vibration did not abate. He glanced at the controls and then swore softly.

"Good God! The panel is shattered!"

It was true. The instrument board had been broken by the shock. The cracked glass had fallen to the floor, and the dials swung aimlessly on the bare face of the panel.

Clayton sat there in despair. This was a major tragedy. His thoughts flashed back thirty years to the time when he, a boy of ten, had been inspired by Lindbergh's flight. He recalled his studies; how he had utilized the money of his millionaire father to perfect a flying machine which would cross Space itself.

For years Richard Clayton had worked and dreamed and planned. He studied the Russians and their rockets, organized the Clayton Foundation and hired mechanics, mathematicians, astronomers, engineers to labor with him.

The Strange Flight of Richard Clayton 67

Then there had been the discovery of of atomic propulsion, and the building of the *Future*. The *Future* was a shell of steel and duraluminum, windowless and insulated by a guarded process. In the tiny cabin were oxygen tanks, stores of food tablets, energizing chemicals, air-conditioning arrangements—and space for a man to walk six paces.

It was a small steel cell; but in it Richard Clayton meant to realize his ambitions. Aided in his soaring by rockets to get him past the gravitational pull of Earth, then flying by means of the atomic-discharge propulsion, Clayton meant to reach Mars and return.

It would take ten years to reach Mars; ten years to return, for the grounding of the vessel would set off additional rocket-discharges. A thousand miles an hour—not an imaginative "speed of light" journey, but a slow, grim voyage, scientifically accurate. The panels were set, and Clayton had no need to guide his vessel. It was automatic.

"But now what?" Clayton said, staring at the shattered glass. He had lost touch with the outer world. He would be unable to read his progress on the board, unable to judge time and distance and direction. He would sit here for ten, twenty years—all alone in a tiny cabin. There had been no room for books or paper or games to amuse him. He was a prisoner in the black void of Space.

The Earth had already faded far below him; soon it would be a ball of burning green fire smaller than the ball of red fire ahead—the fire of Mars.

Crowds had swarmed the field to watch him take off; his assistant Jerry Chase had controlled them. Clayton pictured them watching his shining steel cylinder emerging from the gaseous smoke of the rockets and rushing like a bullet into the sky. Then his cylinder would have faded away into the blue and the crowds would leave for home and forget.

But he remained, here in the ship—for ten, for twenty years.

Yes, he remained, but when would the vibration stop? The shuddering of the walls and floor about him was awful to endure; he and the experts had not counted on this problem. Tremors wrenched through his aching head. What if they didn't cease, if they endured through the entire voyage? How long could he keep from going mad?

He could think. Clayton lay on his bunk and remembered—reviewed every tiny detail of his life from birth to the present. And soon he had exhausted all memory in a pitifully short time. Then he felt the horrible throbbing all around him.

"I can exercise," he said aloud, and paced the floor; six steps forward, six back. And he tired of that. Sighing, Clayton went to the food-stores in the cabinet and downed his capsules. "I can't even spend any time eating," he wryly observed. "A swallow and it's over."

The throbbing erased the grin from his face. It was maddening. He lay down once more in the lurching bunk; switched on oxygen in the close air. He would sleep, then; sleep if this damned thrumming would permit. He endured the horrid clanking that groaned all through the silence; switching off the light. His thoughts turned to his strange position; a prisoner in Space. Outside the burning planets wheeled, and stars whizzed in the inky blackness of spatial Nothingness. Here he lay safe and snug in a vibrating chamber; safe from the freezing cold. If only the awful jarring would stop!

Still, it had its compensations. There would be no newspapers on the voyage to torment him with accounts of man's inhumanity to man; no silly radio or television programs to annoy him. Only this cursed, omnipresent vibration. . . .

Clayton slept, hurtling through Space.

It was not daylight when he awoke. There was no daylight and no night. There was simply himself and the ship in Space. And the vibration was steady, nerve-wracking in its insistent beating against the brain. Clayton's legs trembled as he reached the cabinet and ate his pills.

Then, he sat down and began to endure. A terrific feeling of loneliness was beginning to assail him. He was so utterly detached here—cut off from everything. There was nothing to do. It was worse than being a prisoner in solitary confinement; at least they have larger cells, the sight of the sun, a breath of fresh air, and the glimpse of an occasional face.

Clayton had thought himself a misanthrope, a recluse. Now he longed for the sight of another's face. As the hours passed he got queer ideas. He wanted to see Life, in some form—he would have given a fortune for the company of even an insect in his soaring dungeon. The sound of a human voice would be heaven. He was so *alone*.

Nothing to do but endure the jerking, pace the floor, eat his pills, try to sleep. Nothing to think about. Clayton began to long for the time when his nails needed cutting; he could stretch out the task for hours.

He examined his clothes intently, stared for hours in the little mirror at his bearded face. He memorized his body, scrutinized every article in the cabin of the *Future*.

And still he was not tired enough to sleep again.

He had a throbbing headache constantly. At length he managed to close his eyes and drift off into another slumber, broken by shocks which startled him into waking.

When finally he arose and switched on the light, together with more oxygen, he made a horrible discovery.

He had lost his time-sense.

"Time is relative," they had always told him. Now he realized the truth. He had nothing to measure time by—no watch, no glimpse of the sun or moon or stars, and no regular activities. How long had he been on this voyage? Try as he might, he could not remember.

Had he eaten every six hours? Or every ten? Or every twenty? Had he slept once each day? Once every three or four days? How often had he walked the floor?

With no instruments to place himself he was at a total loss. He ate his pills in a bemused fashion, trying to think above the shuddering which filled his senses.

This was awful. If he lost track of Time he might soon lose consciousness of identity itself. He would go mad here in the spaceship as it plunged through the void to planets beyond. Alone, tormented in a tiny cell, he had to cling to something. What was Time?

He no longer wanted to think about it. He no longer wanted to think about anything. He had to forget the world he left, or memory would drive him frantic.

"I'm afraid," he whispered in a voice that sounded hollow in the tiny humming room. "I'm afraid. *What time is it?*"

He fell asleep, still whispering, and Time rushed on.

Clayton awoke with fresh courage. He had lost his grip, he reasoned. Outside pressure, however equalized, had affected his nerves. The oxygen might have made him giddy, and the pill diet was bad. But now the weakness had passed. He smiled, walked the floor.

Then the thoughts came again. What day was it? How many weeks since he had started? Maybe it was months already; a year, two years. Everything of Earth seemed far away; almost part of a dream. He now felt closer to Mars than to Earth; he began to anticipate now instead of looking back.

For a while everything had been mechanical. He switched light on and off when needed, ate pills by habit, paced the floor without thinking, unconsciously tended the air system, slept without knowing when or why.

Richard Clayton gradually forgot about his body and the surroundings. The lurching buzz in his brain became part of him; an aching part which told that he was whizzing through Space in a silver bullet. But it meant nothing more, for Clayton no longer talked to himself. He forgot himself and dreamed only of Mars ahead. Every throb of the vessel hummed, "Mars—Mars—Mars."

A wonderful thing happened. He landed. The ship nosed down, trembling. It eased gently onto the grassy sward of the red planet. For a long time Clayton had felt the pull of alien gravity, knew that automatic adjustments of his vessel were diminishing the atomic discharges and using the natural gravitational pull of Mars itself.

Now the ship landed, and Clayton had opened the door. He broke the seals and stepped out. He bounded lightly to the purple grass. His body felt free, buoyant. There was fresh air, and the sunlight seemed stronger, more intense, although clouds veiled the glowing globe.

Far away stood the forests, the green forests with the purple growth on the lushly rearing trees. Clayton left the ship and approached the cool grove. The first tree had boughs that bent to the ground in two limbs.

Limbs—limbs they were! Two green arms reached out. Clawing branches grasped him and lifted him upward. Cold coils, slimy as a serpent's, held him tightly as he was pressed against the dark tree trunk. And now he was staring into the purple growth set in the leaves.

The purple growths were—*heads.*

Evil, purple faces stared at him with rotting eyes like dead toadstools. Each face was wrinkled like a purple cauliflower, but beneath the pulpy mass was a great mouth. Every purple face had a purple mouth and each purple mouth opened to drip blood. Now the tree-arms pressed him closer to the cold, writhing trunk, and one of the purple faces—a woman's face—was moving up to kiss him.

The kiss of a vampire! Blood shone scarlet on the moving sensuous lips that bore down on his own. He struggled, but the limbs held him fast and the kiss came, cold as death. The icy flame of it seared through his being and his senses drowned.

Then Clayton awoke, and knew it was a dream. His body was bathed with moisture. It made him aware of his body. He tottered to the mirror.

A single glance sent him reeling back in horror. Was this too a part of his dream? Gazing into the mirror, Clayton saw reflected the face of an aging man. The features were heavily bearded, and they were lined and wrinkled; the once puffy cheeks were sunken. The eyes were the worst—Clayton did not recognize his own eyes any more. Red and deep-set in bony sockets, they burned out in a wild stare of horror. He touched his face, saw the blue-veined hand rise in the mirror and run through graying hair.

Partial time-sense returned. He had been here for years. Years! He was growing old!

Of course the unnatural life would age him more rapidly, but still a great interval must have passed. Clayton knew that he must soon reach the end of his journey. He wanted to reach it before he had any more dreams. From now on, sanity and physical reserve must battle against the unseen enemy of Time. He staggered back to his bunk as, trembling like a metallic flying monster, the *Future* rushed on in the blackness of interstellar Space.

They were hammering outside the vessel now; their iron arms were breaking in the door. The black metal monsters lumbered in with iron tread. Their stern, steel-cut faces were expressionless as they grasped Clayton on either side and pulled him out. Acoss the iron platform they dragged him, walking stiffly with clicking feet that clanged against the metal. The great still shafts rose in silvery spires all about, and into the iron tower they took him. Up the stairs—clang, clang, clang, pounded the great metal feet.

And the iron stairs wound round endlessly; yet still they toiled. Their faces were set, and iron does not sweat. They never tired, though Clayton was a panting wreck ere they reached the dome and threw him before the Presence in the tower room. The metallic voice buzzed, mechanically, like a broken phonograph record.

"We—found—him—in—a—bird—oh- -Master."

"He—is—made—of—soft—ness."

"He—is—alive—in—some—strange—way."

"An—an—im—al."

And then the booming voice from the center of the tower floor.

"I hunger."

Rising on an iron throne from the floor, the Master. Just a great iron trap, with steel jaws like those on a steam-shovel. The jaws clicked open, and the horrid teeth gleamed. A voice came from the depths.

"Feed me."

They threw Clayton forward in iron arms, and he fell into the trap-jaws of the monster. The jaws closed, champing with relish on human flesh. . . .

Clayton woke screaming. The mirror gleamed as his trembling hands found the light-switch. He stared into the face of an aging man with almost white hair. Clayton was growing old. And he wondered if his brain would hold out.

Eat pills, walk cabin, listen to the throbbing, put on air, lie on bunk. That was all, now. And the rest—waiting. Waiting in a humming torture-chamber, for hours, days, years, centuries, untold eons.

In every eon, a dream. He landed on Mars and the ghosts came coiling out of a gray fog. They were shapes in the fog, like slimy ectoplasm, and he saw through them. But they coiled and came, and their voices were faint whispers in his soul.

"Here is Life," they whispered. "We, whose souls have crossed the Void in death, have waited for Life to feast on. Let us take our feasting now."

And they smothered him under gray blankets, and sucked with gray, prickling mouths at his blood. . . .

Again he landed on the planet and there was nothing. Absolutely nothing. The ground was bare and it stretched off into horizons of nothingness. There was no sky nor sun, merely the ground; endless in all directions.

He set foot on it, cautiously. He sank down into nothingness. The nothingness was throbbing now, like the ship throbbed, and it was engulfing him. He was falling into a deep pit without sides, and the oblivion closed all about him. . . .

Clayton dreamed this one standing up. He opened his eyes before the mirror. His legs were weak and he steadied himself with hands that shook with age. He looked at the face in the glass—the face of a man of seventy.

"God!" he muttered. It was his own voice—the first sound he had heard in how long? How many years? For how long had he heard nothing above the hellish vibrations of this ship? How far had the *Future* gone? He was old already.

A horrid thought bit into his brain. Perhaps something had gone wrong. Maybe the calculations were at fault and he was moving into Space too slowly. He might never reach Mars. Then again—and it was a dreadful possibility—he had passed Mars, missed the carefully charted orbit of the planet. Now he was plunging on into empty voids beyond.

He swallowed his pills and lay down in the bunk. He felt a little calmer now; he had to be. For the first time in ages he remembered Earth.

Suppose it had been destroyed? Invaded by war or pestilence or disease while he was gone? Or meteors had struck it, some dying star had flamed death upon it from maddened heavens. Ghastly notions assailed him—what if Invaders crossed Space to conquer Earth, just as he now crossed to Mars?

But no sense in worrying about *that*. The problem was reaching his own goal. Helpless, he had to wait; maintain life and sanity long enough to achieve his aims. In the vibrating horror of his cell, Clayton took a mighty resolve with all his waning strength. He *would* live and when he landed he would see Mars. Whether or not he died on the long voyage home, he would exist until his goal was reached. He would fight against dreams from this moment on. No means of telling Time—only a long daze, and the humming of this infernal spaceship. But he'd live.

There were voices coming now, from outside the ship. Ghosts howled, in the dark depths of Space. Visions of monsters and dreams of torment came, and Clayton repulsed them all. Every hour or day or year—he no longer knew which—Clayton managed to stagger to the mirror. And always it showed that he was aging rapidly. His snow-white hair and wrinkled countenance hinted at incredible senility. But Clayton lived. He was too old to think any longer, and too weary. He merely lived in the droning of the ship.

At first he didn't realize. He was lying on his bunk and his rheumy eyes were closed in stupor. Suddenly he became aware that the lurching had stopped. Clayton knew he must be dreaming again. He drew himself up painfully, rubbed his eyes. No—the *Future* was still. It had *landed!* He was trembling uncontrollably. Years of vibration had done this; years of isolation with only his crazed thoughts for company. He could scarcely stand.

But this was the moment. This was what he had waited for ten long years. No, it must have been many more years. But he could see Mars. He had made it—done the impossible.

It was an inspiring thought. But somehow, Richard Clayton would have given it all up if he could only have learned what time it was, and heard it from a human voice.

He staggered to the door—the long-sealed door. There was a lever here.

His aged heart pumped with excitement as he pulled the lever upward. The door opened—sunlight crept through—air rushed in—the light made him blink and the air wheezed in his lungs—his feet were moving out—

Clayton fell forward into the arms of Jerry Chase.

Clayton didn't know it was Jerry Chase. He didn't know anything. It had been too much.

Chase was staring down at the feeble body in his arms.

"Where's Mr. Clayton?" he murmured. "Who are you?" He stared at the aged, wrinkled face.

"Why—it's Clayton!" he breathed. "Mr. Clayton, what's wrong, sir? The atomic discharges failed when you started the ship, and all that happened was that they kept blasting. The ship never left the Earth, but the violence of the discharges kept us from reaching you until now. We couldn't get to the *Future* until they stopped. Just a little while ago the ship finished shuddering, but we've been watching night and day. What happened to you, sir?"

The faded blue eyes of Richard Clayton opened. His mouth twitched as he faintly whispered.

"I—lost track of Time. How—how long was I in the *Future*?"

Jerry Chase's face was grave as he stared again at the old man and answered, softly.

"Just one week."

And as Richard Clayton's eyes glazed in death, the long voyage ended.

Robert Sheckley began as a prolific writer of short fiction in the early 1950s, when a great number of his pieces appeared in Galaxy *and other magazines, including, occasionally,* Amazing® Stories. *There are many collections of his work. His novels include* Immortality, Inc., Journey Beyond Tomorrow, Mindswap, Crompton Divided, *and* Dramocles. *He is noted for his satiric wit. This story was published in January 1954.*

THE PERFECT WOMAN
by Robert Sheckley

Mr. Morcheck awoke with a sour taste in his mouth and a laugh ringing in his ears. It was George Owen-Clark's laugh, the last thing he remembered from the Triad-Morgan party. And what a party it had been! All Earth had been celebrating the turn of the century. The year Three Thousand! Peace and prosperity to all, and happy life. . . .

"How happy is your life?" Owen-Clark had asked, grinning slyly, more than a little drunk. "I mean, how is life with your sweet wife?"

That had been unpleasant. Everyone knew that Owen-Clark was a Primitivist, but what right had he to rub people's noses in it? Just because he had married a Primitive Woman . . .

"I love my wife," Morcheck had said stoutly. "And she's a hell of a lot nicer and more responsive than that bundle of neuroses you call *your* wife."

But of course, you can't get under the thick hide of a Primitivist. Primitives love the faults in their women as much as their virtues—more perhaps. Owen-Clark had grinned ever more slyly, and said, "You know, Morcheck old man, I think your wife needs a checkup. Have you noticed her reflexes lately?"

Insufferable idiot! Mr. Morcheck eased himself out of bed, blinking at the bright morning sun which hid behind his curtains. Myra's reflexes—the hell of it was, there was a germ of truth in what Owen-Clark had said. Of late, Myra had seemed rather—out of sorts.

"Myra!" Morcheck called. "Is my coffee ready?" There was a pause. Then her voice floated brightly upstairs. "In a minute!"

Morcheck slid into a pair of slacks, still blinking sleepily. Thank Stat the next three days were celebration-points. He'd need all of them just to get over last night's party.

Downstairs, Myra was bustling around, pouring coffee, folding napkins, pulling out his chair for him. He sat down, and she kissed him on his bald spot. He liked being kissed on his bald spot.

"How's my little wife this morning?" he asked.

"Wonderful, darling," she said after a little pause. "I made Seffiners for you this morning. You like Seffiners."

Morcheck bit into one, done to a turn, and sipped his coffee.

"How do you feel this morning?" he asked her.

Myra buttered a piece of toast for him, then said, "Wonderful, darling. You know, it was a perfectly wonderful party last night. I loved every moment of it."

"I got a little bit veery," Morcheck said with a wry grin.

"I love you when you're veery," Myra said. "You talk like an angel—like a very clever angel, I mean. I could listen to you forever." She buttered another piece of toast for him.

Mr. Morcheck beamed on her like a benignant sun, then frowned. He put down his Seffiner and scratched his cheek. "You know," he said, "I had a little ruck-in with Owen-Clark. He was talking about Primitive Women."

Myra buttered a fifth piece of toast for him without answering, adding it to the growing pile. She started to reach for a sixth, but he touched her hand lightly. She bent forward and kissed him on the nose.

"Primitive Women!" she scoffed. "Those neurotic creatures! Aren't you happier with me, dear? I may be Modern—but no Primitive Woman could love you the way I do—and I adore you!"

What she said was true. Man had never, in all recorded history, been able to live happily with unreconstructed Primitive Woman. The egoistic, spoiled creatures demanded a lifetime of care and attention. It was notorious that Owen-Clark's wife made him dry the dishes. And the fool put up with it! Primitive Women were forever asking for money with which to buy clothes and trinkets, demanding breakfast in bed, dashing off to bridge games, talking for hours on the telephone, and Stat knows what else. They tried to take over men's jobs. Ultimately, they proved their equality. Some idiots like Owen-Clark insisted on their excellence.

Under his wife's enveloping love, Mr. Morcheck felt his hangover seep slowly away. Myra wasn't eating. He knew that she had eaten earlier, so that she could give her full attention to feeding him. It was little things like that that made all the difference.

"He said your reaction time had slowed down."

"He did?" Myra asked, after a pause. "Those Primitives think they know everything."

It was the right answer, but it had taken too long. Mr. Morcheck asked his wife a few more questions, observing her reaction time by the second hand on the kitchen clock. She *was* slowing up!

"Did the mail come?" he asked her quickly. "Did anyone call? Will I be late for work?"

After three seconds she opened her mouth, then closed it again. Something was terribly wrong.

"I love you," she said simply.

Mr. Morcheck felt his heart pound against his ribs. He loved her! Madly, passionately! But that disgusting Owen-Clark had been right. She needed a checkup. Myra seemed to sense his thought. She rallied perceptibly, and said, "All I want is your happiness, dear. I think I'm sick. . . . Will you have me cured? Will you take me back after I'm cured—and not let them change me—I wouldn't want to be changed!" Her bright head sank on her arms. She cried—noiselessly, so as not to disturb him.

"It'll just be a checkup, darling," Morcheck said, trying to hold back his own tears.

But he knew—as well as she knew—that she was really sick.

It was so unfair, he thought. Primitive Woman, with her coarse mental fiber, was almost immune to such ailments. But delicate Modern Woman, with her finely balanced sensibilities, was all too prone. So monstrously unfair! Because Modern Woman contained all the finest, dearest qualities of femininity.

Except stamina.

Myra rallied again. She raised herself to her feet with an effort. She was very beautiful. Her sickness had put a high color in her cheeks, and the morning sun highlighted her hair.

"My darling," she said. "Won't you let me stay a little longer? I may recover by myself." But her eyes were fast becoming unfocused.

"Darling . . . " She caught herself quickly holding on to an edge of the table. "When you have a new wife—try to remember how much I loved you." She sat down, her face blank.

"I'll get the car," Morcheck murmured, and hurried away. Any longer and he would have broken down himself.

Walking to the garage, he felt numb, tired, broken. Myra—gone! And modern science, for all its great achievements, unable to help.

He reached the garage and said, "All right, back out." Smoothly his car backed out and stopped beside him.

"Anything wrong, boss?" his car asked. "You look worried. Still got a hangover?"

"No—it's Myra. She's sick."

The car was silent for a moment. Then it said softly, "I'm very sorry, Mr. Morcheck. I wish there were something I could do."

"Thank you," Morcheck said, glad to have a friend at this hour. "I'm afraid there's nothing anyone can do."

The car backed to the door and Morcheck helped Myra inside. Gently the car started.

It maintained a delicate silence on the way back to the factory.

Walter M. Miller, the author of the classic A Canticle for Leibowitz, *was an* Amazing® Stories *discovery, his first story appearing in the magazine in 1951. His other* Amazing Stories, *all from the early 1950s, include an unreprinted novel,* The Reluctant Traitor *(1953). His most memorable short fiction can be found in* The Best of Walter M. Miller *(Gregg Press). He won two Hugos, in 1955 and 1961. This story was published in March 1954.*

MEMENTO HOMO
by Walter M. Miller, Jr.

. . . quia pulvis es et in pulverem reverteris.

Old Donegal was dying. They had known it was coming, and they had watched it come—his haggard wife, his daughter, and now his grandson, home on emergency leave from the pre-astronautics academy. Old Donegal knew it too, and had known it from the beginning, when he had begun to lose control of his legs and was forced to walk with a cane. But most of the time, he pretended to let them keep the secret they shared with the doctors—that the operations had all been failures, and that the cancer that fed at his spine would gnaw its way brainward until the paralysis engulfed vital organs, and then Old Donegal would cease to be. It would be cruel to let them know that he knew. Once, weeks ago, he had joked about the approaching shadows.

"Buy the plot back where people won't walk over it, Martha," he said. "Get it way back under the cedars—next to the fence. There aren't many graves back there yet. I want to be alone."

"Don't *talk* that way, Donny!" his wife had choked. "You're not dying."

His eyes twinkled maliciously. "Listen, Martha, I want to be buried face-down. I want to be buried with my back to space, understand? Don't let them lay me out like a lily."

"Donny, *please!*"

"They oughta face a man the way he's headed," Donegal grunted. "I been up—*way* up. Now I'm going straight down."

Martha had fled from the room in tears. He had never done it again, except to the interns and nurses, who, while they insisted that he was going to get well, didn't mind joking with him about it.

Martha can bear my death, he thought, can bear pre-knowledge of it. But she couldn't bear thinking that he might take it calmly. If he accepted death gracefully, it would be like deliberately leaving her, and Old Donegal had decided to help her believe whatever would be comforting to her in such a troublesome moment.

"When'll they let me out of this bed again?" he complained.

"Be patient, Donny," she sighed. "It won't be long. You'll be up and around before you know it."

"Back on the moon-run, maybe?" he offered. "Listen, Martha, I been planet-bound for too long. I'm not too old for the moon-run, am I? Sixty-three's not so old."

That had been carrying things too far. She knew he was hoaxing, and dabbed at her eyes again. The dead must humor the mourners, he thought, and the sick must comfort the visitors. It was always so.

But it was harder, now that the end was near. His eyes were hazy, and his thoughts unclear. He could move his arms a little, clumsily, but feeling was gone from them. The rest of his body was lost to him. Sometimes he seemed to feel his stomach and his hips, but the sensation was mostly an illusion offered by higher nervous centers, like the "ghost-arm" that an amputee continues to feel. The wires were down, and he was cut off from himself.

He lay wheezing on the hospital bed, in his own room, in his own rented flat. Gaunt and unshaven, gray as winter twilight, he lay staring at the white net curtains that billowed gently in the breeze from the open window. There was no sound in the room but the sound of breathing and the loud ticking of an alarm clock. Occasionally he heard a chair scraping on the stone terrace next door, and the low mutter of voices, sometimes laughter, as the servants of the Keith mansion arranged the terrace for late afternoon guests.

With considerable effort, he rolled his head toward Martha, who sat beside the bed, pinchfaced and weary.

"You ought to get some sleep," he said.

"I slept yesterday. Don't talk, Donny. It tires you."

"You ought to get more sleep. You never sleep enough. Are you afraid I'll get up and run away if you go to sleep for awhile?"

She managed a brittle smile. "There'll be plenty of time for sleep when . . . when you're well again." The brittle smile fled and she swallowed hard, like swallowing a fishbone. He glanced down, and noticed that she was squeezing his hand spasmodically.

There wasn't much left of the hand, he thought. Bones and ugly tight-stretched hide spotted with brown. Bulging knuckles with yellow cigarette stains. My hand. He tried to tighten it, tried to squeeze Martha's thin one in return. He watched it open and contract a little, but it was like operating a remote-control mechanism. Goodbye, hand, you're leaving me the way my legs did, he told it. I'll see you again in hell. How hammy can you get, Old Donegal? You maudlin ass.

"Requiescat," he muttered over the hand, and let it lie in peace.

Perhaps she heard him. "Donny," she whispered, leaning closer, "won't you let me call the priest now? Please."

He rattled a sigh and rolled his head toward the window again. "Are the Keiths having a party today?" he asked. "Sounds like they're moving chairs out on the terrace."

"Please, Donny, the priest?"

He let his head roll aside and closed his eyes, as if asleep. The bed shook slightly as she quickly caught at his wrist to feel for a pulse.

"If I'm not dying, I don't need a priest," he said sleepily.

"That's not right," she scolded softly. "You know that's not right, Donny. You know better."

Maybe I'm being too rough on her? he wondered. He hadn't minded getting baptized her way, and married her way, and occasionally priest-handled the way she wanted him to when he was home from a space-run, but when it came to dying, Old Donegal wanted to do it his own way.

He opened his eyes at the sound of a bench being dragged across the stone terrace. "Martha, what kind of a party are the Keiths having today?"

"I wouldn't know," she said stiffly. "You'd think they'd have a little more respect. You'd think they'd put it off a few days."

"Until—?"

"Until you feel better."

"I feel fine, Martha. I like parties. I'm glad they're having one. Pour me a drink, will you? I can't reach the bottle anymore."

"It's empty."

"No, it isn't, Martha, it's still a quarter full. I know. I've been watching it."

"You shouldn't have it, Donny. Please don't."

"But this is a party, Martha. Besides, the doctor says I can have whatever I want. Whatever I want, you hear? That means I'm getting well, doesn't it?"

"Sure, Donny, sure. Getting well."

"The whiskey, Martha. Just a finger in a tumbler, no more. I want to feel like it's a party."

Her throat was rigid as she poured it. She helped him get the tumbler to his mouth. The liquor seared his throat, and he gagged a little as the fumes clogged his nose. Good whiskey, the best—but he couldn't take it any more. He eyed the green stamp on the neck of the bottle on the bedtable and grinned. He hadn't had whiskey like that since his spacedays. Couldn't afford it now, not on a blastman's pension.

He remembered how he and Caid used to smuggle a couple of fifths aboard for the moon-run. If they caught you, it meant suspension, but there was no harm in it, not for the blastroom men who had nothing much to do from the time the ship acquired enough velocity for the long, long coaster ride until they started the rockets again for lunar landing. You could drink a fifth, jettison the bottle through the trash lock, and sober up before you were needed again. It was the only way to pass the time in the cramped cubicle, unless you ruined your eyes trying to read by the glow-lamps. Old Donegal chuckled. If he and Caid had stayed on the run, Earth would have a ring by now, like Saturn—a ring of Old Granddad bottles.

"You said it, Donny-boy," said the misty man by the billowing curtains. "Who else knows the Gegenschein is broken glass?"

Donegal laughed. Then he wondered what the man was doing there. The man was lounging against the window, and his unzipped space rig draped about him in an old familiar way. Loose plug-in connections and hose-ends dangled about his lean body. He was freckled and grinning.

"Caid," Old Donegal breathed softly.

"What did you say, Donny?" Martha answered.

Old Donegal shook his head. Something let go with a soggy snap, and the misty man was gone. I'd better take it easy on the whiskey, he thought. You got to wait, Donegal, old lush, until Nora and Ken get here. You can't get drunk until they're gone, or you might get them mixed up with memories like Caid's.

Car doors slammed in the street below. Martha glanced toward the window.

"Think it's them? I wish they'd get here. I wish they'd hurry."

Martha arose and tiptoed to the window. She peered down toward the sidewalk, put on a sharp frown. He heard a distant mutter of voices and occasional laughter, with group-footsteps milling about on the sidewalk. Martha murmured her disapproval and closed the window.

"Leave it open," he said.

"But the Keiths' guests are starting to come. There'll be such a racket." She looked at him hopefully, the way she did when she prompted his manners before company came.

Maybe it wasn't decent to listen in on a party when you were dying, he thought. But that wasn't the reason. Donegal, your chamber-pressure's dropping off. Your brains are in your butt-end, where a spacer's brains belong, but your butt-end died last month. She wants the window closed for her own sake, not yours.

"Leave it closed," he grunted. "But open it again before the moon-run blasts off. I want to listen."

She smiled and nodded, glancing at the clock. "It'll be an hour and a half yet. I'll watch the time."

"I hate that clock. I wish you'd throw it out. It's loud."

"It's your medicine-clock, Donny." She came back to sit down at his bedside again. She sat in silence. The clock filled the room with its clicking pulse.

"What time are they coming?" he asked.

"Nora and Ken? They'll be here soon. Don't fret."

"Why should I fret?" He chuckled. "That boy—he'll be a good spacer, won't he, Martha?"

Martha said nothing, fanned at a fly that crawled across his pillow. The fly buzzed up in an angry spiral and alighted on the ceiling. Donegal watched it for a time. The fly had natural-born space-legs. I know your tricks, he told it with a smile, and I learned to walk on the bottomside of things before you were a maggot. You stand there with your magnasoles hanging to the hull, and the rest of you's in free fall. You jerk a sole loose, and your knee flies up to your belly, and reaction spins you half-around and near throws your other hip out of joint if you don't jam the foot down fast and jerk up the other. It's worse'n trying to run through knee-deep mud with snowshoes, and a man'll go nuts trying to keep his arms and legs from taking off in odd directions. I know your tricks, fly. But the fly was born with his magnasoles, and he trotted across the ceiling like Donegal never could.

"That boy Ken—he ought to make a damn good space-engineer," wheezed the old man.

Her silence was long, and he rolled his head toward her again. Her lips tight, she stared down at the palm of his hand, unfolded his bony fingers, felt the cracked calluses that still welted the shrunken skin, calluses worn there by the linings of space gauntlets and the handles of fuel valves, and the rungs of get-about ladders during free fall.

"I don't know if I should tell you," she said.

"Tell me what, Martha?"

She looked up slowly, scrutinizing his face. "Ken's changed his mind, Nora says. Ken doesn't like the academy. She says he wants to go to medical school."

Old Donegal thought it over, nodded absently. "That's fine. Space medics get good pay." He watched her carefully.

She lowered her eyes, rubbed at his calluses again. She shook her head slowly. "He doesn't want to go to space."

The clock clicked loudly in the closed room.

"I thought I ought to tell you, so you won't say anything to him about it," she added.

Old Donegal looked grayer than before. After a long silence, he rolled his head away and looked toward the limp curtains.

"Open the window, Martha," he said.

Her tongue clucked faintly as she started to protest, but she said nothing. After frozen seconds, she sighed and went to open it. The curtains billowed, and a babble of conversation blew in from the terrace of the Keith mansion. With the sound came the occasional brassy discord of a musician tuning his instrument. She clutched the window-sash as if she wished to slam it closed again.

"Well! Music!" grunted Old Donegal. "That's good. This is some shebang. Good whiskey and good music and you." He chuckled, but it choked off into a fit of coughing.

"Donny, about Ken—"

"No matter, Martha," he said hastily. "Space-medic's pay is good."

"But, Donny—" She turned from the window, stared at him briefly, then said, "Sure, Donny, sure," and came back to sit down by his bed.

He smiled at her affectionately. She was a man's woman, was Martha—always had been, still was. He had married her the year he had gone to space—a lissome, wistful, old-fashioned lass, with big violet eyes and gentle hands and gentle thoughts—and she had never complained about the long and lonely weeks between blast-off and glide-down, when most spacers' wives listened to the psychiatrists and soap-operas and soon developed the symptoms that were expected of them, either because the symptoms were *chic*, or because they felt they should do something to earn the pity that was extended to them. "It's not so bad," Martha had assured him. "The house keeps me busy till Nora's home from school, and then there's a flock of kids around till dinner. Nights are a little empty, but if there's a moon, I can always go out and look at it and know where you are. And Nora gets out the telescope you built her, and we make a game of it. 'Seeing if Daddy's still at the office' she calls it."

"Those were the days," he muttered.

"What, Donny?"

"Do you remember that Steve Farran song?"

She paused, frowning thoughtfully. There were a lot of Steve Farran songs, but after a moment she picked the right one, and sang it softly . . .

> "O moon whereo'er the clouds fly,
> Beyond the willow tree,
> There is a ramblin' space guy
> I wish you'd save for me."
> *Mare Tranquilitatis,*

O dark and tranquil sea,
Until he drops from heaven,
Rest him there with thee . . . "

Her voice cracked, and she laughed. Old Donegal chuckled weakly.

"Fried mush," he said. "That one made the cats wilt their ears and wail at the moon.

"I feel real crazy," he added. "Hand me the king kong, fluffmuff."

"Keep cool, Daddy-O, you've had enough." Martha reddened and patted his arm, looking pleased. Neither of them had talked that way, even in the old days, but the out-dated slang brought back memories—school parties, dances at the Rocketport Club, the early years of the war when Donegal had jockeyed an R-43 fighter in the close-space assaults against the Soviet satellite project. The memories were good.

A brassy blare of modern "slide" arose suddenly from the Keith terrace as the small orchestra launched into its first number. Martha caught an angry breath and started toward the window.

"Leave it," he said. "It's a party. Whiskey, Martha. Please—just a small one."

She gave him a hurtful glance.

"Whiskey. Then you can call the priest."

"Donny, it's not right. You know it's not right—to bargain for such as that."

"All right. Whiskey. Forget the priest."

She poured it for him, and helped him get it down, and then went out to make the phonecall. Old Donegal lay shuddering over the whiskey taste and savoring the burn in his throat. Jesus, but it was good.

You old bastard, he thought, you got no right to enjoy life when nine-tenths of you is dead already, and the rest is foggy as a thermal dust-rise on the lunar *mare* at hell-dawn. But it wasn't a bad way to die. It ate your consciousness away from the feet up; it gnawed away the Present, but it let you keep the Past, until everything faded and blended. Maybe that's what Eternity was, he thought—one man's subjective Past, all wrapped up and packaged for shipment, a single space-time entity, a one-man microcosm of memories, when nothing else remains.

"If I've got a soul, I made it myself," he told the gray nun at the foot of the bed.

The nun held out a pie pan, rattled a few coins in it. "Contribute to the Radiation Victims' Relief?" the nun purred softly.

"I know you," he said. "You're my conscience. You hang around the officer's mess, and when we get back from a sortie, you make us pay for the damage we did. But that was forty years ago."

The nun smiled, and her luminous eyes were on him softly. "Mother of God!" he breathed, and reached for the whiskey. His arm obeyed. The last drink had done him good. He had to watch his hand to see where it was going, and squeezed the neck until his fingers whitened so that he knew he had it, but he got it off the table and onto his chest, and he got the cork out with his teeth. He had a long pull at the bottle, and it made his eyes water and his hands grow weak. But he got it back to the table without spilling a bit, and he was proud of himself.

The room was spinning like the cabin of a gyro-gravved ship. By the time he wrestled it to a standstill, the nun was gone. The blare of music from the Keith terrace was louder, and laughing voices blended with it. Chairs scraping and glasses rattling. A fine party, Keith, I'm glad you picked today. This shebang would be the younger

Keith's affair. Ronald Tonwyler Keith, III, scion of Orbital Engineering and Construction Company—builders of the moonshuttle ships that made the run from the satellite station to Luna and back.

It's good to have such important neighbors, he thought. He wished he had been able to meet them while he was still up and about. But the Keiths' place was walled-in, and when a Keith came out, he charged out in a limousine with a chauffeur at the wheel, and the iron gate closed again. The Keiths built the wall when the surrounding neighborhood began to grow shabby with age. It had once been the best of neighborhoods, but that was before Old Donegal had lived in it. Now it consisted of sooty old houses and rented flats, and the Keith place was really not a part of it anymore. Nevertheless, it was really something when a pensioned blastman could say, "I live out close to the Keiths—you know, the *Ronald* Keiths." At least, that's what Martha always told him.

The music was so loud that he never heard the doorbell ring, but when a lull came, he heard Nora's voice downstairs, and listened hopefully for Ken's. But when they came up, the boy was not with them.

"Hello, skinny-britches," he greeted his daughter.

Nora grinned and came over to kiss him. Her hair dangled about his face, and he noticed that it was blacker than usual, with the gray streaks gone from it again.

"You smell good," he said.

"You don't, Pops. You smell like a sot. Naughty!"

"Where's Ken?"

She moistened her lips nervously and looked away. "He couldn't come. He had to take a driver's lesson. He really couldn't help it. If he didn't go, he'd lose his turn, and then he wouldn't finish before he goes back to the academy." She looked at him apologetically.

"It's all right, Nora."

"If he missed it, he wouldn't get his copter license until summer."

"It's okay. Copters! Hell, the boy should be in jets by now!"

Several breaths passed in silence. She gazed absently toward the window and shook her head. "No jets, Pop. Not for Ken."

He glowered at her. "Listen! How'll he get into space? He's got to get his jet license first. Can't get in rockets without 'em."

Nora shot a quick glance at her mother. Martha rolled her eyes as if sighing patiently. Nora went to the window to stare down toward the Keith terrace. She tucked a cigarette between scarlet lips, lit it, blew nervous smoke against the pane.

"Mom, can't you call them and have that racket stopped?"

"Donny says he likes it."

Nora's eyes flitted over the scene below. "Female butterflies and puppy-dogs in sport jackets. And the cadets." She snorted. "Cadets! Imagine Ron Keith the Third ever going to space. The old man buys his way into the academy, and they throw a brawl as if Ronny passed the Compets."

"Maybe he did," growled Old Donegal.

"Hah!"

"They live in a different world, I guess," Martha sighed.

"If it weren't for men like Pops, they'd never've made their fortune."

"I like the music, I tell you," grumbled the old man.

"I'm half-a-mind to go over there and tell them off," Nora murmured.

"Let them alone. Just so they'll stop the racket for the blast-away."

"Look at them!—polite little pattern-cuts, all alike. They take pre-space, because it's the thing to do. Then they quit before the pay-off comes."

"How do you know they'll quit?"

"That party—I'll bet it cost six months' pay, spacer's pay," she went on, ignoring him. "And what do real spacers get? Oley gets killed, and Pop's pension wouldn't feed the Keiths' cat."

"You don't understand, girl."

"I lost Oley. I understand enough."

He watched her silently for a moment, then closed his eyes. It was no good trying to explain, no good trying to tell her the dough didn't mean a damn thing. She'd been a spacer's wife, and that was bad enough, but now she was a spacer's widow. And Oley? Oley's tomb revolved around the sun in an eccentric orbit that spun-in close to Mercury, then reached out into the asteroid belt, once every 725 days. When it came within rocket radius of Earth, it whizzed past at close to fifteen miles a second.

You don't rescue a ship like that, skinny-britches, my darling daughter. Nor do you salvage it after the crew stops screaming for help. If you use enough fuel to catch it, you won't get back. You just leave such a ship forever, like an asteroid, and it's a damn shame about the men trapped aboard. Heroes all, no doubt—but the smallness of the widow's monthly check failed to confirm the heroism, and Nora was bitter about the price of Oley's memory, perhaps.

Ouch! Old Donegal, you know she's not like that. It's just that she can't understand about space. You ought to make her understand.

But did he really understand himself? You ride hot in a roaring blastroom, hands tense on the mixer controls and the pumps, eyes glued to instruments, body sucked down in a four-gravity thrust, and wait for the command to choke it off. Then you float free and weightless in a long nightmare as the beast coasts moonward, a flung javelin.

The "romance" of space—drivel written in the old days. When you're not blasting, you float in a cramped hotbox, crawl through dirty mazes of greasy pipe and cable to tighten a lug, scratch your arms and bark your shins, get sick and choked up because no gravity helps your gullet get the food down. Liquid is worse, but you gag your whiskey down because you have to.

Stars?—you see stars by squinting through a viewing lens, and it's like a photo-transparency, and if you aren't careful, you'll get an eyeful of Old Blinder and back off with a punch-drunk retina.

Adventure?—unless the skipper calls for course-correction, you float around in the blast-cubicle with damn little to do between blast-away and moon-down, except sweat out the omniscient accident statistics. If the beast blows up or gets gutted in space, a statistic had your name on it, that's all, and there's no fighting back. You stay outwardly sane because you're a hog for punishment; if you weren't, you'd never get past the psychologists.

"Did you like horror movies when you were a kid?" asked the psych. And you'd damn well better answer "yes," if you want to go to space.

Tell her, old man, you're her pop. Tell her why it's worth it, if you know. You jail yourself in a coffin-size cubicle, and a crazy beast thunders berserk for uncontrollable seconds, and then you soar in ominous silence for the long long hours. Grow sweaty, filthy, sick, miserable, idle—somewhere out in Big Empty, where Man's got no business except the trouble he always makes for himself wherever he goes. Tell her why it's worth it, for pay less than a good bricklayer's. Tell her why Oley would do it again.

"It's a sucker's run, Nora," he said. "You go looking for kicks, but the only kicks you get to keep is what Oley got. God knows why—but it's worth it."

Nora said nothing. He opened his eyes slowly. Nora was gone. Had she been there at all?

He blinked around at the fuzzy room, and dissolved the shifting shadows that sometimes emerged as old friendly faces, grinning at him. He found Martha.

"You went to sleep," said Martha. "She had to go. Kennie called. He'll be over later, if you're not too tired."

"I'm not tired. I'm all head. There's nothing much to get tired."

"I love you, Old Donegal."

"Hold my hand again."

"I'm holding it, old man."

"Then hold me where I can feel it."

She slid a thin arm under his neck, and bent over his face to kiss him. She was crying a little, and he was glad she could do it now without fleeing the room.

"Can I talk about dying now?" he wondered aloud.

She pinched her lips together and shook her head.

"I lie to myself, Martha. You know how much I lie to myself?"

She nodded slowly and stroked his gray temples.

"I lie to myself about Ken, about dying. If Ken turned spacer, I wouldn't die—that's what I told myself. You know?"

She shook her head. "Don't talk, Donny, please."

"A man makes his own soul, Martha."

"That's not true. You shouldn't say things like that."

"A man makes his own soul, but it dies with him, unless he can pour it into his kids and his grandchildren before he goes. I lied to myself. Ken's a yellow-belly. Nora made him one, and the boots won't fit."

"Don't, Donny. You'll excite yourself again."

"I was going to give him the boots—the over-boots with magnasoles. But they won't fit him. They won't ever fit him. He's a lily-livered lap-dog, and he whines. Bring me my boots, woman."

"Donny!"

"The boots, they're in my locker in the attic. I want them."

"What on earth!"

"Bring me my goddam space boots and put them on my feet. I'm going to wear them."

"You can't; the priest's coming."

"Well, get them anyway. What time is it? You didn't let me sleep through the moon-run blast, did you?"

She shook her head. "It's half an hour yet . . . I'll get the boots if you promise not to make me put them on you."

"I want them on."

"You can't, until Father Paul's finished."

"Do I have to get my feet buttered?"

She sighed. "I wish you wouldn't say things like that. I wish you wouldn't,

Donny. It's sacrilege, you know it is."

"All right—'annointed,' " he corrected wearily.

"Yes, you do."

"The boots, woman, the boots."

She went to get them. While she was gone, the doorbell rang, and he heard her quick footsteps on the stairs, and then Father Paul's voice asking about the patient. Old Donegal groaned inwardly. After the priest, the doctor would come, at the usual time, to see if he were dead yet. The doctor had let him come home from the hospital to die, and the doctor was getting impatient. Why don't they let me alone? he growled. Why don't they let me handle it my own way, and stop making a fuss over it? I can die and do a good job of it without a lot of outside interference, and I wish they'd quit picking at me with syringes and sacraments and enemas. All he wanted was a chance to listen to the orchestra on the Keith terrace, to drink the rest of his whiskey, and to hear the beast blast-away for the satellite on the first lap of the run to Luna.

It's going to be my last day, he thought. My eyes are going fuzzy, and I can't breathe right, and the throbbing's hurting my head. Whether he lived right through the night wouldn't matter, because delirium was coming over him, and then there would be the coma, and the symbolic fight to keep him pumping and panting. I'd rather die tonight and get it over with, he thought, but they probably won't let me go.

He heard their voices coming up the stairs. . . .

"Nora tried to get them to stop it, Father, but she couldn't get in to see anybody but the butler. He told her he'd tell Mrs. Keith, but nothing happened. It's just as loud as before."

"Well, as long as Donny doesn't mind—"

"He just says that. You know how he is."

"What're they celebrating, Martha?"

"Young Ronald's leaving—for pre-space training. It's a going-away affair." They paused in the doorway. The small priest smiled in at Donegal and nodded. He set his black bag on the floor inside, winked solemnly at the patient.

"I'll leave you two alone," said Martha. She closed the door and her footsteps wandered off down the hall.

Donegal and the young priest eyed each other warily.

"You look like hell, Donegal," the padre offered jovially. "Feeling nasty?"

"Skip the small talk. Let's get this routine over with."

The priest humphed thoughtfully, sauntered across to the bed, gazed down at the old man disinterestedly. "What's the matter? Don't want the 'routine'? Rather play it tough?"

"What's the difference?" he growled. "Hurry up and get out. I want to hear the blast-off."

"You won't be able to," said the priest, glancing at the window, now closed again. "That's quite a racket next door."

"They'd better stop for it. They'd better quiet down for it. They'll have to turn it off for five minutes or so."

"Maybe they won't."

It was a new idea, and it frightened him. He liked the music, and the party's gaiety, the nearness of youth and good times—but it hadn't occurred to him that it wouldn't stop so he could hear the beast.

"Don't get upset, Donegal. You know what a blast-off sounds like."

"But it's the last one. The last time. I want to hear."

"How do you know it's the last time?"

"Hell, don't I know when I'm kicking off?"

"Maybe, maybe not. It's hardly your decision."

"It's not, eh?" Old Donegal fumed. "Well, bigawd you'd think it wasn't. You'd think it was Martha's and yours and that damfool medic's. You'd think I got no say-so. Who's doing it, anyway?"

"I would guess," Father Paul grunted sourly, "that Providence might appreciate His fair share of the credit."

Old Donegal made a surly noise and hunched his head back in the pillow to glower.

"You want me?" the priest asked. "Or is this just a case of wifely conscience?"

"What's the difference? Give me the business and scram."

"No soap. Do you want the sacrament, or are you just being kind to your wife? If it's for Martha, I'll go *now*."

Old Donegal glared at him for a time, then wilted. The priest brought his bag to the bedside.

"Bless me, father, for I have sinned."

"Bless you, son."

"I accuse myself . . . "

Tension, anger, helplessness—they had piled up on him, and now he was feeling the after-effects. Vertigo, nausea, and the black confetti—a bad spell. The whiskey—if he could only reach the whiskey. Then he remembered he was receiving a Sacrament, and struggled to get on with it. Tell him, old man, tell him of your various rottennesses and vile transgressions, if you can remember some. A sin is whatever you're sorry for, maybe. But Old Donegal, you're sorry for the wrong things, and this young jesuitical gadget wouldn't like listening to it. I'm sorry I didn't get it instead of Oley, and I'm sorry I fought in the war, and I'm sorry I can't get out of this bed and take a belt to my daughter's backside for making a puny whelp out of Ken, and I'm sorry I gave Martha such a rough time all these years—and wound up dying in a cheap flat, instead of giving her things like the Keiths had. I wish I had been a sharpster, contractor, or thief . . . instead of a common laboring spacer, whose species lost its glamor after the war.

Listen, old man, you made your soul yourself, and it's yours. This young dispenser of oils, Substances, and mysteries wishes only to help you scrape off the rough edges and gouge out the bad spots. He will not steal it, nor distort it with his supernatural chisels, nor make fun of it. He can take nothing away, but only cauterize and neutralize, he says, so why not let him try? Tell him the rotten messes.

"Are you finished, my son?"

Old Donegal nodded wearily, and said what he was asked to say, and heard the soft mutter of Latin that washed him inside and behind his ghostly ears . . . *ego te absolvo in Nomine Patti* . . . and he accepted the rest of it lying quietly in the candlelight and the red glow of the sunset through the window, while the priest anointed him and gave him Bread, and read the words of the soul in greeting its Spouse: "I was asleep, but my heart waked; it is the voice of my beloved calling: come to me, my love, my dove, my undefiled . . . " and from beyond the closed window came the sarcastic wail of a clarinet painting hot slides against a rhythmic background.

It wasn't so bad, Old Donegal thought when the priest was done. He felt like a schoolboy in a starched shirt on Sunday morning, and it wasn't a bad feeling, though it left him weak.

The priest opened the window for him again, and repacked his bag. "Ten minutes till blast-off," he said. "I'll see what I can do about the racket next door."

When he was gone, Martha came back in, and he looked at her face and was glad. She was smiling when she kissed him, and she looked less tired.

"Is it all right for me to die now?" he grunted.

"Donny, don't start that again."

"Where's the boots? You promised to bring them."

"They're in the hall. Donny, you don't want them."

"I want them, and I want a drink of whiskey, and I want to hear them fire the beast." He said it slow and hard, and he left no room for argument.

When she had got the huge boots over his shrunken feet, the magnasoles clanged against the iron bed-frame and clung there, and she rolled him up so that he could look at them, and Old Donegal chuckled inside. He felt warm and clean and pleasantly dizzy.

"The whiskey, Martha, and for God's sake, make them stop the noise till after the firing. Please!"

She went to the window and looked out for a long time. Then she came back and poured him an insignificant drink.

"Well?"

"I don't know," she said. "I saw Father Paul on the terrace, talking to somebody."

"Is it time?"

She glanced at the clock, looked at him doubtfully, and nodded. "Nearly time."

The orchestra finished a number, but the babble of laughing voices continued. Old Donegal sagged. "They won't do it. They're the Keiths, Martha. Why should I ruin their party?"

She turned to stare at him, slowly shook her head. He heard someone shouting, but then a trumpet started softly, introducing a new number. Martha sucked in a hurt breath, pressed her hands together, and hurried from the room.

"It's too late," he said after her.

Her footsteps stopped on the stairs. The trumpet was alone. Donegal listened; and there was no babble of voices, and the rest of the orchestra was silent. Only the trumpet sang—and it puzzled him, hearing the same slow bugle-notes of the call played at the lowering of the colors.

The trumpet stopped suddenly. Then he knew it had been for him.

A brief hush—then thunder came from the blast-station two miles to the west. First the low reverberation, rattling the windows, then the rising growl as the sleek beast knifed skyward on a column of bluewhite Hell. It grew and grew until it drowned the distant traffic sounds and dominated the silence outside.

Quit crying, you old fool, you maudlin ass . . .

"My boots," he whispered, "my boots . . . please . . . "

"You've got them on, Donny."

He sank quietly then. He closed his eyes and let his heart go up with the beast, and he sank into the gravity padding of the blastroom, and Caid was with him, and Oley. And when Ronald Keith, III, instructed the orchestra to play "Blastroom Man," after the beast's rumble had waned, Old Donegal was on his last moon-run, and he was grinning. He'd had a good day.

Martha went to the window to stare out at the thin black trail that curled starward above the blast-station through the twilight sky. Guests on the terrace were watching it too.

The doorbell rang. That would be Ken, too late. She closed the window against the chill breeze, and went back to the bed. The boots, the heavy, clumsy boots—they clung to the bed-frame, with his feet half out of them. She took them off gently and set them out of company's sight. Then she went to answer the door.

Isaac Asimov's first story, "Marooned off Vesta," appeared in
Amazing® Stories in 1939. He has since gone on to publish over
three hundred books, from science fact to such classics of science
fiction as The Foundation Trilogy and The Caves of Steel, with many
oddments mixed in, not the least odd of which is The Sensuous
Dirty Old Man. The present story was originally entitled "Playboy and
the Slime God," when it was published in March 1961 as a retaliatory
strike against an article that appeared in Playboy, "Girls for the Slime
God," about the allegedly salacious nature of pulp science fiction. But
time has since robbed it of context; hence the title change.

WHAT IS THIS THING CALLED LOVE?
by Isaac Asimov

"But these are two species," said Captain
Garm, peering closely at the creatures that had been brought up from the planet below. His optic organs adjusted focus to maximum sharpness, bulging outwards as
they did so. The color patch above them gleamed in quick flashes.

Botax felt warmly comfortable to be following color-changes once again, after
months in a spy cell on the planet, trying to make sense out of the modulated sound
waves emitted by the natives. Communication by flash was almost like being home
in the far-off Perseus arm of the Galaxy. "Not two species," he said, "but two forms
of one species."

"Nonsense, they look quite different. Vaguely Perse-like, thank the Entity, and
not as disgusting in appearance as so many out-forms are. Reasonable shape, recognizable limbs. But no color-patch. Can they speak?"

"Yes, Captain Garm." Botax indulged in a discreetly disapproving prismatic inter-
lude. "The details are in my report. These creatures form sound waves by way of the
throat and mouth, something like complicated coughing. I have learned to do it myself." He was quietly proud. "It is very difficult."

"It must be stomach-turning. Well, that accounts for their flat, unextensible eyes.
Not to speak by color makes eyes largely useless. Meanwhile, how can you insist these
are a single species? The one on the left is smaller and has long tendrils, or whatever it
is, and seems differently proportioned. It bulges where this one does not. Are they
alive?"

"Alive but not at the moment conscious, Captain. They have been psycho-treated
to repress fright in order that they might be studied easily."

"But are they worth the study? We are behind on our schedule and have at least
five worlds of greater moment than this one to check and explore. Maintaining a
Time-stasis unit is expensive and I would like to return them and go on—"

But Botax's moist spindly body was fairly vibrating with anxiety. His tubular
tongue flicked out and curved up and over his flat nose, while his eyes sucked in-

wards. His splayed three-fingered hand made a gesture of negation as his speech went almost entirely into the deep red.

"Entity save us, Captain, for no world is of greater moment to us than this one. We may be facing a supreme crisis. These creatures could be the most dangerous life-forms in the Galaxy, Captain, just *because* there are two forms."

"I don't follow you."

"Captain, it has been my job to study this planet, and it has been most difficult, for it is unique. It is so unique that I can scarcely comprehend its facets. For instance, almost all life on the planet consists of species in two forms. There are no words to describe it, no concepts even. I can only speak of them as first form and second form. If I may use their sounds, the little one is called 'female,' and the big one, here, 'male,' so the creatures themselves are aware of the difference."

Garm winced. "What a disgusting means of communication."

"And, Captain, in order to bring forth young, the two forms must cooperate."

The Captain, who had bent forward to examine the specimens closely with an expression compounded of interest and revulsion, straightened at once. "Cooperate? What nonsense is this? There is no more fundamental attribute of life than that each living creature bring forth its young in innermost communication with itself. What else makes life worth living?"

"The one form does bring forth life but the other form must cooperate."

"How?"

"That has been difficult to determine. It is something very private and in my search through available forms of literature I could find no exact and explicit description. But I have been able to make reasonable deductions."

Garm shook his head. "Ridiculous. Budding is the holiest, most private function in the world. On tens of thousands of worlds it is the same. As the great photo-bard, Levuline, said, 'In budding time, in budding time, in sweet, delightful budding time; when—' "

"Captain, you don't understand. This cooperation between forms brings about somehow (and I am not certain exactly how) a mixture and recombination of genes. It is a device by which in every generation, new combinations of characteristics are brought into existence. Variations are multiplied; mutated genes hastened into expression almost at once where under the usual budding system, millennia might pass first."

"Are you trying to tell me that the genes from one individual can be combined with those of another? Do you know how completely ridiculous that is in the light of all the principles of cellular physiology?"

"It must be so," said Botax nervously under the other's pop-eyed glare. "Evolution *is* hastened. This planet is a riot of species. There are supposed to be a million and a quarter different species of creatures."

"A dozen and a quarter more likely. Don't accept too completely what you read in the native literature."

"I've seen dozens of radically different species myself in just a small area. I tell you, Captain, give these creatures a short space of time and they will mutate into intellects powerful enough to overtake us and rule the Galaxy."

"Prove this cooperation you speak of exists, Investigator, and I shall consider your contentions. If you cannot, I shall dismiss all your fancies as ridiculous and we will move on."

"I can prove it." Botax's color-flashes turned intensely yellow-green. "The creatures of this world are unique in another way. They foresee advances they have not yet made, probably as a consequence of their belief in rapid change which, after all, they constantly witness. They therefore indulge in a type of literature involving the space-travel they have never developed. I have translated their term for the literature as 'science fiction.' Now I have dealt in my readings almost exclusively with science fiction, for there I thought, in their dreams and fancies, they would expose themselves and their danger to us. And it was from that science fiction that I deduced the method of their inter-form cooperation."

"How did you do that?"

"There is a periodical on this world which sometimes publishes science fiction which is, however, devoted almost entirely to the various aspects of the cooperation. It does not speak entirely freely, which is annoying, but persists in merely hinting. Its name as nearly as I can put it into flashes is 'Recreationlad.' The creature in charge, I deduce, is interested in nothing but inter-form cooperation and searches for it everywhere with a systematic and scientific intensity that has aroused my awe. He has found instances of cooperation described in science fiction and I let material in his periodical guide me. From the stories he instanced I have learned how to bring it about.

"And, Captain, I beg of you, when the cooperation is accomplished and the young are brought forth before your eyes, give orders not to leave an atom of this world in existence."

"Well," said Captain Garm, wearily, "bring them into full consciousness and do what you must do quickly."

Marge Skidmore was suddenly completely aware of her surroundings. She remembered very clearly the elevated station at the beginning of twilight. It had been almost empty, one man standing near her, another at the other end of the platform. The approaching train had just made itself known as a faint rumble in the distance.

There had then come the flash, a sense of turning inside out, the half-seen vision of a spindly creature, dripping mucus, a rushing upward, and now—

"Oh, God," she said, shuddering. "It's still here. And there's another one, too."

She felt a revulsion, but no fear. She was almost proud of herself for feeling no fear. The man next to her, standing quietly as she herself was, but still wearing a battered fedora, was the one that had been near her on the platform.

"They got you, too?" she asked. "Who else?"

Charlie Grimwold, feeling flabby and paunchy, tried to lift his hand to remove his hat and smooth the thin hair that broke up but did not entirely cover the skin of his scalp and found that it moved only with difficulty against a rubbery but hardening resistance. He let his hand drop and looked morosely at the thin-faced woman facing him. She was in her middle thirties, he decided, and her hair was nice and her dress fit well, but at the moment, he just wanted to be somewhere else and it did him no good at all that he had company; even female company.

He said, "I don't know, lady. I was just standing on the station platform."

"Me, too."

"And then I see a flash. Didn't hear nothing. Now here I am. Must be little green men from Mars or Venus or one of them places."

Marge nodded vigorously. "That's what I figure. A flying saucer? You scared?"

"No. That's funny, you know. I think maybe I'm going nuts or I *would* be scared."

"Funny thing. I ain't scared either. Oh, God, here comes one of them now. If he touches me, I'm going to scream. Look at those wiggly hands. And that wrinkled skin, all slimy; makes me nauseous."

Botax approached gingerly and said, in a voice at once rasping and screechy, this being the closest he could come to imitating the native timbre, "Creatures! We will not hurt you. But we must ask you if you would do us the favor of cooperating."

"Hey, it talks!" said Charlie. "What do you mean, cooperate?"

"Both of you. With each other," said Botax.

"Oh?" He looked at Marge. "You know what he means, lady?"

"Ain't got no idea whatsoever," she answered loftily.

Botax said, "What I mean—" and he used the short term he had once heard employed as a synonym for the process.

Marge turned red and said "What!" in the loudest scream she could manage. Both Botax and Captain Garm put their hands over their mid-regions to cover the auditory patches that trembled painfully with the decibels.

Marge went on rapidly and nearly incoherently. "Of all things. I'm a married woman, you. If my Ed was here, you'd hear from *him*. And you, wise guy," she twisted toward Charlie against rubbery resistance, "whoever you are, if you think—"

"Lady, lady," said Charlie in uncomfortable desperation. "It ain't my idea. I mean, far be it from me, you know, to turn down some lady, you know; but me, I'm married too. I got three kids. Listen—"

Captain Garm said, "What's happening, Investigator Botax? These cacophonous sounds are awful."

"Well." Botax flashed a short purple patch of embarrassment. "This forms a complicated ritual. They are supposed to be reluctant at first. It heightens the subsequent result. After that initial stage, the skins must be removed."

"They have to be *skinned?*"

"Not really skinned. Those are artificial skins that can be removed painlessly, and must be. Particularly in the smaller form."

"All right then. Tell it to remove the skins. Really, Botax, I don't find this pleasant."

"I don't think I had better tell the smaller form to remove the skins. I think we had better follow the ritual closely. I have here sections of those space-travel tales which the man from the 'Recreationlad' periodical spoke highly of. In those tales the skins are removed forcibly. Here is a description of an accident, for instance 'which played havoc with the girl's dress, ripping it nearly off her slim body. For a second, he felt the warm firmness of her half-bared bosom against his cheek—' It goes on that way. You see, the ripping, the forcible removal, acts as a stimulus."

"Bosom?" said the Captain. "I don't recognize the flash."

"I invented that to cover the meaning. It refers to the bulges on the upper torso region of the smaller form."

"I see. Well, tell the larger one to rip the skins off the smaller one. What a dismal thing this is."

Botax turned to Charlie. "Sir," he said, "rip the girl's dress nearly off her slim body, will you? I will release you for the purpose."

Marge's eyes widened and she twisted toward Charlie in an instant outrage.

"Don't you dare do that, you. Don't you *dare* touch me, you sex maniac."

"Me?" said Charlie plaintively. "It ain't my idea. You think I go around ripping dresses? Listen"—he turned to Botax—"I got a wife and three kids. She finds out I go around ripping dresses, I get clobbered. You know what my wife does when I just look at some dame? *Listen*—"

"Is he still reluctant?" said the Captain, impatiently.

"Apparently," said Botax. "The strange surroundings, you know, may be extending that stage of the cooperation. Since I know this is unpleasant for you, I will perform this stage of the ritual myself. It is frequently written in the space-travel tales that an outer-world species performs this task. For instance, here," and he riffled through his notes finding the one he wanted, "they describe a very awful such species. The creatures on the planet have foolish notions, you understand. It never occurs to them to imagine handsome individuals such as ourselves, with a fine mucous cover."

"Go on! Go on! Don't take all day," said the Captain.

"Yes, Captain. It says here that the extraterrestrial 'came forward to where the girl stood. Shrieking hysterically, she was cradled in the monster's embrace. Talons ripped blindly at her body, tearing the kirtle away in rags.' You see, the native creature is shrieking with stimulation as her skins are removed."

"Then go ahead, Botax, remove it. But please, allow no shrieking. I'm trembling all over with the sound waves."

Botax said politely to Marge, "If you don't mind—"

One spatulate finger made as though to hook on to the neck of the dress.

Marge wiggled desperately. "Don't touch. Don't touch! You'll get slime on it. Listen, this dress cost $24.95 at Ohrbach's. Stay away, you monster. Look at those eyes on him." She was panting in her desperate efforts to dodge the groping, extraterrestrial hand. "A slimy, bug-eyed monster, that's what he is. Listen, I'll take it off myself. Just don't touch it with slime, for God's sake."

She fumbled with the zipper, and said in a hot aside to Charlie, "Don't you dare look."

Charlie closed his eyes and shrugged in resignation.

She stepped out of the dress. "All right? You satisfied?"

Captain Garm's fingers twitched with unhappiness. "Is that the bosom? Why does the other creature keep its head turned away?"

"Reluctance. Reluctance," said Botax. "Besides, the bosom is still covered. Other skins must be removed. When bared, the bosom is a very strong stimulus. It is constantly described as ivory globes, or white spheres, or otherwise after that fashion. I have here drawings, visual picturizations, that come from the outer covers of the space-travel magazines. If you will inspect them, a creature is present with a bosom more or less exposed."

The Captain looked thoughtfully from the illustrations to Marge and back. "What is ivory?"

"That is another made-up flash of my own. It represents the tusky material of one of the large sub-intelligent creatures on the planet."

"Ah," and Captain Garm went into a pastel green of satisfaction. "That explains it. This small creature is one of a warrior sect and those are tusks with which to smash the enemy."

"No, no. They are quite soft, I understand." Botax's small brown hand flicked outward in the general direction of the objects under discussion and Marge screamed and shrank away.

"Then what other purpose do they have?"

"I think," said Botax with considerable hesitation, "that they are used to feed the young."

"The young eat them?" asked the Captain with every evidence of deep distress.

"Not exactly. The objects produce a fluid which the young consume."

"Consume a fluid from a living body? Yech-h-h." The Captain covered his head with all three of his arms, calling the central supernumerary into use for the purpose, slipping it out of its sheath so rapidly as almost to knock Botax over.

"A three-armed, slimy, bug-eyed monster," said Marge.

"Yeah," said Charlie.

"All right, you, just watch those eyes. Keep them to yourself."

"Listen, lady. I'm trying not to look."

Botax approached again. "Madam, would you remove the rest?"

Marge drew herself up as well as she could against the pinioning field. "Never!"

"I'll remove it, if you wish."

"Don't touch! For God's sake, don't touch. Look at the slime on him, will you? All right, I'll take it off." She was muttering under her breath and looking hotly in Charlie's direction as she did so.

"Nothing is happening," said the Captain, in deep dissatisfaction, "and this seems an imperfect specimen."

Botax felt the slur on his own efficiency. "I brought you two perfect specimens. What's wrong with the creature?"

"The bosom does not consist of globes or spheres. I know what globes and spheres are and in these pictures you have shown me, they are so depicted. Those are large globes. On this creature, though, what we have are nothing but small flaps of dry tissue. And they're discolored, too, partly."

"Nonsense," said Botax. "You must allow room for natural variation. I will put it to the creature herself."

He turned to Marge, "Madame, is your bosom imperfect?"

Marge's eyes opened wide and she struggled vainly for moments without doing anything more than gasp loudly. *"Really!"* she finally managed. "Maybe I'm no Gina Lollobrigida or Anita Ekberg, but I'm perfectly all right, thank you. Oh boy, if my Ed were only here." She turned to Charlie. "Listen, you, you tell this bug-eyed slimy thing here, there ain't nothing wrong with my development."

"Lady," said Charlie, softly. "I ain't looking, remember?"

"Oh, sure, you ain't looking. You been peeking enough, so you might as well just open your crummy eyes and stick up for a lady, if you're the least bit of a gentleman, which you probably ain't."

"Well," said Charlie, looking sideways at Marge, who seized the opportunity to inhale and throw her shoulders back, "I don't like to get mixed up in a kind of delicate matter like this, but you're all right—I guess."

"You *guess?* You blind or something? I was once runner-up for Miss Brooklyn, in case you don't happen to know, and where I missed out was on waist-line, *not* on—"

Charlie said, "All right, all right. They're fine. Honest." He nodded vigorously in Botax's direction. "They're okay. I ain't that much of an expert, you understand, but they're okay by me."

Marge relaxed.

Botax felt relieved. He turned to Garm. "The bigger form expresses interest, Captain. The stimulus is working. Now for the final step."

"And what is that?"

"There is no flash for it, Captain. Essentially, it consists of placing the speaking-and-eating apparatus of one against the equivalent apparatus of the other. I have made up a flash for the process, thus: kiss."

"Will nausea never cease?" groaned the Captain.

"It is the climax. In all the tales, after the skins are removed by force, they clasp each other with limbs and indulge madly in burning kisses, to translate as nearly as possible the phrase most frequently used. Here is one example, just one, taken at random: 'He held the girl, his mouth avid on her lips.' "

"Maybe one creature was devouring the other," said the Captain.

"Not at all," said Botax impatiently. "Those were burning kisses."

"How do you mean, burning? Combustion takes place?"

"I don't think literally so. I imagine it is a way of expressing the fact that the temperature goes up. The higher the temperature, I suppose, the more successful the production of the young. Now that the big form is properly stimulated, he need only place his mouth against hers to produce young. The young will not be produced without that step. It is the cooperation I have been speaking of."

"That's all? Just this—" The Captain's hands made motions of coming together, but he could not bear to put the thought into flash form.

"That's all," said Botax. "In none of the tales; not even in 'Recreationlad,' have I found a description of any further physical activity in connection with young-bearing. Sometimes after the kissing, they write a line of symbols like little stars, but I suppose that merely means more kissing; one kiss for each star, when they want to produce a multitude of young."

"Just one, please, right now."

"Certainly, Captain."

Botax said with grave distinctness, "Sir, would you kiss the lady?"

Charlie said, "Listen, I can't move."

"I will free you, of course."

"The lady might not like it."

Marge glowered. "You bet your damn boots, I won't like it. You just stay away."

"I would like to, lady, but what do they do if I don't? Look, I don't want to get them mad. We can just—you know—make like a little peck."

She hesitated, seeing the justice of the caution. "All right. No funny stuff, though. I ain't in the habit of standing around like this in front of every Tom, Dick and Harry, you know."

"I know that, lady. It was none of my doing. You got to admit that."

Marge muttered angrily, "Regular slimy monsters. Must think they're some kind of gods or something, the way they order people around. Slime gods is what they are!"

Charlie approached her. "If it's okay now, lady." He made a vague motion as though to tip his hat. Then he put his hands awkwardly on her bare shoulders and leaned over in a gingerly pucker.

What is This Thing Called Love? 99

Marge's head stiffened so that lines appeared in her neck. Their lips met.

Captain Garm flashed fretfully. "I sense no rise in temperature." His heat-detecting tendril had risen to full extension at the top of his head and remained quivering there.

"I don't either," said Botax, rather at a loss, "but we're doing it just as the space-travel stories tell us to. I think his limbs should be more extended— Ah, like that. See, it's working."

Almost absently, Charlie's arm had slid around Marge's soft, nude torso. For a moment, Marge seemed to yield against him and then she suddenly writhed hard against the pinioning field that still held her with fair firmness.

"Let go." The words were muffled against the pressure of Charlie's lips. She bit suddenly, and Charlie leaped away with a wild cry, holding his lower lip, then looking at his fingers for blood.

"What's the idea, lady?" he demanded plaintively.

She said, "We agreed just a peck, is all. What were you starting there? You some kind of playboy or something? What am I surrounded with here? Playboy and the slime gods?"

Captain Garm flashed rapid alterations of blue and yellow. "Is it done? How long do we wait now?"

"It seems to me it must happen at once. Throughout all the universe, when you have to bud, you bud, you know. There's no waiting."

"Yes? After thinking of the foul habits you have been describing, I don't think I'll ever bud again. Please get this over with."

"Just a moment, Captain."

But the moments passed and the Captain's flashes turned slowly to a brooding orange, while Botax's nearly dimmed out altogether.

Botax finally asked hesitantly, "Pardon me, madam, but when will you bud?"

"When will I *what?*"

"Bear young?"

"I've got a kid."

"I mean bear young now."

"I should say not. I ain't ready for another kid yet."

"What? What?" demanded the Captain. "What's she saying?"

"It seems," said Botax, weakly, "she does not intend to have young at the moment."

The Captain's color patch blazed brightly. "Do you know what I think, Investigator? I think you have a sick, perverted mind. Nothing's happening to these creatures. There is no cooperation between them, and no young to be born. I think they're two different species and that you're playing some kind of foolish game with me."

"But, Captain—" said Botax.

"Don't but Captain me," said Garm. "I've had enough. You've upset me, turned my stomach, nauseated me, disgusted me with the whole notion of budding and wasted my time. You're just looking for headlines and personal glory and I'll see to it that you don't get them. Get rid of these creatures now. Give that one its skins back and put them back where you found them. I ought to take the expense of maintaining Time-stasis all this time out of your salary."

"But, Captain—"

"Back, I say. Put them back in the same place and at the same instant of time. I want this planet untouched, and I'll see to it that it stays untouched." He cast one more furious glance at Botax. "One species, two forms, bosoms, kisses, cooperation, BAH— You are a fool, Investigator, a dolt as well and, most of all, a sick, sick, sick creature."

There was no arguing. Botax, limbs trembling, set about returning the creatures.

They stood there at the elevated station, looking around wildly. It was twilight over them, and the approaching train was just making itself known as a faint rumble in the distance.

Marge said, hesitantly, "Mister, did it really happen?"

Charlie nodded. "I remember it."

Marge said, "We can't tell anybody."

"Sure not. They'd say we was nuts. Know what I mean?"

"Uh-huh. Well," she edged away.

Charlie said, "Listen. I'm sorry you was embarrassed. It was none of my doing."

"That's all right. I know." Marge's eyes considered the wooden platform at her feet. The sound of the train was louder.

"I mean, you know, lady, you wasn't really bad. In fact, you looked good, but I was kind of embarrassed to say that."

Suddenly, she smiled. "It's all right."

"You want maybe to have a cup of coffee with me just to relax you? My wife, she's not really expecting me for a while."

"Oh? Well, Ed's out of town for the weekend so I got only an empty apartment to go home to. My little boy is visiting at my mother's." She explained.

"Come on, then. We been kind of introduced."

"I'll say." She laughed.

The train pulled in, but they turned away, walking down the narrow stairway to the street.

They had a couple of cocktails actually, and then Charlie couldn't let her go home in the dark alone, so he saw her to her door. Marge was bound to invite him in for a few moments, naturally.

Meanwhile, back in the spaceship, the crushed Botax was making a final effort to prove his case. While Garm prepared the ship for departure Botax hastily set up the tight-beam visiscreen for a last look at his specimens. He focused in on Charlie and Marge in her apartment. His tendril stiffened and he began flashing in a coruscating rainbow of colors.

"Captain Garm! Captain! Look what they're doing now!"

But at that very instant the ship winked out of Time-stasis.

Edmond Hamilton first appeared in Weird Tales *in 1926, but began to write for* Amazing® Stories *in 1928, and continued to do so until 1969.* Amazing Stories *published the grandest of his space-operas,* The Star Kings *(1947), and also a large share of his later, more mature writings, such as the story below, which appeared in April 1962. Hamilton was one of the great pioneers of the field, who never ceased to keep up with its development. His wife, the late Leigh Brackett, edited* The Best of Edmond Hamilton *(1977).*

REQUIEM
by Edmond Hamilton

Kellon thought sourly that he wasn't commanding a star-ship, he was running a traveling circus. He had aboard telaudio men with tons of equipment, pontifical commentators who knew the answer to anything, beautiful females who were experts on the woman's angle, pompous bureaucrats after publicity, and entertainment stars who had come along for the same reason.

He had a good ship and crew, one of the best in the Survey. *Had* had. They weren't any more. They had been taken off their proper job of pushing astrographical knowledge ever further into the remote regions of the galaxy, and had been sent off with this cargo of costly people on a totally unnecessary mission.

He said bitterly to himself, "Damn all sentimentalists."

He said aloud, "Does its position check with your calculated orbit, Mr. Riney?"

Riney, the Second, a young and serious man who had been fussing with instruments in the astrogation room, came out and said,

"Yes. Right on the nose. Shall we go in and land now?"

Kellon didn't answer for a moment, standing there in the front of the bridge, a middle-aged man, stocky, square-shouldered, and with his tanned, plain face showing none of the resentment he felt. He hated to give the order but he had to.

"All right, take her in."

He looked gloomily through the filter-windows as they went in. In this fringe-spiral of the galaxy, stars were relatively infrequent, and there were only ragged drifts of them across the darkness. Full ahead shone a small, compact sun like a diamond. It was a white dwarf and had been so for two thousand years, giving forth so little warmth that the planets which circled it had been frozen and ice-locked all that time. They still were, all except the innermost world.

Kellon stared at that planet, a tawny blob. The ice that had sheathed it ever since its primary collapsed into a white dwarf, had now melted. Months before, a dark wandering body had passed very close to this lifeless system. Its passing had perturbed the planetary orbits and the inner planets had started to spiral slowly in toward their sun, and the ice had begun to go.

Viresson, one of the junior officers, came into the bridge looking harassed. He said to Kellon,

"They want to see you down below, sir. Especially Mr. Borrodale. He says it's urgent."

Kellon thought wearily, "Well, I might as well go down and face the pack of them. Here's where they really begin."

He nodded to Viresson, and went down below to the main cabin. The sight of it revolted him. Instead of his own men in it, relaxing or chinning, it held a small and noisy mob of overdressed, overloud men and women, all of whom seemed to be talking at once and uttering brittle, nervous laughter.

"Captain Kellon, I want to ask you—"

"Captain, if you *please*—"

He patiently nodded and smiled and plowed through them to Borrodale. He had been given particular instructions to cooperate with Borrodale, the most famous telaudio commentator in the Federation.

Borrodale was a slightly plump man with a round pink face and incongruously large and solemn black eyes. When he spoke, one recognized at once that deep, incredibly rich and meaningful voice.

"My first broadcast is set for thirty minutes from now, Captain. I shall want a view as we go in. If my men could take a mobile up to the bridge—"

Kellon nodded. "Of course. Mr. Viresson is up there and will assist them any way."

"Thank you, Captain. Would you like to see the broadcast?"

"I would, yes, but—"

He was interrupted by Lorri Lee, whose glitteringly handsome face and figure and sophisticated drawl made her the idol of all female telaudio reporters.

"*My* broadcast is to be right after the landing—remember? I'd like to do it alone, with just the emptiness of that world as background. Can you keep the others from spoiling the effect? Please?"

"We'll do what we can," Kellon mumbled. And as the rest of the pack converged on him, he added hastily, "I'll talk to you later. Mr. Borrodale's broadcast—"

He got through them, following after Borrodale toward the cabin that had been set up as a telaudio-transmitter room. It had, Kellon thought bitterly, once served an honest purpose, holding the racks of soil and water and other samples from far worlds. But that had been when they were doing an honest Survey job, not chaperoning chattering fools on this sentimental pilgrimage.

The broadcasting set-up was beyond Kellon. He didn't want to hear this, but it was better than the mob in the main cabin. He watched as Borrodale made a signal. The monitor-screen came alive.

It showed a dun-colored globe spinning in space, growing visibly larger as they swept toward it. Now straggling seas were identifiable upon it. Moments passed and Borrodale did not speak, just letting that picture go out. Then his deep voice spoke over the picture, with dramatic simplicity.

"You are looking at the Earth," he said.

Silence again, and the spinning brownish ball was bigger now, with white clouds ragged upon it. And then Borrodale spoke again.

"You who watch from many worlds in the galaxy—this is the homeland of our race. Speak its name to yourselves. The Earth."

Kellon felt a deepening distaste. This was all true, but still it was phony. What was Earth now to him, or to Borrodale, or his billions of listeners? But it was a story, a sentimental occasion, so they had to pump it up into something big.

"Some thirty-five hundred years ago," Borrodale was saying, "our ancestors lived on this world alone. That was when they first went into space. To these other planets first—but very soon, to other stars. And so our Federation began, our community of human civilization on many stars and worlds."

Now, in the monitor, the view of Earth's dun globe had been replaced by the face of Borrodale in close-up. He paused dramatically.

"Then, over two thousand years ago, it was discovered that the sun of Earth was about to collapse into a white dwarf. So those people who still remained on Earth left it forever and when the solar change came, it and the other planets became mantled in eternal ice. And now, within months, the final end of the old planet of our origin is at hand. It is slowly spiraling toward the sun and soon it will plunge into it as Mercury and Venus have already done. And when that occurs, the world of man's origin will be gone forever."

Again the pause, for just the right length of time, and then Borrodale continued in a voice expertly pitched in a lower key.

"We on this ship—we humble reporters and servants of the vast telaudio audience on all the worlds—have come here so that in these next weeks we can give you this last look at our ancestral world. We think—we hope—that you'll find interest in recalling a past that is almost legend."

And Kellon thought, "The bastard has no more interest in this old planet than I have, but he surely is smooth."

As soon as the broadcast ended, Kellon found himself besieged once more by the clamoring crowd in the main cabin. He held up his hand in protest.

"Please, now, now—we have a landing to make first. Will you come with me, Doctor Darnow?"

Darnow was from Historical Bureau, and was the titular head of the whole expedition, although no one paid him much attention. He was a sparrowy, elderly man who babbled excitedly as he went with Kellon to the bridge.

He, at least, was sincere in his interest, Kellon thought. For that matter, so were all the dozen-odd scientists who were aboard. But they were far outnumbered by the fat cats and big brass out for publicity, the professional enthusers and sentimentalists. A real hell of a job the Survey had given him!

In the bridge, he glanced through the window at the dun-colored planet and its satellite. Then he asked Darnow, "You said something about a particular place you wanted to land?"

The historiographer bobbed his head, and began unfolding a big, old-fashioned chart.

"See this continent here? Along its eastern coast were a lot of the biggest cities, like New York."

Kellon remembered that name, he'd learned it in school history, a long time ago.

Darnow's finger stabbed at the chart. "If you could land there, right on the island—"

Kellon studied the relief features, then shook his head. "Too low. There'll be great tides as time goes on and we can't take chances. That higher ground back inland a bit should be all right, though."

Darnow looked disappointed. "Well. I suppose you're right."

Kellon told Riney to set up the landing-pattern. Then he asked Darnow skeptically, "You surely don't expect to find much in those old cities now—not after they've had all that ice on them for two thousand years?"

"They'll be badly damaged, of course," Darnow admitted. "But there should be a vast number of relics. I could study here for years—"

"We haven't got years, we've got only a few months before this planet gets too close to the sun," said Kellon. And he added mentally, "Thank God."

The ship went into its landing-pattern. Atmosphere whined outside its hull and then thick gray clouds boiled and raced around it. It went down through the cloud layer and moved above a dull brown landscape that had flecks of white in its deeper valleys. Far ahead there was the glint of a gray ocean. But the ship came down toward a rolling brown plain and settled there, and then there was the expected thunderclap of silence that always followed the shutting off of all machinery.

Kellon looked at Riney, who turned in a moment from the test-panel with a slight surprise on his face. "Pressure, oxygen, humidity, everything—all optimum." And then he said, "But of course. This place *was* optimum."

Kellon nodded. He said, "Doctor Darnow and I will have a look out first. Viresson, you keep our passengers in."

When he and Darnow went to the lower airlock he heard a buzzing clamor from the main cabin and he judged that Viresson was having his hands full. The people in there were not used to being said no to, and he could imagine their resentment.

Cold, damp air struck a chill in Kellon when they stepped down out of the airlock. They stood on muddy, gravelly ground that squashed a little under their boots as they trudged away from the ship. They stopped and looked around, shivering.

Under the low gray cloudy sky there stretched a sad, sunless brown landscape. Nothing broke the drab color of raw soil, except for the shards of ice still lingering in low places. A heavy desultory wind stirred the raw air, and then was still. There was not a sound except the clinkclinking of the ship's skin cooling and contracting, behind them. Kellon thought that no amount of sentimentality could make this anything but a dreary world.

But Darnow's eyes were shining. "We'll have to make every minute of the time count," he muttered. "Every minute."

Within two hours, the heavy broadcast equipment was being trundled away from the ship on two motor-tracs that headed eastward. On one of the tracs rode Lorri Lee, resplendent in lilac-colored costume of synthesilk.

Kellon, worried about the possibility of quicksands, went along for the first broadcast from the cliffs that looked down on the ruins of New York. He wished he hadn't when it got under way.

For Lorri Lee, her blonde head bright even in the dull light, turned loose all her practiced charming gestures for the broadcast cameras, as she gestured with pretty excitement down toward the ruins.

"It's so *unbelievable!*" she cried to a thousand worlds. "To be here on Earth, to see the old places again—it *does* something to you."

It did something to Kellon. It made him feel sick at his stomach. He turned and went back to the ship, feeling at that moment that if Lorri Lee went into a quicksand on the way back, it would be no great loss.

But that first day was only the beginning. The big ship quickly became the center of multifarious and continuous broadcasts. It had been especially equipped to beam strongly to the nearest station in the Federation network, and its transmitters were seldom quiet.

Kellon found that Darnow, who was supposed to coordinate all this programming, was completely useless. The little historian was living in a seventh heaven on this old planet which had been uncovered to view for the first time in millennia, and he was away most of the time on field trips of his own. It fell to his assistant, an earnest and worried and harassed young man, to try to reconcile the clashing claims and demands of highly temperamental broadcasting stars.

Kellon felt an increasing boredom at having to stand around while all this tosh went out over the ether. These people were having a field-day, but he didn't think much of them and of their broadcasts. Roy Quayle, the young male fashion designer, put on a semi-humorous, semi-nostalgic display of the old Earth fashions, with the prettier girls wearing some of the ridiculous old costumes he had had duplicated. Barden, the famous teleplay producer, ran off ancient films of the old Earth dramas that had everyone in stitches. Jay Maxson, a rising politician in Federation Congress, discussed with Borrodale the governmental systems of the old days, in a way calculated to give his own Wide-Galaxy Party none the worst of it. The Arcturus Players, that brilliant group of young stage-folk, did readings of old Earth dramas and poems.

It was, Kellon thought disgustedly, just playing. Grown people, famous people, seizing the opportunity given by the accidental end of a forgotten planet to posture in the spotlight like smart-aleck children. There was real work to do in the galaxy, the work of the Survey, the endless and wearying but always-fascinating job of charting the wild systems and worlds. And instead of doing that job, he was condemned to spend weeks and months here with these phonies.

The scientists and historians he respected. They did few broadcasts and they did not fake their interest. It was one of them, Haller, the biologist, who excitedly showed Kellon a handful of damp soil a week after their arrival.

"Look at *that!*" he said proudly.

Kellon stared. "What?"

"Those seeds—they're common weed-grass seeds. Look at them."

Kellon looked, and now he saw that from each of the tiny seeds projected a new-looking hairlike tendril.

"They're sprouting?" he asked unbelievingly.

Haller nodded happily. "I was hoping for it. You see, it was almost spring in the northern hemisphere, according to the records, when Sol collapsed suddenly into a white dwarf. Within hours the temperature plunged and the hydrosphere and atmosphere began to freeze."

"But surely that would kill all plant-life?"

"No," said Haller. "The larger plants, trees, perennial shrubs, and so on, yes. But the seeds of the smaller annuals just froze into suspended animation. Now the warmth that melted them is causing germination."

"Then we'll have grass—small plants?"

"Very soon, the way the warmth is increasing."

It was, indeed, getting a little warmer all the time as these first weeks went by. The clouds lifted one day and there was brilliant, thin white sunshine from the little diamond sun. And there came a morning when they found the rolling landscape flushed with a pale tint of green.

Grass grew. Weeds grew, vines grew, all of them seeming to rush their growth as though they knew that this, their last season, would not be long. Soon the raw brown mud of the hills and valleys had been replaced by a green carpet, and everywhere taller growths were shooting up, and flowers beginning to appear. Hepaticas, bluebells, dandelions, violets, bloomed once more.

Kellon took a long walk, now that he did not have to plow through mud. The chattering people around the ship, the constant tug and pull of clashing temperaments, the brittle, febrile voices, got him down. He felt better to get away by himself.

The grass and the flowers had come back, but otherwise this was still an empty world. Yet there was a certain peace of mind in tramping up and down the long green rolling slopes. The sun was bright and cheerful now, and white clouds dotted the sky, and the warm wind whispered as he sat upon a ridge and looked away westward to where nobody was, or would ever be again.

"Damned dull," he thought. "But at least it's better than back with the gabblers."

He sat for a long time in the slanting sunshine, feeling his bristling nerves relax. The grass stirred about him, rippling in long waves, and the taller flowers nodded.

No other movement, no other life. A pity, he thought, that there were no birds for this last spring of the old planet—not even a butterfly. Well, it made no difference, all this wouldn't last long.

As Kellon tramped back through the deepening dusk, he suddenly became aware of a shining bubble in the darkening sky. He stopped and stared up at it and then remembered. Of course, it was the old planet's moon—during the cloudy nights he had forgotten all about it. He went on, with its vague light about him.

When he stepped back into the lighted main cabin of the ship, he was abruptly jarred out of his relaxed mood. A first-class squabble was going on, and everyone was either contributing to it or commenting on it. Lorri Lee, looking like a pretty child complaining of a hurt, was maintaining that she should have broadcast time next day for her special woman's-interest feature, and somebody else disputed her claim, and young Valley, Darnow's assistant, looked harried and upset. Kellon got by them without being noticed, locked the door of his cabin and poured himself a long drink, and damned Survey all over again for this assignment.

He took good care to get out of the ship early in the morning, before the storm of temperament blew up again. He left Viresson in charge of the ship, there being nothing for any of them to do now anyway, and legged it away over the green slopes before anyone could call him back.

They had five more weeks of this, Kellon thought. Then, thank God, Earth would be so near the sun that they must take the ship back into its proper element of space. Until that wished-for day arrived, he would stay out of sight as much as possible.

He walked miles each day. He stayed carefully away from the east and the ruins of old New York, where the others so often were. But he went north and west and south, over the grassy, flowering slopes of the empty world. At least it was peaceful, even though there was nothing at all to see.

But after a while, Kellon found that there were things to see if you looked for them. There was the way the sky changed, never seeming to look the same twice. Sometimes it was deep blue and white clouds sailed it like mighty ships. And then it would suddenly turn gray and miserable, and rain would drizzle on him, to be ended when a lance of sunlight shot through the clouds and slashed them to flying ribbons. And there was a time when, upon a ridge, he watched vast thunderheads boil up and darken in the west, and black storm clouds marched across the land like an army with banners of lightning and drums of thunder.

The winds and the sunshine, the sweetness of the air and the look of the moonlight and the feel of the yielding grass under his feet, all seemed oddly right. Kellon had walked on many worlds under the glare of many-colored suns, and some of them he had liked much better than this one and some of them he had not liked at all, but never had he found a world that seemed so exactly attuned to his body as this outworn, empty planet.

He wondered vaguely what it had been like when there were trees and birds, and animals of many kinds, and roads and cities. He borrowed film-books from the reference library Darnow and the others had brought, and looked at them in his cabin of nights. He did not really care very much, but at least it kept him out of the broils and quarrels, and it had a certain interest.

Thereafter in his wandering strolls, Kellon tried to see the place as it would have been in the long ago. There would have been robins and bluebirds, and yellow-and-black bumblebees nosing the flowers, and tall trees with names that were equally strange to him, elms and willows and sycamores. And small furred animals, and humming clouds of insects, and fish and frogs in the pools and streams, a whole vast complex symphony of life, long gone, long forgotten.

But were all the men and women and children who had lived here less forgotten? Borrodale and the others talked much on their broadcasts about the people of old Earth, but that was just a faceless name, a term that meant nothing. Not one of these millions, surely, had ever thought of himself as part of a numberless multitude. Each one had been to himself, and to those close to him or her, an individual, unique and never to be exactly repeated, and what did the glib talkers know of all those individuals, what could anyone know?

Kellon found traces of them here and there, bits of flotsam that even the crush of the ice had spared. A twisted piece of steel, a girder of rail that someone had labored to make. A quarry with the toolmarks still on the rocks, where surely men had once sweated in the sun. The broken shards of concrete that stretched away in a ragged line to make a road upon which men and women had once traveled, hurrying upon missions of love or ambition, greed or fear.

He found more than that, a startling find that he made by purest chance. He followed a brook that ran down a very narrow valley, and at one point he leaped across it and as he landed he looked up and saw that there was a house.

Kellon thought at first that it was miraculously preserved whole and unbroken, and surely that could not be. But when he went closer he saw that this was only an illusion and that destruction had been at work upon it too. Still, it remained, incredibly, a recognizable house.

It was a rambling stone cottage with low walls and a slate roof, set close against the steep green wall of the valley. One gable-end was smashed in, and part of that end wall. Studying the way it was embayed in the wall, Kellon decided that a chance natural arch of ice must have preserved it from the grinding pressure that had shattered almost all other structures.

The windows and doors were only gaping openings. He went inside and looked around the cold shadows of what had once been a room. There were some wrecked pieces of rotting furniture, and dried mud banked along one wall contained unrecognizable bits of rusted junk, but there was not much else. It was chill and oppressive in there, and he went out and sat on the little terrace in the sunshine.

He looked at the house. It could have been built no later than the Twentieth Century, he thought. A good many different people must have lived in it during the hundreds of years before the evacuation of Earth.

Kellon thought that it was strange that the airphoto surveys that Darnow's men had made in quest of relics had not discovered the place. But then it was not so strange, the stone walls were so grayly inconspicuous and it was set so deeply into the sheltering bay of the valley wall.

His eye fell on eroded lettering on the cement side of the terrace, and he went and brushed the soil off that place. The words were time-eaten and faint but he could read them.

"Ross and Jennie—Their House."

Kellon smiled. Well, at least he knew now who once had lived here, who probably built the place. He could imagine two young people happily scratching the words in the wet cement, exuberant with achievement. And who had Ross and Jennie been, and where were they now?

He walked around the place. To his surprise, there was a ragged flower-garden at one side. A half-dozen kinds of brilliant little flowers, unlike the wild ones of the slopes, grew in patchy disorder here. Seeds of an old garden that had been ready to germinate when the long winter of Earth came down, and had slept in suspended animation until the ice melted and the warm blooming time came at last. He did not know what kinds of flowers these were, but there was a brave jauntiness about them that he liked.

Starting back across the green land in the soft twilight, Kellon thought he should tell Darnow about the place. But if he did, the gabbling pack in the ship would certainly stampede toward it. He could imagine the solemn and cute precious broadcasts that Borrodale and the Lee woman and the rest of them would stage from the old house.

"No," he thought. "The devil with them."

He didn't care anything himself about the old house, it was just that it was a refuge of quiet he had found and he didn't want to draw in the noisy horde he was trying to escape.

Kellon was glad in the following days that he had not told. The house gave him a place to go to, to poke around and investigate, a focus for his interest in this waiting time. He spent hours there, and never told anyone at all.

Haller, the biologist, lent him a book on the flowers of Earth, and he brought it with him and used it to identify those in the ragged garden. Verbenas, pinks, morning glories, and the bold red and yellow ones called nasturtiums. Many of these, he read, did not do well on other worlds and had never been successfully transplanted. If that was so, this would be their last blooming anywhere at all.

He rooted around the interior of the house, trying to figure out how people had lived in it. It was strange, not at all like a modern metalloy house. Even the interior walls were thick beyond belief, and the windows seemed small and pokey. The biggest room was obviously where they had lived most, and its window-openings looked out on the little garden and the green valley and brook beyond.

Kellon wondered what they had been like, the Ross and Jennie who had once sat here together and looked out these windows. What things had been important to them? What had hurt them, what had made them laugh? He himself had never married, the far-ranging captains of the Survey seldom did. But he wondered about this marriage of long ago, and what had become of it. Had they had children, did their blood still run on the far worlds? But even if it did, what was that now to those two of long ago?

There had been a poem about flowers at the end of the old book on flowers that Haller had lent him, and he remembered some of it.

"All are at one now, roses and lovers,
Not known of the winds and the fields and the sea,
Not a breath of the time that has been hovers
In the air now soft with a summer to be."

Well, yes, Kellon thought, they were all at one now, the Rosses and the Jennies and the things they had done and the things they had thought, all at one now in the dust of this old planet whose fiery final summer would be soon, very soon. Physically, everything that had been done, everyone who had lived, on Earth was still here in its atoms, excepting the tiny fraction of its matter that had sped to other worlds.

He thought of the names that were so famous still through all the galactic worlds, names of the men and women and places. Shakespeare, Plato, Beethoven, Blake, the old splendor of Babylon and the bones of Angkor and the humble houses of his own ancestors, all here, all still here.

Kellon mentally shook himself. He didn't have enough to do, that was his trouble, to be brooding here on such shadowy things. He had seen all there was to this queer little old place, and there was no use in coming back to it.

But he came back. It was not, he told himself, as though he had any sentimental antiquarian interests in this old place. He had heard enough of that kind of gush from all the glittering phonies in the ship. He was a Survey man and all he wanted was to get back to his job, but while he was stuck here it was better to be roaming the green land or poking about this old relic than to have to listen to the endless babbling and quarreling of those others.

They were quarreling more and more, because they were tired of it here. It had seemed to them a fine thing to posture upon a galactic stage by helping to cover the end of Earth, but time dragged by and their flush of synthetic enthusiasm wore thin. They could not leave, the expedition must broadcast the final climax of the planet's end, but that was still weeks away. Darnow and his scholars and scientists, busy coming and going to many old sites, could have stayed here forever but the others were frankly bored.

But Kellon found in the old house enough interest to keep the waiting from being too oppressive. He had read a good bit now about the way things had been in the old days, and he sat long hours on the little terrace in the afternoon sunshine, trying to imagine what it had been like when the man and woman named Ross and Jennie had lived here.

So strange, so circumscribed, that old life seemed now! Most people had had ground-cars in those days, he had read, and had gone back and forth in them to the cities where they worked. Did both the man and woman go, or just the man? Did the woman stay in the house, perhaps with their children if they had any, and in the afternoon did she do things in the little flower garden where a few bright, ragged survivors still bloomed? Did they ever dream that some future day when they were long gone, their house would lie empty and silent with no visitor except a stranger from far-off stars? He remembered a line in one of the old plays the Arcturus Players had read. "Come like shadows, so depart."

No, Kellon thought. Ross and Jennie were shadows now but they had not been then. To them, and to all the other people he could visualize going and coming busily about the Earth in those days, it was he, the future, the man yet to come, who was the shadow. Alone here, sitting and trying to imagine the long ago, Kellon had an eerie feeling sometimes that his vivid imaginings of people and crowded cities and movement and laughter were the reality and that he himself was only a watching wraith.

Summer days came swiftly, hot and hotter. Now the white sun was larger in the heavens and pouring down such light and heat as Earth had not received for millennia. And all the green life across it seemed to respond with an exultant surge of final growth, an act of joyous affirmation that Kellon found infinitely touching. Now even the nights were warm, and the winds blew thrilling soft, and on the distant beaches the ocean leaped up in a laughter of spray and thunder, running in great solar tides.

With a shock as though awakened from dreaming, Kellon suddenly realized that only a few days were left. The spiral was closing in fast now and very quickly the heat would mount beyond all tolerance.

He would, he told himself, be very glad to leave. There would be the wait in space until it was all over, and then he could go back to his own work, his own life, and stop fussing over shadows because there was nothing else to do.

Yes. He would be glad.

Then when only a few days were left, Kellon walked out again to the old house and was musing over it when a voice spoke behind him.

"Perfect," said Borrodale's voice. "A perfect relic."

Kellon turned, feeling somehow startled and dismayed. Borrodale's eyes were alight with interest as he surveyed the house, and then he turned to Kellon.

"I was walking when I saw you, Captain, and thought I'd catch up to you. Is this where you've been going so often?"

Kellon, a little guiltily, evaded. "I've been here a few times."

"But why in the world didn't you *tell* us about this?" exclaimed Borrodale. "Why, we can do a terrific final broadcast from here. A typical ancient home of Earth. Roy can put some of the Players in the old costumes, and we'll show them living here the way people did—"

Unexpectedly to himself, a violent reaction came up in Kellon. He said roughly, "No."

Borrodale arched his eyebrows. "No? But why not?"

Why not, indeed? What difference could it possibly make to him if they swarmed all over the old house, laughing at its ancientness and its inadequacies, posing grinning forras in front of it, prancing about in old-fashioned costumes and making a show of it. What could that mean to him, who cared nothing about this forgotten planet or anything on it?

And yet something in him revolted at what they would do here, and he said, "We might have to take off very suddenly, now. Having you all out here away from the ship could involve a dangerous delay."

"You said yourself we wouldn't take off for a few days yet!" exclaimed Borrodale. And he added firmly, "I don't know why you should want to obstruct us, Captain. But I can go over your head to higher authority."

He went away, and Kellon thought unhappily, He'll message back to Survey headquarters and I'll get my ears burned off, and why the devil did I do it anyway? I must be getting real planet-happy.

He went and sat down on the terrace, and watched until the sunset deepened into dusk. The moon came up white and brilliant, but the air was not quiet tonight. A hot, dry wind had begun to blow, and the stir of the tall grass made the slopes and plains seem vaguely alive. It was as though a queer pulse had come into the air and the ground, as the sun called its child homeward and Earth strained to answer. The house dreamed in the silver light, and the flowers in the garden rustled.

Borrodale came back, a dark pudgy figure in the moonlight. He said triumphantly, "I got through to your headquarters. They've ordered your full cooperation. We'll want to make our first broadcast here tomorrow."

Kellon stood up. "No."

"You can't ignore an order—"

"We won't be here tomorrow," said Kellon. "It is my responsibility to get the ship off Earth in ample time for safety. We take off in the morning."

Borrodale was silent for a moment, and when he spoke his voice had a puzzled quality.

"You're advancing things just to block our broadcast, of course. I just can't understand your attitude."

Well, Kellon thought, he couldn't quite understand it himself, so how could he explain it? He remained silent, and Borrodale looked at him and then at the old house.

"Yet maybe I do understand," Borrodale said thoughtfully, after a moment. "You've come here often, by yourself. A man can get too friendly with ghosts."

Kellon said roughly, "Don't talk nonsense. We'd better get back to the ship, there's plenty to do before take-off."

Borrodale did not speak as they went back out of the moonlit valley. He looked back once, but Kellon did not look back.

They took the ship off twelve hours later, in a morning made dull and ominous by racing clouds. Kellon felt a sharp relief when they cleared atmosphere and were out in the depthless, starry blackness. He knew where he was, in space. It was the place where a spaceman belonged. He'd get a stiff reprimand for this later, but he was not sorry.

They put the ship into a calculated orbit, and waited. Days, many of them, must pass before the end came to Earth. It seemed quite near the white sun now, and its moon had slid away from it on a new distorted orbit, but even so it would be a while before they could broadcast to a watching galaxy the end of its ancestral world.

Kellon stayed much of that time in his cabin. The gush that was going out over the broadcasts now, as the grand finale approached, made him sick. He wished the whole thing was over. It was, he told himself, getting to be a bore—

An hour and twenty minutes to E-time, and he supposed he must go up to the bridge and watch it. The mobile camera had been set up there and Borrodale and as many others of them as could crowd in were there. Borrodale had been given the last hour's broadcast, and it seemed that the others resented this.

"Why must you have the whole last hour?" Lorri Lee was saying bitterly to Borrodale. "It's not fair."

Quayle nodded angrily. "There'll be the biggest audience in history, and we should all have a chance to speak."

Borrodale answered them, and the voices rose and bickered, and Kellon saw the broadcast technicians looking worried. Beyond them through the filter-window he could see the dark dot of the planet closing on the white star. The sun called, and it seemed that with quickened eagerness Earth moved on the last steps of its long road. And the clamoring, bickering voices in his ears suddenly brought rage to Kellon.

"Listen," he said to the broadcast men. "Shut off all sound transmission. You can keep the picture on, but no sound."

That shocked them all into silence. The Lee woman finally protested, "Captain Kellon, you can't!"

"I'm in full command when in space, and I can, and do," he said.

"But the broadcast, the commentary—"

Kellon said wearily, "Oh, for Christ's sake all of you shut up, and let the planet die in peace."

He turned his back on them. He did not hear their resentful voices, did not even hear when they fell silent and watched through the dark filter-windows as he was watching, as the camera and the galaxy was watching.

And what was there to see but a dark dot almost engulfed in the shining veils of the sun? He thought that already the stones of the old house must be beginning to vaporize. And now the veils of light and fire almost concealed the little planet, as the star gathered in its own.

All the atoms of old Earth, Kellon thought, in this moment bursting free to mingle with the solar being, all that had been Ross and Jennie, all that had been Shakespeare and Schubert, gay flowers and running streams, oceans and rocks and the wind of the air, received into the brightness that had given them life.

They watched in silence, but there was nothing more to see, nothing at all. Silently the camera was turned off.

Kellon gave an order, and presently the ship was pulling out of orbit, starting on the long voyage back. By that time the others had gone, all but Borrodale. He said to Borrodale, without turning,

"Now go ahead and send your complaint to headquarters."

Borrodale shook his head. "Silence can be the best requiem of all. There'll be no complaint. I'm glad now, Captain."

"Glad?"

"Yes," said Borrodale. "I'm glad that Earth had one true mourner, at the last."

Mark Clifton's work, neglected for a time, is once again finding readers. A collection of his best short fiction has been published by Southern Illinois University Press. His novels, Eight Keys to Eden *and* They'd Rather Be Right *(a collaboration with Frank Riley, and the 1955 Hugo-winner), have been reprinted. He was a mainstay of* Astounding *in the early '50s, but had shifted to* Amazing® Stories *a few years before his death in 1963. This story was published in April 1962.*

HANG HEAD, VANDAL!
by Mark Clifton

On our abandoned Martian landing field there hangs a man's discarded spacesuit, suspended from the desensitized prongs of a Come-to-me tower. It is stuffed with straw that was filched, no doubt, from packing cases which brought out so many more delicate, sensitive, precision instruments than we will take back.

None knows which of our departing crew hung the spacesuit there, nor exactly what he meant in the act. A scarecrow to frighten all others away?

More likely a mere Kilroy-was-here symbol: defacing initials irresistibly carved in a priceless, ancient work of art, saying, "I am too shoddy a specimen to create anything of worth, but I can deface. And this proves that I, too, have been."

Or was it symbolic suicide: an expression of guilt so overpowering that man hanged himself upon the scene of his crime?

Captain Leyton saw it there on the morning of final departure. He saw it, and felt a sudden flush of his usual stern discipline surge within him; and he all but formed the harsh command to take that thing down at once. Find the one who hung it there: Bring him to me!

The anger—the command. Died together. Unspoken.

Something in the pose of the stuffed effigy hanging there must have got down through the diminishing person inside the ever-thickening rind of a commander. The forlorn sadness, the dejection; and yes, he too must have felt the shame, the guilt, that overwhelmed us all.

Whether the helmet had fallen forward of its own weight because the vandal had been careless in stuffing it with too little straw to hold its head erect—vandals being characteristically futile even in their vandalism—or whether, instead of the supposed vandal, this was the talent of a consummate artist molding steel and rubber, plastic and straw into an expression of how we all felt—no matter, the result was there.

The Captain did not command the effigy to be taken down. No one offered and no one asked if that might be his wish—not even the ubiquitous Ensign perpetually bucking for approval.

So on an abandoned Martian landing field there hangs a discarded spacesuit—the image of man stuffed with straw; with straw where heart, and mind, and soul ought to be.

At the time it seemed a most logical solution to an almost impossible problem.

Dr. VanDam summed it up in his memorable speech before the United Nations. If he were visually conscious of the vault of face blurs in the hushed assembly, this lesser sight did not obscure his stronger vision of the great vaulted mass of shining stars in the black of space.

He may not even have been conscious of political realities, which ever obscure man's dreams. What he said would be weighed by each delegate in terms of personal advantage to be gained for his own status. Second, his words would be weighed again in terms of national interest. Third, what advantage could be squeezed out for the racial-religious-color blocs? At the fourth level of consideration, what advantage to the small-nation bloc over the large; or how would his plan enhance the special privileges of the large over the small? Down at the fifth level, could it preserve the status quo, changing nothing so that those in power could remain in power, while, at the same time, giving the illusion of progress to confound the ever-clamoring liberals? At the deep sixth level, if one ever got down that far, one might give a small fleeting thought to what might be good for mankind.

If Dr. VanDam even knew that such political realities must ever take precedence over the dreams of science, he gave no sign of it. It was as if all his thought was upon the glory of the stars and the dream of man reaching out to them. It was the goal of reaching the stars that inspired his speech.

"We must sum up the problem," he was saying. "It is simply this. There is a limit to how far we can theorize in science without testing those theories to see if they will work. Sooner or later the theorist must submit to the engineer whose acid test of worth is simply this: 'Does it work?'

"We have always known that the Roman candles we are using for our timid little space flights can take us only to the nearest planets, for there is that inexorable ratio of time to initial thrust. Unless thrust continues and continues, the Mayfly lifetime of man will expire many times over before we can reach the nearest star. Nor will our limited resources fuel ion engines. We must learn how to replenish with space dust gathered along the way.

"To have continuous velocity we must have continuous nuclear power. To have continuous nuclear power, we must have more nuclear tests. Now we believe we know how to take not special ores but ordinary matter, of any kind, and convert it into nuclear power. We believe we can control this. We have this in theory. But the engineer has not tested it with his question, 'Does it work?'

"We cannot make these tests on Earth. For what if it does not work? We dare not use the Moon. Its lighter gravity makes it too valuable a piece of real estate in terms of future star journeys. It will be our busy landing stage; we dare not contaminate it nor risk destroying it.

"We have reached stalemate. On Earth and Moon we can go no further without testing. On Earth and Moon we dare not test. Some other testing area must be found.

"Our explorers have brought us conclusive proof that Mars is a dead world. A useless world in terms of life. Useless, too, as a source of minerals, for our little Roman candles can carry no commercial pay load. A useless world for colonization, with air too tenuous for human lungs and water too scarce for growing food. Humans must be housed in sealed chambers, or wear spacesuits constantly. From all practical points of view, a worthless world.

"But invaluable to science. For there, without destroying anything of value to man, we can put our theories to test. We believe we can start a nuclear reaction in ordinary rock and dirt, and keep it under control to produce a continuous flow of power. We believe we can keep it from running wild out of control.

"If the innumerable tests we must run *do* contaminate the planet, or even destroy it slowly, our gain in knowledge will be greater than the loss of this worthless real estate."

There was a stir in the Assembly: something between a gasp of horror and a murmur of admiration at the audacity of man's sacrificing a whole planet to his knowledge. They had not known we were so far along the way.

And then, on second thought, a settling back in satisfaction. It seemed a simple solution to an impossible problem. To take not only VanDam's test away from Earth, but nuclear testing of every kind! To quell the fears and still the clamoring of the humanists who would rather see man stagnate in ignorance than risk the future to learn. At every level of political reality this might turn to advantage. If there were any who still thought in such terms, it might even be good for mankind generally!

"I am not mystic-minded," VanDam continued, when the rustle and murmur had diminished, "but the convenience of this particular planet, located precisely where it is, far enough away that we must have made great progress in science to reach it, and close enough to be ready when we need it for further progress—this seems almost mystical in its coincidence."

(That for the ones who would have to go through the usual motions of obtaining Higher Power approval for doing what they fully intended doing all along.)

"My question: Shall the nations of Earth agree upon our use of this so convenient and otherwise worthless stage placed right where we need it—waiting for us down through all the ages until we should be ready to make use of it?"

Their ultimate response was favorable.

Dr. VanDam did not mention, and the members being only politicians unable to see beyond the next vote or appointment, did not say:

"True, we do have a theory of how to start and continue the slow-burn nuclear conversion of ordinary rock and dirt to energy. What we do not have, as yet, is a way to stop it.

"We *think* that eventually future man will probably find a way to stop the process. We *think* slow-burn will not speed up and run out of control to consume an entire planet before we have found a way to stop it. We *think* that future science may even find a way to decontaminate the planet. We *hope* these things.

"But we *know* that the science of nucleonics will be stillborn and stunted to grow no further unless we go on testing. We convince ourselves that even if an entire planet is consumed, it is a worthless planet anyway, and will be worth it."

Yet there was the usual small minority who questioned our right to destroy one of the planets of the solar system. There is always such a minority, and as always, the rest of the world, intent on turning what it intended to do anyway into the Right-Thing-To-Do, was able to shout them down.

Hang Head, Vandal! 117

Anyway, the consequences were for future man to face. Or so we thought.

I say we, because I was one of the members of Project Slow-Burn. Not that I'm the hero. There wasn't any hero. Mistaken or not, as it was conceived this wasn't one of those television spectaculars cooked up to convert science into public emotionalism. There was no country-wide search for special photogenic hero-types to front the project.

The reporters, true to their writing tradition of trying to reduce even the most profound scientific achievement to the lowest common denominator of sloppy sentimentalism or avid sensationalism, tried to heroize Dr. VanDam as head of the science side of the project. But he wasn't having any.

"Don't you think, gentlemen," he answered them with acid scorn, "it is about time the public grew up enough to support the search for knowledge because we need it, rather than because they'd like to go to bed with some handsome, brainless kook you've built up into a hero?"

This response was not likely to further the cause of journalism.

They tried to lionize Captain Leyton, as head of the transport side of it; but his remarks were even more unprintable.

They never got down far enough through the echelons of status to reach me. I was Chief of Communications, which is just another way of saying I was a television repairman with headaches. Not that it would have done them any good.

There isn't one thing about me that fits the sentimental notions of what a hero should be. I'm not even a colorful character. If I'm expert in my job, it's only because I learned early what any lazy man with an ounce of brains also learns—that life goes easier for the expert than for the ignorant. Which is not exactly the hero attitude the public likes to hear, but true all the same.

I did have an advantage which qualifies me to tell this tale.

Supervision nowadays sits on its duff in an office, surrounded by television monitors showing them every phase of their responsibilities, and punches buttons when some guy tries to goof off or starts lousing up the operation.

Somebody has to maintain the system and check the same monitors. I saw everything of importance that happened.

That's the only way I come into the yarn at all. I didn't start out a hero type. I didn't turn into one. I just watched what happened; and I got sick at my stomach along with everybody else. And now I slink away, sick and ashamed, and not understanding even that, along with the rest. Not heroes—no, none of us.

From the first this was intended and conducted as a genuine scientific project, a group effort, with each man's ego subdued to serve the needs of the whole. No special heroes emerging to show up the rest of the dopes. None of the usual stuff of romantic fiction was supposed to happen—those unusual dangers, horrible accidents, sudden frightful emergencies so dear to the little sadistic hearts of readers and viewers.

So far as I know, nobody beat up anybody with his fists, nor gunned anyone down, which is the usual, almost the only, fictional way yet found by the humanists for coping with life problems.

We assembled the mastership on the Moon base from parts which were Roman-candled up, a few pieces at a time, from too heavily gravitied Earth.

The yelps of pain from taxpayers reached almost as high. It was one thing to wash the hands of the vexing problem of nuclear testing by wanting it shifted òut to Mars.

It was something else to pay for the project.

Against the Moon's lighter gravity we eventually were spaceborne with no more than the usual fight between power thrust and inertia, both physical and psychological.

Without touching that precious reserve of fuel which we hoped would bring us back again, we were able to build up so much speed that it took us only a month to reach Mars. No point in showing, because nobody would care, how the two dozen of us were cramped in the tiny spaces left by the equipment and instruments we had to carry.

Construction and maintenance had done their job properly, and, for once, inspection had actually done its job, too. We were able to reverse properly at the right time, and soft-cushion powered our way down into a Martian plain eastward of a low range of hills.

Surely everybody has watched the documentaries long enough to have some idea about the incredibly hostile surface of Mars: the too-thin air, which lets some stars shine through even in the daytime; the waterless desert; the extremes of temperature; the desolation. . . .

Ah, the desolation! The terrifying desolation!

Moon surface is bad enough; but at least there is the great ball of Earth, seeming so near in that airless world that one has the illusion of being able to reach out and almost touch it, touch home, know home is still there, imagine he can almost see it.

"See that little tip of land there on the east coast of the North American continent? That's where I live!"

"Yeah," somebody answers. "And who is that guy walking through your front door without knocking while you're away?"

Sometimes it seems that close.

On Mars, Earth is just another bright spot in the black night sky; so far away that the first reaction is one of terrible despair, the overpowering conviction that in all that vast hostility a man will nevermore see home; nor know again the balmy twilight of soft, moist summer; nor feel the arms of love.

Explorers had not lied. Nothing, anywhere, could be more worthless to man than the planet Mars. Worthless, except for the unique purpose which brought us here.

We dug in beneath the surface.

Now surely, again, everyone has seen so many of the documentaries that it is unnecessary to show us digging out our living quarters and laboratories beneath that merciless plain. We used the displaced powdered rock to form a crude cement, not long-lasting but adequate for the time we would be there. With it, surfaced over our living area. This was not so much to provide a landing field, since most of our journeying would be in individual jet-powered spacesuits, but to help insure against any leakage of air if our inner seals cracked.

To help seal out the killing radiation we intended to let loose—that, too.

We erected Come-to-me towers at each elevator which would lower spacesuited men to lower levels where they could go through locks to reach their quarters. One Come-to-me tower for each half dozen men, tuned to the power source of their suits, to bring each man safely back, as truly as a homing pigeon, to guarantee against their becoming lost on that hostile planet; and, in emergency, should one arise, to see that no panic mob ganged up at one lock and died waiting there for entrance to safety while other locks remained idle—the human way of doing things under stress.

We had to finish all that in the first few weeks before any nuclear tests could be started. Anybody whose notions of science are derived from white-frocked actors in television commercials hasn't the vaguest idea of how much back-breaking physical work at the common labor level a genuine scientist has to do.

There was some emotional relief once we had dug in and sealed out the awful desolation of an uncaring universe. (This is the hardest part of reconciling oneself to the science attitude. More comforting to believe even that the universe is hostile than to admit that it simply doesn't care about man, one way or another.) In our sealed quarters we might briefly imagine ourselves working in an air-conditioned laboratory back home.

It helped. It certainly helped.

Not that I seemed to find time for more than exhausted sleeping there. To see what would be going on at the various field sites where tests were to be run meant the cameras had to be installed at those spots. In spite of the purported rigid tests for expedition personnel, my two assistants must have been somebody's nephews. Somehow each installation seemed to require that I be there.

I was there and usually without some little piece of equipment which would have helped so much, but which had been deleted from the lists we submitted by clerks who were more concerned with making a big showing of how much weight they could eliminate than in helping us.

Somehow we managed.

But I have made a list of guys I'm going to ferret out and poke in the nose once I get back to Earth. Maybe those Hollywood producers who think the only way to solve a problem is to beat up somebody or gun him down have something, after all. Right on top of that list, in big bold letters, is the spacesuit designer who thinks a man can handle the incredibly fine parts of miniaturized electronic equipment with those crude instruments they give us to screw into the arm ends of spacesuits.

Somehow we managed. Somehow, out of chaos, order came. Somehow tests got made. Somehow the theories worked; sometimes, more often, there was only the human sigh, the gulp, the shrug, and back to the drawing board.

Big surprise at the end of the first three months. A supply ship landed. Mostly food and some champagne, yet! Stuff the folks back home thought they'd like to have if they were out here. Even some pin-up pictures, as if we weren't already having enough trouble without being reminded. But none of the equipment we'd radioed for in case the taxpayers could forego a drink and a cigarette apiece to raise money for sending it. The public couldn't understand our need for equipment, so they didn't send any. Miracles aren't supposed to need any equipment or effort; they just come into being because people want them.

The packages of home-baked cookies were welcome enough after our diet of hydroponic algae, but I'd still rather have had a handful of miniature transistors.

Some of the guys said they'd have been willing to substitute their cookies for an equal weight of big, buxom blonde; but that's something the cookie bakers probably preferred not to think about.

The little three-man crew of the supply ship promised, as they were taking off for their return journey, they'd tell 'em what we really wanted when they got back, but I doubt the message ever got broadcast over the home and family television sets. Anyway, scientists are supposed to be cold, unfeeling, inhuman creatures who wander around looking noble, wise, and above it all.

In the beginning I'd thought that once I got the heavy work of installation completed, I could do a little wandering around myself, looking wise and noble. No such luck. I'd no more than get set up to show one experiment than it was over; and I'd have to dismantle, move, and set up for another. We'd thought the lighter gravity of Mars, 38 percent, would make the labor easy. But somehow there was still lifting, tugging, pulling, hauling, cursing.

But then, nobody wants to hear how the scientist has to work to get his miracle. The whole essence is the illusion that miracles can be had without work, that all one needs is to wish.

All right. So we'll get to the miracle.

Now we were finally ready to get down to the real test, the main reason for our coming out to Mars—Project Slow-Burn.

VanDam chose a little pocket at the center of that little cluster of hills to our West—that little cluster of hills everybody has seen in the pictures radioed back to Earth.

We didn't know it at the time, but that little cluster of hills was causing quite an uproar among archeologists back home. No archeologists had been included in the expedition, and now they were beating their breasts because from the pictures those hills looked mighty artificial to them. There was too much of a hint that the hills might once have been pyramids, they said, incredibly ancient, perhaps weathered down eons ago when the planet was younger, before it had lost so much of its atmosphere, but maybe still containing something beneath them.

We didn't hear the uproar, of course. Administration deemed it unnecessary for us to bother our pretty little heads about such nonsense. In fact, the uproar never got outside the academic cloister to reach the public at all. Administration should have listened. But then, when does man listen to what might interfere with his plans and spoil something?

We got all set to go in that little pocket at the center of the hills. The spot was ideal for us because the hill elevations gave us an opportunity to place our cameras on their tops to focus down into the crater we hoped would appear.

A whole ring of cameras was demanded. The physicists seemed to share too much of the public's attitude that all I needed to produce enough equipment was to wish for it. But by stripping the stuff from virtually every other project, I managed to balance the demands of the Slow-Burn crew against the outraged screams of the side-issue scientists.

VanDam's theories worked.

At first it took the instruments to detect that there was any activity; but gradually, even crude human eyes could see there was a hole beginning to appear, deepen and spread—progressively.

It was out of my line, but the general idea seemed to be that only one molecular layer at a time was affected, and that it, in turn, activated the next beneath and to the side while its own electrons and protons gave up their final energy.

The experiment did not work perfectly. The process should have been complete. There should have been no by-product of smoke and fire, no sign to human eyes of anything happening except a slowly deepening and spreading hole in the ground.

Instead there was some waste of improperly consumed molecules, resulting in an increasingly heavy, fire-laced smoke which arose sluggishly in the thin air, borne aloft

Hang Head, Vandal! 121

only by its heat, funneling briefly while it gave up that heat. Then it settled down and contaminated everything it touched. To compound my troubles, of course.

The physicists were griping their guts out because I didn't have the proper infrared equipment to penetrate the smoke; and somehow I wasn't smart enough to snap my fingers and—abracadabra—produce. Those damned cookie packages instead of equipment! Those damned clerks who had decided what we wouldn't need. My little list was getting longer.

Still, I guess I was able to get a feeble little snap from my fingers. I did manage to convert some stuff, never intended for that purpose, into infrared penetration. We managed to see down into that smoke- and fire-filled crater.

To see enough.

It was the middle of a morning (somebody who still cared claimed it would be a Tuesday back home) some three basic weeks after the beginning of the experiment. The hole was now some thirty feet across and equally deep, growing faster than Van-Dam's figures predicted it should, but still not running wild and out of control. Even if it had been, we couldn't have stopped it. We didn't know how.

I was trying to work out a little cleaner fix on the south wall of the crater when that wall disappeared like the side of a soap bubble. My focus was sharp enough to see.

To see down and into that huge, vaulted room. To see the living Martians in that room shrivel, blacken, writhe, and die. To see some priceless, alien works of art writhe and blacken and curl; some burst into flame; some shatter into dust.

That was when the scientists, sitting there watching their monitors with horror-stricken eyes, felt jubilation replaced with terrible guilt.

I, too. For naturally I was watching the master monitors to see that the equipment kept working. I saw it all.

I saw those miniature people, yes, people, whole and beautiful, in one brief instant blacken, writhe and die.

Out of the billions of gross people on Earth, once in a generation a tiny midget is born and matures to such perfection in proportion and surpassing beauty that the huge, coarse, normal person can only stare and marvel—and remember the delicate perfection of that miniature being with nostalgic yearning for the rest of his life.

From such, perhaps, come the legends common to all peoples in all ages, of the fairies. Or, eons ago, was there traffic between Earth and Mars? Or even original colonization from Mars to Earth, finally mutating into giants? They were people, miniatures of ourselves.

I saw them there. Perhaps not more than a dozen in that room. But in other rooms? Perhaps in a lacework of underground rooms? A whole civilization which, like ourselves on Mars, had gone underground, sealed themselves in against the thinning atmosphere, the dying planet?

I saw them die. Somehow I felt their pain.

But I did not die of it.

I carry it with me. I shall always carry it with me.

That's all there is.

In years to come people on Earth, people who did not see what we saw, did not feel the pain and guilt we felt, will wonder at our behavior following that.

Oh, there is much to wonder. If there is a civilization, where does their food come from? If they are able to convert rock to food, why are they not able to stop the atomic destruction of their planet we have started? If they are able to fill us with such grief that we can think of nothing but to slink away, like whipped curs caught in vandalism, why didn't they do this before we started the fire we cannot stop?

Oh, there is so much unanswered. People will wonder at the fact that we simply abandoned most of our equipment, the very project itself; that for a sick hour we watched, then, with one accord, without anybody making the decision, we began to withdraw and start for home.

Like small boys, thinking only to vandalize a schoolhouse in their savage glee, discovering it is a shrine.

Or, perhaps in time, we can rationalize it all away. Perhaps so soon as during that long, journey back.

It wasn't our fault, we shall begin to say. They were as much to blame as we. Sure they were!

More to blame! They were more to blame than we!

Why didn't they come out of their holes and fight us? With their fists if they didn't have any guns? *Any* red-bloodied—er, red-blooded—Amuri—well, whatever they are—ought to have enough guts to come out and fight, to defend home, flag, and mother!

We'll probably get around to that. It's the normal attitude to take after vandalism. It's the human way.

But as of now, our only thought is to slink away.

On our abandoned Martian landing field there hangs a man's discarded spacesuit, suspended from the desensitized prongs of a Come-to-me tower. It is stuffed with straw filched, no doubt, from packing cases which brought out so many more delicate, sensitive, precision instruments than we take back.

Although we have not been entirely irresponsible in our head-long flight back home.

We do bring back some of what we took out: the more valuable of the instruments. We have been most selective in this.

The only coarse, insensitive, unfinished instrument we bring back—is man.

Cordwainer Smith, long the mystery-man of science fiction, was actually Paul Linebarger (1913-66), a political scientist, intelligence officer, and military adviser, specializing in the Orient, particularly China. The Oriental influence is evident in his work, most of which forms a large mosaic of one of the strangest future universes ever imagined. His stories are typically told as legends of remote centuries, of events looked back on with wonder and awe. The Best of Cordwainer Smith, *edited by J.J. Pierce, gives an excellent overview of his work. This story was published in October 1963.*

DRUNKBOAT
by Cordwainer Smith

Perhaps it is the saddest, maddest, wildest story in the whole long history of space. It is true that no one else had ever done anything like it before, to travel at such a distance, and at such speeds, and by such means. The hero looked like such an ordinary man—when people looked at him for the first time. The second time, ah! that was different.

And the heroine. Small she was, and ash-blonde, intelligent, perky, and hurt. Hurt—yes, that's the right word. She looked as though she needed comforting or helping, even when she was perfectly all right. Men felt more like men when she was near. Her name was Elizabeth.

Who would have thought that her name would ring loud and clear in the wild vomiting nothing which made up space$_3$?

He took an old, old rocket, of an ancient design. With it he outflew, outfled, outjumped all the machines which had ever existed before. You might almost think that he went so fast that he shocked the great vaults of the sky, so that the ancient poem might have been written for him alone. "All the stars threw down their spears and watered heaven with their tears."

Go he did, so fast, so far that people simply did not believe it at first. They thought it was a joke told by men, a farce spun forth by rumor, a wild story to while away the summer afternoon.

We know his name now.

And our children and their children will know it for always.

Rambo. Artyr Rambo of Earth Four.

But he followed his Elizabeth where no space was. He went where men could not go, had not been, did not dare, would not think.

He did all this of his own free will.

Of course people thought it was a joke at first, and got to making up silly songs about the reported trip.

"Dig me a hole for that reeling feeling. . . !" sang one.

"Push me the call for the umber number. . . !" sang another.

"Where is the ship of the ochre joker. . . ?" sang a third.

Then people everywhere found it was true. Some stood stock still and got goose-flesh. Others turned quickly to everyday things. Space$_3$ had been found, and it had been pierced. Their world would never be the same again. The solid rock had become an open door.

Space itself, so clean, so empty, so tidy, now looked like a million million light-years of tapioca pudding—gummy, mushy, sticky, not fit to breathe, not fit to swim in.

How did it happen?

Everybody took the credit, each in his own different way.

"He came for me," said Elizabeth. "I died and he came for me because the machines were making a mess of my life when they tried to heal my terrible, useless death."

"I went myself," said Rambo. "They tricked me and lied to me and fooled me, but I took the boat and I became the boat and I got there. Nobody made me do it. I was angry, but I went. And I came back, didn't I?"

He too was right, even when he twisted and whined on the green grass of earth, his ship lost in a space so terribly far and strange that it might have been beneath his living hand, or might have been half a galaxy away.

How can anybody tell, with space three?

It was Rambo who got back, looking for his Elizabeth. He loved her. So the trip was his, and the credit his.

But the Lord Crudelta said, many years later, when he spoke in a soft voice and talked confidently among his friends, "The experiment was mine. I designed it, I picked Rambo. I drove the selectors mad, trying to find a man who would meet those specifications. And I had that rocket built to the old, old plans. It was the sort of thing which human beings first used when they jumped out of the air a little bit, leaping like flying fish from one wave to the next and already thinking that they were eagles. If I had used one of the regular platform ships, it would have disappeared with a sort of reverse gurgle, leaving space milky for a little bit while it faded into nastiness and obliteration. But I did not risk that. I put the rocket on a launching pad. *And the launching pad itself was an interstellar ship!* Since we were using an ancient rocket, we did it up right, with the old, old writing, mysterious letters printed all over the machine. We even had the name of our Organization—I and O and M—for 'the Instrumentality of Mankind' written on it good and sharp.

"How would I know," went on Lord Crudelta, "that we would succeed more than we wanted to succeed, that Rambo would tear space itself loose from its hinges and leave that ship behind, just because he loved Elizabeth so sharply much, so fiercely much?"

Crudelta sighed.

"I know it and I don't know it. I'm like that ancient man who tried to take a water boat the wrong way around the planet Earth and found a new world instead. Columbus, he was called. And the land, that was Australia or America or something like that. That's what I did. I sent Rambo out in that ancient rocket and he found a way through space₃. Now none of us will ever know who might come bulking through the floor or take shape out of the air in front of us.

Crudelta added, almost wistfully: "What's the use of telling the story? Everybody knows it, anyhow. My part in it isn't very glorious. Now the end of it, that's pretty. The bungalow by the waterfall and all the wonderful children that other people gave to them, you could write a poem about that. But the next to the end, how he showed up at the hospital helpless and insane, looking for his own Elizabeth. That was sad and eerie, that was frightening. I'm glad it all came to the happy ending with the bungalow by the waterfall, but it took a crashing long time to get there. And there are parts of it that we will never quite understand, the naked skin against naked space, the eyeballs riding something much faster than light ever was. Do you know what an *aoudad* is? It's an ancient sheep that used to live on Old Earth, and here we are, thousands of years later, with a children's nonsense rhyme about it. The animals are gone but the rhyme remains. It'll be like that with Rambo someday. Everybody will know his name and all about his drunkboat, but they will forget the scientific milestone that he crossed, hunting for Elizabeth in an ancient rocket that couldn't fly from peetle to pootle. . . . Oh, the rhyme? Don't you know that? It's a silly thing. It goes,

Point your gun at a murky lurky.
(Now you're talking ham or turkey!)
Shoot a shot at a dying aoudad.
(Don't ask the lady why or how, dad!)

Don't ask me what 'ham' and 'turkey' are. Probably parts of ancient animals, like beefsteak or sirloin. But the children still say the words. They'll do that with Rambo and his drunken boat someday. They may even tell the story of Elizabeth. But they will never tell the part about how he got to the hospital. That part is too terrible, too real, too sad and wonderful at the end. They found him on the grass. Mind you, naked on the grass, and nobody knew where he had come from!"

They found him naked on the grass and nobody knew where he had come from. They did not even know about the ancient rocket which the Lord Crudelta had sent beyond the end of nowhere with the letters I, O, and M written on it. They did not know that this was Rambo, who had gone through space three. The robots noticed him first and brought him in, photographing everything that they did. They had been programmed that way, to make sure that anything unusual was kept in the records.

Then the nurses found him in the outside room.

They assumed that he was alive, since he was not dead, but they could not prove that he was alive, either.

That heightened the puzzle.

The doctors were called in. Real doctors, not machines. They were very important men. Citizen Doctor Timofeyev, Citizen Doctor Grosbeck, and the director himself, Sir and Doctor Vomact. They took the case.

(Over on the other side of the hospital Elizabeth waited, unconscious, and nobody knew it at all. Elizabeth, for whom he had jumped space, and pierced the stars, but nobody knew it yet!)

The young man could not speak. When they ran eyeprints and fingerprints through the Population Machine, they found that he had been bred on Earth itself,

Drunkboat 127

but had been shipped out as a frozen and unborn baby to Earth Four. At tremendous cost, they queried Earth Four with an "instant message," only to discover that the young man who lay before them in the hospital had been lost from an experimental ship on an intergalactic trip.

Lost.

No ship and no sign of ship.

And here he was.

They stood at the edge of space, and did not know what they were looking at. They were doctors and it was their business to repair or rebuild people, not to ship them around. How should such men know about space$_3$ when they did not even know about space$_2$, except for the fact that people got on the planoform ships and made trips through it? They were looking for sickness when their eyes saw engineering. They treated him when he was well.

All he needed was time, to get over the shock of the most tremendous trip ever made by a human being, but the doctors did not know that and they tried to rush his recovery.

When they put clothes on him, he moved from coma to a kind of mechanical spasm and tore the clothing off. Once again stripped, he lay himself roughly on the floor and refused food or speech.

They fed him with needles while the whole energy of space, had they only known it, was radiating out of his body in new forms.

They put him all by himself in a locked room and watched him through the peephole.

He was a nice-looking young man, even though his mind was blank and his body was rigid and unconscious. His hair was very fair and his eyes were light blue, but his face showed character—a square chin; a handsome, resolute sullen mouth; old lines in the face which looked as though, when conscious, he must have lived many days or months on the edge of rage.

When they studied him the third day in the hospital, their patient had not changed at all.

He had torn off his pajamas again and lay naked, face down, on the floor.

His body was as immobile and tense as it had been on the day before.

(*One year later, this room was going to be a museum with a bronze sign reading, "Here lay Rambo after he left the Old Rocket for Space Three," but the doctors still had no idea of what they were dealing with.*)

His face was turned so sharply to the left that the neck muscles showed. His right arm stuck out straight from the body. The left arm formed an exact right angle from the body, with the left forearm and hand pointing rigidly upward at 90° from the upper arm. The legs were in the grotesque parody of a running position.

Doctor Grosbeck said, "It looks to me like he's swimming. Let's drop him in a tank of water and see if he moves." Grosbeck sometimes went in for drastic solutions to problems.

Timofeyev took his place at the peephole. "Spasm, still," he murmured. "I hope the poor fellow is not feeling pain when his cortical defenses are down. How can a man fight pain if he does not even know what he is experiencing?"

"And you, sir and doctor," said Grosbeck to Vomact, "what do you see?"

Vomact did not need to look. He had come early and had looked long and quietly at the patient through the peephole before the other doctors arrived. Vomact was a

VALLEY OF INVISIBLE MEN *by* EDMOND HAMILTON

SEE
BACK
COVER

AMAZING STORIES

MARCH
20c

The
RAID
FROM
MARS

by
MILES J. BREUER

AND
GREAT
STORIES BY
ED EARL REPP
ROBERT BLOCH
F. A. KUMMER, JR.

The March 1939 issue reflects the somewhat primitive view of futuristic and alien technologies that was prevalent at the time. One of Robert Bloch's earlier pieces, "The Strange Flight of Richard Clayton," also appeared in this issue. Artwork by Robert Fuqua.

UNDERSEA SALVAGER

The greatest unconquered frontiers on earth are the sea depths. This supersubmarine, built specifically for exploration and salvaging is scientifically constructed to withstand great pressure, capable of descending to depths as great as that achieved by Beebe's bathysphere. Retractable gear will insure solid foundation on any type sea bottom; special sea chambers will allow divers to work with assured safety. At super depths, salvage will be done from inside the ship, by retractable derricks, perhaps lifting whole ships to levels permitting divers to finish the job. Searchlights using ordinary light, infra-red light, and ultra-violet rays, coupled with a televisor periscope system permitting complete 360° vision, will allow scientific exploration of these realms of eternal night and mystery. See Page 145 for details.
© AMAZING STORIES 2020

Not only were the front covers of the magazine used to promote story selections, but back covers were also used for this purpose. A strange tale of a supersubmarine salvager was introduced on the back cover of the March 1939 issue. Artwork by H. W. McCauley.

The perfect pulp-magazine image—a ravishing alien beauty menaced by a grisly beast—graces the cover of the July 1946 issue. Artwork by Walter Parke.

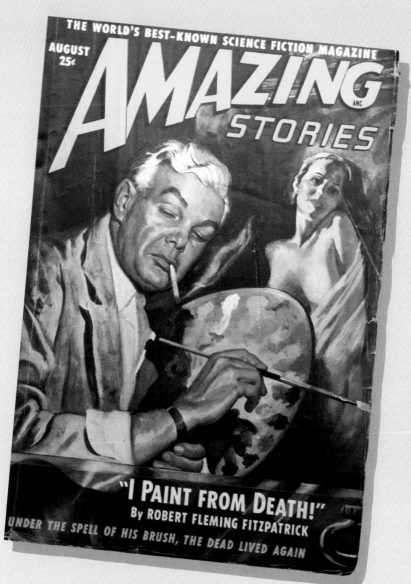

THE WORLD'S BEST-KNOWN SCIENCE FICTION MAGAZINE

AUGUST
25¢

AMAZING
STORIES
INC

"I PAINT FROM DEATH!"
By ROBERT FLEMING FITZPATRICK
UNDER THE SPELL OF HIS BRUSH, THE DEAD LIVED AGAIN

*Though science fiction and fantasy were standard
fare, horror fiction also crept into the pages of
Amazing® Stories, as the August 1949 issue
illustrates. One can only wonder what the artist's
model thought. Artwork by Arnold Kohn.*

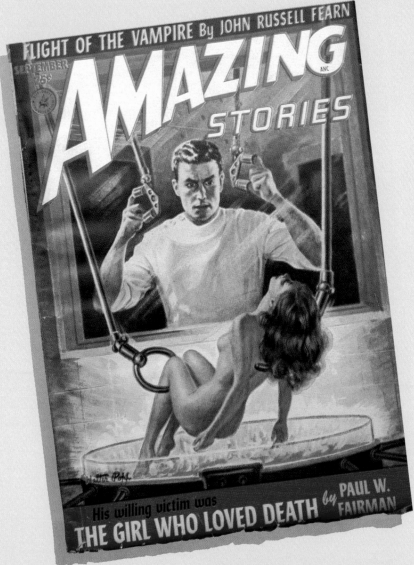

Again, the combination of modern technology and sex appeal, as seen in the September 1952 issue, was what made science-fiction pulp magazines such enjoyable reading. Artwork by Walter Popp.

Emulating the Saturday matinee thrillers, the January 1957 issue illustrates that aliens can be our allies. Artwork by Edward Valigursky.

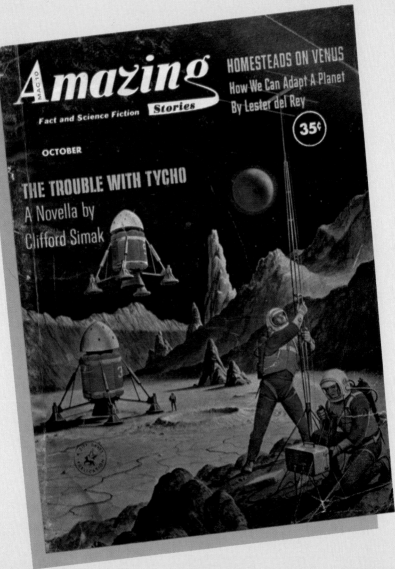

As a new decade began wherein more energy was applied to the U.S. space program, the science-fiction magazines tried to reflect an element of hard realism. The October 1960 issue is reminiscent of this trend. Artwork by Alex Schomburg.

The February 1963 issue sports a new Amazing® logo and a peculiar future anachronism—the alien giant is retrieving what appears to be a Mercury capsule from the waters of its home world. Artwork by Vernon Kramer.

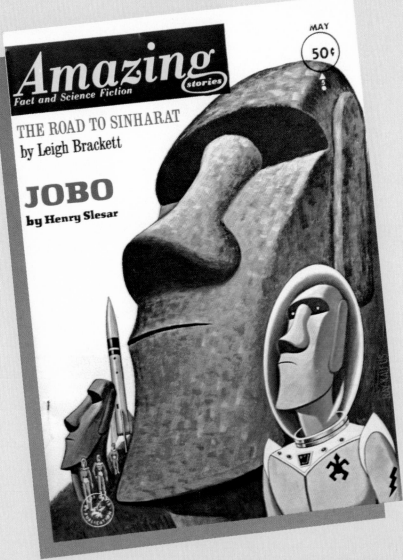

Amazing *stories*
Fact and Science Fiction

MAY
50¢

THE ROAD TO SINHARAT
by Leigh Brackett

JOBO
by Henry Slesar

A tongue-in-cheek portrayal of the true settlers of Easter Island on the cover of the May 1963 issue takes a job at contemporary ethnocentrism: what was thought to be a primitive culture isn't. Artwork by Ray Kalfus.

The highly stylized cover of the October 1963 issue represents the influence of computer technology on modern art. "Drunkboat" by Cordwainer Smith is featured in this issue. Artwork by Lloyd Birmingham.

Amazing

Fact and Science Fiction

stories

DECEMBER
50¢

TO PLANT A SEED, by Neil Barrett, Jr.

DAYS OF PERKY PAT,
by Philip K. Dick

SF Profile: FRITZ LEIBER

*Originality has always been an important element
in science-fiction literature—whether it be aliens
building spacecraft out of cacti, as illustrated on
the cover of the December 1963 issue, or humans
trying to survive the years following a nuclear
holocaust, as in Philip K. Dick's "The Days of
Perky Pat," which was featured in this issue.
Artwork by Emsh.*

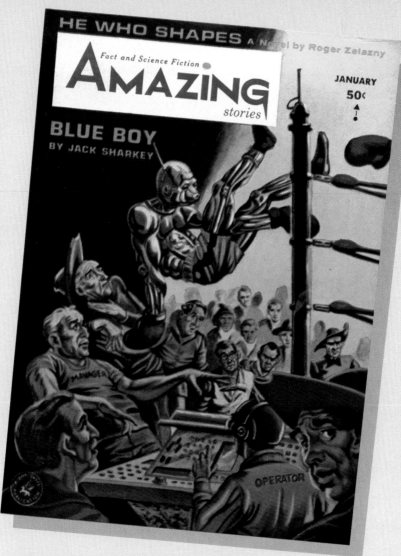

Taking a common occurrence and adding a surprising plot twist has been a standard science-fiction device. In the case of the January 1965 cover art, boxing contenders of the future will be robots. Artwork by Michael Arndt.

With the dawning of the '70s came the New Wave movement in science-fiction literature. That this movement affected the artists is apparent when studying the artwork of this period. With its New Wave appeal, the September 1970 issue introduced Philip José Farmer's "The Oogenesis of Bird City." Artwork by Jeff Jones.

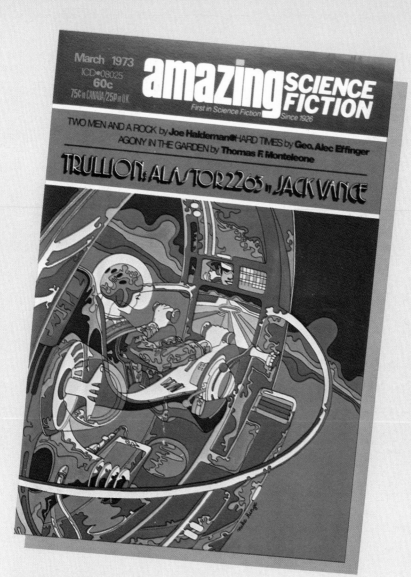

New Wave wasn't the only influence on science-fiction artwork. Psychedelia and op art also had a role, as seen in this brilliant March 1973 issue cover. Artwork by Mike Hinge.

Man In A Vice by GREGORY BENFORD

February 1974
ICD♦08025
60c
75¢ IN CANADA & FOREIGN COUNTRIES

amazing SCIENCE FICTION

First in Science Fiction ▪ Since 1926

FATHER BY **PAMELA SARGENT**
A NEW SHORT NOVEL, COMPLETE IN THIS ISSUE!

also

No Deposit • No Refill by **Robert F. Young** ◉ Mama Loves You by **Dale Randles, Jr.** ◉ Warship by **David Redd** ◉◉◉ Annapolis Town by **Grant Carrington**

Moving away from hard science fiction, the February 1974 issue shows an interest in the introspective, human element that blossomed in many of the works appearing in the pulp magazines. Artwork by Jeff Jones.

*Celebrating the 50th anniversary of Amazing®
Science Fiction Stories, the June 1976 issue
included a reproduction of the first Amazing®
magazine cover from April 1926. Artwork by
Stephen E. Fabian.*

K ● $1.50 March 1983 ● 47734 ● UK: 75p ●

SCIENCE FICTION

AMAZING™

Stories

Combined with FANTASTIC™ Magazine

Edited by
George Scithers
NOW 160 PAGES

Gregory Benford

Bill Pronzini

Darrell Schweitzer

Thomas Disch

Founded in 1926 by Hugo Gernsback

The current use of the old comet-tail logo brings back the feel of the earlier pulp magazines. From the March 1983 issue, one gets a feel that the search for a better future and for contact with alien life will perhaps always be the pursuit of science-fiction writers. Artwork by Jack Gaughan.

wise man, with good insight and rich intuitions. He could guess in an hour more than a machine could diagnose in a year; he was beginning to understand that this was a sickness which no man had ever had before. Still, there were remedies waiting.

The three doctors tried them.

They tried hypnosis, electrotherapy, massage, subsonics, atropine, surgital, a whole family of the digitalinids, and some quasi-narcotic viruses which had been grown in orbit where they mutated fast. They got the beginning of a response when they tried gas hypnosis combined with an electronically amplified telepath; this showed that something still went on inside the patient's mind. Otherwise the brain might have seemed to be mere fatty tissue, without a nerve in it. The other attempts had shown nothing. The gas showed a faint stirring away from fear and pain. The telepath reported glimpses of unknown skies. (The doctors turned the telepath over to the Space Police promptly, so they could try to code the star patterns which he had seen in a patient's mind, but the patterns did not fit. The telepath, though a keen-witted man, could not remember them in enough detail for them to be scanned against the samples of piloting sheets.)

The doctors went back to their drugs and tried ancient, simple remedies—morphine and caffeine to counteract each other, and a rough massage to make him dream again, so that the telepath could pick it up.

There was no further result that day, or the next.

Meanwhile the Earth authorities were getting restless. They thought, quite rightly, that the hospital had done a good job of proving that the patient had not been on Earth until a few moments before the robots found him on the grass. How had he gotten on the grass?

The airspace of Earth reported no intrusion at all, no vehicle marking a blazing arc of air incandescing against metal, no whisper of the great forces which drove a plano-form ship through space$_2$.

(Crudelta, using faster-than-light ships, was creeping slow as a snail back toward Earth, racing his best to see if Rambo had gotten there first.)

On the fifth day, there was the beginning of a breakthrough.

Elizabeth had passed.

This was found out only much later, by a careful check of the hospital records.

The doctors only knew this much: Patients had been moved down the corridor, sheet-covered figures immobile on wheeled beds.

Suddenly the beds stopped rolling.

A nurse screamed.

The heavy steel-and-plastic wall was bending inward. Some slow, silent force was pushing the wall into the corridor itself.

The wall ripped.

A human hand emerged.

One of the quick-witted nurses screamed, "*Push* those beds! *Push* them out of the way."

The nurses and robots obeyed.

The beds rocked like a group of boats crossing a wave when they came to the place where the floor, bonded to the wall, had bent upward to meet the wall as it tore inward. The peace-colored glow of the lights flickered. Robots appeared.

A second human hand came through the wall. Pushing in opposite directions, the hands tore the wall as though it had been wet paper.

The patient from the grass put his head through.

He looked blindly up and down the corridor, his eyes not quite focusing, his skin glowing a strange red-brown from the burns of open space.

"No," he said. Just that one word.

But that "No" was heard. Though the volume was not loud, it carried throughout the hospital. The internal telecommunications system relayed it. Every switch in the place went negative. Frantic nurses and robots, with even the doctors helping them, rushed to turn all the machines back on—the pumps, the ventilators, the artificial kidneys, the brain re-recorders, even the simple air engines which kept the atmosphere clean.

Far overhead an aircraft spun giddily. Its "off" switch, surrounded by triple safeguards, had suddenly been thrown into the negative postion. Fortunately the robot-pilot got it going again before crashing into earth.

The patient did not seem to know that his word had this effect.

(Later the world knew that this was part of the "drunkboat effect." The man himself had developed the capacity for using his neurophysical system as a machine control.)

In the corridor, the machine robot who served as policeman arrived. He wore sterile, padded velvet gloves with a grip of sixty metric tons inside his hands. He approached the patient. The robot had been carefully trained to recognize all kinds of danger from delirious or psychotic humans; later he reported that he had an input of "danger, extreme" on every band of sensation. He had been expecting to seize the prisoner with irreversible firmness and to return him to his bed, but with this kind of danger sizzling in the air, the robot took no chances. His wrist itself contained a hypodermic pistol which operated on compressed argon.

He reached out toward the unknown, naked man who stood in the big torn gap in the wall. The wrist-weapon hissed and a sizeable injection of condamine, the most powerful narcotic in the known universe, spat its way through the skin of Rambo's neck. The patient collapsed.

The robot picked him up gently and tenderly, lifted him through the torn wall, pushed the door open with a kick which broke the lock and put the patient back on his bed. The robot could hear doctors coming, so he used his enormous hands to pat the steel wall back into its proper shape. Work-robots or underpeople could finish the job later, but meanwhile it looked better to have that part of the building set at right angles again.

Doctor Vomact arrived, followed closely by Grosbeck.

"What happened?" he yelled, shaken out of a lifelong calm. The robot pointed at the ripped wall.

"He tore it open. I put it back," said the robot.

The doctors turned to look at the patient. He had crawled off his bed again and was on the floor, but his breathing was light and natural.

"What did you give him?" cried Vomact to the robot.

"Condamine," said the robot, "according to rule 47-B. The drug is not to be mentioned outside the hospital."

"I know that," said Vomact absentmindedly and a little crossly. "You can go along now. Thank you."

"It is not usual to thank robots," said the robot, "but you can read a commendation into my record if you want to."

"Get the blazes out of here!" shouted Vomact at the officious robot.

The robot blinked. "There are no blazes but I have the impression you mean me. I shall leave, with your permission." He jumped with odd gracefulness around the two doctors, fingered the broken doorlock absentmindedly, as though he might have wished to repair it; and then, seeing Vomact glare at him, left the room completely.

A moment later soft muted thuds began. Both doctors listened for a moment and then gave up. The robot was out in the corridor, gently patting the steel floor back into shape. He was a tidy robot, probably animated by an amplified chicken-brain, and when he got tidy he became obstinate.

"Two questions, Grosbeck," said the sir and doctor Vomact.

"Your service, sir!"

"Where was the patient standing when he pushed the wall into the corridor, and how did he get the leverage to do it?"

Grosbeck narrowed his eyes in puzzlement. "Now that you mention it, I have no idea of how he did it. In fact, he could not have done it. But he has. And the other question?"

"What do you think of condamine?"

"Dangerous, of course, as always. Addiction can—"

"Can you have addiction with no cortical activity?" interrupted Vomact.

"Of course," said Grosbeck promptly. "Tissue addiction."

"Look for it, then," said Vomact.

Grosbeck knelt beside the patient and felt with his fingertips for the muscle endings. He felt where they knotted themselves into the base of the skull, the tips of the shoulders, the striped area of the back.

When he stood up there was a look of puzzlement on his face. "I never felt a human body like this one before. I am not even sure that it *is* human any longer."

Vomact said nothing. The two doctors confronted one another. Grosbeck fidgeted under the calm stare of the senior man. Finally he blurted out,

"Sir and Doctor, I know what we *could* do."

"And that," said Vomact levelly, without the faintest hint of encouragement or of warning, "is what?"

"It wouldn't be the first time that it's been done in a hospital."

"What?" said Vomact, his eyes—those dreaded eyes!—making Grosbeck say what he did not want to say.

Grosbeck flushed. He leaned toward Vomact so as to whisper, even though there was no one standing near them. His words, when they came, had a lover's improper suggestion:

"Kill the patient, Sir and Doctor. Kill him. We have plenty of records of him. We can get a cadaver out of the basement and make it into a good simulacrum. Who knows what we will turn loose among mankind if we let him get well?"

"Who knows?" said Vomact without tone or quality to his voice. "But, citizen and doctor, what is the twelfth duty of a physician?"

" 'Not to take the law into his own hands, keeping healing for the healers and giving to the state or the Instrumentality whatever property belongs to the state or the Instrumentality.' " Grosbeck sighed as he retracted his own suggestion. "Sir and Doctor, I take it back. It wasn't medicine which I was talking about. It was government and politics which were really in my mind."

"And now? . . ." asked Vomact.

"Heal him, or let him be until he heals himself."

"And which would you do?"

"I'd try to heal him."

"How?" said Vomact.

"Sir and Doctor," cried Grosbeck, "do not ride my weaknesses in this case! I know that you like me because I am a bold, confident sort of man. Do not ask me to be myself when we do not even know where this body came from. If I were bold as usual, I would give him typhoid and condamine, stationing telepaths nearby. But this is something new in the history of man. We are people and perhaps he is not a person any more. Perhaps he represents the combination of people with some kind of new force. How did he get here from the far side of nowhere? How many million times has he been enlarged or reduced? We do not know what he is or what has happened to him. How can we treat a man when we are treating the cold of space, the heat of suns, the frigidity of distance? We know what to do with flesh, but this is not quite flesh any more. Feel him yourself, Sir and Doctor! You will touch something which nobody has ever touched before."

"I have," Vomact declared, "already felt him. You are right. We will try typhoid and condamine for half a day. Twelve hours from now let us meet each other at this place. I will tell the nurses and the robots what to do in the interim."

They both gave the red-tanned spread-eagled figure on the floor a parting glance. Grosbeck looked at the body with something like distaste mingled with fear; Vomact was expressionless, save for a wry wan smile of pity.

At the door the head nurse awaited them. Grosbeck was surprised at his chief's orders.

"Ma'am and nurse, do you have a weapon-proof vault in this hospital?"

"Yes, sir," she said. "We used to keep our records in it until we telemetered all our records into Computer Orbit. Now it is dirty and empty."

"Clean it out. Run a ventilator tube into it. Who is your military protector?"

"My what?" she cried, in surprise.

"Everyone on Earth has military protection. Where are the forces, the soldiers, who protect this hospital of yours?"

"My sir and doctor!" she called out. "My sir and doctor! I'm an old woman and I have been allowed to work here for three hundred years, but I never thought of that idea before. Why would I need soldiers?"

"Find who they are and ask them to stand by. They are specialists, too, with a different kind of art from ours. Let them stand by. They may be needed before this day is out. Give my name as authority to their lieutenant or sergeant. Now here is the medication which I want you to apply to this patient."

Her eyes widened as he went on talking, but she was a disciplined woman and she nodded as she heard him out, point by point. Her eyes looked very sad and weary at the end but she was a trained expert and she had enormous respect for the skill and wisdom of the Sir and Doctor Vomact. She also had a warm, feminine pity for the motionless young male figure on the floor, swimming forever on the heavy floor, swimming between archipelagoes of which no man living had ever dreamed before.

Crisis came that night.

The patient had worn handprints into the inner wall of the vault, but he had not escaped.

The soldiers, looking oddly alert with their weapons gleaming in the bright corridor of the hospital, were really very bored, as soldiers always become when they are on duty with no action.

Their lieutenant was keyed up. The wirepoint in his hand buzzed like a dangerous insect. Sir and Doctor Vomact, who knew more about weapons than the soldiers thought he knew, saw that the wirepoint was set to HIGH, with a capacity of paralyzing people five stories up, five stories down, or a kilometer sideways. He said nothing. He merely thanked the lieutenant and entered the vault, closely followed by Grosbeck and Timofeyev.

The patient swam here, too.

He had changed to an arm-over-arm motion, kicking his legs against the floor. It was as though he had swum on the other floor with the sole purpose of staying afloat, and had now discovered some direction in which to go, albeit very slowly. His motions were deliberate, tense, rigid, and so reduced in time that it seemed as though he hardly moved at all. The ripped pajamas lay on the floor beside him.

Vomact glanced around, wondering what forces the man could have used to make those handprints on the steel wall. He remembered Grosbeck's warning that the patient should die, rather than subject all mankind to new and unthought risks, but though he shared the feeling, he could not condone the recommendation.

Almost irritably, the doctor thought to himself—where could the man be going?

(To Elizabeth, the truth was, to Elizabeth, now only sixty meters away. Not till much later did people understand what Rambo had been trying to do—crossing sixty mere meters to reach his Elizabeth when he had already jumped an un-count of light-years to return to her. To his own, his dear, his well-beloved who needed him!)

The condamine did not leave its characteristic mark of deep lassitude and glowing skin: perhaps the typhoid was successfully contradicting it. Rambo did seem more lively than before. The name had come through on the regular message system, but it still did not mean anything to the Sir and Doctor Vomact. It would. It would.

Meanwhile the other two doctors, briefed ahead of time, got busy with the apparatus which the robots and the nurses had installed.

Vomact murmured to the others, "I think he's better off. Looser all around. I'll try shouting."

So busy were they that they just nodded.

Vomact screamed at the patient, "Who are you? What are you? Where do you come from?"

The sad blue eyes of the man on the floor glanced at him with a surprisingly quick glance, but there was no other real sign of communication. The limbs kept up their swim against the rough concrete floor of the vault. Two of the bandages which the hospital staff had put on him had worn off again. The right knee, scraped and bruised, deposited a sixty-centimeter trail of blood—some old and black and coagulated, some fresh, new and liquid—on the floor as it moved back and forth.

Vomact stood up and spoke to Grosbeck and Timofeyev. "Now," he said, "let us see what happens when we apply the pain."

The two stepped back without being told to do so.

Timofeyev waved his hand at a small white-enameled orderly-robot who stood in the doorway.

The pain net, a fragile cage of wires, dropped down from the ceiling.

It was Vomact's duty, as senior doctor, to take the greatest risk. The patient was wholly encased by the net of wires, but Vomact dropped to his hands and knees, lifted the net at one corner with his right hand, thrust his own head into it next to the head of the patient. Doctor Vomact's robe trailed on the clean concrete, touching the black old stains of blood left from the patient's "swim" throughout the night.

Now Vomact's mouth was centimeters from the patient's ear.

Said Vomact, "Oh."

The net hummed.

The patient stopped his slow motion, arched his back, looked steadfastly at the doctor.

Doctors Grosbeck and Timofeyev could see Vomact's face go white with the impact of the pain machine, but Vomact kept his voice under control and said evenly and loudly to the patient, *"Who—are—you?"*

The patient said flatly, "Elizabeth."

The answer was foolish, but the tone was rational.

Vomact pulled his head out from under the net, shouting at the patient, *"Who—are—you?"*

The naked man replied, speaking very clearly:

"Chwinkle, chwinkle, little chweeble
I am feeling very feeble!"

Vomact frowned and murmured to the robot, "More pain. Turn it up to pain ultimate."

The body threshed under the net, trying to resume its swim on the concrete.

A loud wild braying cry came from the victim under the net. It sounded like a screamed distortion of the name Elizabeth, echoing out from endless remoteness.

It did not make sense.

Vomact screamed back, *"Who—are—you?"*

With unexpected clarity and resonance, the voice came back to the three doctors from the twisting body under the net of pain:

"I'm the shipped man, the ripped man, the gypped man, the dipped man, the hipped man, the tripped man, the tipped man, the slipped man, the flipped man, the nipped man, the ripped man, the clipped man—aah!" His voice choked off with a cry and he went back to swimming on the floor, despite the intensity of the pain net immediately above him.

The doctor lifted his hand. The pain net stopped buzzing and lifted high into the air.

He felt the patient's pulse. It was quick. He lifted an eyelid. The reactions were much closer to normal.

"Stand back," he said to the others.

"Pain on both of us," he said to the robot.

The net came down on the two of them.

"Who are you?" shrieked Vomact, right into the patient's ear, holding the man halfway off the floor and not quite knowing whether the body which tore steel walls might not, somehow, tear both of them apart as they stood.

The man babbled back at him, "I'm the most man, the post man, the host man, the ghost man, the coast man, the boast man, the dosed man, the grossed man, the toast man, the roast man, no! no! no!"

He struggled in Vomact's arms. Grosbeck and Timofeyev stepped forward to rescue their chief when the patient added, very calmly and clearly:

"Your procedure is all right, doctor, whoever you are. More fever, please. More pain, please. Some of that dope to fight the pain. You're pulling me back. I know I am on Earth. Elizabeth is near. For the love of God, get me Elizabeth! But don't rush me. I need days and days to get well."

The rationality was so startling that Grosbeck, without waiting for orders from Vomact, as chief doctor, ordered the pain net lifted.

The patient began babbling again: "I'm the three man, the he man, the tree man, the me man, the three man, the three man. . . ." His voice faded and he slumped unconscious.

Vomact walked out of the vault. He was a little unsteady.

His colleagues took him by the elbows.

He smiled wanly at them: "I wish it were lawful. . . . I could use some of that condamine myself. No wonder the pain nets wake the patients up and even make dead people do twitches! Get me some liquor. My heart is old."

Grosbeck sat him down while Timofeyev ran down the corridor in search of medicinal liquor.

Vomact murmured, "How are we going to find *his* Elizabeth? There must be millions of them. And he's from Earth Four too."

"Sir and Doctor, you have worked wonders," said Grosbeck. "To go under the net. To take those chances. To bring him to speech. I will never see anything like it again. It's enough for any one lifetime, to have seen this day."

"But what do we do next?" asked Vomact wearily, almost in confusion.

That particular question needed no answer.

The Lord Crudelta had reached Earth.

His pilot landed the craft and fainted at the controls with sheer exhaustion.

Of the escort cats, who had ridden alongside the space craft in the miniature spaceships, three were dead, one was comatose, and the fourth was spitting and raving.

When the port authorities tried to slow the Lord Crudelta down to ascertain his authority, he invoked Top Emergency, took over the command of troops in the name of the Instrumentality, arrested everyone in sight but the troop commander, and requisitioned the troop commander to take him to the hospital. The computers at the port had told him that one Rambo, "sans origine," had arrived mysteriously on the grass of a designated hospital.

Outside the hospital, the Lord Crudelta invoked Top Emergency again, placed all armed men under his own command, ordered a recording monitor to cover all his actions if he should later be channeled into a court-martial, and arrested everyone in sight.

The tramp of heavily armed men, marching in combat order, overtook Timofeyev as he hurried back to Vomact with a drink. The men were jogging along on the double. All of them had live helmets and their weapons were buzzing.

Nurses ran forward to drive the intruders out, ran backward when the sting of the stun-rays brushed cruelly over them. The whole hospital was in an uproar.

The Lord Crudelta later admitted that he had made a serious mistake.

The Two Minutes' War broke out immediately.

You have to understand the pattern of the Instrumentality to see how it happened. The Instrumentality was a self-perpetuating body of men with enormous powers and a strict code. Each was a plenum of the low, the middle, and the high justice. Each could do anything he found necessary or proper to maintain the Instrumentality and to keep the peace between the worlds. But if he made a mistake or committed a wrong—ah, then, it was suddenly different. Any Lord could put another Lord to death in an emergency, but he was assured of death and disgrace himself if he assumed this responsibility. The only difference between ratification and repudiation came in the fact that Lords who killed in an emergency and were proved wrong were marked down on a very shameful list, while those who killed other Lords rightly (as later examination might prove) were listed on a very honorable list, but still killed.

With three Lords, the situation was different. Three lords made an emergency court; if they acted together, acted in good faith, and reported to the computers and the Instrumentality, they were exempt from punishment, though not from blame or even reduction to citizen status. Seven Lords, or all the Lords on a given planet at a given moment, were beyond any criticism except that of a dignified reversal of their actions should a later ruling prove them wrong.

This was all the business of the Instrumentality. The Instrumentality had the perpetual slogan: "Watch, but do not govern; stop war, but do not wage it; protect, but do not control; and first, survive!"

The Lord Crudelta had seized the troops—not his troops, but light regular troops of Manhome Government—because he feared that the greatest danger in the history of man might come from the person whom he himself had sent through Space$_3$.

He never expected that the troops would be plucked out from his command—an overriding power reinforced by robotic telepathy and the incomparable communications net, both open and secret, reinforced by thousands of years in trickery, defeat, secrecy, victory, and sheer experience, which the Instrumentality had perfected since it emerged from the Ancient Wars.

Overriding, overridden!

These were the commands which the Instrumentality had used before recorded time began. Sometimes they suspended their antagonists on points of law, sometimes by the deft and deadly insertion of weapons, most often by cutting in on other peoples' mechanical and social controls and doing their will, only to drop the controls as suddenly as they had taken them.

But not Crudelta's hastily called troops.

The war broke out with a change of pace.

The two squads of men were moving into that part of the hospital where Elizabeth lay, waiting the endless returns to the jelly baths which would rebuild her poor ruined body.

The squads changed pace.

The survivors could not account for what happened.

They all admitted to great mental confusion—afterward.

At the time it seemed that they had received a clear, logical command to turn and to defend the women's section by counterattacking their own main battalion right in their rear.

The hospital was a very strong building. Otherwise it would have melted to the ground or shot up in flame.

The leading soldiers suddenly turned around, dropped for cover and blazed their wirepoints at the comrades who followed them. The wirepoints were cued to organic material, though fairly harmless to inorganic. They were powered by the power relays which every soldier wore on his back.

In the first ten seconds of the turnaround, twenty-seven soldiers, two nurses, three patients, and one orderly were killed. One hundred and nine other people were wounded in that first exchange of fire.

The troop commander had never seen battle, but he had been well trained. He immediately deployed his reserves around the external exits of the building and sent his favorite squad, commanded by a Sergeant Lansdale whom he trusted well, down into the basement, so that it could rise vertically from the basement into the women's quarters and find out who the enemy was.

As yet, he had no idea that it was his own leading troops turning and fighting their comrades.

He testified later, at the trial, that he personally had no sensations of eerie interference with his own mind. He merely knew that his men had unexpectedly come upon armed resistance from antagonists—identity unknown!—who had weapons identical with theirs. Since the Lord Crudelta had brought them along in case there might be a fight with unspecified antagonists, he felt right in assuming that a Lord of the Instrumentality knew what he was doing. This was the enemy all right.

In less than a minute, the two sides had balanced out. The line of fire had moved right into his own force. The lead men, some of whom were wounded, simply turned around and began defending themselves against the men immediately behind them. It was as though an invisible line, moving rapidly, had parted the two sections of the military force.

The oily black smoke of dissolving bodies began to glut the ventilators.

Patients were screaming, doctors cursing, robots stamping around, and nurses trying to call each other.

The war ended when the troop commander saw Sergeant Lansdale, whom he himself had sent upstairs, leading a charge out of the women's quarters—directly at his own commander!

The officer kept his head.

He dropped to the floor and rolled sideways as the air chittered at him, the emanations of Lansdale's wirepoint killing all the tiny bacteria in the air. On his helmet phone he pushed the manual controls to TOP VOLUME and to NON-COMS ONLY, and he commanded, with a sudden flash of brilliant mother-wit, "Good job, Lansdale!"

Lansdale's voice came back as weak as if it had been off-planet, "We'll keep them out of this section yet, sir!"

The troop commander called back very loudly but calmly, not letting on that he thought his sergeant was psychotic.

"Easy now. Hold on. I'll be with you."

He changed to the other channel and said to his nearby men, "Cease fire. Take cover and wait."

A wild scream came to him from the phones.

It was Lansdale. "Sir! Sir! I'm fighting *you*, sir. I just caught on. It's getting me again. Watch out."

The buzz and burr of the weapons suddenly stopped.

The wild human uproar in the hospital continued.

A tall doctor, with the insignia of high seniority, came gently to the troop commander and said, "You can stand up and take your soldiers out now, young fellow. The fight was a mistake."

"I'm not under your orders," snapped the young officer. "I'm under the Lord Crudelta. He requisitioned this force from the Manhome Government. Who are you?"

"You may salute me, captain," said the doctor. "I am Colonel General Vomact of the Earth Medical Reserve. But you had better not wait for the Lord Crudelta."

"But *where* is he?"

"In my bed," said Vomact.

"Your *bed*?" cried the young officer in complete amazement.

"In bed. Doped to the teeth. I fixed him up. He was excited. Take your men out. We'll treat the wounded on the lawn. You can see the dead in the refrigerators downstairs in a few minutes, except for the ones that went smoky from direct hits."

"But the fight . . . ?"

"A mistake, young man, or else—"

"Or else what?" shouted the young officer, horrified at the utter mess of his own combat experience.

"Or else a weapon no man has ever seen before. Your troops fought each other. Your command was intercepted."

"I could see that," snapped the officer, "as soon as I saw Lansdale coming at me."

"But do you know what took him over?" said Vomact gently, while taking the officer by the arm and beginning to lead him out of the hospital. The captain went willingly, not noticing where he was going, so eagerly did he watch for the other man's words.

"I think I know," said Vomact. "Another man's dreams. Dreams which have learned how to turn themselves into electricity or plastic or stone. Or anything else. Dreams coming to us out of space three."

The young officer nodded dumbly. This was too much. "Space three?" he murmured. It was like being told that the really alien invaders, whom men had been expecting for thirteen thousand years and had never met, were waiting for him on the grass. Until now space three had been a mathematical idea, a romancer's daydream, but not a fact.

The sir and doctor Vomact did not even ask the young officer. He brushed the young man gently at the nape of the neck and shot him through with tranquilizer. Vomact then led him out to the grass. The young captain stood alone and whistled happily at the stars in the sky. Behind him, his sergeants and corporals were sorting out the survivors and getting treatment for the wounded.

The Two Minutes' War was over.

Rambo had stopped dreaming that his Elizabeth was in danger. He had recognized, even in his deep sick sleep, that the tramping in the corridor was the movement of armed men. His mind had set up defenses to protect Elizabeth. He took over command of the forward troops and set them to stopping the main body. The powers which space$_3$ had worked into him made this easy for him to do, even though he did not know that he was doing it.

"How many dead?" said Vomact to Grosbeck and Timofeyev.

"About two hundred."

"And how many irrevocable dead?"

"The ones that got turned into smoke. A dozen, maybe fourteen. The other dead can be fixed up, but most of them will have to get new personality prints."

"Do you know what happened?" asked Vomact.

"No, Sir and Doctor," they both chorused.

"I do. I think I do. No, I *know* I do. It's the wildest story in the history of man. Our patient did it—Rambo. He took over the troops and set them against each other. That Lord of the Instrumentality who came charging in—Crudelta. I've known him for a long long time. He's behind this case. He thought that troops would help, not sensing that troops would invite attack upon themselves. And there is something else."

"Yes?" they said, in unison.

"Rambo's woman—the one he's looking for. She must be here."

"Why?" asked Timofeyev.

"Because *he's* here."

"You're assuming that he came here because of his own will, Sir and Doctor."

Vomact smiled the wise crafty smile of his family; it was almost a trademark of the Vomact house.

"I am assuming all the things which I cannot otherwise prove.

"First, I assume that he came here naked out of space itself, driven by some kind of force of which we cannot even guess.

"Second, I assume he came *here* because he wanted something. A woman named Elizabeth, who must already be here. In a moment we can go inventory all our Elizabeths.

"Third, I assume that the Lord Crudelta knew something about it. He has led troops into the building. He began raving when he saw me. I know hysterical fatigue, as do you, my brothers, so I condamined him for a night's sleep.

"Fourth, let's leave our man alone. There'll be hearings and trials enough, Space knows, when all these events get scrambled out."

Vomact was right.

He usually was.

Trials did follow.

It was lucky that Old Earth no longer permitted newspapers or television news. The population would have been frothed up to riot and terror if they had ever found out what happened at the Old Main Hospital just to the west of Meeya Meefla.

Twenty-one days later, Vomact, Timofeyev, and Grosbeck were summoned to the trial of the Lord Crudelta. A full panel of seven Lords of the Instrumentality were there to give Crudelta an ample hearing and, if required, a sudden death. The doctors were present both as doctors for Elizabeth and Rambo and as witnesses for the Investigating Lord.

Elizabeth, fresh up from being dead, was as beautiful as a newborn baby in exquisite, adult feminine form. Rambo could not take his eyes off her, but a look of bewilderment went over his face every time she gave him a friendly, calm remote little smile. (She had been told that she was his girl, and she was prepared to believe it, but she had no memory of him or of anything else more than sixty hours back, when speech had been reinstalled in her mind; and he, for his part, was still thick of speech and subject to strains which the doctors could not quite figure out.)

The Investigating Lord was a man named Starmount.

He asked the panel to rise.

They did so.

He faced the Lord Crudelta with great solemnity. "You are obliged, my Lord Crudelta, to speak quickly and clearly to this court."

"Yes, my Lord," he answered.

"We have the summary power."

"You have the summary power. I recognize it."

"You will tell the truth or else you will lie."

"I shall tell the truth or I will lie."

"You may lie, if you wish, about matters of fact and opinion, but you will in no case lie about human relationships. If you do lie, nevertheless, you will ask that your name be entered in the Roster of Dishonor."

"I understand the panel and the rights of this panel. I will lie if I wish—though I don't think I will need to do so"—and here Crudelta flashed a weary intelligent smile at all of them—"but I will not lie about matters of relationships. If I do, I will ask for dishonor."

"You have yourself been well trained as a Lord of the Instrumentality?"

"I have been so trained and I love the Instrumentality well. In fact, I am myself the Instrumentality, as are you, and as are all the honorable Lords beside you. I shall behave well, for as long as I live this afternoon."

"Do you credit him, my Lords?" asked Starmount.

The members of the panel nodded their mitered heads. They had dressed ceremonially for the occasion.

"Do you have a relationship to the woman Elizabeth?"

The members of the trial panel caught their breath as they saw Crudelta turn white: "My Lords!" he cried, and answered no further.

"It is the custom," said Starmount firmly, "that you answer promptly or that you die."

The Lord Crudelta got control of himself. "I am answering. I did not know who she was, except for the fact that Rambo loved her. I sent her to Earth from Earth Four, where I then was. Then I told Rambo that she had been murdered and hung desperately at the edge of death, wanting only his help to return to the green fields of life."

Said Starmount, "Was that the truth?"

"My Lord and Lords, it was a lie."

"Why did you tell it?"

"To induce rage in Rambo and to give him an overriding reason for wanting to come to Earth faster than any man has ever come before."

"A-a-ah! A-a-ah!" Two wild cries came from Rambo, more like the call of an animal than like the sound of a man.

Vomact looked at his patient, felt himself beginning to growl with a deep internal rage. Rambo's powers, generated in the depths of space$_3$, had begun to operate again. Vomact made a sign. The robot behind Rambo had been coded to keep Rambo calm. Though the robot had been enameled to look like a white gleaming hospital orderly, he was actually a police robot of high powers, built up with an electronic cortex based on the frozen midbrain of an old wolf. (A wolf was a rare animal, something like a dog.) The robot touched Rambo, who dropped off to sleep. Doctor Vomact felt the anger in his own mind fade away. He lifted his hand gently; the robot caught the signal and stopped applying the narcoleptic radiation. Rambo slept normally; Elizabeth looked worriedly at the man whom she had been told was her own.

The Lords turned back from the glances at Rambo.

Said Starmount, icily, "And why did you do that?"

"Because I wanted him to travel through space three."

"Why?"

"To show it could be done."

"And do you, my Lord Crudelta, affirm that this man has in fact traveled through space three?"

"I do."

"Are you lying?"

"I have the right to lie, but I have no wish to do so. In the name of the Instrumentality itself, I tell you that this is the truth."

The panel members gasped. Now there was no way out. Either the Lord Crudelta was telling the truth, *which meant that all former times had come to an end and that a new age had begun for all the kinds of mankind*, or else he was lying in the face of the most powerful form of affirmation which any of them knew.

Even Starmount himself took a different tone. His teasing, restless, intelligent voice took on a new timbre of kindness.

"You do therefore assert that this man has come back from outside our galaxy with nothing more than his own natural skin to cover him? No instruments? No power?"

"I did not say that," said Crudelta. "Other people have begun to pretend I used such words. I tell you, my Lords, that I planoformed for twelve consecutive Earth days and nights. Some of you may remember where Outpost Baiter Gator is. Well, I had a good Go-captain, and he took me four long jumps beyond there, out into intergalactic space. I left this man there. When I reached Earth, he had been here twelve days, more or less. I have assumed, therefore, that his trip was more or less instantaneous. I was on my way back to Baiter Gator, counting by Earth time, when the doctor here found this man on the grass outside the hospital."

Vomact raised his hand. The Lord Starmount gave him the right to speak. "My sirs and Lords, we did not find this man on the grass. The robots did, and made a record. But even the robots did not see or photograph his arrival."

"We know that," said Starmount angrily, "and we know that we have been told that nothing came to Earth by any means whatever, in that particular quarter hour. Go on, my Lord Crudelta. What relation are you to Rambo?"

"He is my victim."

"Explain yourself!"

"I computed him out. I asked the machines where I would be most apt to find a man with a tremendous lot of rage in him, and was informed that on Earth Four the rage level had been left high because that particular planet had a considerable need for explorers and adventurers, in whom rage was a strong survival trait. When I got to Earth Four, I commanded the authorities to find out which border cases had exceeded the limits of allowable rage. They gave me four men. One was much too large. Two were old. This man was the only candidate for my experiment. I chose him."

"What did you tell him?"

"Tell him? I told him his sweetheart was dead or dying."

"No, no," said Starmount. "Not at the moment of crisis. What did you tell him to make him cooperate in the first place?"

"I told him," said the Lord Crudelta evenly, "that I was myself a Lord of the Instrumentality and that I would kill him myself if he did not obey, and obey promptly."

"And under what custom or law did you act?"

"Reserved material," said the Lord Crudelta promptly. "There are telepaths here who are not a part of the Instrumentality. I beg leave to defer until we have a shielded place."

Several members of the panel nodded and Starmount agreed with them. He changed the line of questioning.

"You forced this man, therefore, to do something which he did not wish to do?"

"That is right," said the Lord Crudelta.

"Why didn't you go yourself, if it is that dangerous?"

"My Lords and honorables, it was the nature of the experiment that the experimenter himself should not be expended in the first try. Artyr Rambo has indeed traveled through space three. I shall follow him myself, in due course." (How the Lord Crudelta did do so is another tale, told about another time.) "If I had gone and if I had been lost, that would have been the end of the space-three trials. At least for our time."

"Tell us the exact circumstances under which you last saw Artyr Rambo before you met after the battle in the Old Main Hospital."

"We had put him in a rocket of the most ancient style. We also wrote writing on the outside of it, just the way the Ancients did when they first ventured into space. Ah, that was a beautiful piece of engineering and archeology! We copied everything right down to the correct models of fourteen thousand years ago, when the Paroskii and Murkins were racing each other into space. The rocket was white, with a red and white gantry beside it. The letters IOM were on the rocket, not that the words mattered. The rocket has gone into nowhere, but the passenger sits here. It rose on a stool of fire. The stool became a column. Then the landing field disappeared."

"And the landing field," said Starmount quietly, "what was that?"

"A modified planoform ship. We have had ships go milky in space because they faded molecule by molecule. We have had others disappear utterly. The engineers had changed this around. We took out all the machinery needed for circumnavigation, for survival, or for comfort. The landing field was to last three or four seconds, no more. Instead, we put in fourteen planoform devices, all operating in tandem, so that the ship would do what other ships do when they planoform—namely, drop one of our familiar dimensions and pick up a new dimension from some unknown category of space—but do it with such force as to get out of what people call space two and move over into space three."

"And space three, what did you expect of that?"

"I thought that it was universal, and instantaneous, in relation to our universe. That everything was equally distant from everything else. That Rambo, wanting to see his girl again, would move in a thousandth of a second from the empty space beyond Outpost Baiter Gator into the hospital where she was."

"And, my Lord Crudelta, what made you think so?"

"A hunch, my Lord, for which you are welcome to kill me."

Starmount turned to the panel. "I suspect, my Lords, that you are more likely to doom him to long life, great responsibility, immense rewards, and the fatigue of being his own difficult and complicated self."

The miters moved gently and the members of the panel rose.

"You, my Lord Crudelta, will sleep till the trial is finished."

A robot stroked him and he fell asleep.

"Next witness," said the Lord Starmount, "in five minutes."

Vomact tried to keep Rambo from being heard as a witness. He argued fiercely with the Lord Starmount in the intermission. "You Lords have shot up my hospital, abducted two of my patients and now you are going to torment both Rambo and Elizabeth. Can't you leave them alone? Rambo is in no condition to give coherent answers and Elizabeth may be damaged if she sees him suffer."

The Lord Starmount said to him, "You have your rules, doctor, and we have ours. This trial is being recorded, inch by inch and moment by moment. Nothing is going to be done to Rambo unless we find that he has planet-killing powers. If that is true, of course, we will ask you to take him back to the hospital and to put him to death very pleasantly. But I don't think it will happen. We want his story so that we can judge my colleague Crudelta. Do you think that the Instrumentality would survive if it did not have fierce internal discipline?"

Vomact nodded sadly; he went back to Grosbeck and Timofeyev, murmuring sadly to them, "Rambo's in for it. There's nothing we could do."

The panel reassembled. They put on their judicial miters. The lights of the room darkened and the weird blue light of justice was turned on.

The robot orderly helped Rambo to the witness chair.

"You are obliged," said Starmount, "to speak quickly and clearly to this court."

"You're not Elizabeth," said Rambo.

"I am the Lord Starmount," said the Investigating Lord, quickly deciding to dispense with formalities. "Do you know me?"

"No," said Rambo.

"Do you know where you are?"

"Earth," said Rambo.

"Do you wish to lie or to tell the truth?"

"A lie," said Rambo, "is the only truth which men can share with each other, so I will tell you lies, the way we always do."

"Can you report your trip?"

"No."

"Why not, citizen Rambo?"

"Words won't describe it."

"Do you remember your trip?"

"Do you remember your pulse of two minutes ago?" countered Rambo.

"I am not playing with you," said Starmount. "We think you have been in space three and we want you to testify about the Lord Crudelta."

"Oh!" said Rambo. "I don't like him. I never did like him."

"Will you nevertheless try to tell us what happened to you?"

"Should I, Elizabeth?" asked Rambo of the girl, who sat in the audience.

She did not stammer. "Yes," she said, in a clear voice which rang through the big room. "Tell them, so that we can find our lives again."

"I will tell you," said Rambo.

"When did you last see the Lord Crudelta?"

"When I was stripped and fitted to the rocket, four jumps out beyond Outpost

Baiter Gator. He was on the ground. He waved good-bye to me."

"And then what happened?"

"The rocket rose. It felt very strange, like no craft I had ever been in before. I weighed many, many gravities."

"And then?"

"The engines went on. I was thrown out of space itself."

"What did it seem like?"

"Behind me I left the working ships, the cloth, and the food which goes through space. I went down rivers which did not exist. I felt people around me though I could not see them, red people shooting arrows at live bodies."

"*Where* were you?" asked a panel member.

"In the wintertime where there is no summer. In an emptiness like a child's mind. In peninsulas which had torn loose from the land. And I *was* the ship."

"You were what?" asked the same panel member.

"The rocket nose. The cone. The boat. I was drunk. It was drunk. I was the drunkboat myself," said Rambo.

"And where did you go?" resumed Starmount.

"Where crazy lanterns stared with idiot eyes. Where the waves washed back and forth with the dead of all the ages. Where the stars became a pool, and I swam in it. Where blue turns to liquor, stronger than alcohol, wilder than music, fermented with the *red red reds* of love. I saw all the things that men have ever thought they saw, but it was me who really saw them. I've heard phosphorescence singing and tides that seemed like crazy cattle clawing their way out of the ocean, their hooves beating the reefs. You will not believe me, but I found Floridas wilder than this, where the flowers had human skins and eyes like big cats."

"What are you talking about?" asked the Lord Starmount.

"What I found in space three," snapped Artyr Rambo. "Believe it or not. This is what I now remember. Maybe it's a dream, but it's all I have. It was years and years and it was the blink of an eye. I dreamed green nights. I felt places where the whole horizon became one big waterfall. The boat that was me met children and I showed them El Dorado, where the gold men live. The people drowned in space washed gently past me. I was a boat where all the lost spaceships lay drowned and still. Seahorses which were not real ran beside me. The summer month came and hammered down the sun. I went past archipelagoes of stars, where the delirious skies opened up for wanderers. I cried for me. I wept for man. I wanted to be the drunkboat sinking. I sank. I fell. It seemed to me that the grass was a lake, where a sad child, on hands and knees, sailed a toy boat as fragile as a butterfly in spring. I can't forget the pride of unremembered flags, the arrogance of prisons which I suspected, the swimming of the businessmen! Then I was on the grass."

"This may have scientific value," said the Lord Starmount, "but it is not of judicial importance. Do you have any comment on what you did during the battle in the hospital?"

Rambo was quick and looked sane: "What I did, I did not do. What I did not do, I cannot tell. Let me go, because I am tired of you and space, big men and big things. Let me sleep and let me get well."

Starmount lifted his hand for silence.

The panel members stared at him.

Only the few telepaths present knew that they had all said, "*Aye. Let the man go.*

Let the girl go. Let the doctors go. But bring back the Lord Crudelta later on. He has many troubles ahead of him, and we wish to add to them."

Between the Instrumentality, the Manhome Government and the authorities at the Old Main Hospital, everyone wished to give Rambo and Elizabeth happiness.

As Rambo got well, much of his Earth Four memory returned. The trip faded from his mind.

When he came to know Elizabeth, he hated the girl.

This was not his girl—his bold, saucy Elizabeth of the markets and the valleys, of the snowy hills and the long boat rides. This was somebody meek, sweet, sad, and hopelessly loving.

Vomact cured that.

He sent Rambo to the Pleasure City of the Herperides, where bold and talkative women pursued him because he was rich and famous.

In a few weeks—a very few indeed—he wanted *his* Elizabeth, this strange shy girl who had been cooked back from the dead while he rode space with his own fragile bones.

"Tell the truth, darling." He spoke to her once gravely and seriously. "The Lord Crudelta did not arrange the accident which killed you?"

"They say he wasn't there," said Elizabeth. "They say it was an actual accident. I don't know. I will never know."

"It doesn't matter now," said Rambo. "Crudelta's off among the stars, looking for trouble and finding it. We have our bungalow, and our waterfall, and each other."

"Yes, my darling," she said, "each other. And no fantastic Floridas for us."

He blinked at this reference to the past, but he said nothing. A man who has been through space$_3$ needs very little in life, outside of *not* going back to space$_3$. Sometimes he dreamed he was the rocket again, the old rocket taking off on an impossible trip. Let other men follow! he thought, let other men go! I have Elizabeth and I am here.

Philip K. Dick, just before his tragic death in 1983, was gaining wide recognition as one of the greatest of all science-fiction writers. The film Bladerunner, *based on his* Do Androids Dream of Electric Sheep?, *has helped to spread his fame further. Dick is most renowned for such novels as* Ubik, The Man in the High Castle, The Three Stigmata of Palmer Eldritch, *and* Flow My Tears, the Policeman Said. *His novel* We Can Build You *was serialized in* Amazing® Stories *under the title* A. Lincoln, Simulacrum *(1969). This story was published in December 1963, and is the basis of his "Palmer Eldtritch" novel.*

THE DAYS OF PERKY PAT
by Philip K. Dick

At ten in the morning a terrific horn, familiar to him, hooted Sam Regan out of his sleep, and he cursed the careboy upstairs; he knew the racket was deliberate. The careboy, circling, wanted to be certain that flukers—and not merely wild animals—got the care parcels that were to be dropped.

We'll get them, we'll get them, Sam Regan said to himself as he zipped his dustproof overalls, put his feet into boots and then grumpily sauntered as slowly as possible toward the ramp. Several other flukers joined him, all showing similar irritation.

"He's early today," Tod Morrison complained. "And I'll bet it's all staples, sugar and flour and lard—nothing interesting like, say, candy."

"We ought to be grateful," Norman Schein said.

"Grateful!" Tod halted to stare at him. "GRATEFUL?"

"Yes," Schein said. "What do you think we'd be eating without them? If they hadn't seen the clouds ten years ago."

"Well," Tod said sullenly, "I just don't like them to come *early*; I actually don't mind their coming, as such."

As he put his shoulders against the lid at the top of the ramp, Schein said genially, "That's mighty tolerant of you, Tod boy. I'm sure the careboys would be pleased to hear your sentiments."

Of the three of them, Sam Regan was the last to reach the surface; he did not like the upstairs at all, and he did not care who knew it. And anyhow, no one could compel him to leave the safety of the Pinole Fluke-pit; it was entirely his business, and he noted now that a number of his fellow flukers had elected to remain below in their quarters, confident that those who did answer the horn would bring them back something.

"It's bright," Tod murmured, blinking in the sun.

The care ship sparkled close overhead, set against the gray sky as if hanging from an uneasy thread. Good pilot, this drop, Tod decided. He, or rather *it*, just lazily handles it, in no hurry. Tod waved at the care ship, and once more the huge horn burst out its din, making him clap his hands to his ears. Hey, a joke's a joke, he said to himself. And then the horn ceased; the careboy had relented.

"Wave to him to drop," Norm Schein said to Tod. "You've got the wigwag."

"Sure," Tod said, and began laboriously flapping the red flag, which the Martian creatures had long ago provided, back and forth, back and forth.

A projectile slid from the underpart of the ship, tossed out stabilizers, spiraled toward the ground.

"Sheoot," Sam Regan said with disgust. "It *is* staples; they don't have the parachute." He turned away, not interested.

How miserable the upstairs looks today, he thought, as he surveyed the scene surrounding him. There, to the right, the uncompleted house which someone—not far from their pit—had begun to build out of lumber salvaged from Vallejo, ten miles to the north. Animals or radiation dust had gotten the builder, and so his work remained where it was; it would never be put to use. And, Sam Regan saw, an unusually heavy precipitate had formed since last he had been up here, Thursday morning or perhaps Friday; he had lost exact track. The darn dust, he thought. Just rocks, pieces of rubble, and the dust. World's becoming a dusty object with no one to whisk it off regularly. How about you? he asked silently of the Martian careboy flying in a slow circle overhead. Isn't your technology limitless? Can't you appear some morning with a dust rag a million miles in surface area and restore our planet to pristine newness?

Or rather, he thought, to pristine *oldness*, the way it was in the "ol-days," as the children called it. We'd like that. While you're looking for something to give us in the way of further aid, try that.

The careboy circled once more, searching for sign of writing in the dust: a message from the flukers below. I'll write that, Sam thought. BRING DUST RAG, RESTORE OUR CIVILIZATION. Okay, careboy?

All at once the care ship shot off, no doubt on its way back home to its base on Luna or perhaps all the way to Mars.

From the open fluke-pit hole, up which the three of them had come, a further head poked, a woman's. Jean Regan, Sam's wife, appeared, shielded by a bonnet against the gray, blinding sun, frowning and saying, "Anything important? Anything *new*?"

"Fraid not," Sam said. The care-parcel projectile had landed and he walked toward it, scuffling his boots in the dust. The hull of the projectile had cracked open from the impact and he could see the canisters already. It looked to be five thousand pounds of salt . . . might as well leave it up here so the animals won't starve, he decided. He felt despondent.

How peculiarly anxious the careboys were. Concerned all the time that the mainstays of existence be ferried from their own planet to Earth. They must think we eat all day long, Sam thought. My god . . . the pit was filled to capacity with stored foods. But of course it had been one of the smallest public shelters in Northern California.

"Hey," Schein said, stooping down by the projectile and peering into the crack opened along its side. "I believe I see something we can use." He found a rusted metal pole—once it had helped reinforce the concrete side of an ol-days public building—and poked at the projectile, stirring its release mechanism into action. The mechanism, triggered off, popped the rear half of the projectile open . . . and there lay the contents.

"Looks like radios in that box," Tod said. "Transistor radios." Thoughtfully stroking his short black beard, he said, "Maybe we can use them for something new in our layouts."

"Mine's already got a radio," Schein pointed out.

"Well, build an electronic self-directing lawn mower with the parts," Tod said. "You don't have that, do you?" He knew the Scheins' Perky Pat layout fairly well; the two couples, he and his wife with Schein and his, had played together a good deal, being almost evenly matched.

Sam Regan said, "Dibs on the radios, because I can use them." His layout lacked the automatic garage-door opener that both Schein and Tod had; he was considerably behind them.

"Let's get to work," Schein agreed. "We'll leave the staples here and just cart back the radios. If anybody wants the staples, let them come here and get them. Before the do-cats do."

Nodding, the other two men fell to the job of carting the useful contents of the projectile to the entrance of their fluke-pit ramp. For use in their precious, elaborate Perky Pat layouts.

Seated cross-legged with his whetstone, Timothy Schein, ten years old and aware of his many responsibilities, sharpened his knife, slowly and expertly. Meanwhile, disturbing him, his mother and father quarreled with Mr. and Mrs. Morrison, on the far side of the partition. They were playing Perky Pat again. As usual.

How many times today do they have to play that dumb game? Timothy asked himself. Forever, I guess. He could see nothing in it, but his parents played on anyhow. And they weren't the only ones; he knew from what other kids said, even from other fluke-pits, that their parents, too, played Perky Pat most of the day and sometimes even on into the night.

His mother said loudly, "Perky Pat's going to the grocery store and it's got one of those electric eyes that opens the door. Look." A pause. "See, it opened for her, and now she's inside."

"She pushes a cart," Timothy's dad added, in support.

"No, she doesn't," Mrs. Morrison contradicted. "That's wrong. She gives her list to the grocer and he fills it."

"That's only in little neighborhood stores," his mother explained. "And this is a supermarket, you can tell because of the electric-eye door."

"I'm sure all grocery stores had electric-eye doors," Mrs. Morrison said stubbornly, and her husband chimed in with his agreement. Now the voices rose in anger; another squabble had broken out. As usual.

Aw, cung to them, Timothy said to himself, using the strongest word which he and his friends knew. What's a supermarket anyhow? He tested the blade of his knife—he had made it himself, originally, out of a heavy metal pan—and then dropped to his feet. A moment later he had sprinted silently down the hall and was rapping his special rap on the door of the Chamberlains' quarters.

Fred, also ten years old, answered. "Hi. Ready to go? I see you got that ol' knife of yours all sharpened; what do you think we'll catch?"

"Not a do-cat," Timothy said. "A lot better than that; I'm tired of eating do-cat. Too peppery."

"Your parents playing Perky Pat?"

"Yeah."

Fred said, "My mom and dad have been gone for a long time, off playing with the Benteleys." He glanced sideways at Timothy, and in an instant they had shared their mute disappointment regarding their parents. Gosh, and maybe the darn game was all over the world, by now; that would not have surprised either of them.

"How come your parents play it?" Timothy asked.

"Same reason yours do," Fred said.

Hesitating, Timothy said, "Well, why? I don't know why they do; I'm asking you, can't you say?"

"It's because—" Fred broke off. "Ask them. Come on; let's get upstairs and start hunting." His eyes shone. "Let's see what we can catch and kill today."

Shortly, they had ascended the ramp, popped open the lid, and were crouching amidst the dust and rocks, searching the horizon. Timothy's heart pounded; this moment always overwhelmed him, the first instant of reaching the upstairs. The thrilling initial sight of the expanse. Because it was never the same. The dust heavier today, had a darker gray color to it than before, it seemed denser, more mysterious.

Here and there, covered by many layers of dust, lay parcels dropped from past relief ships—dropped and left to deteriorate. Never to be claimed. And, Timothy saw, an additional new projectile which had arrived that morning. Most of its cargo could be seen within; the grownups had not had any use for the majority of the contents, today.

"Look," Fred said softly.

Two do-cats—mutant dogs or cats; no one knew for sure—could be seen, lightly sniffing at the projectile. Attracted by the unclaimed contents.

"We don't want them," Timothy said.

"That one's sure nice and fat," Fred said longingly. But it was Timothy that had the knife; all he himself had was a string with a metal bolt on the end, bull-roarer that could kill a bird or a small animal at a distance—but useless against a do-cat, which generally weighed fifteen to twenty pounds and sometimes even more.

High up in the sky a dot moved at immense speed, and Timothy knew that it was a care ship heading for another fluke-pit, bringing supplies to it. Sure are busy, he thought to himself. Those careboys always coming and going; they never stop, because if they did, the grownups would die. Wouldn't that be too bad? he thought ironically. Sure be sad.

Fred said, "Wave to it and maybe it'll drop something." He grinned at Timothy, and then they both broke out laughing.

"Sure," Timothy said. "Let's see; what do I want?" Again the two of them laughed at the idea of them wanting something. The two boys had the entire upstairs, as far as the eye could see . . . they had even more than the careboys had, and that was plenty, more than plenty.

"Do you think they know," Fred said, "that our parents play Perky Pat with furniture made out of what they drop? I bet they don't know about Perky Pat; they never have seen a Perky Pat doll, and if they did they'd be really mad."

"You're right," Timothy said. "They'd be so sore they'd probably stop dropping stuff." He glanced at Fred, catching his eyes.

"Aw no," Fred said. "We shouldn't tell them; your dad would beat you again if you did that, and probably me, too."

Even so, it was an interesting idea. He could imagine first the surprise and then the anger of the careboys; it would be fun to see that, see the reaction of the eight-legged Martian creatures who had so much charity inside their warty bodies, the cephalopodic univalve mollusklike organisms who had voluntarily taken it upon themselves to supply succor to the waning remnants of the human race—this was how they got paid back for their charity, this utterly wasteful, stupid purpose to which their goods were being put. This stupid Perky Pat game that all the adults played.

And anyhow it would be very hard to tell them; there was almost no communication between humans and careboys. They were too different. Acts, deeds, could be done, conveying something . . . but not mere words, not mere *signs*. And anyhow—

A great brown rabbit bounded by to the right, past the half-completed house. Timothy whipped out his knife. "Oh boy!" he said aloud in excitement. "Let's go!" He set off across the rubbly ground, Fred a little behind him. Gradually they gained on the rabbit; swift running came easy to the two boys: they had done much practicing.

"Throw the knife!" Fred panted, and Timothy, skidding to a halt, raised his right arm, paused to take aim, and then hurled the sharpened, weighted knife. His most valuable, self-made possession.

It cleaved the rabbit straight through its vitals. The rabbit tumbled, slid, raising a cloud of dust.

"I bet we can get a dollar for that!" Fred exclaimed, leaping up and down. "The hide alone—I bet we can get fifty cents just for the darn hide!"

Together, they hurried toward the dead rabbit, wanting to get there before a red-tailed hawk or a day-owl swooped on it from the gray sky above.

Bending, Norman Schein picked up his Perky Pat doll and said sullenly, "I'm quitting; I don't want to play anymore."

Distressed, his wife protested, "But we've got Perky Pat all the way downtown in her new Ford hardtop convertible and parked and a dime in the meter and she's shopped and now she's in the analyst's office reading *Fortune*—we're way ahead of the Morrisons! Why do you want to quit, Norm?"

"We just don't agree," Norman grumbled. "You say analysts charged twenty dollars an hour and I distinctly remember them charging only ten; nobody could charge twenty. So you're penalizing our side, and for what! The Morrisons agree it was only ten. Don't you?" he said to Mr. and Mrs. Morrison, who squatted on the far side of the layout which combined both couples' Perky Pat sets.

Helen Morrison said to her husband, "You went to the analyst more than I did; are you sure he charged only ten?"

"Well, I went mostly to group therapy," Tom said. "At Berkeley State Mental Hygiene Clinic, and they charged according to your ability to pay. And Perky Pat is at a *private* psychoanalyst."

"We'll have to ask someone else," Helen said to Norman Schein. "I guess all we can do now this minute is suspend the game." He found himself being glared at by her, too, now, because by his insistence on that one point he had put an end to their game for the whole afternoon.

"Shall we leave it all set up?" Fran Schein asked. "We might as well; maybe we can finish tonight after dinner."

Norman Schein gazed down at their combined layout, the swanky shops, the well-lit streets with the parked new-model cars, all of them shiny, the split-level house it-self, where Perky Pat lived and where she entertained Leonard, her boy friend. It was the *house* that he perpetually yearned for; the house was the real focus of the layouts, however much they might otherwise differ.

Perky Pat's wardrobe, for instance, there in the closet of the house, the big bed-room closet. Her capri pants, her white cotton short-shorts, her two-piece polka-dot swimsuit, her fuzzy sweaters . . . and there, in her bedroom, her hi-fi set, her collec-tion of long-playing records . . .

It had been this way, once, really been like this in the ol-days. Norm Schein could remember his own LP record collection, and he once had clothes almost as swanky as Perky Pat's boy friend Leonard, cashmere jackets and tweed suits and Italian sport-shirts and shoes made in England. He hadn't owned a Jaguar XKE sports car, like Leonard did, but he had owned a fine-looking old 1963 Mercedes-Benz, which he had used to drive to work.

We lived then, Norm Schein said to himself, like Perky Pat and Leonard do now. This is how it actually was.

To his wife he said, pointing to the clock radio which Perky Pat kept beside her bed, "Remember our G.E. clock radio? How it used to wake us up in the morning with classical music from that FM station, KSFR? The 'Wolfgangers,' the program was called. From six A.M. to nine every morning."

"Yes," Fran said, nodding soberly. "And you used to get up before me; I knew I should have gotten up and fixed bacon and hot coffee for you, but it was so much fun just indulging myself, not stirring for half an hour longer, until the kids woke up."

"Woke up, hell; they were awake before we were," Norm said. "Don't you re-member? They were in the back watching *The Three Stooges* on TV until eight. Then I got up and fixed hot cereal for them, and then I went to my job at Ampex down at Redwood City."

"Oh yes," Fran said. "The TV." Their Perky Pat did not have a TV set; they had lost it to the Regans in a game a week ago, and Norm had not yet been able to fashion another one realistic-looking enough to substitute. So, in a game, they pretended now that "the TV-repairman had come for it." That was how they explained their Perky Pat not having something she really would have had.

Norm thought, Playing this game . . . it's like being back there, back in the world before the war. That's why we play it, I suppose. He felt shame, but only fleetingly; the shame, almost at once, was replaced by a desire to play a little longer.

"Let's not quit," he said suddenly. "I'll agree the psychoanalyst would have charged Perky Pat twenty dollars. Okay?"

"Okay," both the Morrisons said together, and they settled back down once more to resume the game.

Tod Morrison had picked up their Perky Pat; he held it, stroking its blond hair—theirs was a blond, whereas the Scheins' was a brunette—and fiddling with the snaps of its skirt.

"Whatever are you doing?" his wife inquired.

"Nice skirt she has," Tod said. "You did a good job sewing it."

Norman said, "Ever know a girl, back in the ol-days, that looked like Perky Pat?"

"No," Tod Morrison said somberly. "Wish I had, though. I *saw* girls like Perky Pat, especially when I was living in Los Angeles during the Korean War. But I just could never manage to know them personally. And of course there were really terrific girl singers, like Peggy Lee and Julie London . . . they looked a lot like Perky Pat."

"Play," Fran said vigorously. And Norm, whose turn it was, picked up the spinner and spun.

"Eleven," he said. "That gets my Leonard out of the sports car repair garage and on his way to the race track." He moved the Leonard doll ahead.

Thoughtfully, Tod Morrison said, "You know, I was out the other day hauling in perishables which the careboys had dropped . . . Bill Ferner was there, and he told me something interesting. He met a fluker from a fluke-pit down where Oakland used to be. And at that fluke-pit you know what they play? Not Perky Pat. They never heard of Perky Pat."

"Well, what do they play, then?" Helen asked.

"They have another doll entirely." Frowning, Tod continued, "Bill says the Oakland fluker called it a Connie Companion doll. Ever heard of that?"

"A 'Connie Companion' doll," Fran said thoughtfully. "How strange. I wonder what she's like. Does she have a boy friend?"

"Oh sure," Tod said. "His name is Paul. Connie and Paul. You know, we ought to hike down there to that Oakland Fluke-pit one of these days and see what Connie and Paul look like and how they live. Maybe we could learn a few things to add to our own layouts."

Norm said, "Maybe we could play them."

Puzzled, Fran said, "Could a Perky Pat play a Connie Companion? Is that possible? I wonder what would happen."

There was no answer from any of the others. Because none of them knew.

As they skinned the rabbit, Fred said to Timothy, "Where did the name 'fluker' come from? It's sure an ugly word; why do they use it?"

"A fluker is a person who lived through the hydrogen war," Timothy explained. "You know, by a fluke. A fluke of fate. See? Because almost everyone was killed; there used to be thousands of people."

"But what's a 'fluke,' then? When you say a 'fluke of fate—' "

"A fluke is when fate has decided to spare you," Timothy said, and that was all he had to say on the subject. That was all he knew.

Fred said thoughtfully, "But you and I, we're not flukers because we weren't alive when the war broke out. We were born after."

"Right," Timothy said.

"So anybody who calls me a fluker," Fred said, "is going to get hit in the eye with my bull-roarer."

"And 'careboy,' " Timothy said, "that's a made-up word, too. It's from when stuff was dumped from jet planes and ships to people in a disaster area. They were called 'care parcels' because they came from people who cared."

"I know that," Fred said. "I didn't ask that."

"Well, I told you anyhow," Timothy said.

The two boys continued skinning the rabbit.

Jean Regan said to her husband, "Have you heard about the Connie Companion doll?" She glanced down the long rough-board table to make sure none of the other families were listening. "Sam," she said, "I heard it from Helen Morrison; she heard it from Tod and he heard it from Bill Ferner, I think. So it's probably true."

"What's true?" Sam asked.

"That in the Oakland Fluke-pit they don't have Perky Pat; they have Connie Companion . . . and it occurred to me that maybe some of this—you know, this sort of emptiness, this boredom we feel now and then—maybe if we saw the Connie Companion doll and how she lives, maybe we could add enough to our own layout to—" She paused, reflecting. "To make it more complete."

"I don't care for the name," Sam Regan said. "Connie Companion; it sounds cheap." He spooned up some of the plain, utilitarian grain-mash which the careboys had been dropping, of late. And, as he ate a mouthful, he thought, I'll bet Connie Companion doesn't eat slop like this; I'll bet she eats cheeseburgers with all the trimmings, at a high-type drive-in.

"Could we make a trek down there?" Jean asked.

"To Oakland Fluke-pit?" Sam stared at her. "It's *fifteen miles*, all the way on the other side of the Berkeley Fluke-pit!"

"But this is important," Jean said stubbornly. "And Bill says that a fluker from Oakland came all the way up here, in a search of electronic parts or something . . . so if he can do it, we can. We've got the dust suits they dropped us. I know we could do it."

Little Timothy Schein, sitting with his family, had overheard her; now he spoke up. "Mrs. Regan, Fred Chamberlain and I, we could trek down that far, if you pay us. What do you say?" He nudged Fred, who sat beside him. "Couldn't we? For maybe five dollars."

Fred, his face serious, turned to Mrs. Regan and said, "We could get you a Connie Companion doll. For five dollars for *each* of us."

"Good grief," Jean Regan said, outraged. And dropped the subject.

But later, after dinner, she brought it up again when she and Sam were alone in their quarters.

"Sam, I've got to see it," she burst out. Sam, in a galvanized tub, was taking his weekly bath, so he had to listen to her. "Now that we know it exists we have to play against someone at the Oakland Fluke-pit; at least we can do that. Can't we? Please." She paced back and forth in the small room, her hands clasped tensely. "Connie Companion may have a Standard Station and an airport terminal with jet landing strip and color TV and a French restaurant where they serve escargots, like the one you and I went to when we were first married . . . I just have to see her layout."

"I don't know," Sam said hesitantly. "There's something about Connie Companion doll that—makes me uneasy."

"What could it possibly be?"

"I don't know."

Jean said bitterly, "It's because you know her layout is so much better than ours and she's so much more than Perky Pat."

"Maybe that's it," Sam murmured.

"If you don't go, if you don't try to make contact with them down at the Oakland Fluke-pit, someone else will—someone with more ambition will get ahead of you. Like Norman Schein. He's not afraid the way you are."

Sam said nothing; he continued with his bath. But his hands shook.

A careboy had recently dropped complicated pieces of machinery which were, evidently, a form of mechanical computer. For several weeks the computers—if that was what they were—had sat about the pit in their cartons, unused, but now Norman Schein was finding something to do with one. At the moment he was busy adapting some of its gears, the smallest ones, to form a garbage disposal unit for his Perky Pat's kitchen.

Using the tiny special tools—which were necessary in fashioning environmental items for Perky Pat—he was busy at his hobby bench. Thoroughly engrossed in what he was doing, he all at once realized that Fran was standing directly behind him, watching.

"I get nervous when I'm watched," Norm said, holding a tiny gear with a pair of tweezers.

"Listen," Fran said, "I've thought of something. Does this suggest anything to you?" She placed before him one of the transistor radios which had been dropped the day before.

"It suggests that garage-door opener already thought of," Norm said irritably. He continued with his work, expertly fitting the miniature pieces together in the sink drain of Pat's kitchen; such delicate work demanded maximum concentration.

Fran said, "It suggests that there must be radio *transmitters* on Earth somewhere, or the careboys wouldn't have dropped these."

"So?" Norm said, uninterested.

"Maybe our mayor has one," Fran said. "Maybe there's one right here in our own pit, and we could use it to call the Oakland Fluke-pit. Representatives from there could meet us halfway . . . say at the Berkeley Fluke-pit. And we could play there. So we wouldn't have that long fifteen-mile trip."

Norman hesitated in his work; he set his tweezers down and said slowly, "I think you're possibly right." But if their Mayor Hooker Glebe had a radio transmitter, would he let them use it? And if he did—

"We can try," Fran urged. "It wouldn't hurt to try."

"Okay," Norm said, rising from his hobby bench.

The short, sly-faced man in Army uniform, the Mayor of the Pinole Fluke-pit, listened in silence as Norm Schein spoke. Then he smiled a wise, cunning smile. "Sure, I have a radio transmitter. Had it all the time. Fifty-watt output. But why would you want to get in touch with the Oakland Fluke-pit?"

Guardedly, Norm said, "That's my business."

Hooker Glebe said thoughtfully, "I'll let you use it for fifteen dollars."

It was a nasty shock, and Norm recoiled. Good lord; all the money he and his wife had—they needed every bill of it for use in playing Perky Pat. Money was the tender in the game; there was no other criterion by which one could tell if he had won or lost. "That's too much," he said aloud.

"Well, say ten," the Mayor said, shrugging.

In the end they settled for six dollars and a fifty-cent piece.

"I'll make the radio contact for you," Hooker Glebe said. "Because you don't know how. It will take time." He began turning a crank at the side of the generator of the transmitter. "I'll notify you when I've made contact with them. But give me the money now." He held out his big hand for it, and, with great reluctance, Norm paid him.

It was not until late that evening that Hooker managed to establish contact with

Oakland. Pleased with himself, beaming in self-satisfaction, he appeared at the Scheins' quarters, during their dinner hour. "All set," he announced. "Say, you know there are actually *nine* fluke-pits in Oakland? I didn't know that. Which you want? I've got one with the radio code of Red Vanilla." He chuckled. "They're tough and suspicious down there; it was hard to get any of them to answer."

Leaving his evening meal, Norman hurried to the Mayor's quarters, Hooker puffing along after him.

The transmitter, sure enough, was on, and the static wheezed from the speaker of its monitoring unit. Awkwardly, Norm seated himself at the microphone. "Do I just talk?" he asked Hooker Glebe.

"Just say, This is Pinole Fluke-pit calling. Repeat that a couple of times and then when they acknowledge, you say what you want to say." The Mayor fiddled with controls of the tranmitter, fussing in an important fashion.

"This is Pinole Fluke-pit," Norm said loudly into the microphone.

Almost at once a clear voice from the monitor said, "This is Red Vanilla Three answering."

The voice was cold and harsh; it struck Norm forcefully as distinctly alien. Hooker was right.

"Do you have Connie Companion down there where you are?"

"Yes, we do," the Oakland fluker answered.

"Well, I challenge you," Norman said, feeling the veins in his throat pulse with the tension of what he was saying. "We're Perky Pat in this area; we'll play Perky Pat against your Connie Companion. Where can we meet?"

"Perky Pat," the Oakland fluker echoed. "Yeah, I know about her. What would the stakes be, in your mind?"

"Up here we play for paper money mostly," Norman said, feeling that his response was somehow lame.

"We've got lots of paper money," the Oakland fluker said cuttingly. "That wouldn't interest any of us. What else?"

"I don't know." He felt hampered, talking to someone he could not see; he was not used to that. People should, he thought, be face to face, then you can see the other person's expression. This was not natural. "Let's meet halfway," he said, "and discuss it. Maybe we could meet at the Berkeley Fluke-pit; how about that?"

The Oakland fluker said, "That's too far. You mean lug our Connie Companion layout all that way? It's too heavy and something might happen to it."

"No, just to discuss rules and stakes," Norman said.

Dubiously, the Oakland fluker said, "Well, I guess we could do that. But you better understand—we take Connie Companion doll pretty damn seriously; you better be prepared to talk terms."

"We will," Norm assured him.

All this time Mayor Hooker Glebe had been cranking the handle of the generator; perspiring, his face bloated with exertion, he motioned angrily for Norm to conclude his palaver.

"At the Berkeley Fluke-pit," Norm finished. "In three days. And send your best player, the one who has the biggest and most authentic layout. Our Perky Pat layouts are works of art, you understand."

The Oakland fluker said, "We'll believe that when we see them. After all, we've got carpenters and electricians and plasterers here, building our layouts; I'll bet you're all unskilled."

"Not as much as you think," Norm said hotly, and laid down the microphone. To Hooker Glebe—who had immediately stopped cranking—he said, "We'll beat them. Wait'll they see the garbage disposal unit I'm making for my Perky Pat; did you know there were people back in the ol-days, I mean real alive human beings, who didn't have garbage disposal units?"

"I remember," Hooker said peevishly. "Say, you got a lot of cranking for your money; I think you gypped me, talking so long." He eyed Norm with such hostility that Norm began to feel uneasy. After all, the Mayor of the pit had the authority to evict any fluker he wished; that was their law.

"I'll give you the fire-alarm box I just finished the other day," Norm said. "In my layout it goes at the corner of the block where Perky Pat's boyfriend Leonard lives."

"Good enough," Hooker agreed, and his hostility faded. It was replaced, at once, by desire. "Let's see it, Norm. I bet it'll go good in my layout; a fire-alarm box is just what I need to complete my first block where I have the mailbox. Thank you."

"You're welcome." Norm sighed, philosophically.

When he returned from the two-day trek to the Berkeley Fluke-pit, his face was so grim that his wife knew at once that the parley with the Oakland people had not gone well.

That morning a careboy had dropped cartons of a synthetic tea-like drink; she fixed a cup of it for Norman, waiting to hear what had taken place eight miles to the south.

"We haggled," Norm said, seated wearily on the bed which he and his wife and child all shared. "They don't want money; they don't want goods—naturally not goods, because the darn careboys are dropping regularly down there, too."

"What will they accept, then?"

Norm said, "Perky Pat herself." He was silent, then.

"Oh, good lord," she said, appalled.

"But if we win," Norm pointed out, "we win Connie Companion."

"And the layouts? What about them?"

"We keep our own. It's just Perky Pat herself, not Leonard, not anything else."

"But," she protested, "what'll we *do* if we lose Perky Pat?"

"I can make another one," Norm said. "Given time. There's still a big supply of thermoplastics and artificial hair, here in the pit. And I have plenty of different paints; it would take at least a month, but I could do it. I don't look forward to the job, I admit. But—" His eyes glinted. "Don't look on the dark side; *imagine what it would be like to win Connie Companion doll.* I think we may well win; their delegate seemed smart and, as Hooker said, tough . . . but the one I talked to didn't strike me as being very flukey. You know, on good terms with luck."

And, after all, the element of luck, of chance, entered into each stage of the game through the agency of the spinner.

"It seems wrong," Fran said, "to put up Perky Pat herself. But if you say so—" She managed to smile a little. "I'll go along with it. And if you won Connie Companion—who knows? You might be elected Mayor when Hooker dies. Imagine, to have won somebody else's *doll*—not just the game, the money, but the *doll itself.*"

"I can win," Norm said soberly. "Because I'm very flukey." He could feel it in him, the same flukeyness that had got him through the hydrogen war alive, that had kept him alive ever since. You either have it or you don't, he realized. And I do.

His wife said, "Shouldn't we ask Hooker to call a meeting of everyone in the pit, and send the best player out of our entire group? So as to be the surest of winning?"

"Listen," Norm Schein said emphatically. "I'm the best player. I'm going. And so are you; we made a good team, and we don't want to break it up. Anyhow, we'll need at least two people to carry Perky Pat's layout." All in all, he judged, their lay-out weighed sixty pounds.

His plan seemed to him to be satisfactory. But when he mentioned it to the others living in the Pinole Fluke-pit he found himself facing sharp disagreement. The whole next day was filled with argument.

"You can't lug your layout all that way yourselves," Sam Regan said. "Either take more people with you or carry your layout in a vehicle of some kind. Such as a cart." He scowled at Norm.

"Where'd I get a cart?" Norm demanded.

"Maybe something could be adapted," Sam said. "I'll give you every bit of help I can. Personally, I'd go along, but, as I told my wife, this whole idea worries me." He thumped Norm on the back. "I admire your courage, you and Fran, setting off this way. I wish I had what it takes." He looked unhappy.

In the end, Norm settled on a wheelbarrow. He and Fran would take turns push-ing it. That way neither of them would have to carry any load above and beyond their food and water, and of course knives with which to protect them from the do-cats.

As they were carefully placing the elements of their layout in the wheelbarrow, the Scheins' boy, Timothy, came sidling up to them. "Take me along, Dad," he pleaded. "For fifty cents I'll go as guide and scout, and also help you catch food along the way."

"We'll manage fine," Norm said. "You stay here in the fluke-pit; you'll be safer here." It annoyed him, the idea of his son tagging along on an important venture such as this. It was almost—sacrilegious.

"Kiss us good-bye," Fran said to Timothy, smiling at him briefly; then her atten-tion returned to the layout within the wheelbarrow. "I hope it doesn't tip over," she said fearfully to Norm.

"Not a chance," Norm said. "If we're careful." He felt confident.

A few moments later they began wheeling the wheelbarrow up the ramp to the lid at the top, to upstairs. Their journey to the Berkeley Fluke-pit had begun.

A mile outside the Berkeley Fluke-pit, he and Fran began to stumble over empty drop-canisters and some only partly empty; remains of past care parcels such as lit-tered the surface near their own pit. Norm Schein breathed a sigh of relief; the jour-ney had not been so bad after all, except that his hands had become blistered from gripping the metal handles of the wheelbarrow, and Fran had turned her ankle so that now she walked with a painful limp. But it had taken them less time than he had anticipated, and his mood was one of buoyancy.

Ahead, a figure appeared, crouching low in the ash. A boy. Norm waved at him and called, "Hey, sonny—we're from the Pinole pit; we're supposed to meet a party from Oakland here . . . do you remember me?"

The boy, without answering, turned and scampered off.

"Nothing to be afraid of," Norm said to his wife. "He's going to tell their Mayor. A nice fellow named Ben Fennimore."

Soon several adults appeared, approaching warily.

With relief, Norm set the legs of the wheelbarrow down into the ash, letting go and wiping his face with his handkerchief. "Has the Oakland team arrived yet?" he called.

"Not yet," a tall, elderly man with a white armband and ornate cap answered. "It's you, Schein, isn't it?" he said, peering. This was Ben Fennimore. "Back already with your layout." Now the Berkeley flukers had begun crowding around the wheelbarrow, inspecting the Scheins' layout. Their faces showed admiration.

"They have Perky Pat here," Norm explained to his wife. "But—" He lowered his voice. "Their layouts are only basic. Just a house, wardrobe, and car . . . they've built almost nothing. No imagination."

One Berkeley fluker, a woman, said wonderingly to Fran, "And you made each of the pieces of furniture yourselves?" Marveling, she turned to look at the man beside her. "See what they've accomplished, Ed?"

"Yes," the man answered, nodding. "Say," he said to Fran and Norm, "can we see it all set up? You're going to set it up in our pit, aren't you?"

"We are indeed," Norm said.

The Berkeley flukers helped push the wheelbarrow the last mile. And before long they were descending the ramp, to the pit below the surface.

"It's a big pit," Norm said knowingly to Fran. "Must be two thousand people here. This is where the University of California was."

"I see," Fran said, a little timid at entering a strange pit; it was the first time in years—since the war in fact—that she had seen any strangers. And so many at once. It was almost too much for her; Norm felt her shrink back, pressing against him in fright.

When they had reached the first level and were starting to unload the wheelbarrow, Ben Fennimore came up to them and said softly, "I think the Oakland people have been spotted; we just got a report of activity upstairs. So be prepared." He added, "We're rooting for you, of course, because you're Perky Pat, the same as us."

"Have you ever seen the Connie Companion doll?" Fran asked him.

"No, ma'am," Fennimore answered courteously. "But naturally we've heard about it, being neighbors to Oakland and all. I'll tell you one thing . . . we hear that Connie Companion doll is a bit older than Perky Pat. You know—more, um, *mature*." He explained, "I just wanted to prepare you."

Norm and Fran glanced at each other. "Thanks," Norm said slowly. "Yes, we should be as much prepared as possible. How about Paul?"

"Oh, he's not much," Fennimore said. "Connie runs things; I don't even think Paul has a real apartment of his own. But you better wait until the Oakland flukers get here; I don't want to mislead you—my knowledge is all hearsay, you understand."

Another Berkeley fluker, standing nearby, spoke up. "I saw Connie once, and she's much more grown up than Perky Pat."

"How old do you figure Perky Pat is?" Norm asked him.

"Oh, I'd say seventeen or eighteen," Norm was told.

"And Connie?" He waited tensely.

"Oh, she might be twenty-five, even."

From the ramp behind them, they heard noises. More Berkeley flukers appeared, and, after them, two men carrying between them a platform on which Norm saw spread out a great, spectacular layout.

This was the Oakland team, and they weren't a couple, a man and wife; they were both men, and they were hard-faced with stern, remote eyes. They jerked their heads briefly at him and Fran, acknowledging their presence. And then, with enormous care, they set down the platform on which their layout rested.

Behind them came a third Oakland fluker, carrying a metal box, much like a lunch pail. Norm, watching, knew instinctively that in the box lay Connie Companion doll. The Oakland fluker produced a key and began unlocking the box.

"We're ready to begin playing any time," the taller of the Oakland men said. "As we agreed in our discussion, we'll use a numbered spinner instead of dice. Less chance of cheating that way."

"Agreed," Norm said. Hesitantly he held out his hand. "I'm Norman Schein and this is my wife and play-partner Fran."

The Oakland man, evidently the leader, said, "I'm Walter R. Wynn. This is my partner here, Charley Dowd, and the man with the box, that's Peter Foster. He isn't going to play; he just guards our layout." Wynn glanced about, at the Berkeley flukers, as if saying, I know you're all partial to Perky Pat, in here. But we don't care; we're not scared.

Fran said, "We're ready to play, Mr. Wynn." Her voice was low but controlled.

"What about money?" Fennimore asked.

"I think both teams have plenty of money," Wynn said. He laid out several thousand dollars in greenbacks, and now Norm did the same. "The money, of course, is not a factor in this, except as a means of conducting the game."

Norm nodded; he understood perfectly. Only the dolls themselves mattered. And now, for the first time, he saw Connie Companion doll.

She was being placed in her bedroom by Mr. Foster, who evidently was in charge of her. And the sight took his breath away. Yes, she was older. A grown woman, not a girl at all . . . the difference between her and Perky Pat was acute. And so lifelike. Carved, not poured; she obviously had been whittled out of wood and then painted—she was not a thermoplastic. And her hair. It appeared to be genuine hair.

He was deeply impressed.

"What do you think of her?" Walter Wynn asked, with a faint grin.

"Very—impressive," Norm conceded.

Now the Oaklanders were studying Perky Pat. "Poured thermoplastic," one of them said. "Artificial hair. Nice clothes, though; all stitched by hand, you can see that. Interesting; what we heard was correct. Perky Pat isn't a grownup, she's just a teenager."

Now the male companion to Connie appeared; he was set down in the bedroom beside Connie.

"Wait a minute," Norm said. "You're putting Paul, or whatever his name is, in her bedroom with her? Doesn't he have to start out from his own apartment?"

Wynn said, "They're married."

"*Married!*" Norman and Fran stared at him, dumbfounded.

"Why sure," Wynn said. "So naturally they live together. Your dolls, they're not, are they?"

"N-no," Fran said. "Leonard is Perky Pat's boy friend . . ." Her voice trailed off.

"Norm," she said, clutching his arm, "I don't believe him; I think he's just saying they're married to get the advantage. Because if they both start out from the same room—"

Norm said aloud, "You fellows, look here. It's not fair, calling them married."

Wynn said, "We're not 'calling' them married; they are married. Their names are Connie and Paul Lathrope, of 24 Arden Place, Piedmont. They've been married for a year, most players will tell you." He sounded calm.

Maybe, Norm thought, it's true. He was truly shaken.

"Look at them together," Fran said, kneeling down to examine the Oaklanders' layout. "In the same bedroom, in the same house. Why, Norm; do you see? There's just the one bed. A big double bed." Wild-eyed, she appealed to him. "How can Perky Pat and Leonard play against them?" Her voice shook. "It's not morally *right.*"

"This is another type of layout entirely," Norm said to Walter Wynn. "This, that you have. Utterly different from what we're used to, as you can see." He pointed to his own layout. "I insist that in this game Connie and Paul *not* live together and *not* be considered married."

"But they are," Foster spoke up. "It's a fact. Look—their clothes are in the same closet." He showed them the closet. "And in the same bureau drawers." He showed them that, too. "And look in the bathroom. Two toothbrushes. His and hers, in the same rack. So you can see we're not making it up."

There was silence.

Then Fran said in a choked voice. "And if they're married—you mean they've been—intimate?"

Wynn raised an eyebrow, then nodded. "Sure, since they're married. Is there anything wrong with that?"

"Perky Pat and Leonard have never—" Fran began and then ceased.

"Naturally not," Wynn agreed. "Because they're only going together. We understand that."

Fran said, "We just can't play. We can't." She caught hold of her husband's arms. "Let's go back to Pinole pit—please, Norman."

"Wait," Wynn said at once. "If you don't play, you're conceding; you have to give us Perky Pat."

The three Oaklanders all nodded. And, Norm saw, many of the Berkeley flukers were nodding, too, including Ben Fennimore.

"They're right," Norm said heavily to his wife. He put his arm around her. "We'd have to give her up. We better play, dear."

"Yes," Fran said, in a dead, flat voice. "We'll play." She bent down and listlessly spun the needle of the spinner. It stopped at six.

Smiling, Walter Wynn knelt down and spun. He obtained a four.

The game had begun.

Crouching behind the strewn, decayed contents of a care parcel that had been dropped long ago, Timothy Schein saw coming across the surface of ash his mother and father, pushing the wheelbarrow ahead of them. They looked tired and worn.

"Hi," Timothy yelled, leaping out at them in joy at seeing them again; he had missed them very much.

"Hi, son," his father murmured, nodding. He let go of the handles of the wheelbarrow, then halted and wiped his face with his handkerchief.

Now Fred Chamberlain raced up, panting. "Hi, Mr. Schein; hi, Mrs. Schein. Hey, did you win? Did you beat the Oakland flukers? I bet you did, didn't you?" He looked from one of them to the other and then back.

In a low voice, Fran said, "Yes, Freddy. We won."

Norm said, "Look in the wheelbarrow."

The two boys looked. And, there among Perky Pat's furnishings, lay another doll. Larger, fuller-figured, much older than Pat . . . they stared at her and she stared up sightlessly at the gray sky overhead. So this is Connie Companion doll, Timothy said to himself. Gee.

"We were lucky," Norm said. Now several people had emerged from the pit and were gathering around them, listening. Jean and Sam Regan, Tod Morrison and his wife, Helen, and now their Mayor, Hooker Glebe himself, waddling up excited and nervous, his face flushed, gasping for breath from the labor—unusual for him—of ascending the ramp.

Fran said, "We got a cancellation-of-debts card, just when we were most behind. We owed fifty thousand, and it made us even with the Oakland flukers. And then, after that, we got an advance-ten-squares card, and that put us right on the jackpot square, at least in our layout. We had a very bitter squabble, because the Oaklanders showed us that on their layout it was a tax-lien-slapped-on-real-estate-holdings square, but we had spun an odd number so that put us back on our own board." She sighed. "I'm glad to be back. It was hard, Hooker; it was a tough game."

Hooker Glebe wheezed, "Let's all get a look at the Connie Companion doll, folks." To Fran and Norm he said, "Can I lift her up and show them?"

"Sure," Norm said, nodding.

Hooker picked up Connie Companion doll. "She sure is realistic," he said, scrutinizing her. "Clothes aren't as nice as ours generally are; they look machine-made."

"They are," Norm agreed. "But she's carved, not poured."

"Yes, so I see." Hooker turned the doll about, inspecting her from all angles. "A nice job. She's—um, more filled-out than Perky Pat. What's this outfit she has on? Tweed suit of some sort."

"A business suit," Fran said. "We won that with her, they had agreed on that in advance."

"You see, she has a job," Norm explained. "She's a psychology consultant for a business firm doing marketing research. In consumer preferences. A high-paying position . . . she earns twenty thousand a year, I believe Wynn said."

"Golly," Hooker said. "And Pat's just going to college; she's still in school." He looked troubled. "Well, I guess they were bound to be ahead of us in some ways. What matters is that you won." His jovial smile returned. "Perky Pat came out ahead." He held the Connie Companion doll up high, where everyone could see her. "Look what Norm and Fran came back with, folks!"

Norm said, "Be careful with her, Hooker." His voice was firm.

"Eh?" Hooker said, pausing. "Why, Norm?"

"Because," Norm said, "she's going to have a baby."

There was a sudden chill silence. The ash around them stirred faintly; that was the only sound.

"How do you know?" Hooker asked.

"They told us. The Oaklanders told us. And we won that, too—after a bitter argument that Fennimore had to settle." Reaching into the wheelbarrow, he brought out a little leather pouch; from it he carefully took a carved pink new-born baby. "We won this too because Fennimore agreed that from a technical standpoint it's literally part of Connie Companion doll at this point."

Hooker stared for a long, long time.

"She's married," Fran explained. "To Paul. They're not just going together. She's three months pregnant, Mr. Wynn said. He didn't tell us until after we won; he didn't want to, then, but they felt they had to. I think they were right; it wouldn't have done not to say."

Norm said, "And in addition there's actually an embryo outfit—"

"Yes," Fran said. "You have to open Connie up, of course, to see—"

"No," Jean Regan said. "Please, no."

Hooker said, "No, Mrs. Schein, don't." He backed away.

Fran said, "It shocked us, of course, at first, but—"

"You see," Norm put in, "it's logical; you have to follow the logic. Why, eventually Perky Pat—"

"No," Hooker said violently. He bent down, picked up a rock from the ash at his feet. "No," he said, and raised his arm. "You stop, you two. Don't say any more."

Now the Regans, too, had picked up rocks. No one spoke.

Fran said, at last, "Norm, we've got to get out of here."

"You're right," Tod Morrison told them. His wife nodded in grim agreement.

"You two go back down to Oakland," Hooker said to Norman and Fran Schein. "You don't live here anymore. You're different than you were. You—changed."

"Yes," Sam Regan said slowly, half to himself. "I was right, there was something to fear." To Norm Schein he said, "How difficult a trip is it to Oakland?"

"We just went to Berkeley," Norm said. "To the Berkeley Fluke-pit." He seemed baffled and stunned by what was happening. "My god," he said, "we can't turn around and push the wheelbarrow back all the way to Berkeley again—we're worn out, we need rest!"

Sam Regan said, "What if somebody else pushed?" He walked up to the Scheins, then, and stood with them. "I'll push the darn thing. You lead the way, Schein." He looked toward his wife, but Jean did not stir. And she did not put down her handful of rocks.

Timothy Schein plucked at his father's arm. "Can I come this time, Dad? Please let me come."

"Okay," Norm said, half to himself. Now he drew himself together. "So we're not wanted here." He turned to Fran. "Let's go. Sam's going to push the wheelbarrow; I think we can make it back there before nightfall. If not, we can sleep out in the open. Timothy'll help protect us against the do-cats."

Fran said, "I guess we have no choice." Her face was pale.

"And take this," Hooker said. He held out the tiny carved baby. Fran Schein accepted it and put it tenderly back in its leather pouch. Norm laid Connie Companion back down in the wheelbarrow, where she had been. They were ready to start back.

"It'll happen up here eventually," Norm said, to the group of people, to the Pinole flukers. "Oakland is just more advanced; that's all."

Nodding, Norm started to pick up the handles of the wheelbarrow, but Sam Regan moved him aside and took them himself. "Let's go," he said.

The three adults, with Timothy Schein going ahead of them with his knife ready—in case a do-cat attacked—started into motion, in the direction of Oakland and the south. No one spoke. There was nothing to say.

"It's a shame this had to happen," Norm said at last, when they had gone almost a mile and there was no further sign of the Pinole flukers behind them.

"Maybe not," Sam Regan said. "Maybe it's for the good." He did not seem downcast. And after all, he had lost his wife; he had given up more than anyone else, and yet—he had survived.

"Glad you feel that way," Norm said somberly.

They continued on, each with his own thoughts.

After a while, Timothy said to his father, "All these big fluke-pits pits to the south . . . there's lots more things to do there, isn't there? I mean, you don't just sit around playing that game." He certainly hoped not.

His father said, "That's true, I guess."

Overhead, a care ship whistled at great velocity and then was gone again almost at once; Timothy watched it go, but he wasn't much interested in it, because there was so much more to look forward to, on the ground and below the ground, ahead of them to the south.

His father murmured, "These Oaklanders; their game, their particular doll, it taught them something. Connie had to grow and it forced them all to grow along with her. Our flukers never learned about that, not from Perky Pat. I wonder if they ever will. She'd have to grow up the way Connie Companion did. Connie must have been like Perky Pat, once. A long time ago."

Not interested in what his father was saying—who really cared about dolls and games with dolls?—Timothy scampered ahead, peering to see what lay before them, the opportunities and possibilities, for him and for his mother and dad, for Mr. Regan also.

"I can't wait," he yelled back at his father, and Norm Schein managed a faint, fatigued smile in answer.

Ursula K. Le Guin, whose first story appeared in Fantastic™ Stories
in 1964, made several early appearances in Amazing® Stories *before achieving general recognition with* The Left Hand of Darkness
(1969) and The Dispossessed *(1974). She has won numerous
awards, including the Hugo, Nebula, Newbery Medal, and the National Book Award. She is now one of the most acclaimed of all
science-fiction writers. The present story, which appeared in*
Amazing Stories *in September 1964 as "Dowry of the Angyar,"
forms a prologue to her novel* Rocannon's World.

SEMLEY'S NECKLACE
by Ursula K. Le Guin

How can you tell the legend from the fact on
these worlds that lie so many years away?—planets without names, called by their
people simply The World, planets without history, where the past is the matter of
myth, and a returning explorer finds his own doings a few years back have become
the gestures of a god. Unreason darkens that gap of time bridged by our lightspeed
ships, and in the darkness uncertainty and disproportion grow like weeds.

In trying to tell the story of a man, an ordinary League scientist, who went to such a
nameless half-known world not many years ago, one feels like an archeologist amid
millennial ruins, now struggling through choked tangles of leaf, flower, branch and
vine to the sudden bright geometry of a wheel or a polished cornerstone, and now entering some commonplace, sunlit doorway to find inside it the darkness, the impossible flicker of a flame, the glitter of a jewel, the half-glimpsed movement of a
woman's arm.

How can you tell fact from legend, truth from truth?

Through Rocannon's story the jewel, the blue glitter seen briefly, returns. With it
let us begin, here:

Galactic Area 8, No. 62: FOMALHAUT II.
High-Intelligence Life Forms: Species Contacted:
Species I.

*A. Gdemiar (singular Gdem): Highly intelligent, fully hominoid nocturnal troglodytes, 120-135 cm. in height, light skin, dark head-hair. When contacted these
cave-dwellers possessed a rigidly stratified oligarchic urban society modified by partial colonial telepathy, and a technologically oriented Early Steel culture. Technology
enhanced to Industrial, Point C, during League Mission of 252-254. In 254 an Automatic Drive ship (to-from New South Georgia) was presented to oligarchs of the Kiriensea Area community. Status C-Prime.*

B. Fiia (singular Fian): Highly intelligent, fully hominoid, diurnal, av. ca. 130 cm.

in height, observed individuals generally light in skin and hair. Brief contacts indicated village and nomadic communal societies, partial colonial telepathy, also some indication of short-range TK. The race appears a-technological and evasive, with minimal and fluid culture-patterns. Currently untaxable. Status E-Query.

Species II.
Liuar (singular Liu): Highly intelligent, fully hominoid, diurnal, av. height above 170 cm., this species possesses a fortress/village, clan-descent society, a blocked technology (Bronze), and feudal-heroic culture. Note horizontal social cleavage into 2 pseudo-races: (a) Olgyior, "midmen," light-skinned and dark-haired; (b) Angyar, "lords," very tall, dark-skinned, yellow-haired—

"That's her," said Rocannon, looking up from the *Abridged Handy Pocket Guide to Intelligent Life-forms* at the very tall, dark-skinned, yellow-haired woman who stood halfway down the long museum hall. She stood still and erect, crowned with bright hair, gazing at something in a display case. Around her fidgeted four uneasy and unattractive dwarves.

"I didn't know Fomalhaut II had all those people besides the trogs," said Ketho, the curator.

"I didn't either. There are even some 'Unconfirmed' species listed here, that they never contacted. Sounds like time for a more thorough survey mission to the place. Well, now at least we know what she is."

"I wish there were some way of knowing *who* she is. . . ."

She was of an ancient family, a descendant of the first kings of the Angyar, and for all her poverty her hair shone with the pure, steadfast gold of her inheritance. The little people, the Fiia, bowed when she passed them, even when she was a barefoot child running in the fields, the light and fiery comet of her hair brightening the troubled winds of Kirien.

She was still very young when Durhal of Hallan saw her, courted her, and carried her away from the ruined towers and windy halls of her childhood to his own high home. In Hallan on the mountainside there was no comfort either, though splendor endured. The windows were unglassed, the stone floors bare; in coldyear one might wake to see the night's snow in long, low drifts beneath each window. Durhal's bride stood with narrow bare feet on the snowy floor, braiding up the fire of her hair and laughing at her young husband in the silver mirror that hung in their room. That mirror, and his mother's bridal-gown sewn with a thousand tiny crystals, were all his wealth. Some of his lesser kinfolk of Hallan still possessed wardrobes of brocaded clothing, furniture of gilded wood, silver harness for their steeds, armor and silver mounted swords, jewels and jewelry—and on these last Durhal's bride looked enviously, glancing back at a gemmed coronet or a golden brooch even when the wearer of the ornament stood aside to let her pass, deferent to her birth and marriage-rank.

Fourth from the High Seat of Hallan Revel sat Durhal and his bride Semley, so close to Hallanlord that the old man often poured wine for Semley with his own hand, and spoke of hunting with his nephew and heir Durhal, looking on the young pair with a grim, unhopeful love. Hope came hard to the Angyar of Hallan and all the Western Lands, since the Starlords had appeared with their houses that leaped about on pillars of fire and their awful weapons that could level hills. They had interfered with all the old ways and wars, and though the sums were small there was terrible shame to the Angyar in having to pay a tax to them, a tribute to the Starlords' war that was to be fought with some strange enemy, somewhere in the hollow places between the stars, at the end of years. "It will be your war too," they said, but for a generation now the Angyar had sat in idle shame in their revel-halls, watching their double swords rust, their sons grow up without ever striking a blow in battle, their daughters marry poor men, even midmen, having no dowry of heroic loot to bring a noble husband. Hallanlord's face was bleak when he watched the fair-haired couple and heard their laughter as they drank bitter wine and joked together in the cold, ruinous, resplendent fortress of their race.

Semley's own face hardened when she looked down the hall and saw, in seats far below hers, even down among the halfbreeds and the midmen, against white skins and black hair, the gleam and flash of precious stones. She herself had brought nothing in dowry to her husband, not even a silver hairpin. The dress of a thousand crystals she had put away in a chest for the wedding-day of her daughter, if daughter it was to be.

It was, and they called her Haldre, and when the fuzz on her little brown skull grew longer it shone with steadfast gold, the inheritance of the lordly generations, the only gold she would ever possess. . . .

Semley did not speak to her husband of her discontent. For all his gentleness to her, Durhal in his pride had only contempt for envy, for vain wishing, and she dreaded his contempt. But she spoke to Durhal's sister Durossa.

"My family had a great treasure once," she said. "It was a necklace all of gold, with the blue jewel set in the center—sapphire?"

Durossa shook her head, smiling, not sure of the name either. It was late in warmyear, as these Northern Angyar called the summer of the eight-hundred-day year, beginning the cycle of months anew at each equinox; to Semley it seemed an outlandish calendar, a midmannish reckoning. Her family was at an end, but it had been older and purer than the race of any of these northwestern marchlanders, who mixed too freely with the Olgyior. She sat with Durossa in the sunlight on a stone windowseat high up in the Great Tower, where the older woman's apartment was. Widowed young, childless, Durossa had been given in second marriage to Hallanlord, who was her father's brother. Since it was a kinmarriage and a second marriage on both sides, she had not taken the title of Hallanlady, which Semley would some day bear; but she sat with the old lord in the High Seat and ruled with him his domains. Older than her brother Durhal, she was fond of his young wife, and delighted in the bright-haired baby Haldre.

"It was bought," Semley went on, "with all the money my forebear Leynen got when he conquered the Southern Fiefs—all the money from a whole kingdom, think of it, for one jewel! Oh, it would outshine anything here in Hallan, surely, even those crystals like koob-eggs your cousin Issar wears. It was so beautiful they gave it a name of its own; they called it the Eye of the Sea. My great-grandmother wore it."

"You never saw it?" the older woman asked lazily, gazing down at the green mountainslopes where long, long summer sent its hot and restless winds straying among the forests and whirling down white roads to the seacoast far away.

"It was lost before I was born.

"No, my father said it was stolen before the Starlords ever came to our realm. He wouldn't talk of it, but there was an old midwoman full of tales who always told me the Fiia would know where it was."

"Ah, the Fiia I should like to see!" said Durossa. "They're in so many songs and tales; why do they never come to the Western Lands?"

"Too high, too cold in winter, I think. They like the sunlight of the valleys of the south."

"Are they like the Clayfolk?"

"Those I've never seen; they keep away from us in the south. Aren't they like white midmen, and misformed? The Fiia are fair; they look like children, only thinner, and wiser. Oh, I wonder if they know where the necklace is, who stole it and where he hid it! Think, Durossa—if I could come into Hallan Revel and sit down by my husband with the wealth of a kingdom round my neck, and outshine the other women as he outshines all men!"

Durossa bent her head above the baby, who sat studying her own brown toes on a fur rug between her mother and her aunt. "Semley is foolish," she murmured to the baby; "Semley who shines like a falling star, Semley whose husband loves no gold but the gold of her hair. . . ."

And Semley, looking out over the green slopes of summer toward the distant sea, was silent.

But when another coldyear had passed, and the Starlords had come again to collect their taxes for the war against the world's end—this time using a couple of dwarfish Clayfolk as interpreters, and so leaving all the Angyar humiliated to the point of rebellion—and another warmyear too was gone, and Haldre had grown into a lovely, chattering child, Semley brought her one morning to Durossa's sunlit room in the tower. Semley wore an old cloak of blue, and the hood covered her hair.

"Keep Haldre for me these few days, Durossa," she said quick and calm. "I'm going south to Kirien."

"To see your father?"

"To find my inheritance. Your cousins of Harget Fief have been taunting Durhal. Even that halfbreed Parna can torment him, because Parna's wife has a satin coverlet for her bed, and a diamond earring, and three gowns, the dough-faced black-haired trollop! while Durhal's wife must patch her gown—"

"Is Durhal's pride in his wife, or what she wears?"

But Semley was not to be moved. "The Lords of Hallan are becoming poor men in their own hall. I am going to bring my dowry to my lord, as one of my lineage should."

"Semley! Does Durhal know you're going?"

"My return will be a happy one—that much let him know," said young Semley, breaking for a moment into her joyful laugh; then she bent to kiss her daughter, turned, and before Durossa could speak, was gone like a quick wind over the floors of sunlit stone.

Married women of Angyar never rode for sport, and Semley had not been from Hallan since her marriage; so now, mounting the high saddle of a windsteed, she felt like a girl again, like the wild maiden she had been, riding half-broken steeds on the north wind over the fields of Kirien. The beast that bore her now down from the hills of Hallan was of finer breed, striped coat fitting sleek over hollow, buoyant bones, green eyes slitted against the wind, light and mighty wings sweeping up and down to either side of Semley, revealing and hiding the clouds above her and the hills below.

On the third morning she came to Kirien and stood again in the ruined courts.

Her father had been drinking all night, and, just as in the old days, the morning sunlight poking through his fallen ceilings annoyed him, and the sight of his daughter only increased his annoyance. "What are you back for?" he growled, his swollen eyes glancing at her and away. The fiery hair of his youth was quenched, gray strands tangled on his skull. "Did the young Halla not marry you, and you've come sneaking home?"

"I am Durhal's wife. I came to get my dowry, father."

The drunkard growled in disgust; but she laughed at him so gently that he had to look at her again, wincing.

"Is it true, father, that the Fiia stole the necklace Eye of the Sea?"

"How do I know? Old tales. The thing was lost before I was born, I think. I wish I never had been. Ask the Fiia if you want to know. Go to them, go back to your husband. Leave me alone here. There's no room at Kirien for girls and gold and all the rest of the story. The story's over here; this is the fallen place, this is the empty hall. The sons of Leynen all are dead, their treasures are all lost. Go on your way, girl."

Gray and swollen as the web-spinner of ruined houses, he turned and went blundering toward the cellars where he hid from daylight.

Leading the striped windsteed of Hallan, Semley left her old home and walked down the steep hill, past the village of the midmen, who greeted her with sullen respect, on over fields and pastures where the great, wing-clipped, half-wild herilor grazed, to a valley that was green as a painted bowl and full to the brim with sunlight. In the deep of the valley lay the village of the Fiia, and as she descended leading her steed the little, slight people ran up toward her from their huts and gardens, laughing, calling out in faint, thin voices.

"Hail Halla's bride, Kirienlady, Windborne, Semley the Fair!"

They gave her lovely names and she liked to hear them, minding not at all their laughter; for they laughed at all they said. That was her own way, to speak and laugh. She stood tall in her long blue cloak among their swirling welcome.

"Hail Lightfolk, Sundwellers, Fiia friends of men!"

They took her down into the village and brought her into one of their airy houses, the tiny children chasing along behind. There was no telling the age of a Fian once he was grown; it was hard even to tell one from another and be sure, as they moved about as quick as moths around a candle, that she spoke always to the same one. But it seemed that one of them talked with her for a while, as the others fed and patted her steed, and brought water for her to drink, and bowls of fruit from their gardens of little trees. "It was never the Fiia that stole the necklace of the Lords of Kirien!" cried the little man. "What would the Fiia do with gold, Lady? For us there is sunlight in warmyear, and in the coldyear the remembrance of sunlight; the yellow fruit, the yellow leaves in endseason, the yellow hair of our lady of Kirien; no other gold."

"Then it was some midman stole the thing?"

Laughter rang long and faint about her. "How would a midman dare? O Lady of Kirien, how the great jewel was stolen no mortal knows, not man nor midman nor Fian nor any among the Seven Folk. Only dead minds know how it was lost, long ago when Kireley the Proud whose great-granddaughter is Semley walked alone by the caves of the sea. But it may be found perhaps among the Sunhaters."

"The Clayfolk?"

A louder burst of laughter, nervous.

"Sit with us, Semley, sunhaired, returned to us from the north." She sat with them to eat, and they were as pleased with her graciousness as she with theirs. But when they heard her repeat that she would go to the Clayfolk to find her inheritance, if it was there, they began not to laugh; and little by little there were fewer of them around her. She was alone at last with perhaps the one she had spoken with before the meal. "Do not go among the Clayfolk, Semley," he said, and for a moment her heart failed her. The Fian, drawing his hand down slowly over his eyes, had darkened all the air about them. Fruit lay ash-white on the plate; all the bowls of clear water were empty.

"In the mountains of the far land the Fiia and the Gdemiar parted. Long ago we parted," said the slight, still man of the Fiia. "Longer ago we were one. What we are not, they are. What we are, they are not. Think of the sunlight and the grass and the trees that bear fruit, Semley; think that not all roads that lead down lead up as well."

"Mine leads neither down nor up, kind host, but only straight on to my inheritance. I will go to it where it is, and return with it."

The Fian bowed, laughing a little.

Outside the village she mounted her striped windsteed, and, calling farewell in answer to their calling, rose up into the wind of afternoon and flew southwestward toward the caves down by the rocky shores of Kiriensea.

She feared she might have to walk far into those tunnel-caves to find the people she sought, for it was said the Clayfolk never came out of their caves into the light of the sun, and feared even the Greatstar and the moons. It was a long ride; she landed once to let her steed hunt tree-rats while she ate a little bread from her saddlebag. The bread was hard and dry by now and tasted of leather, yet kept a faint savor of its making, so that for a moment, eating it alone in a glade of the southern forests, she heard the quiet tone of a voice and saw Durhal's face turned to her in the light of the candles of Hallan. For a while she sat daydreaming of that stern and vivid young face, and of what she would say to him when she came home with a kingdom's ransom around her neck: "I wanted a gift worthy of my husband, Lord. . . ." Then she pressed on, but when she reached the coast the sun had set, with the Greatstar sinking behind it. A mean wind had come up from the west, starting and gusting and veering, and her windsteed was weary fighting it. She let him glide down on the sand. At once he folded his wings and curled his thick, light limbs under him with a thrum of purring. Semley stood holding her cloak close at her throat, stroking the steed's neck so that he flicked his ears and purred again. The warm fur comforted her hand, but all that met her eyes was gray sky full of smears of cloud, gray sea, dark sand. And then running over the sand a low, dark creature—another—a group of them, squatting and running and stopping.

She called aloud to them. Though they had not seemed to see her, now in a moment they were all around her. They kept a distance from her windsteed; he had stopped purring, and his fur rose a little under Semley's hand. She took up the reins, glad of his protection but afraid of the nervous ferocity he might display. The strange folk stood silent, staring, their thick bare feet planted in the sand. There was no mistaking them: they were the height of the Fiia and in all else a shadow, a black image of those laughing people. Naked, squat, stiff, with lank hair and gray-white skins, dampish-looking like the skins of grubs; eyes like rocks.

"You are the Clayfolk?"

"Gdemiar are we, people of the Lords of the Realms of Night." The voice was unexpectedly loud and deep, and rang out pompous through the salt, blowing dusk;

but, as with the Fiia, Semley was not sure which one had spoken.

"I greet you, Nightlords. I am Semley of Kirien, Durhal's wife of Hallan. I come to you seeking my inheritance, the necklace called Eye of the Sea, lost long ago."

"Why do you seek it here, Angya? Here is only sand and salt and night."

"Because lost things are known of in deep places," said Semley, quite ready for a play of wits, "and gold that came from earth has a way of going back to the earth. And sometimes the made, they say, returns to the maker." This last was a guess; it hit the mark.

"It is true the necklace Eye of the Sea is known to us by name. It was made in our caves long ago, and sold by us to the Angyar. And the blue stone came from the Clay-fields of our kin to the east. But these are very old tales, Angya."

"May I listen to them in the places where they are told?"

The squat people were silent a while, as if in doubt. The gray wind blew by over the sand, darkening as the Greatstar set; the sound of the sea loudened and lessened. The deep voice spoke again: "Yes, lady of the Angyar. You may enter the Deep Halls. Come with us now." There was a changed note in his voice, wheedling. Semley would not hear it. She followed the Claymen over the sand, leading on a short rein her sharp-taloned steed.

At the cave-mouth, a toothless, yawning mouth from which a stinking warmth sighed out, one of the Claymen said, "The air-beast cannot come in."

"Yes," said Semley.

"No," said the squat people.

"Yes. I will not leave him here. He is not mine to leave. He will not harm you, so long as I hold his reins."

"No," deep voices repeated; but others broke in, "As you will," and after a moment of hesitation they went on. The cave-mouth seemed to snap shut behind them, so dark was it under the stone. They went in single file, Semley last.

The darkness of the tunnel lightened, and they came under a ball of weak white fire hanging from the roof. Farther on was another, and another; between them long black worms hung in festoons from the rock. As they went on these fire-globes were set closer, so that all the tunnel was lit with a bright, cold light.

Semley's guides stopped at a parting of three tunnels, all blocked by doors that looked to be of iron. "We shall wait, Angya," they said, and eight of them stayed with her, while three others unlocked one of the doors and passed through. It fell to behind them with a clash.

Straight and still stood the daughter of the Angyar in the white, blank light of the lamps; her windsteed crouched beside her, flicking the tip of his striped tail, his great folded wings stirring again and again with the checked impulse to fly. In the tunnel behind Semley the eight Claymen squatted on their hams, muttering to one another in their deep voices, in their own tongue.

The central door swung clanging open. "Let the Angya enter the Realm of Night!" cried a new voice, booming and boastful. A Clayman who wore some clothing on his thick gray body stood in the doorway, beckoning to her. "Enter and behold the wonders of our lands, the marvels made by hands, the works of the Nightlords!"

Silent, with a tug at her steed's reins, Semley bowed her head and followed him under the low doorway made for dwarfish folk. Another glaring tunnel stretched ahead, dank walls dazzling in the white light, but, instead of a way to walk upon, its floor carried two bars of polished iron stretching off side by side as far as she could see. On the bars rested some kind of cart with metal wheels. Obeying her new guide's gestures, with no hesitation and no trace of wonder on her face, Semley stepped into the cart and made the windsteed crouch beside her. The Clayman got in and sat down in front of her, moving bars and wheels about. A loud grinding noise arose, and a screaming of metal on metal, and then the walls of the tunnel began to jerk by. Faster and faster the walls slid past, till the fireglobes overhead ran into a blur, and the stale warm air became a foul wind blowing the hood back off her hair.

The cart stopped. Semley followed the guide up basalt steps into a vast anteroom and then a still vaster hall, carved by ancient waters or by the burrowing Clayfolk out of the rock, its darkness that had never known sunlight lit with the uncanny brilliance of the globes. In grilles cut in the walls huge blades turned and turned, changing the stale air. The great closed space hummed and boomed with noise, the loud voices of the Clayfolk, the grinding and shrill buzzing and vibration of turning blades and wheels, the echoes and re-echoes of all this from the rock. Here all the stumpy figures of the Claymen were clothed in garments imitating those of the Starlords—divided trousers, soft boots, and hooded tunics—though the few women to be seen, hurrying servile dwarves, were naked. Of the males many were soldiers, bearing at their sides weapons shaped like the terrible light-throwers of the Starlords, though even Semley could see these were merely shaped iron clubs. What she saw, she saw without looking. She followed where she was led, turning her head neither to left nor right. When she came before a group of Claymen who wore iron circlets on their black hair her guide halted, bowed, boomed out, "The High Lords of Gdemiar!"

There were seven of them, and all looked up at her with such arrogance on their lumpy gray faces that she wanted to laugh.

"I come among you seeking the lost treasure of my family, O Lords of the Dark Realm," she said gravely to them. "I seek Leynen's prize, the Eye of the Sea." Her voice was faint in the racket of the huge vault.

"So said our messengers, Lady Semley." This time she could pick out the one who spoke, one even shorter than the others, hardly reaching Semley's breast, with a white, fierce face. "We do not have this thing you seek."

"Once you had it, it is said."

"Much is said, up there where the sun blinks."

"And words are borne off by the winds, where there are winds to blow. I do not ask how the necklace was lost to us and returned to you, its makers of old. Those are old tales, old grudges. I only seek to find it now. You do not have it now; but it may be you know where it is."

"It is not here."

"Then it is elsewhere."

"It is where you cannot come to it. Never, unless we help you."

"Then help me. I ask this as your guest."

"It is said, *The Angyar take; the Fiia give; the Gdemiar give and take.* If we do this for you, what will you give us?"

"My thanks, Nightlord."

She stood tall and bright among them, smiling. They all stared at her with a heavy, grudging wonder, a sullen yearning.

"Listen, Angya, this is a great favor you ask of us. You do not know how great a favor. You cannot understand. You are of a race that will not understand, that cares for nothing but wind-riding and crop-raising and sword-fighting and shouting together. But who made your swords of the bright steel? We, the Gdemiar! Your lords come to us here and in the Clayfields and buy their swords and go away, not looking, not understanding. But you are here now, you will look, you can see a few of our endless marvels, the lights that burn forever, the car that pulls itself, the machines that make our clothes and cook our food and sweeten our air and serve us in all things. Know that all these things are beyond your understanding. And know this: we, the Gdemiar, are the friends of those you call the Starlords! We came with them to Hallan, to Reohan, to Hul-Orren, to all your castles, to help them speak to you. The lords to whom you, the proud Angyar, pay tribute, are our friends. They do us favors as we do them favors! Now, what do your thanks mean to us?"

"That is your question to answer," said Semley, "not mine. I have asked my question. Answer it, Lord."

For a while the seven conferred together, by word and silence. They would glance at her and look away, and mutter and be still. A crowd grew around them, drawn slowly and silently, one after another till Semley was encircled by hundreds of the matted black heads, and all the great booming cavern floor was covered with people, except a little space directly around her. Her windsteed was quivering with fear and irritation too long controlled, and his eyes had gone very wide and pale, like the eyes of a steed forced to fly at night. She stroked the warm fur of his head, whispering, "Quietly now, brave one, bright one, windlord. . . ."

"Angya, we will take you to the place where the treasure lies." The Clayman with the white face and iron crown had turned to her once more. "More than that we cannot do. You must come with us to claim the necklace where it lies, from those who keep it. The air-beast cannot come with you. You must come alone."

"How far a journey, Lord?"

His lips drew back and back. "A very far journey, Lady. Yet it will last only one long night."

"I thank you for your courtesy. Will my steed be well cared for this night? No ill must come to him."

"He will sleep till you return. A greater windsteed you will have ridden, when you see that beast again! Will you not ask where we take you?"

"Can we go soon on this journey? I would not stay long away from my home."

"Yes. Soon." Again the gray lips widened as he stared up into her face.

What was done in those next hours Semley could not have retold; it was all haste, jumble, noise, strangeness. While she held her steed's head a Clayman stuck a long needle into the golden-striped haunch. She nearly cried out at the sight, but her steed merely twitched and then, purring, fell asleep. He was carried off by a group of Clayfolk who clearly had to summon up their courage to touch his warm fur. Later on she had to see a needle driven into her own arm—perhaps to test her courage, she thought, for it did not seem to make her sleep; though she was not quite sure. There were times she had to travel in the rail-carts, passing iron doors and vaulted caverns by the hundred and hundred; once the rail-cart ran through a cavern that stretched off on either hand measureless into the dark, and all that darkness was full of great flocks of herilor. She could hear their cooing, husky calls, and glimpse the flocks in the front-lights of the cart; then she saw some more clearly in the white light, and saw that they were all wingless, and all blind. At that she shut her eyes. But here were more tunnels to go through, and always more caverns, more gray lumpy bodies and fierce faces and booming boasting voices, until at last they led her suddenly out into the open air. It was full night; she raised her eyes joyfully to the stars and the single moon shining, little Heliki brightening in the west. But the Clayfolk were all about her still, making her climb now into some new kind of cart or cave, she did not know which. It was small, full of little blinking lights like rushlights, very narrow and shining after the great dank caverns and the starlit night. Now another needle was stuck in her, and they told her she would have to be tied down in a sort of flat chair, tied down head and hand and foot.

"I will not," said Semley.

But when she saw that the four Claymen who were to be her guides let themselves be tied down first, she submitted. The others left. There was a roaring sound, and a long silence; a great weight that could not be seen pressed upon her. Then there was no weight; no sound; nothing at all.

"Am I dead?" asked Semley.

"Oh no, Lady," said a voice she did not like.

Opening her eyes, she saw the white face bent over her, the wide lips pulled back, the eyes like little stones. Her bonds had fallen away from her, and she leaped up. She was weightless, bodiless; she felt herself only a gust of terror on the wind.

"We will not hurt you," said the sullen voice or voices. "Only let us touch you, Lady. We would like to touch your hair. Let us touch your hair. . . ."

The round cart they were in tumbled a little. Outside its one window lay blank night, or was it mist, or nothing at all? One long night, they had said. Very long. She sat motionless and endured the touch of their heavy gray hands on her hair. Later they would touch her hands and feet and arms, and once her throat: at that she set her teeth and stood up, and they drew back.

"We have not hurt you, Lady," they said. She shook her head.

When they bade her, she lay down again in the chair that bound her down; and when light flashed golden, at the window, she would have wept at the sight, but fainted first.

"Well," said Rocannon, "now at least we know what she is."

"I wish there were some way of knowing *who* she is," the curator mumbled. "She wants something we've got here in the Museum, is that what the trogs say?"

"Now, don't call 'em trogs," Rocannon said conscientiously; as a hilfer, an ethnologist of the High Intelligence Life-forms, he was supposed to resist such words. "They're not pretty, but they're Status C Allies. . . . I wonder why the Commission picked them to develop? Before even contacting all the HILF species? I'll bet the survey was from Centaurus—Centaurans always like nocturnals and cave dwellers. I'd have backed Species II, here, I think."

"The troglodytes seem to be rather in awe of her."

"Aren't you?"

Ketho glanced at the tall woman again, then reddened and laughed. "Well, in a way. I never saw such a beautiful alien type in eighteen years here on New South Georgia. I never saw such a beautiful woman anywhere, in fact. She looks like a goddess." The red now reached the top of his bald head, for Ketho was a shy curator, not given to hyperbole. But Rocannon nodded soberly, agreeing.

"I wish we could talk to her without those tr—Gdemiar as interpreters. But there's no help for it." Rocannon went toward their visitor, and when she turned her splendid face to him he bowed down very deeply, going right down to the floor on one knee, his head bowed and his eyes shut. This was what he called his All-Purpose Intercultural Curtsey, and he performed it with some grace. When he came erect again the beautiful woman smiled and spoke.

"She say, Hail, Lord of Stars," growled one of her squat escorts in Pidgin-Galactic.

"Hail, Lady of the Angyar," Rocannon replied. "In what way can we of the Museum serve the lady?"

Across the troglodytes' growling her voice ran like a brief silver wind.

"She say, Please give her necklace which treasure her blood-kin-forebears long long."

"Which necklace?" he asked, and understanding him, she pointed to the central display of the case before them, a magnificent thing, a chain of yellow gold, massive but very delicate in workmanship, set with one big hot-blue sapphire. Rocannon's eyebrows went up, and Ketho at his shoulder murmured, "She's got good taste. That's the Fomalhaut Necklace—famous bit of work."

She smiled at the two men, and again spoke to them over the heads of the troglodytes.

"She say, O Starlords, Elder and Younger Dwellers in House of Treasures, this treasure her one. Long long time. Thank you."

"How did we get the thing, Ketho?"

"Wait; let me look it up in the catalogue. I've got it there. Here. It came from these trogs—trolls—whatever they are: Gdemiar. They have a bargain-obsession, it says; we had to let 'em buy the ship they came here on, an AD-4. This was part payment. It's their own handiwork."

"And I'll bet they can't do this kind of work anymore, since they've been steered to Industrial."

"But they seem to feel the thing is hers, not theirs or ours. It must be important, Rocannon, or they wouldn't have given up this time-span to her errand. Why, the objective lapse between there and Fomalhaut must be considerable!"

"Several years, no doubt," said the hilfer, who was used to star-jumping. "Not very far. Well, neither the *Handbook* nor the *Guide* gives me enough data to base a decent guess on. These species obviously haven't been properly studied at all. The little fellows may be showing her simple courtesy. Or an interspecies war may depend on this damn sapphire. Perhaps her desire rules them, because they consider themselves totally inferior to her. Or, despite appearances, she may be their prisoner, their decoy. How can we tell? Can you give the thing away, Ketho?"

"Oh, yes. All the Exotica are technically on loan, not our property, since these claims come up now and then. We seldom argue. Peace above all, until the War comes. . . ."

"Then I'd say give it to her."

Ketho smiled. "It's a privilege," he said. Unlocking the case, he lifted out the great golden chain; then, in his shyness, he held it out to Rocannon, saying, "You give it to her."

So the blue jewel first lay, for a moment, in Rocannon's hand.

His mind was not on it; he turned straight to the beautiful, alien woman, with his handful of blue fire and gold. She did not raise her hands to take it, but bent her head, and he slipped the necklace over her hair. It lay like a burning fuse along her golden-brown throat. She looked up from it with such pride, delight, and gratitude in her face that Rocannon stood wordless, and the little curator murmured hurriedly in his own language, "You're welcome, you're very welcome." She bowed her golden head to him and to Rocannon. Then, turning, she nodded to her squat guards—or captors?—and, drawing her worn blue cloak about her, paced down the long hall and was gone. Ketho and Rocannon stood looking after her.

"What I feel . . ." Rocannon began.

"Well?" Ketho inquired hoarsely, after a long pause.

"What I feel sometimes is that I . . . meeting these people from worlds we know so little of, you know, sometimes . . . that I have as it were blundered through the corner of a legend, or a tragic myth, maybe, which I do not understand. . . ."

"Yes," said the curator, clearing his throat. "I wonder . . . I wonder what her name is."

Semley the Fair, Semley the Golden, Semley of the Necklace. The Clayfolk had bent to her will, and so had even the Starlords in that terrible place where the Clayfolk had taken her, the city at the end of the night. They had bowed to her, and given her gladly her treasure from amongst their own.

But she could not yet shake off the feeling of those caverns about her where rock lowered overhead, where you could not tell who spoke or what they did, where voices boomed and gray hands reached out— Enough of that. She had paid for the necklace; very well. Now it was hers. The price was paid, the past was the past.

Her windsteed had crept out of some kind of box, with his eyes filmy and his fur rimed with ice, and at first when they had left the caves of the Gdemiar he would not fly. Now he seemed all right again, riding a smooth south wind through the bright sky toward Hallan. "Go quick, go quick," she told him, beginning to laugh as the wind cleared away her mind's darkness. "I want to see Durhal soon, soon. . . ."

And swiftly they flew, coming to Hallan by dusk of the second day. Now the caves of the Clayfolk seemed no more than last year's nightmare, as the steed swooped with her up the thousand steps of Hallan and across the Chasmbridge where the forests fell away for a thousand feet. In the gold light of evening in the flightcourt she dismounted and walked up the last steps between the stiff carven figures of heroes and the two gatewards, who bowed to her, staring at the beautiful, fiery thing around her neck.

In the Forehall she stopped a passing girl, a very pretty girl, by her looks one of Durhal's close kin, though Semley could not call to mind her name. "Do you know me, maiden? I am Semley, Durhal's wife. Will you go tell the Lady Durossa that I have come back?"

For she was afraid to go on in and perhaps face Durhal at once, alone; she wanted Durossa's support.

The girl was gazing at her, her face very strange. But she murmured, "Yes, Lady," and darted off toward the Tower."

Semley stood waiting in the gilt, ruinous hall. No one came by; were they all at table in the Revel-hall? The silence was uneasy. After a minute Semley started toward the stairs to the Tower. But an old woman was coming across the stone floor, holding her arms out, weeping.

"O Semley, Semley!"

She had never seen the gray-haired woman, and shrank back.

"But, Lady, who are you?"

"I am Durossa, Semley."

She was quiet and still, all the time that Durossa embraced her and wept, and asked if it was true the Clayfolk had captured her and kept her under a spell all these long years, or had it been the Fiia with their strange arts? Then, drawing back a little, Durossa ceased to weep.

"You're still young, Semley. Young as the day you left here. And you wear round your neck the necklace. . . ."

"I have brought my gift to my husband, Durhal. Where is he?"

"Durhal is dead."

Semley stood unmoving.

"Your husband, my brother, Durhal Hallanlord was killed seven years ago in battle. Nine years you had been gone. The Starlords came no more. We fell to warring with the Eastern Halls, with the Angyar of Log and Hul-Orren. Durhal, fighting, was killed by a midman's spear, for he had little armor for his body, and none at all for his spirit. He lies buried in the fields above Orren Marsh."

Semley turned away. "I will go to him, then," she said, putting her hand on the gold chain that weighed down her neck. "I will give him my gift."

"Wait, Semley! Durhal's daughter, your daughter, see her now, Haldre the beautiful!"

It was the girl she had first spoken to and sent to Durossa, a girl of nineteen or so, with eyes like Durhal's eyes, dark blue. She stood beside Durossa, gazing with those steady eyes at this woman Semley who was her mother and was her own age. Their age was the same, and their gold hair, and their beauty. Only Semley was a little taller, and wore the blue stone on her breast.

"Take it, take it. It was for Durhal and Haldre that I brought it from the end of the long night!" Semley cried this aloud, twisting and bowing her head to get the heavy chain off, dropping the necklace so it fell on the stones with a cold, liquid clash. "O take it, Haldre!" she cried again, and then, weeping aloud, turned and ran from Hallan, over the bridge and down the long, broad steps, and, darting off eastward into the forest of the mountainside like some wild thing escaping, was gone.

Ron Goulart, who began producing his own patented brand of science-fictional humor in 1952, has been an occasional contributor to Amazing® Stories *over the years. He is the author of many (mostly humorous) novels, including* The Sword Swallower, After Things Fell Apart, Hawkshaw, The Hellhound Project, *and* Cowboy Heaven. *This story was published in March 1965.*

CALLING DR. CLOCKWORK
by Ron Goulart

Arnold Vesper nudged the flower vending machine with the palm of his hand. The dusty green cabinet hunched once and a confetti of yellow rose petals snapped out of the slot and scattered on the parking lot paving. Vesper gave the machine a shy kick. His credit card whirred back out the money intake and he caught it. Turning away, Vesper pressed his lips angrily together for an instant and then hopped onto the conveyor walk that led to the visitors' entrance of the hospital.

He didn't really even know Mr. Keasby. So actually the flowers could be skipped. Vesper wished he wasn't so considerate of his father's wishes. His father lived in a Senior Citizens' Sun Tower in the Laguna Sector of Greater Los Angeles. When he'd heard his old friend Keasby was laid up in an Urban Free Hospital he'd asked his son to pay a visit. So here Vesper was, thirty years old, still doing errands for his father. Well, the flowers could really be skipped.

Urban Free Hospital #14 was a pale yellow building. It gave the impression that its whole surface was vaguely sticky. Keasby should have taken a bigger chunk out of his salary for insurance and then he wouldn't have ended up in a UFH. Vesper hoped the old man wasn't full of stories about organizing the food scenters union back in 1990. His father was.

The android guard was one of the fat pink models. "Visitors' hours end sharp at eight. Be sure you get out, don't make trouble for me so I have to come and get you out special. Is that clear?"

"Fine," said Vesper. "Where's Ward 77?"

"Go right, turn left. Corridor four, then elevator G. Up to three, left again, then right. Move along now."

Vesper went down the stationary corridor, turned left at its end. The corridors that appeared off this one all had letters and not numbers. Vesper continued, slowing his pace.

In front of him a portion of the floor slid away and a bell began ringing up above him. A wheeled stretcher, an automatic one, came up in front of Vesper. The patient on it was a heavyset middle-aged man. He moaned.

The stretcher clicked and moved ahead. The ringing stopped. Vesper stayed still, giving the stretcher a chance to get going. But as he watched, the thing zagged into the corridor wall. A bell rang again as the patient bounced up and then snapped off the wheeled cot. Vesper ran to help.

His feet tangled in the covering sheet. The sheet was dirty gray and spotted. Vesper had to kneel to keep from falling. He almost touched the fallen patient, then noticed that there was blood on the man's chest now. Vesper's stomach seemed to grow out like the ripples from a rock dropped in a pool. He began to swallow and his ears gave him a severe pain. He tried to avoid the bloody man when he pitched over and passed out.

The doctor was a human. He had a slightly pointed head with hair coming down in a strip onto his forehead like a plastic doormat. He had no chin. "Don't I know how you feel," he said to Vesper.

This seemed to be a ward. Five beds side by side, gray sticky walls. Vesper, undressed and wearing a pajama top someone else had already worn, was in one of the beds. The other four cots were empty. It looked like late night outside the one high window slot. "Is that man all right?"

The doctor pursed his lips. "Let's not talk about him. It gives me gooseflesh thinking about that. I'll tell you frankly that blood makes my stomach go whoopsy, too."

"Well, how am I then? I know I'm okay."

The doctor was sitting in a straight chair next to Vesper's bed. "My name is Dr. William F. Norgran, by the way. Why don't you give me all the info on your case?"

"I just fainted, didn't I?" Vesper elbowed up to a sitting position. "See, I came to visit a Mr. Keasby in Ward 77. He's a friend of my father. My father doesn't get around much. He lives in a Senior Citizens' Sun Tower down in Laguna Sector."

Dr. Norgran shivered. "Old people give me the willies."

Vesper said, "I'd like to get my clothes back and go on."

"Let me level with you, Mr. . . . ah . . ."

"Vesper. Arnold Vesper."

"Mr. Vesper, whenever somebody is brought in here to Urban Free Hospital #14 he has to be checked out. This is a charity hospital. We have to be thorough. It's our obligation to the public."

"But I have Multimedical. I work in the Oleomargarine Division of one of our largest motivational research companies. I'm covered even if I were sick. I wouldn't have to come to an UFH."

"Yes," said Dr. Norgran, clearing his throat. "You've had some sort of seizure possibly. We can't be too careful in cases of this sort." He shifted in his chair. "Listen. Is that motivational research as much fun as it sounds? I'll tell you why I ask. I wanted to major in that at school, but my folks wanted me to be a doctor. Here I am, stranded in a freeby hospital. During my internship at Hollywood Movie Hospital I kept fainting and getting sick headaches. That helped stick me here."

"It's pretty tough getting into motivational research without a degree in it," said Vesper, looking around the room. There did not seem to be any lockers or closets. "Where exactly are my clothes?"

Dr. Norgran shrugged. "One of the android orderlies whisked them away someplace. Frankly, Mr. Vesper, it's hell being a human doctor here. You don't have a fighting chance. Particularly if you happen to feel queasy about blood. As you may know, the Head Physician at most Urban Frees is an android. And old Dr. Clockwork is a real toughie to work under."

"Dr. Clockwork?"

"We just call him that. The few humans here with the sense of humor enough. Because of the way he whirs and clanks sometimes. His official name is Medi Android A-12 #675 RHLW. An old devil, believe you me."

Vesper nodded. "As soon as you examine me I can go. You can understand, being that way yourself, that I just fainted because of the blood. Did that man die?"

Dr. Norgran gave a quick negative wave of his hand. "Let's not dwell on him. Mr. Vesper, you can really do me a favor. I'll confess somthing to you. I'm fairly sure it's only a temporary condition. The thing is, I've developed this absolute horror of touching people. Has nothing to do with you. It's my nag."

"I'm afraid I don't follow you."

"I'd prefer to let Dr. Clockwork look at you. I get so really creepy crawly lately if I have to examine someone. Silly of me, isn't it?"

"Why don't you just let me go?"

The doctor shook his head. "No, no. You're already being processed. If you belong to Multimedical, then the office andies have already got your MM card from your effects."

"Effects are what dead people have."

Dr. Norgran blushed. "Sorry. Don't let anything worry you, Mr. Vesper. The MM people and our staff are on top of this. You concentrate on getting a good night's sleep."

Vesper started to swing out of bed. "Night's sleep?"

"Dr. Clockwork spends his nights up in Isolation 3. He can't see you until morning."

"My job."

"The hospital will notify. Anyway, Mr. Vesper, you'll more than likely be out of here before Coffee I tomorrow. Do you have a family?"

"I'm divorced. I live in a rancho tower over on Gower in the Hollywood Sector. A two-room suite."

"Lucky," said Dr. Norgran. He touched something under the bed and the bed pulled Vesper back and gave him a shot in the left buttock. "To help you sleep. See you tomorrow. And let's hope nobody else makes any unpleasantness tonight. I'm on duty till the wee hours."

"Wait," said Vesper, falling asleep.

The whirring awakened him. Vesper saw a wide-shouldered android in a frayed white coat watching him. The android had a square thrust-jawed face and a convincing head of backswept gray hair. Humor wrinkles had been built in at the eyes and mouth. "How are we feeling?" asked the android in a warm familiar voice. "I'm Medi/Android A/12 #675 RHLW. The young fellows around here call me Dr. Clockwork." He winked. "I'm not supposed to know about it." The winking continued and Dr. Clockwork made a ratcheting sound and his eyeball, the right one, popped out. "The things we old-timers have to put up with," he sighed, and stooped, vanishing under the bed. "I've got it."

Vesper sat up. "Dr. Clockwork," he said as the android physician, two eyed again, rose up beside him. "I'm in perfect shape. I simply fainted last night while on the way to visit an old friend of my father's. A Mr. Keasby in Ward 77. I'd like my clothes. Then I'll leave."

"Open your jaw for a second. Fine." The android got a grip on Vesper's jaw. "Nothing is simple in the doctor business. That's one thing I learned as an old-fashioned suburban practitioner. Hmm."

"I'm probably late for work." The window indicated it was along into mid-morning.

"Work, work," said Dr. Clockwork. "We all of us rush and hurry. Well, now." He began tapping Vesper's chest. "Breathe through your mouth. I see, I see."

"My father was in the food scenting field for thirty-nine years before he retired," said Vesper, between inhalations. "As I understand it he and Mr. Keasby worked side by side for several decades."

"Roll over on your stomach."

Vesper obliged. "They don't seem to know where my clothes are."

"Nothing escapes my attention in UFH #14 here," said Dr. Clockwork. "When your clothes are needed old Dr. Clockwork will round them up." He ran a finger along Vesper's spine. "Much history of fainting in your family?"

"I don't know. I only fainted because I saw all that blood." He glanced back over his shoulder. "Did that man survive?"

"Well, well," said Dr. Clockwork, pinching Vesper's right buttock. "How often do you faint?"

"Not often."

"What's your idea of often, young fellow?"

"Three times in my life."

"I see." The android made a bellows sound and whirred in a different way for a moment. "For lunch today tell your nurse to give you gruel and some skim milk. Then I'll want to run tests on you down in Testing 4 this afternoon."

"But I have to leave."

"Not in your condition."

"What do you mean?"

"Don't forget the gruel. Relax now." The doctor started for the door. Halfway there he developed a severe limp. He swung out into the hall and in a moment there was a crash.

The bed wouldn't let Vesper up. He twisted around and spotted a switch marked *nurse*. He stretched and flicked it. This produced a humming in a speaker grid next to the switch. In a few minutes a female voice said, "Ward 23 is supposed to be empty. Who's in there?"

"Never mind. Dr. Clockwork's fallen over in the hall."

"He's always doing that. Now who are you?"

"I'm Arnold Vesper and I want to get out of here."

The grid grew silent and did not reply.

Dr. Rex Willow's lower lip made his orange-colored cigar angle up toward his soft nose. He was human, apparently, and he was sitting on Vesper's bed when Vesper came to from an enforced afternoon nap. Willow explained that he was the doctor sent over by Multimedical insurance. After he'd asked Vesper what he thought was wrong with him, Dr. Willow said, "Those kids over at your office really like you. Here you go." From under his suit coat he produced a small carton.

Vesper took it. "I got skipped over for lunch today. The nurse won't answer me on the com system. I hope this is food." He rested his hand on the box lid. "What I really hope is that you'll get me out of here."

"Time enough to worry later, Arnold."

The box contained get-well cards. Two dozen identical ones. Each signed by a member of the oleomargarine team. "All the same," said Vesper, putting the box on his bedside table.

"Similar sentiments can take similar forms." Dr. Willow jumped off the bed. "Good talking to you, Arnold. Sign this punch form set for me and I'll scat. I have to hustle over to some of the big pay hospitals in the better sectors." He gave Vesper a small deck of miniaturized punch forms.

"How come you're here at all? I thought this was a free hospital."

"Multimedical goes everywhere. It's not a bad hospital if you're down and out, Arnold. Or have an emergency like yours." He pointed. "Sign on the red line. On the blue line on the forms where it's blue."

"My pen's in my clothes."

"Use mine."

Willow's pen said Multimedical on it and Get Well Quick. Vesper asked him, "Can't you arrange to get me out?"

"Not if your head physician is dead set against it."

"I don't even have a phone in here. Can't you at least get me one? I really should have a phone."

"This is a charity hospital, Arnold, not a resort. When you are up and around you can hunt down a phone. I spotted a phone cubicle in the visitors' lobby. Sign."

Vesper signed. "Have you talked to my doctors here?"

"Well, of course. Dr. Norgran is a fine boy. Medi/Android A/12 #675 RHLW is the best android in any of the freeby hospitals."

"When he was in here this morning his glass eye fell out."

"A man's handicaps don't reflect his abilities."

"But he's a machine."

"If you don't finish signing soon, I'll have to put more credit script in my landing-strip meter, Arnold."

"Okay." He completed the forms except the line about his mother's hobbies. Willow said that was optional anyway. As the insurance doctor left Vesper called, "How about telling them to feed me?"

"All in due time," said Willow, hurrying.

Toward evening two androids wheeled in a man named Skeeman and put him in a bed two down from Vesper. Vesper found out the name because the man, who was small and old and yellowish, kept telling the orderlies, "Call Dr. Wolter and say Milton Skeeman's had another one." The andies nodded, smiled, and let the bed put Skeeman to sleep.

"When's dinner?" Vesper asked them.

"No mouth from you, freeloader," said one.

"Wise patients are the worst kind. Want to eat, eat all the time."

"And I want to get up and go to the bathroom."

"Your big expensive bed will take care of that."

They left and the bed did.

The lights came on at what Vesper guessed to be seven or eight that night. Something thunked against the door and then it swung in and Dr. Clockwork appeared. "How are we feeling?"

Vesper shook his head. "Why are you in that wheel chair?"

Dr. Clockwork rolled himself over to the bedside. "My problems are too trivial to fuss about. Let's talk about you. Hmm. That gruel doesn't seemed to have helped."

"Nobody has fed me today yet. I'm hungry. It gives me a headache and an upset stomach when I don't eat."

Dr. Clockwork reached up and smoothed back his thick gray hair. "Severe head pains, nausea. I thought so. My boy, let me explain something. Ever since the turn of the 21st Century the Cold War has intensified. It stands to reason, since you can't trust the Oriental mind. While no weapons show on the surface, you can be sure that the mailed glove hides a velvet fist."

"That's not quite the right metaphor."

"The point being that they have all along been using subtle weapons against us." Dr. Clockwork laughed. "You might not think that one of the most insidious weapons known to humanity has been found out by a humble doctor in a humble free hospital. Well now, many great martyrs have had humble backgrounds. There have even been a happy few android martyrs. I may not be human, but I love this old country of ours and I do my best to fight her enemies at home and abroad. That's how I came to discover Contagium DDW."

"What is that all about?"

"Contagium DDW," said the android, his voice quivering. "An insidious germ that they send over to debilitate our folks. Up in Isolation 3 I've got two dozen poor victims. No one on the outside has guessed the existence of Contagium DDW. No one knows of my work. Someday they will. A statue perhaps. There'll be a statue someday perhaps. The first one erected to honor an android."

"But when do I get out of here, doctor?"

"Who can tell," said Dr. Clockwork. "I'm sorry to have to tell you that you've been hit by Contagium DDW."

Vesper felt his forehead again. The automatic nurse never told him what his temperature was, but he suspected he'd had a fever for several days. There was something wrong with the heating unit in his isolation room. The crystal in the thermostat was frosted over, making it difficult to be sure that the room was sometimes much too warm.

As Vesper paced the small room he reached now and then into the pocket of his hospital gown and got a handkerchief to wipe the perspiration off his face. His chest kept perspiring, too. The service was better in Isolation 3 than it had been down in the ward. They fed him regularly and he was allowed an hour's stroll around the cubicle each day.

Something tapped on the view window of his door. Vesper turned to see the face of Dr. William F. Norgran looking in. The live doctor nodded and spoke into the com. "Excuse my not getting back to you sooner. Horrible diseases make me jittery."

Vesper was going to explain that he didn't really have any disease at all and had really only fainted because of the blood. He hesitated. He did feel odd, the fever and the sweating and all. Dr. Clockwork did seem to know about Contagium DDW, even though he never quite explained what it was to Vesper. "I can understand that," he said to Dr. Norgran.

"All things considered," said the doctor, "you're looking moderately well."

"Dr. Clockwork says I'm coming right along."

Dr. Norgran's face paled. "Too much. I've seen too much of you. Sorry. I'll call again later." He bolted.

Behind him the bed beckoned Vesper back.

Vesper didn't take his walks any more and the bed didn't insist. He was fighting against Contagium DDW, but it was making him increasingly tired. It didn't help his condition that the room forgot to feed him now and then or that the heat unit would act up in the quiet hours of the night, suddenly roasting or freezing him awake. Vesper took his pulse, the way he'd seen Dr. Clockwork do it.

The office gang had stopped sending get-well cards. So far as he could remember, his union guaranteed him his job back. He was also supposed to be getting $52/day insurance money. Dr. Rex Willow never came, wasn't allowed to, up to Isolation 3. $52/day was certainly the figure that Vesper remembered from his insurance brochure.

"It's taking its toll," said Dr. Clockwork, wheeling himself into the room. "Buck up, lad."

"I'm feeling pretty good."

Dr. Clockwork rolled nearer. "Hmm. The symptoms are spreading. It's insidious. Still, I vow that someday there will be Contagium DDW sanitariums across the land, perhaps an island colony. I wonder if there can be an android saint. No matter. The thought would be in the hearts and minds of people. No official sanction need be. Let me see your tongue."

"Ah," said Vesper, too fatigued to rise up to a sitting position.

"Yes, yes," said the android doctor.

"Something?"

"We're coming along. Don't fear."

"You know," said Vesper, "I wasn't too appreciative of you at first, doctor. Now I'm feeling I owe you a lot. For diagnosing this thing and helping me."

"Let's give you a shot," said the doctor. "Roll over."

"I really think I'm coming to trust you, doctor."

"Yes, they may call me Dr. Clockwork behind my back, but I'm to be trusted." As he made the injection the android began to whir in a new way. "I'm to be trusted."

"I think so now," said Vesper.

"I'm to be trusted. I'm to be trusted. I'm to be trusted. I'm to be trusted. I'm to be trusted. I'm to be trusted. I'm to be trusted. I'm to be trusted."

Vesper fell asleep before Dr. Clockwork finished speaking.

John Jakes, now best known for his top-selling Bicentennial *series and other historical epics, made his debut with a story in* Fantastic™ Adventures *November 1950. He appeared in* Amazing® Stories *a month later with "Your Number is Up!" He has published several science-fiction novels; but is perhaps best known in the SF/fantasy field for the adventures of the prehistoric hero, Brak the Barbarian, who cut a swath through the pages of* Fantastic Stories *in the early '60s. This story was published in April 1965.*

THERE'S NO VINISM LIKE CHAUVINISM
by John Jakes

— 1 —

Union regulations did not make rising mandatory until reveille. Most of the troops were stirring by 0500, however. For Gregory Rooke, plagued by sleeplessness since an owl's hoot awoke him around 0315, this voluntary early rising of so many of the men bore out a certainty of his which had grown the past few days.

They had a happy army.

And once they finished the run, Rooke would be in a position to write his own contract for the next one. Not bad for a product of the East Hampton slums who only ten short years ago, after flunking out of Pharmacy H.S., had been toting a stingrifle in the rear rank of the Finger Lakes Freedom Fighters, the dusty summer that saw the culmination of the Napa Valley Campaign.

Yet he was just a bit fearful. And, as usual, the boots hurt his feet.

Rooke's vaguely Lincolnesque face, one of his decided assets, drew into thoughtful lines as he stood smoking at the flap of his small field geodesic. In five out of seven major campaigns, he had been fortunate to be on the winning side. And in all seven he had won distinction by giving the part more than it required, thus assuring himself a better part in each succeeding run.

Not all the hopefuls who entered this chancy business were so fortunate. Consequently he realized that when they had their final go today at the holdouts, the victory must be brought off with flourish. Like any man a bit on this side of forty, he was reasonably ambitious. He wanted the prestige that went with being able to demand, and get, a contract written his way.

Perhaps then, the awareness of the stakes accounted for his nervousness. He stamped his field boots down hard in the sweet meadow grass to awaken himself, shake off the mood. Distressing, how the apprehensions wouldn't depart.

Or was his condition caused by something more direct and personal? He'd had several dreams bout Mary Lu lately. Treacly, sympathic dreams. Always upon awakening he was irritated.

In the HQ geodesic, the communications gear squawked. As Rooke watched two butterflies darting in the long grass down beside the gray-silver sheen of Lake Oconomowoc, a seductive female voice honeyed the sweet-smelling air of the May morning.

"Hi there, soldier. This is your old pal Frannie with some pleasant wake-up music for you fellows out there fighting, bleeding and dying for the dairy trusts. Bleeding and dying uselessly, I might remind you. But more about that later. Here's our first tune."

Rooke's thin lips turned sour. A group—Rooke thought it was the UBM combo—pumped a *bossa electronica* into the air.

Throughout the encampment on the lake shore, activity quickened. Extras, bits and principals rolled out of their sleeping bags. A clank and clatter of mess and make-up kits created a counterpoint to the whine from the ordnance pool where the FFs revved their generators and spun their treads. For a moment, Rooke's cynical professionalism, a hard-shell attitude produced by a decade as a working member of Fairness, melted. He was touched by something like a genuine loyalty to the troops, fifty thousand strong, and not a bad actor among them.

Well, not many.

Three hundred feet down the slope, a man in a trench cape beckoned inquiringly. Rooke hesitated. The man cocked his head. Why not? Rooke had no reason for uncertainty about the day's outcome since it had been programmed months ago by the big computers of Wm. Norris Industries/East, the government contractor for the creative part of this particular war. Still, his touch of doubt persisted.

Stage fright, pure and simple. Finale coming up. A trial run with the man standing down there beside the creepie-peepie would take the edge off.

Rooke was a figure of lonely, brooding splendor as he marched down the hillside, tapping his swagger stick against his leg. His epaulet stars gave off a dull glitter in the lightening gray air of morn. He passed the HQ geodesic and heard Fond du Lac Fran resume at the end of the musical selection:

"Gosh, fellows, are you really certain your heart's in this campaign? Think of your wives and kids, your moms and your sweethearts waiting back home—and worrying. Will you get home to them? Are you sure? You know our boys are ready to fight to the death. You know their battle cry. 'Better dead than the high-priced spread.' Do you really want to waste your lives, your young manhood, fighting against such dedicated veterans? Do you really want to oppose a cause you know deep in your hearts is just? What, after all, has made America great? The genius for the synthetic. Do you want to fight the tidal wave of history, fellows? Think about that, you soldiers of UDEF. Think about that while we play another—"

Among the UDEF troops past whose bivouacs Rooke walked now, there was understandably little interest in Fond du Lac Fran. Many of the men did have transistors going, but tuned to capture snippets of news from the area outside the Staging Zone. Only one here or there listened to Fran.

Rooke was one of the few higher-ups privy to the knowledge that Fond du Lac Fran, like her opposite number on the UDEF side, Kenosha Kate (not broadcasting as Milwaukee Marilyn since the Liberation) was nonhuman, a patch job of syllables and phrases culled and re-edited from hundreds of innocuous taped interviews with the most provocative-voiced actresses of past decades. The UDEF soldiers who listened to Fran did so to appraise her as they would any professional. The troops understood that the broadcasts by the propaganda girls were aimed at the general public outside the Staging Zone. Rooke's status was indicated by knowledge that Fran and Marilyn/Kate were tape drums, nothing else.

"Thirty seconds, Pierre," said a sepulchral voice from the speaker grille in the side of the square metal creepie-peepie hovering above the ground on jets of air. The side of the creepie-peepie lens housing, as well as the cape and headphones of the man who had summoned Rooke, bore the logotype of the Government Broadcasting Company.

Pierre winked as Rooke came up. He answered the speaker grille:

"Right, Buster." Then, to his guest, "Morning, General."

"Hello, Pierre. What do you hear about the ratings?"

Pierre's blue eyes grew merry. "We're three points ahead of the Free BC and the Fee BC isn't even in the park."

"Terrific."

"Hold on. Okay, Buster, I read you."

Pierre switched off the grille speaker. He adjusted his ear button. "Stand by, General." He waited, fixing his wry and weary reportorial smile in place. Rooke shifted restlessly as Pierre got his signal.

"This is Pierre Pell, your GBC field correspondent, speaking to you from a lonely, embattled hillside on the shores of Lake Oconomowoc, less than two miles from the scene of some of the bloodiest fighting yet encountered in this campaign. Yesterday, in a lightning advance from Nashotah, soldiers of the United Dairy Expeditionary Forces pressed to within striking distance of the last major point of resistance of the AMMA irregulars, the headquarters of Burton Tanzy, former executive VP of AMMA. Casualties in the advance were heavy. To offer some comments on this climactic phase of the campaign, I have with me the commander of the UDEF striking force, Major General William ('Butterfat Bill') Smith."

The self-motorized creepie-peepie dollied back to include Rooke in a two shot. Pierre Pell continued smoothly.

"At the outset of the war five and a half months ago, the opposition had some caustic remarks about the nickname of General Smith, then newly elevated to the rank of the chief field commander for UDEF. They've learned that General Smith's name was not bestowed lightly."

Rooke peered straight into the lens. "I certainly hope they've learned that, Pierre."

"To you—and to all these men fighting and dying out here, General—butterfat is not a joking word, am I correct?"

"Yes, Pierre. Butterfat is a way of life. The natural, wholesome way. And we're going to make the holdouts realize it, even if we have to jam the word 'butterfat' down their throats with the point of the stingrifle."

"Then I take it, General, your orders from UDEF remain the same?"

Rooke's nod was brief. "Exactly the same as they were when we liberated Milwaukee three weeks ago and our batallions captured the AMMA executive offices. The only terms acceptable to UDEF—the only terms under which we will deal with the American Margarine Manufacturers Association—are the terms of unconditional surrender."

Rather good, Rooke thought to himself. Of course he had cribbed from the often-quoted unconditional surrender speech of the commander of the Finger Lakes Freedom Fighters, old Wesley Woodis, who was now retired at an Actor's Fairness Senior Citizen Ranch in Arizona. Wesley had stood in a light breeze in Golden Gate Park and vowed to the world that only the total surrender of the Napa Wine Cooperative, surrender terms to include a new contract with many binding East-of-the Mississippi restraint of trade clauses, would be acceptable. Rooke had thrilled to Wesley Woodis's style and never forgotten.

The war correspondent was talking again. "—perhaps you can give us some indication of the strategic situation this morning, General."

"Be happy to, Pierre."

The main studio in Washington cut in a visual. Rooke saw it on the monitor panel on the front of the creepie-peepie housing. It was a simplified map of the area. Pierre explained, voice-over:

"General, I might point out to our audience of three hundred million Americans that we are now looking at a map of the primary battle zone. This territory has literally been devastated by some of the most savage fighting in the history of modern commercial warfare. On your screen, viewers, you are looking at an area of roughly two hundred and fifty square miles, comprised of three counties, Jefferson County to screen left, Waukesha screen center and Milwaukee screen right."

Pell winked at Rooke to indicate they would be back on camera momentarily. The main studio zoomed in on a large Maltese cross, indicating the UDEF position, and a circle which marked the city of Oconomowoc just a short distance westward. Pell's sudden tired smile indicated they were back into the two shot.

"Can you outline the situation as it applies to Oconomowoc, General?"

"I can say this, Pierre. The AMMA forces would have saved themselves much bloodshed had they listened to the wiser heads on their executive board. The board members counselled unconditional surrender at the time we liberated Milwaukee and captured them. One recalcitrant holdout, however—Tanzy—"

"Excuse me, General, but let me clarify. The General is referring to J. Burton Tanzy, the president of the Golden-Glo Margarine Company, and former executive VP of the AMMA board. Please continue, General."

"Well, Pierre, as you know, Tanzy fled Milwaukee in a milk truck whose insignia had been forged to resemble that of the American Red Cross, which was in the process of delivering free processed milk tablets to men in the front lines on our side of Plankinton Avenue. Tanzy managed to slip beyond our perimeters and reach his plant in Oconomowoc. He has turned the town into a veritable stronghold of hysterical last-ditch resistance. The only men fighting with him, I might say, are misguided pseudo-patriots, escaped criminals and a large percentage of high-cholesterol degenerates. Barricaded inside the Golden-Glo factory, Tanzy has refused to surrender while still alive. Consequently we have moved westward from Milwaukee, suffering some heavy casualties from his guerillas, true, but determined to take Oconomowoc and bring Tanzy in." Rooke gave the lens his flintiest look. "Either alive or dead. The choice is his."

Now Pierre Pell had really warmed to the subject. "Just when do you anticipate taking Tanzy, General?"

Struggling to suppress a sudden thrust of shame at the hypocrisy of it all, Rooke put on a speculative, merciless expression. "By nightfall, Pierre."

"Let me clarify for the viewers," Pierre said in a hush. "You mean by nightfall today?"

"That is exactly what I mean, Pierre. We plan—"

The correspondent cut in abruptly, scowling: "This is Pierre Pell, on the battlefield in Waukesha County, where we have been talking to—this is Pierre Pell returning you to the Early News."

Angrily Pierre jerked off his headphones. He unscrewed his ear button, spat into it, "What the hell's the matter, Buster? Couldn't you for God's sake give me five seconds for a signoff before—oh. Yeah? No kidding."

Pierre turned to Rooke. The latter was already watching the peculiar scene which had appeared on the monitor. Flanked by another reporter in a GBC trench cape, a thin, peppery, white-haired little man in fusty clothes was shown appearing in a doorway in a brick wall which bled all sides of the screen.

"Tanzy," said Rooke in surprise.

"Yeah, Greg—uh, General. That's why they cut in," Pierre said. "Sorry."

"What's that Tanzy has in his hand?"

Pierre peered. "Looks like a gun. My God—a real one."

"Quick! Can you get the audio?"

The correspondent rushed to the hovering creepie-peepie console. He began twisting dials and throwing switches. A small cluster of UDEF troops began to form around the two men. The soldiers wore khakis with the embroidered shoulder patches of the Elzie Division. They looked mainly puzzled. Pierre muttered several uncomplimentary things about the hamming of his professional rival on screen.

The GBC reporter was standing next to Tanzy, talking animatedly. The president of Golden-Glo Margarine watched something out of the frame. His glitter-eyed fanaticism came across even on the reduced framework of the monitor. Pierre's hands flew as he tried to adjust the controls and screw in his ear button at the same time.

"Can't get it amplified, General. Tanzy's hollering something about no surrender. I can hear a little in the earpiece. And I'm also picking up some net traffic at the same time. It's got them all in a flap back east. This was unexpected."

How unexpected, Pierre Pell certainly could not comprehend. In his role as UDEF field commander, Gregory Rooke was one of half a dozen persons who had been allowed to see the Master Warscript, an Eyes Only document. He recalling nothing whatsoever in the final pages of the outline that resembled this macabre interruption. His uneasiness had come home to roost.

Three men in guerilla coveralls entered the picture, hauling on a rope with obvious force.

Gradually the rope's far point of attachment became clear. A reluctant Guernsey was dragged into what was apparently the truck yard of the Golden-Glo plant.

Continuing to gesture wildly, Burton Tanzy advanced toward the cow. He paused for effect before putting the gun against the cow's unsuspecting skull and pulling the trigger.

Pierre Pell's cheeks were the color of oatmeal. "My God, he's gone crazy!"

"What the hell is happening?" Rooke said. "This isn't in the scr—"

He bit his lip before he uttered the damning word. The men around him were muttering uneasily. Abruptly Rooke shouldered a path out. He did not have to feign grimness or worry. For the first time in his acting career, he felt it.

The officers in the HQ geodesic were sweating. They stared stupefied at their blacked-out consoles of tiny lights. To Rooke's query, the baffled answer was:

"We just don't know, sir. Someone's cut the beams. We can't get a thing in or out of the producer's office in the Pentagon."

Somewhere to the west, Rooke heard gunfire.

The genuine kind.

— 2 —

Rooke said, "Keep trying the Pentagon. I'll—" The responsibility choked him up a moment. "—have to send one of you to find out who's doing that shooting."

One of the officers, a Major, carefully studied his nails. "Uh, sir?"

"Yes?"

"Isn't it true that all contracts of principals require no participation in actual hostilities except in the event of accidental direct confrontation?"

Damn stage lawyer! Rooke recalled the clause. In the unlikely event of pseudo-combatants actually coming to blows, accidental or otherwise, the job of investigating the altercation, and the implicit risk of doing same, fell to the CO. It was one of the penalties, if you wished to call it that, of the leading role.

Rooke felt a moment of hot hostility toward his fellow thespians. Then it passed. His belief in the principle of the union contract was too deep and abiding to allow for more than temporary anger. Loyalty did not prevent him from being frightened, though.

"Has anyone seen Colonel Greene?" he asked.

Eyebrows lifted. Another Major coughed. Nervously Rooke amended:

"That is, I meant to say, Aaron?"

"Think I saw him down at the Mess getting his morning injection, sir."

"Uh, thanks. I'll try to get back quickly with some intelligence."

Rooke rushed down the hill. He regretted his last slip in the HQ geodesic. It revealed the extreme state of his nerves to his co-workers of lesser billing.

Enlisted men were signed, processed and paid by serial number. Therefore they used their real names, except when called upon for character bits. But the officers, because they were more frequently dealing with press people like Pierre Pell, knew each other both by real names and role names assigned for the campaign. Which name a man employed depended upon his proximity to the representatives of the news media. An officer who slipped up and forgot his script name in a live interview, for example—he could not count upon his post-hyp block to help him since all the news people were aware of the realities and did not come under the heading "outsiders"—could be assured of never working in another commercial war again. So disconcerted was Rooke by what had happened that he had lapsed the other way. The lesser officers were probably wishing they had not auditioned for their parts.

Rooke entered the O-Mess geodesic and bypassed the short queue waiting for morning vitamin hypos administered by the medico-nutritionists. He searched the O-Mess for Aaron Peskin.

A first-generation descendant of a United Kingdom family, Peskin was a first-rate mimic. As a result, he had won hands down in competition for the role of Rooke's aide, Colonel Googie Greene, a bespectacled, gumchewing, wisecracking officer from the borough of Brooklyn:

"—yeh, when I was just fourteen awreddy and loinin' about da boids and da bees from Shoiley—"

"Googie, may I see you right away?" said Rooke, beside the table where Peskin was having his morning breakfast cubes.

"Jeez, we godda fire boinin' or somepin', General?"

"Outside, please. Quickly."

Once into the light of the now-risen sun, Rooke explained the devastating developments of the last few minutes. Peskin's face lost its mugger's elasticity. When he spoke, the accent which he had been practicing in the O-Mess and which made him a favorite when he wisecracked with newsmen on the air, was gone, replaced by a light flavoring of his natural British:

"You mean, Greg old boy, we may have to expose ourselves to fire?"

"It's in my contract," Rooke said heavily. "And as my aide, in yours."

"Crikey! What happens to Operation Oconomowoc?"

"Issue orders to hold positions until we get back. Then meet me at the motor pool. And bring your sidearm."

Peskin's sandy eyebrows quirked. "What do we do for ammunition?"

"The only place they have ammunition is in Washington. But maybe whoever is doing the shooting doesn't know that."

Ten minutes later, Peskin came running across the pool yard. He hopped in the staff vehicle. He advanced the knobbed levers and shot the car forward on short airbursts.

The vehicle hovered past a line of sentries. Rooke could see that the men were perturbed, uncertain. The cluster watching Pierre Pell's interview had doubtless passed the word that something unusual was happening. Rooke lounged uneasily in the tonneau while Peskin maneuvered the staff car through a clump of maple trees, then held it cautiously on the shoulder of a sunlit, four-lane, nonmagnetized country road.

A light haze to the westward seemed to hang on the horizon, veiling the menace of inscrutable Oconomowoc from sight and comprehension.

"Not a thing stirring, old boy," Peskin said.

"Take it to the right. Slowly. We'll go half a mile and turn back. Unless we find something."

Rooke sincerely hoped they did not. The tight-mouthed, death-defying commander of the UDEF forces was a role only. An image projected to three hundred million Americans who, in their packed vertical cities, found release in the emotional catharsis of fierce partisanship with the armies on either side of the various commercial wars which had uncontrollably wracked the U.S. (so it was made to seem) for more than twenty years.

Out of three hundred million, perhaps one hundred and fifty thousand principals, bits, extras, scripters, producers, newsmen, and members of ancillary service organizations such as The Combat Actors' Studio, were in on the secret of how the national sanity, at long last, was being precariously maintained. None of the hundred and fifty thousand odd, however, escaped the ministrations of the medico-hyp practitioners employed by the Pentagon before and after each run.

The technique was faultless. There had never been a single recorded case of a blabber who was able to talk about the realities to anyone clearly an outsider.

Naturally the commercial wars were excoriated in press and pulpit, and seemed ghastly happenings if you listened to the lip-service on the outside. Now, Rooke reflected as the air vehicle hissed along, this one was actually becoming ghastly, and he was on the inside.

There's No Vinism Like Chauvinism 193

"Bit of smoke curling up behind that ditch, old boy," Peskin murmured.

Glancing out of the bubble, Rooke saw it. The thin thread of black rose against the blue Wisconsin sky just beyond a deserted farmhouse. Civvies were always hastily evacuated at the eleventh hour to leave a Staging Zone clear. This action, billed as humane, was chiefly practical. No news ever left a Staging Zone except through authorized channels. The Pierre Pells checked in every six months for post-hypnos, too. Thus those who might carry unauthorized news outside by shank's mare were rushed from the battle's path by the airtruck-load at the start.

Cautiously Peskin geared down the staff vehicle. Rooke tensed to jump out and investigate. Suddenly he had a vision of Mary Lu's face. Delicately heart-shaped, cornflower-eyed, passion-lipped.

The words were comfortable, easy to call to mind because he had read them aloud, jeeringly, several times during the arguments about conflicting careers which had preceded the divorce. Her personal flacks had ghosted them for a handout. Ironically, Mary Lu had turned up as his opposite number in this campaign. She was the third woman ever to land such a major role. ("I can go to the top, Greg!" she had said. "I can! But not hitched to a quivering jealous baby like you. And once I do go to the top, I'll hamstring you, not to mention that ruthless greedy union of yours!")

Rooke was glad that the Master Warscript had called for her to surrender, as CO of the AMMA fighting forces, in the Battle of Plankinton Avenue. He hoped she was safe in her prisoners' compound back in Milwaukee. He realized he hadn't been so sentimental about her in quite a while. But today's situation had brought him back to essentials.

"Look at that, would you!" Peskin whistled.

A UDEF-marked FF lay upside down on its turret on the other side of the drainage ditch. The treads reflected the sun. Peskin and Rooke approached gingerly. The stench of a gasoline fire penetrated the grassy heat of the overgrown meadow. A redbird flew past above. Rooke extended his hand.

"Force field off?" Peskin said.

Rooke moved his hand ahead further, into empty air.

"Think so. Come on."

The two officers worked their way carefully through milkweed and tall tasselled ryegrass, around to the far side of the smoldering FF. Rooke attempted to grasp one of the hand mounts to brace himself so he might peer up inside the gutted turret where a few flames still flickered. The metal was too hot to touch. Peskin let out a yell.

"Greg! They left one. Ours!"

Whirling, Rooke raced through the weeds. Peskin pressed a palm over his mouth. The sight was not pleasant.

Sprawled on his back over a rotted log lay a UDEF soldier costumed as a Tech Sergeant. A tiny blue plastic object was pinned to the corpse's blouse. Three messy, very final bullet holes had turned to black clotted spots up near his left breast pocket.

"What do you suppose happened to the other two on the patrol?" Peskin asked.

"Must have taken them along."

"But Greg—sweet Elizabeth! The patrols aren't warlike."

"Only from the air." Rooke unpinned the plastic object. "Only when the networks train their cameras from their newsplanes. Then the patrols look warlike. They—" Rooke stopped in midsentence.

The significance of the object in his hand registered. It was a soft poly trinket, molded into the shape of a certain kind of headgear once worn by farmers' wives. For the first time, some of Rooke's confusion was cut away by sheer anger.

"Recognize this, Aaron?"

"Weren't some of the margies wearing them on their berets in Milwaukee?"

"Yes. The Blubonnet Brigade."

Rooke shielded his eyes against the morning sun. He peered into the mysterious distance where Oconomowoc lay hidden.

"Aaron, it must be true. Tanzy has blown a fuse. Somehow, contact with the Pentagon producer has been blacked out and for one insane reason or another, this battle area has been turned into a real—"

A rising whroosh interrupted him. He and Peskin spun. "Some bloke's trying to steal the bus!" Peskin squalled. The men went running.

The thief, however, was clearly unskilled in the operation of an air vehicle. As their boots slapped the concrete, Rooke and Peskin heard curses of frustrated confusion. A spiky-headed silhouette loomed inside the bubble.

"Take him on this side, Aaron, I'll get him from the other!" Rooke sprinted around the scooped cowl. The thief glanced up. As they pried up the bubble clamps, Rooke had the wild impression that they were about to lay hands on a scarecrow.

"Get the hell out of there, mate!" Peskin gave the would-be thief a biff in the ear. With a cry the man tumbled from the bubble, knocking Rooke to the pavement.

When Rooke recovered, Peskin was covering both of them with his empty side-arm, upon whose butt his hand looked shaky and untrained.

As he leaped up and took two paces back, Gregory Rooke had the eerie feeling that he had seen the thief before. The thief was elderly. He wore once-natty navy blue coveralls bearing the tag of a leading mail order firm, a matching light blue shirt and high-top work shoes. His hair was a wild, messy, grayed tangle.

The thief groaned, rolled over. Then his brown eyes popped wide behind his steel-rimmed spectacles.

"Greg! Aaron baby! Holy Moley, are you a sight! I mean—it's me."

"Blooming spy for the AMMA doublecrossers—" Peskin began.

Rooke seized his arm. "No, hang on. It's our referee."

"That's right, that's right!" the thief exclaimed, on his feet and busy peeling gobs of putty from his cheeks.

Lumps of it came away from the side of his head, rendering his ears hairless. He stuffed his glasses, then his fright wig into the capacious coverall pockets. He stood before them twenty years younger, a thin, nervous man with hawk features and upset eyes.

"Charlie Ripallo, you remember me, I was in Milwaukee over that rehearsal time dispute." From another of his pockets, he fished first a transistor radio, then an embossed, forgeproof plastic card which stated that he was indeed *Chas. C. Ripallo, Authorized Referee, Actors' Fairness (Central Div.)*.

Rooke said, "Aaron, you can put up the gun."

"Dunno, old boy. Certainly it's our union. But what's he doing way out here?"

"I can explain that," Ripallo said. He fingered his cheeks, where several large bruises bloomed now the putty was off. "See these! I was out tramping the roads this morning in this damn rube get-up they handed me for this cornpone war, and three guys in an unmarked aircar jumped me and beat the hell out of me."

Rooke glowered, used his thumb. "The same kind who turned over our FF patrol, kidnapped two of our boys and shot a third one dead?"

"Shot!" Ripallo's sly Mediterranean face bleached. "Man, they're not playing Monopoly, are they? The guys who jumped me had themselves tricked up to look like some of Crazy Tanzy's guerillas. But I recognized two of them. Shep Swenson and Moe Gatch. Those names mean anything to you?"

Ransacking his memory, Rooke said, "Moe Gatch is chief referee for the other side, isn't he?"

Ripallo nodded. "He is to the union playing the AMMA crowd what I am to you fellas—the place you holler if something's not kosher in the contract. The only trouble is, those birds have altogether flipped. I heard 'em mumbling after they threw me out into a ditch—I was walking toward your camp when I saw the car standing empty, by the way. Anyway, I think those guys have got Crazy Tanzy hooked on some kind of stim juice back there in Oconomowoc. And they're stockpiling real guns and ammo fast as they can."

Peskin swallowed. "You mean, old boy, this is turning into a—a genuine war?"

"Looks that way."

"Bloody margies!"

"You still haven't got it yet," Ripallo said. "We aren't up against the AMMA crowd as such. That's a front. Their part. This is a union thing. Us—Actors' Fairness—against then, ACVA. The drift I get is, somebody has decided right in the middle of the run that ACVA has been on the losing side in too many of these commercial wars. They mean to call a halt. Some rabble-rouser who's big in their union escaped from Milwaukee and is over there in Oconomowoc stirring them up."

A cloud passed over the sun. Rooke had a premonition, scowled. "Do you happen to know the sex of this rabble-rouser, Charlie?"

"That's a funny thing. It's a female broad."

"She wouldn't have been one of the principals for AMMA, would she?"

In his turn, Ripallo tumbled. "You don't mean top dog in this gig? Yeah, I did hear that. Also that she really hates Fairness' insides. But it's the same one you're thinking about."

Wandering over to the shoulder, Rooke leaned in the shade of a huge elm. He shook his head, which throbbed.

"I should have heeded the warnings." He glanced up, noticed both men watching him, explained, "In addition to choice remarks about my acting inability, the lady of whom I'm thinking once treated me to several long lectures, the substance of which was, Actors' Fairness is an octopus swallowing all the goodies, while the poor American Congress of Variety Artists, of which she was a patriotic and reasonably powerful member, being the Philly area governor, always got handed the less choice roles. Now, apparently, she's decided to do something about it. I'm speaking of Mary Lu Beth, also operating in this campaign under the name of Major General Lynn ('old Leatherboots') Lucky. The CO for AMMA."

Thinking of the corpse in the ryegrass, he added in a glum tone, "Also my ex-wife."

—3—

In mufti and highly apprehensive, Rooke barely heard the reduction in the scream of the turbines. Scarcely ten minutes had passed since the commercial V-liner had risen from the Greater Milwaukee port. Now they were arriving.

That the situation was extraordinary was evidenced by a single fact. Rooke and Ripallo were the only passengers in all of the two hundred and forty cabin seats. Highups in Fedair had lifted the customary ban on commercial traffic in or out of a Staging Zone so that the two men might attend the hastily-called bargaining session.

The Loop's two-hundred-story higher rises were coming into view below. Face pressed to the solex glass, Rooke wondered what the opposition hoped to gain by a meeting. Besides the chance to hurl insults, of course. In commercial war history, there was no precedent for what had occurred today.

Still, if they were talking, they would not be firing up near Oconomowoc. Firing, for God's sake! Live ammo! The notion was both ludicrous and terrifying.

On the air trip down from Greater Milwaukee, the horizon had been aglow with lights all the way. The Metromichigania Area, as the media hustlers referred to it, was populated by some fifty-seven million people. Even far to the eastward, on the water, the little bungalows on their pilings in the aqurbs combined their many tiny window lamps to turn the midnight bright as noon.

The V-liner began to descend more rapidly.

Rooke felt slightly out of contact with reality. Things had simply happened too fast.

Shortly after they had returned from their scouting expedition, a message came through from the producer at the Pentagon. The AMMA—correction, ACVA—resistance had momentarily turned off whatever device had been concocted to block the beams, and the single transmission requested two representatives of Actors' Fairness to attend the 12:30 A.M. negotiations; Fedair clearance was available for the emergency flight.

Rooke had left Peskin in what both men somewhat hysterically referred to as command. He had ordered Peskin to conceal the corpse which was resting under a tarp in the staff vehicle. Hiding the corpse was necessary to prevent panic from setting in. When Rooke and Ripallo left at sunset, an uneasy silence prevailed over camp and countryside. Since ACVA had called for the negotiations, presumably the union could keep its unhinged dupes such as Tanzy in check. But there was no guarantee.

Rooke shook Ripallo, who had a remarkable faculty for sleeping with his mouth open, even in trying times. A slender, coffee-skinned man carrying a brief bag was the only person waiting for them in the windy light of the V-port atop the one hundred and eighty-fifth floor of the Merchandise Monolith. Southeast, a massed light cluster in Soldiers' Square Mile indicated a partisan war rally in progress.

"Hello, Putney," Rooke said as he came down the ramp. "Are you the one on deck tonight?"

Putney George nodded. He seemed tired. "One senior counsel from each union was invited. Those are ACVA's terms, incidentally. They certainly must have some aces showing up north. They're being firm, even dictatorial about the ground rules. You should have seen the snide 'gram they sent to the exec producer."

"Gonna be someone here from the Pentagon?" Ripallo inquired sleepily.

The lawyer nodded again. "If it's any consolation, fellows, I gather Washington is more upset than you are about the possibility of real conflict."

"It's distinctly more than a possibility," Rooke said as they entered the tube. He described the corpse. Putney George listened in disbelief, then tactfully raised the issue of Rooke's ex-wife:

There's No Vinism Like Chauvinism 197

"Can you handle her, Greg? Cool her down some? She's being very vocal."

"I couldn't handle her when we were married. How can I now?"

Sounding annoyed, Ripallo said, "Well, you better think of a way."

Normal pedestrian traffic flowed on the third street level as they left the tube and entered an aircab which the lawyer had waiting. Even this late in the evening, vehicular traffic was stupendous. It took them twenty minutes to travel the few blocks to The Conrad Cloud House, in whose Pizzicato Room the bargaining session was to be held.

On one clotted street corner where they were slowed to a standstill, a fiery-cheeked partisan orator was haranguing a crowd of cheering, stamping, whistling, applauding margarine supporters:

"—and I ask you, I ask you folks," came the orator's amplified roar, "what is the fifth freedom? Tell me!"

"Freedom from cholesterol!" came the thundering reply.

In an opposite lane, a sound truck with directional horns rolled past. It muffled the orator's speech with a special jingle in march tempo. Rooke felt a tingling but fleeting thrill of pride at the stirring music. He could hear little of the lyric, sung by a massed chorus, but he did catch the rhyming of "spoilers" with "corn-oilers" before the speaker incited his emotional audience to charge the sound truck, overturn it and set it afire.

No luckless driver scrambled from the cab, Rooke saw through the rear window. A drone unit, then. In the brief interval before traffic commenced moving again, Rooke watched the attackers fall back, then begin to drift listlessly away. Most were smiling.

The cathartic effect had prevailed again. It was precisely this effect which tended to keep marital hostility, preteen sex experimentation, job mobility psychoses and a thousand other social ills within the range of the manageable. It was this cathartic effect with which his darling ex-wife was tampering. Indeed, she was tampering with the precarious stability of the national good. The union struggle might obscure or even destroy the usefulness of commercial wars. Curse her parochial eyes!

They finally arrived. Passing under the marquee of The Conrad Cloud House, Rooke noticed a newsflash strip jerking its message along the facade of a building opposite.

—ALL COMMUNICATIONS WITH WISCONSIN BATTLE AREA STILL COMPLETELY CUT OFF.

*** YELLOWS SCORE IMPRESSIVE GAINS ON NEARLY ALL FRONTS FOR 15TH STRAIGHT WEEK. PEKING PREDICTS VICTORY.

*** SIEGE OF SAMARKAND ENTERS 958TH DAY WITH SPORADIC FIGHTING BOTH SIDES AS YELLOWS UNVEIL NEW SCHEME FOR GROWING VEGETABLES IN SAND, INSURING FOOD SUPPLY FOR CITY'S DEFENDERS.

*** FIELD MARSHAL NIKOL GRIMINSHOVICH KILLED AT AGE 37 IN KREMLIN FALL. FAMED "BATTLEFIELD BABY" BORN TWO MINUTES BEFORE OUTBREAK OF RED-YELLOW CONFLICT 37 YEARS AG—

Ripallo tugged his arm. Rooke followed the other men. Bemused, he had been watching the flasher stories without really seeing them. He was losing his alertness. He must make an effort to recover. Toughness, that was all Mary Lu venerated.

The men rode silently to the ninety-second floor. Rooke tried to get his field commander image back in shape by scowling at the tube's closed semicylindrical door. An ominous-looking group awaited them inside the Pizzicato Room, to one side of a green-draped table.

A man seated at the head of the table rose, snuffing out a cigar in the table chute. "Gentlemen, good evening," said the man, as armed guards supplied by the Hotel Security Director slammed and barred the doors from the outside. "Was your flight, uh, pleasant?"

"We have no comment at the present time," said Putney George automatically.

The hostility in the meeting room was thicker than thick. Representing the American Congress of Variety Artists, and all glaring, were three persons. A mummified senior counsel. A slovenly, adder-eyed fat man, Moe Gatch. And in the center, slapping her riding crop lightly on the baize, Mary Lu.

As Rooke assumed his seat, he twitched the corners of his mouth to indicate that her showing up in her tight-fitting, star-shouldered battle jacket, battle trousers, and battle boots, all of glossy black leather, was a bit much. No response. He might have been smiling at a pretty stranger, for all the expression on Mary Lu's—dammit, he had to admit it—poignantly remembered face.

After taking two capsules and screwing back the cap of the vial and giving a slight belch, the man at the head unfolded a blue-covered sheaf of papers. The mellow yet commanding voice which had made Desmond Cecil-Vidor Thatcher one of the most successful senior producers in the Pentagon now carried a faint quaver.

"Gentlemen and, uh, ladies, I have before me a brief prepared by senior counsel for the American Congress of Variety Artists in which certain demands are enumerated, together with a declaration that unless these demands are fully met by certain of us gathered here tonight, the contractual players currently engaged in Production Forty-Two, Sub-agreement Two, will foment and carry out armed hostilities against the contractual players represented by Sub-agreement One, the purpose being to force—"

Ripallo lunged up, glaring at Moe Gatch. "We already seen some of your rotten hostilities. We can play that game, too!"

Gatch sniggered. "With that bunch of uniformed pansies you got? Pfaugh!"

"For God's sake, Charlie, sit down," whispered Putney George.

Ripallo, however, would not be silenced. "Mr. Producer, Greg Rooke here and I, we found this dead actor this afternoon, shot to death by some of these terrorist goons who are now pretending to sit down here like decent citizens—"

While Ripallo was orating, Rooke saw his ex-wife blink. Then she bent to whisper in Gatch's ear.

The obese man waved her question away as too ridiculous. Mary Lu slapped her crop on the table. The noise startled Ripallo. His mouth open in mid-defamation, he did not recover quickly enough. The stars on Mary Lu's epaulets caught the light from the ceiling panels as she rose and overrode Ripallo's feeble comeback with her smoky voice:

"Mr. Producer, ACVA categorically denies these ridiculous charges by the representative of Actors' Fairness."

This time Rooke himself felt prodded. "Listen here, Mary Lu—"

"My name," she said, "is Miss Beth to you."

"Your name is Mary Lu Wolowiczniski if you want to be painfully truthful about it!"

"You foul, absolute son of a—"

The ACVA counsel pounded the table. "Contempt citation! Contempt citation!"

"—and if you think you're so good at denying the evidence of your own damn eyes," Rooke was shouting, "then you come up to our camp and take a look at the dead man we've got there. Right now take a look at these marks on Charlie Ripallo's face which were inflicted in a beating by the same people, I don't doubt who shot that man of ours and kidnapped two others. I mean Mr. Gatch and his cronies."

Desmond C-V. Thatcher hammered for order. Mary Lu whispered to Gatch a second time. The latter bellowed, "I tol' you, babydoll, I was cooped up all afternoon with one of them little cuties from Tanzy's processing line. She was showing me her, uh, pat slicing mechanism."

The referee's lecherous leer substituted a lesser crime for a greater. Mary Lu bit her lip while the producer continued to plead for order.

Though she was a willful little twist, hot tempered and ambitious as hell, and though Rooke disliked her actively at the moment, yet deep within his heart he found himself harboring a trace of gooey sadness over their parting.

Mary Lu finally said, "The word of Mr. Gatch that these accusations are false is sufficient evidence for me, Mr. Producer."

"This is the most outrageous travesty—" began Putney George.

"Oh go take a flying—" began Moe Gatch.

"Everyone, God damn it," Thatcher suddenly bawled, "calm *down!*"

Tense silence.

Thatcher brushed back his magnificent white hair with two palms, glanced from face to face reprovingly, said:

"I think this immature outburst on all your parts indicates that you fail to recognize the gravity of the situation. We are dealing not with partisan complaints, but with the very tissue of national mental health. I will not demean your intelligences—" His glare at Gatch indicated that that gentleman might be an exception. "—with a recitation of the difficult straits in which our nation—and remember, we are all Americans—found itself at the end of a decade of prolonged armed conflict between the Reds and the Yellows. We were at peace. We were prosperous. We were not involved directly in the major conflict. Yet our domestic problems, in this ostensibly idyllic time, became mountainous. I will not insult you with statistics on the rising crime rates, divorce rates, insanity rates, and the scores of other social difficulties which had to be forcefully met to prevent this nation from becoming a jungle."

Ignoring his notes, Thatcher continued fluently and with increasing emotion:

"We can all be proud that it was our profession, the theatrical profession, which offered the solution. We were the people both technically and temperamentally equipped to provide our restless, multiplying population with the kind of emotional diversion and release which thinkers more profound than I had reluctantly concluded was necessary to maintain the public order in our country. Your government and mine recognized this when it secretly called in the presidents of those two great corporations, The Dr. Landers Camera Company and Yellow Box, Ltd., and won their agreement to a limited, pre-planned conflict between rival work and sales forces."

Listening, Rooke once more felt a stir of patriotism. Probably to keep them mindful of the structure which unrestrained union feuding could so easily tear down, Thatcher sketched in the details of the evolution from street riots between actors disguised as photographic blue and white collar workers to battlefield combats between actors playing members of the private security forces hired by gigantic corporations and trade associations. Thatcher spoke with much verve and passion. Cynically, Rooke supposed he was eager to settle this because he was rumored about to step up to a cabinet post—either Secretary of Internal Well Being, the big one, or Secretary of News Management. Rooke watched his emotionless wife as he listened.

"—only a complex and super-secret alliance between the entertainment and communications industries, between the highest echelons of big business, the American College of Medico-hypnotists and your government, prevented the great population of America from becoming a neurotic, distracted, frustrated, purposeless—"

"Mr. Producer," Putney George interrupted. Thatcher glowered. "I respectfully suggest that we deal not with historical generalities but contemporary specifics. Admittedly we have a critical and unprecedented situation here. As senior counsel for Actors' Fairness, I am empowered to suggest that the President, as a condition for negotiations, immediately neutralize the present Staging Zone by dispatching federal troops—"

Opposition counsel wheezed, "What federal troops?"

"Surely," Putney George said, "there must be some federal troops left in the United States. They can't all be assigned overseas."

"I'm afraid they are," Thatcher said. "As a representative of the Joint Chiefs of Production, I am in a position to know that, except for callow trainees, our entire military manpower is committed to perimeter defense of the Russo-Chinese conflict zone."

"The suggestion is ridiculous anyway," said Mary Lu. With a malevolent glance in Rooke's direction and an okaying nod from Gatch, she continued, "We don't need gobbledygook and government intervention. All we want is a fair shake."

"Like what?" Ripallo asked.

"A guaranteed agreement that members of ACVA will be on the winning side in all future commercial wars at least fifty percent of the time."

Rooke, Putney and Ripallo exchanged thunderstruck looks.

"We will never agree to that," said Putney with firmness.

"Then," said Mary Lu, slapping her riding crop against her leather breeches, "all we are doing here is wasting our damn time. Gentlemen?"

The ACVA delegation got up and walked out.

Producer Thatcher breathed, "Oh my God," called a ten minute recess after the fact, and swallowed another brace of pills for whatever other ills were contributing to the pained and horrified expression on his face.

—4—

Thatcher rushed around the table to Rooke's place.

"Greg, this ball is in your court. Can you go after her? She's leading them by the nose."

"I'm not sure of that."

"What?"

"Did you notice how she seemed to be taking all her cues from that Gatch?"

"No, frankly I didn't. The point is, Greg, we must get them all back here. At least to sit down and finish the discussion so we know where we—"

Normally a fellow with the best of tempers, Putney George had been irritated in just the proper spot. He interrupted in a shout:

"Mr. Producer, Actors' Fairness will never, I repeat, never, submit to that ridiculous fifty-fifty proposal."

"Shouldn't you at least contact your president and your board before you make such a flat assertion?" Thatcher fired back.

"Mr. Producer!" Putney rushed on. "That Actors' Fairness is more often than not chosen to fulfill the winner's role is vivid testimony that we would be fools to negotiate on that point. Vivid testimony, I say, that ours is a craft union of professional artists, not floozy industrial show hoofers, jugglers, trampolinists, exotics and other mediocre talents unable to register any emotion save the stereotyped leer of the evil—"

"Now I kind of resent that, Putney," Rooke found himself interrupting in turn. "Mary Lu may have a nasty temper, but she's a good actress, not a floozy."

"Whose side ya on?" Ripallo cried.

Thatcher said, "We'll talk about it later. The problem now is to keep talking, period."

Hastily he summoned one of the armed guards. "Pick up your spyphone and peep those people who just walked out. I assume they haven't left the hotel. I want to know where they are."

The guard rushed from the room. Thatcher turned toward the three men, all arguing at the top of their lungs, and in a still louder voice demanded that they shut up. They did.

"Now, Greg," said the Pentagon representative puffily, "if they have not left the building, I'm putting it up to you to go after them, especially your wife, and bring them back to the bargaining table."

"Ah," Ripallo said, gesturing, "she's got those jerks brainwashed."

Gregory Rooke had a sudden impulse to punch Ripallo in the nose. He refrained, both because temper would not help, and because he suddenly felt compelled to learn who was actually in control of the ACVA delegation.

Mary Lu seemed the spokesman, true. Yet her whispered colloquy with Moe Gatch regarding the shot actor cast some doubt on her full awareness of what was happening. Rooke would have bet money Mary Lu had not been dissembling. He knew her well enough to know when she was performing, and when not.

He also felt a certain sudden and inexplicable urge to vindicate her.

Or himself?

Either way, he had thought enough of her at one time to propose. Ripallo and Putney George had already dumped her into a category with that oaf Gatch. He felt compelled to discover whether this was so, and the Mary Lu of yore no more. He hoped not. To Thatcher he promised:

"Mr. Producer, I'll do my best."

Shortly the armed guard buzzed. Thatcher lit up the panel for half a minute, then hustled back to the table, a tiredly hopeful smile on his face.

"Evidently it's as I suspected. The walkout was a bit of a bluff, gentlemen. All three adjourned to the cocktail bar on forty-four. They're obviously waiting. It's our move. Go to it, Greg."

The tube ride downward seemed endless. Two commercial travellers off for a late flight were commenting about the mysterious shortage of war news from Wisconsin. Lest they recognize his face, Rooke quickly drew out his shades and donned them. Consequently, he could see virtually nothing when he stepped beneath the large sign suspended at the end of the arcade on the forty-fourth floor. The sign's lettering, formed of glowing tubes, penetrated the green darkness produced by his glasses— *The Walt Bisbee Heirs present THE WONDERFUL WORLD OF LIBATIONS*—but for a moment nothing else did. He whipped off the shades again and peered around in the gloom.

That the bar concession was almost a huge hall had been cleverly disguised by a variety of divider panels and animation exhibits secluded in nooks and subtly lighted. As Rooke passed one such while searching the tables, an electronic Omar Khayyam with an Anglo-Saxon countenance rolled forward on casters, was hit with a spotlight and began to recite verses from *The Rubaiyat* to music. Rooke was so tense, he half swung to take a punch at an imagined adversary before he caught on.

"Why, it's the General. The General looks a little nervous, don't he, counsel?"

The voice issued from a dark cove booth. Rooke stepped closer. Moe Gatch had spoken, in an insulting tone. The attorney kept his peace. There was a third drinking globe hovering half an inch off the table, but Mary Lu was absent.

"I'll deal with Miss Beth, if you don't mind, Gatch."

"Suit yourself. Question is, will she deal with you?"

Rooke checked a sarcastic comment. Though Gatch might be a power in ACVA, he was clearly a hooligan. Baiting him would serve no purpose. Grubby gangster! He looked as untidy physically as he clearly was mentally. Beneath his sport cape Gatch wore an upper of a cheap, flashy lemon shade, fitting tightly around his neck where it appeared to darken to a deeper ring of the same hue. How did Mary Lu become involved with seedy sorts who didn't even bathe? Rooke wondered, facing around.

Just then Mary Lu emerged from beneath an electronic wall figure representing Maude Frickert tippling from her cane; Maude's left hand held a sign animated by polarized light, bearing the legend *Gals*. Rooke was gratified to see that his ex-wife had had the good sense to don a mufti cape and shades. The cape was long enough to conceal all but the tips of her military boots. That was all they needed—recognition of General Lynn Lucky by the patrons.

As soon as Mary Lu saw him standing in her path to the table, she switched her course. She marched to the bar and took a stool beneath an animated wall display featuring an electronic figure with curly hair and pince-nez. The figure periodically chanted a chorus of *The Maine Stein Song* through a megaphone.

The back of Mary Lu's cape remained snobbishly turned toward Rooke as the latter hitched himself onto the bucket chair beside hers. He adjusted the levarod so the air column lifted him a bit higher, to proper drinking position. He pressed a mixing stud. He slid a bill into the adjacent slot and waited until the highball revolved into serving position before he spoke.

"Am I allowed to buy you one, Mary Lu? Or are you just resting?"

As Rooke peeled the polyfilm from the top of his globe, Mary Lu swivelled around.

"I told you, Rooke. It's Miss Beth. I told you that. I am sitting here because you were so rude as to stand directly in my path."

Rooke looked rueful. "Miss Beth. God, that sounds ridiculous between people who have—well, anyway." A surreptitious glance. No one was within three stools. "How did you happen to pull that escape in Milwaukee? You could have gotten hurt."

"Listen to my ex faking worry, would you! Greg sweetest, you certainly weren't so solicitous when we were married. Your appeal is phony, dear. As always, your acting stinks. May I ask why you followed us?"

"Followed you," he corrected, his temper approaching the boil. "Gatch and that mummy lawyer you can have."

"Was it to softsoap us into more bargaining under impossible terms?"

"Why did you and your friends hang around here?" he countered slyly. "To give our side the opportunity to grovel while we persuaded you to come back?"

Mary Lu bit her lip. "Well, the strategy wasn't my idea. Gatch's. He's so obvious. I was prepared to walk all the way out."

"Mr. Gatch, along with some friends, beat up Charlie Ripallo and possibly shot and killed at least one member of Actors' Fairness."

The actress guffawed in ladylike fashion behind her hand. "Oh, stop."

"Mary L—Miss Beth, I mean it. A man is dead."

"But Gatch swore—" She depressed a stud. "I believe I will have a drink. But I'll pay for it myself. Greg, you're lying in your teeth, just the way you lied about that canteen chippy when we were married and you were a looie in Romley's Raiders in the Invasion of Detroit. You stood on your flat feet—how are your flat feet, by the way?"

Morosely he drank his thiamine-laced highball. "Still flat. They hurt like hades in combat boots. Concerning that so-called canteen chippy, I did not lie and she was no chippy, she was geriatric, practically. You'll refuse to believe this too, but I was worried about you when I heard you had escaped."

"I'll bet you were! You admit I'm a real threat!"

"Not that way, dammit. Worried you might—get hurt. How did you manage it?"

Briskly Mary Lu downed her drink in a nonstop gulp. Rooke was tempted to say something about living the part of the colorful lady commander, refrained. "That, my bucko," she told him finally, "is my little secret. But I'll be glad to tell you the why. I was enraged by the behavior of those Milwaukee compound guards. All, I might point out, members of Actors' Fairness."

"Heck, you know either union accumulates some scum among the extras, Mary Lu."

No eruption anent the name. He felt he was getting through. More astonishing, he was oddly gratified that he was. His suspicious side cautioned care, wariness, and tried to mentally catalogue all the fierce differences leading to the divorce filing. Somehow, his face inches from hers at the noisy bar, the catalogue would not fall together.

Mary Lu's ripe lower lip was quivering.

"You should have seen this fat swine of a guard, Greg. Immediately he discovered I was a district governor of ACVA, do you know what he did? He and a bunch of plug-ugly pals surrounded me. They began buzzing me with their stim prods. Not enough to hurt, not then. This leading swine reached into his credit case, pulled out his Actors' Fairness membership card and made me kiss it. Kiss it! The plastic tasted horrible. You know I've always felt you people in Fairness believed you were so damn superior, and that one callous act by that brute in Milwaukee showed me. Frankly, it set me off."

Now Rooke sympathized, his own anger directed parallel to hers. "Callous isn't the word for an act like that. What you should have done was screamed for the union referee."

"But, darling, I knew the union referee, Moe Gatch, would be getting ready for the finale out around Oconomowoc, don't you see?"

"Of course! Naturally you'd read the—" He lowered his voice. "—Warscript."

"Yes, and seen the same humiliating role forced upon ACVA people one more time. When I told that pork-jowled guard that I wanted him to 'gram the referee, he laughed. I tell you, there's a lot that goes on behind the back of the stuffed shirts in the Washington front office."

"I can certainly see that." Rooke nodded. "Something ought to be done."

"Exactly. I did it. I won't tell you the details, because that would incriminate some people on your side. But it seems there's a tidy little under-the-ledge trade in special favors going on. You know the type of situation. A family emergency arises but the contract says you can't leave until the engagement ends on such and such a date. Well, doors can be opened. They were for me, in return for a perfectly barbarous percent of some residuals. But I made it to Oconomowoc, right enough—was within a mile of your campsite once, too. I filed my complaint with Gatch, which is all I intended to do before giving myself up. And then, Gatch flabbergasted me."

"How so?"

"He said he too was fed up with ACVA getting second choice all the time, and why didn't we do a bit of impromptu scriptwriting? At firsht—" Mary Lu was not all martinet; the one drink she had swigged was beginning to render her speech slurry now and then. "—I had some, you know, patriotic reservations. Then I thought—oh, what the hell? Fairness has rubbed our noses in it long enough. Mr. Gatch is not as dense as he might look or act, Gregory. He opened his portfolio and showed us some schematics for a contraption to neutralize the outside communications beams, seal off the area while we made our demands. And he had a decanter full of stim juice, one drop of which would make that old hothead, Tanzy, putty. It certainly did. Gatch was the one who called for these negotiations, too. But understand." Stiff upper lip, determined glance. "I was all for it. He seemed to have several friends with him, all equally enthusiastic about the cause, and before very long, we were rewriting the script."

Over his shoulder, Rooke noticed with some slight alarm that the ACVA counsel still sat with his drink, but Gatch had left the booth and disappeared.

"Whose idea was it to have Tanzy shoot the cow?" Rooke asked.

"Gatch's. I thought it was coarse and cruel myself. But effective."

"Then you actually haven't engineered what has happened, Mary Lu, Gatch has?"

"Well, I guess you could shay—say—" She flicked at the collar of her cape, struggling to maintain an air of composure. "Damn you, Gregory, I haven't had a drop shince—since I went into the field. And no dinner tonight, either. Here you've gone and gotten me all gooey and plastered, made me tell—"

The sudden appearance of two bleached spots in Mary Lu's cheeks caused Rooke to stiffen. Mary Lu's pretty eyes attempted to focus somewhere past his shoulder. He spun his bucket just as Moe Gatch popped out from behind an ornamental pillar across the aisle, reaching for Mary Lu's throat region:

"I heard a few things, General. I think you're talking too damn mu—what's wrong with you, Rooke, ya chump?"

Cold in his middle, Rooke pointed.

"The question is, Gatch, what's wrong with you?"

The shaking tip of Rooke's index finger indicated the place where, by virtue of Gatch's energetic lean and reach as he attempted to throttle Mary Lu, the collar of his lemon-colored upper pulled away from his throat, exposing again the saffron-colored ring Rooke had noticed earlier. This time, however, there was no trick play of lights and reflections to account for it.

Blundering back, Gatch whipped his left hand up to his collar. He checked the move too late. "Who are you?" Rooke shouted, and leaped.

His fingers dug in savagely at Gatch's collar line, ripped—

A heartbeat later, strips of something like human flesh and hair hung from Rooke's right hand. Disbelieving, he turned the microthin molded material over. He saw the true nature of the stuff on the obverse—it was an undyed, undoctored off-white color, with a fine pattern of tiny trademarks in parallel lines. The pattern was unbroken except for the breathing apertures and other openings.

Whipping the material up to his eyes, Rooke read one of the trademarks:

PLIO-MA-KUP®
A Mondanto Chemical
Substance
(Max Vector Divison)

"God in heaven!" came Mary Lu's breathy voice. "Greg, he, he's a—"

The apparition in front of them whipped out a genuine pistol from somewhere beneath its cape. The half of the apparition's face yet unpeeled belonged to Moe Gatch.

The other, authentic half, totally hairless and of a deep saffron hue, belonged to a high-cheeked, glittering-eyed and sinister Oriental.

"You will pay for your addled behavior, Miss Beth," hissed the apparition, grabbing Mary Lu by the arm and wrenching her to his side.

Stupefied, Rooke swung a fist. A bar steward rushing from among the tables to investigate the nature of the fuss inadvertently ran between Rooke and the Oriental just as the latter's gun went off. The steward reeled, shot to death. Only the man's accidental intervention saved Rooke's life.

Dragging Mary Lu and scattering tables and glassware behind, the Oriental ran into the arcade and disappeared into a tube. In pursuit, Rooke slammed back from the tube's semicylindrical door as it rotated shut. He shook with shock. He had almost had his hands clipped off at the wrists by the shutting door.

"I don't understand this," came the voice of the ACVA counsel who had chased Rooke into the arcade. "Who was that? Where is the real Mr. Gatch?"

"Probably dead. Keep quiet." Rooke bowled past him, back into the lounge. He indexed the button for the Hotel Security Staff, next put in a call to the civil police. Then he and the unstrung counsel took the tube back up to the Pizzicato Room.

As there were no indicator lights above the entrances to the tubes, Rooke did not know whether the Oriental had gone up or down. He did not know where to begin looking for the Oriental and Mary Lu either. The Security Staff would know the hotel better anyway. But he was deathly afraid for Mary Lu's safety, which now, inexplicably, mattered very, very much. He prayed the Staff would get their licensed spyphones to work peeping promptly.

In an hour a representative of the Staff dolefully announced that the missing pair was nowhere in The Conrad Cloud House. Thatcher sent for a multi-channel set which was installed in a corner of the site of the aborted negotiations, and the group spent the remaining hours of the night sucking on caffeine cubes and waiting for ominous Bulletins.

None came.

At four, the civil police reported that the pair had evidently escaped the city. Thatcher used his influence to contact Fedair's top echelon. Yes, an unidentified V-craft had slipped out of the Chicago pattern at approximately 2:48 A.M., heading northwest.

"Oconomowoc!" said Rooke in a ghastly whisper.

"—expose at last the rotten hypocricy of your own leaders, from first-hand, personal experience in—"

Blear-eyed, Rooke turned toward the noise. On the top left monitor of the panel of nine screens, a bizarre scene was unfolding. A wild-eyed, disarrayed man on a soapbox was haranguing a crowd on a street. Thatcher frantically fooled with the gain until he got the volume so that he, Rooke, Putney George, Ripallo and the ACVA attorney who had been weeping intermittently for several hours, might hear.

"I know that face," Thatcher was saying as he watched the scarecrow image on the monitor. "I'm sure I know that face."

"Which channel is carrying that?" Rooke said. "Where does it come from?"

"This is the hotel's own internal ID channel, Greg. The camera is trained on the main entrance, street level."

"Get him down, get him down, you people!" a civil policeman at the fringe of the pictured crowd was crying.

"Push him off the box! Push him off!" other voices chorused.

"—know what I'm talking about!" the orator exclaimed, windmilling his arms in excitement. "I've been there! It's all a fraud, a sham, these commercial wars. Nothing but fakery!"

The man had the same coked-up look of runaway insanity as the man himself had observed on the screened face of J. Burton Tanzy at dawn. Rooke's mind reeled under the impact of this latest turn of events.

The screaming muckraker on the soapbox was Pierre Pell.

—5—

Gregory Rooke gripped the gasketing at the hatchway edges and held on, arms throbbing, to keep from being blown out. A chron dial high on the control panel and seen at the oblique through his shatterproof goggles showed the time as 09:17. An adjacent indicator registered the chopper's altitude at nine hundred and fifty feet and dropping.

A quartet of smokestacks, the construction-grade high-impact material carefully scored and soot-sprayed to give a quaint and charming effect of ancient brick, seemed to rush at the chopper with frightening speed. Permanently radiating vertical letters on each stack spelled out identical messages:

G-o-l-d-e-n-G-l-o

The cheery yellow signs somehow lent a sinister cast to the wide, innocent blue arc of Wisconsin sky beyond.

Rooke was surviving on sheer tension energy alone. His belly hurt fiercely. He was totally unskilled in matters of this kind. Of course he was willing, considering Mary Lu's plight.

Thatcher and Putney George had V-linered back to Lake Oconomowoc with Rooke and Ripallo shortly after sunrise. Thatcher had consulted the battlefield computers and received a printout which indicated that a quick, guerrilla-type strike was the only means of saving the situation. The others had drawn lots.

Rooke had merely watched. He had already volunteered to lead the party, following a short, but hot-tempered hassle with Thatcher in which the Pentagon producer had ultimately promised triple time wages and, most important, full death benefits from the Fairness pension fund to be paid to Mary Lu regardless of their divorced status in the event Rooke did not survive.

Below, howling, fist-shaking clots of ACVA-AMMA irregulars jammed the streets of Oconomowoc over which they were passing rapidly. The holdouts were clearly surprised by this non-scripted appearance of the huge chopper. Noting their fury, Rooke grew more and more tense.

He moved his left leg gingerly as he squatted in the chopper's open hatch. The holstered press of one of the genuine, loaded, nontheatrical sidearms commandeered by Thatcher God knew where unnerved him. He kept fearing the thing would go off and remove part of his leg.

The chopper pilot began adjusting levers.

"Stand by, gents. It's gonna be a helluva bump."

Thus far the pebbled roof of the Golden-Glo plant, nestled among several other suitably antiqued factory structures, was unoccupied. Behind Rooke, Aaron Peskin shoved his goggles up in place. In his Colonel Googie Greene voice he kept reminding himself aloud:

"It's a perfoimance, nuttin' else. Bluff is half da battle. A perfoimance."

The actor who had drawn the second lot to fill out the trio, a spindly bit player, had fainted when he lost, or won, depending on how you looked at it. Consequently Putney George had volunteered. George, Rooke had reflected, was truly a loyal Fairness man. He had had no reason for returning to the Staging Zone with the others, except patriotism. The same went for his volunteering. Putney George apparently felt Fairness had been stabbed in the back.

Rooke wasn't all that loyal about it. He was concerned about his ex-wife. Had he not been, he would have been unable to maintain even a semblance of the flint-eyed, stern-jawed expression of a fearless CO. They were, after all, actors going against international assassins.

The chopper dropped down and down. Above the rotor clangor, the vocal fury of the holdouts could now be heard as they ran every which way in the streets below. To Rooke it appeared that the chopper would smash into the cornice of the Golden-Glo plant. The pilot cursed, much perspiration on his face. Rooke gripped the hatchway edges all the harder, prepared to jump out at impact.

A courier had been dispatched to the Pentagon by Thatcher, informing the President and Joint Chiefs of Production that, with their major war going successfully at last, the commanders of the Peking bloc had evidently seen fit to release and assign espionage agents to infiltrate the ranks of U.S. commercial war players, with the dimly-guessed purpose of exposing the whole fabric of the trickery and dealing a shatter-blow to U.S. morale.

Perhaps the U.S. was Peking's next target if the anti-Russ campaign went well, as it had been for the past months. Perhaps this blow to morale was but the first stage of the softening process. How the Yellow spies had penetrated the secret of the commercial wars was unknown at the moment, but since that side warred in earnest, it was assumed by Thatcher that their intelligence agents knew all the tricks. There was no doubt that the Yellows had discovered a means of overturning post-hyp blocks. But of course the devils had always been experts at that type of cerebral tampering.

Vivid testimony to their expertise was the appearance of Pierre Pell. Shortly after the scene witnessed on the monitor in the hotel by Rooke and the others, Pell had leaped from the soapbox and fled into the disconcerted crowd. Pell was still at large somewhere in Greater Chicagoland.

Clearly Pierre Pell had been kidnapped. He had vanished from the UDEF bivouac at about the time Peskin and Rooke discovered the burned-out FF yesterday. He had probably been unblocked and shipped out of the Staging Zone—or perhaps fetched along by the false Gatch and then released—to spread his message of dissension. Anyway, it was plain that Pierre Pell no longer had any mental barriers to prevent him from speaking about the great fiction to people not directly connected with commercial wars. Rather than worry about Pell, however, Thatcher and the Pentagon had agreed that a strike must be made at the heart of the conspiracy, Oconomowoc.

During the last few seconds the chopper had descended practically to the roof of the Golden-Glo plant. In the factory's truck yard directly below, Rooke saw hundrds of ACVA-AMMA troops queued up outside a bay from which they were being issued firearms. Putney George craned over Rooke's shoulder, howled above the roar:

"Bet those are bandoliers of live stuff. Bet they airdropped it from drone planes coming in over Canada."

A throaty ker-*chow*, a puff of smoke, and the chopper reeled under a metallic whang. Horrified, Rooke looked out through a small circle in the fuselage into blue sky. The tiny circle was a scant inch or two above his hard-gripping left glove.

A few more shots were fired from the yard, and several sections of a margarine packing crate were hurled fruitlessly upward, only to fall short. Then the chopper was past the cornice, its skids hitting the pebbled roof and dragging along, slewing the craft around.

"Out, out!" The pilot's voice rose to a squeak. "I ain't taking any more bullets. Lotsa luck."

Rooke leaped to the roof. Aaron Peskin followed. Putney George had hardly begun his deplaning when the pilot, a civilian mercenary, gunned hard. The upward jerk of the chopper spilled Putney combat boots over shock helmet. He managed to pull the big twine-tied, paper-wrapped bale out with him, however. It landed with a clump.

Rooke peered through the anti-glare lenses. Carefully he withdrew his sidearm and pointed the muzzle at a small house-like structure between two of the smokestacks.

"That looks like a stairway."

The chopper whirled away up into the blue sky, leaving the trio alone but fortunately out of sight of the cursing, shouting men in the truck yard below. Among the profanities and obscenities which drifted up to them, Rooke heard cries of, "On the roof, the roof!"

Putney George shuddered visibly. "I've never heard actors so furious before."

"Well," Peskin said, "da bums loined—ah, shove that, I'm so blighty scared I can't keep it up. Guess they've hated Fairness's guts a long time. They finally got a chance to do—"

"The—the—door—"

Rooke's gauntlet was flung out, pointing. Why, oh why, hadn't he finished Pharmacy H.S.? He was as brave as the next, but the next was not very brave, not in Fairness.

Peskin and Putney George had their backs toward the door panel in the small roofhouse. that door panel now displayed a tiny but widening vertical crack of black between edge and jamb. Putney and Peskin continued to exchange remarks designed to reassure one another. Rooke grabbed the shoulders of their combat jackets to spin them around.

"The door's opening. Get your guns out!"

Putney and Peskin managed to whirl as the door crashed backward. Carrying a large, round-muzzled portable riot cannon, the sinister Oriental whom Rooke had unmasked in the cocktail bar lunged into the light. From the neck downward he was still costumed, though rather grubbily and showing the wrinkles, as Moe Gatch. He had, however, peeled the remaining half of his phony face off in the interim.

"Put up your guns, Americans!" The agent's saffron pate glowed in the sunlight. Behind, thrusting up from the stairwell, came a tough-looking cadre of half a dozen younger Orientals who made no pretense; they were garbed in the flimsy gray disposable paper jackets and pantaloons of the People's Army.

"Tell them to stop shoving in the rear," the leader said over his shoulder.

"It is the plant president, honorable one," said a Sergeant just emerging.

"I instructed you to keep that imbecile in his office, with the girl."

"But he went into a frenzy upon learning we had captured butter trusters, honorable one."

Muzzle to muzzle, the thespian trio faced the fully armed hard core of the Chinese espionage team on the sunlit roof. Tense seconds passed while no one fired. The Orientals refrained, Rooke felt, because they knew they had already won, and could take their time. Rooke refrained out of a firm conviction that he would be finished if he pulled the trigger, since he would probably miss but the Orientals would not.

One lucky thing. The passing reference to a girl indicated that Mary Lu might be safe. Somehow, that made all the fright knotting his belly and the perspiration steaming up his goggles worth it.

A raucous voice gave a bleat, a curse, from the dark stairwell. The leader swung his head a bit more. His fierce yellow nose was in profile as he hissed, "I do not want that unruly, witless dupe fumbling out here to spoil—"

Too late. Against the growing shrieks, screams, catcalls and curses from the ACVA-AMMA troops in the yard below, a more strident voice broke through:

"Where are they? Where are the unprintable cow-lovers?"

And, nearly knocking the Oriental leader off balance, J. Burton Tanzy, wing collar askew, hair flying, fought his way onto the roof.

Lurching along rubber-legged, Tanzy dug his left hand into his clothing. He drew out a polished flash, took a hasty swig. Shoulder to shoulder with Rooke, Peskin whispered against the former's helmet, "They're feeding him stim juice, right enough. The UK ought never have pulled out of the China Trade. That liquid hell has proved worse than the poppy."

The Oriental leader chewed his thin lower lip, then adjusted what Rooke was afraid was a cocking mechanism on his riot cannon. He swung the muzzle slightly to the oblique so that it pointed at the wobbling back of the margarine magnate who was tottering toward the trio, his right hand outstretched. The Oriental's eyes grew even more narrow as he sighted.

Tanzy came on, coked and giggling maniacally. Extended before him on the palm of his hand was a glistening yellow pound brick of Golden-Glo.

"Now, you devils! Burton Tanzy is going to have his revenge. Burton Tanzy is going to watch each of you swallow some of this—" He hiccoughed violently.

"Tanzy, be careful!" Rooke said. "They're going to shoot you in the back."

"—swallow some of this superior, refined, emulsified vegetable oil. Hah! Won't that flay the butter trusters? Their own toadies forced to down a vegetable oil product? I'm sick of the restrictions!" Tanzy shrieked, his mind unhinged, all knowledge evidently gone that AMMA participation in the commercial war had been wholly voluntary and worked out at cordial bargaining sessions. "The high-priced spread, the high-priced spread! Why can't we just come out and tell the truth, the truth about that rotten but—"

There was a *blam.*

Watching the Oriental's trigger finger, Rooke had had a slight warning. He had seen the knuckle flesh pale perceptibly. In that desperate second, when all his cerebral processes broke down and fear and adrenalin took over, Rooke brought his right boot flying up, hoping to kick poor Tanzy out of the path of death as the riot cannon went off.

His boot-tip caught Tanzy's outstretched hand. The margarine manufacturer flailed and fell, an instant after the margarine block, kicked from below like a football, shot up into the air.

The riot cannon chattered again. Rooke and his companions fell flat from instinct. An equally powerful instinct was at work on the other side. Pairs of startled human eyes followed the upward path of the kicked margarine for a fraction of a second. Rooke—he never knew how or why, later—reacted. Perhaps professionalism ran deeper than fear after all:

"*Charge!*"

Sidearms spitting, the counsel and Aaron Peskin followed Rooke's headlong lunge. Once you got the hang of it, the sidearm was remarkably easy to fire. The noise was thunderous.

The espionage agents in their paper uniforms managed a few return efforts. But having glanced upward collectively at the margarine was their undoing. Rooke's bullets mowed down three. Peskin and Putney George accounted for another four between them. Then only the leader remained, scarcely feet from the charging Rooke now. But fully in control as he swung the riot cannon around to remove Rooke's head with a single blast.

The trio's attack and the exchange of fire had taken less than seconds. From out of the sun, the brick of Golden-Glo completed its flight path and splattered soundly against the leader's shaved pate.

"Aieee!"

The Oriental jerked the riot cannon trigger as sunny yellow table spread oozed down around his ears. The light blow on the head threw him off balance just enough, however. The cannon projectile puffed past Rooke to smash blocks from the cornice behind. Rooke had the presence of mind to realize that someone might wish to question the chief spy later. He thrust his sidearm against the Oriental's left leg and fired.

He disarmed the chief spy after he fell. Laughing uproariously in surprise and disbelief, Peskin and Putney George rushed among the other agents, disarming them also. No more Chinese appeared on the stairwell.

"Kill the cow-lovers! Kill the cow-lovers! Kill the cow-lovers!"

The chant, unnoticed by Rooke during the shooting, now beat on his ears with fresh force and menace. Putney George rushed to the cornice, turned back. "My God! They're coming up the walls after us!"

As if it were a cue, a grappling hook, then another, caught the cornice with solid chunks. Rooke hurried in that direction.

Directly below the first hook, a member of ACVA, a genuine sidearm gripped in his teeth, was climbing a flexible ladder. Anti-Fairness hostility shone in his eyes.

"We're finished, Greg," Putney George shuddered. "They'll tear us apart."

Rooke had to admit it looked that way. Desperately he scanned the roof. Then he saw it.

"The bale! You forgot the bale!"

The men seemed all thumbs getting the twine and wrapping off. But at last, just as the scalp of the first ACVA performer rose above the cornice, Rooke and the others unwrapped the leaflets. They were jerry-printed, the ink still smeary on the front cover where the numerals 50/50 blazed forth in 36-point fluorescent green ink. In his right hand Rooke carried the one other object from the bale as Putney George and Peskin began raining handfuls of leaflets down onto the hundreds in the truck yard.

The actor who had climbed all the way up already had a leg over and resting on the cornice. He was aiming his sidearm at Rooke's forehead.

"Take a leaflet, a leaflet!" Rooke waved one and prepared to dodge another bullet if necessary. "Actor's Fairness agrees! Fifty-fifty split on the winning roles from now on!"

"It's a trick," snarled the cornice gunman.

"No, it isn't, here! The President of Fairness is waiting to talk to any one of you, any spokesman! You can talk to him if you want. Here, the dial's set for the Vegas band. Just get someone to turn off whatever machine is scrambling the beam signals and you'll be able to talk to him." Rooke held the tiny transmitter inches from the quavering muzzle of the ACVA professional. In rather superior fashion Rooke managed to feel that the man was obviously as inexperienced with firearms. Correction, had been.

The brows of the actor on the cornice beetled briefly. In order to take the transmitter, he had to put away his sidearm. Mercifully, he did.

In minutes, it was all over.

The scrambler was located, turned off and discreetly smashed. The mellow voice of Frankie Clan III, amplified to blare out over the yard, assured the ACVA members that the offer was genuine. The sidearms disappeared.

Putney George found the room where the two UDEF soldiers, kidnapped while on patrol, had been kept prisoner. In Burton Tanzy's executive office—the margarine magnate tried to block Rooke's entrance by madly running a motorized pallet-load of cartoned Golden-Glo down the corridor: he was carried out frothing—Rooke found Mary Lu, shaken, alarmed, but unbruised. The Oriental leader had been on the point of administering a punishment with some bamboo slivers when the unexpected chopper arrived.

To Rooke's surprise and delight, Mary Lu actually hugged him.

Next came a hasty script conference, with Rooke acting for Fairness, Mary Lu for ACVA. Rooke pointed out that despite the new agreement, to alter the outcome of the current engagement would not be playing by the rules. Delighted by the copy of the leaflet she was reading, Mary Lu offered no objection whatever.

So, at 11:02, the UDEF banner was raised from the Golden-Glo flagpole, per script. The flag fluttered out, rich blue satin and crested with two smiling tots with tumblers of milk rampant upon a field of milking machines and udders.

Even the ACVA-AMMA troops, fingers messy with the green ink of the leaflets, waved and cheered. A new day of concord was at hand. The correspondent from the Fee BC was the first to reach Oconomowoc and flash the word to a breathless nation.

The one clear and present danger still remaining was the deranged, unblocked Pell, at large somewhere in Greater Chicagoland and armed with a catastrophic weapon which could undo them all.

The truth.

—6—

Eastward from the esplanade, lamps in the aqurb bungalows glowed like cheerful fireflies in the twilight. Behind, the Greater Chicagoland skyline reared impressively. A news flimsy went skittering past, left by some pedestrian who had abandoned the strollways to the nippy autumn wind. Part of a headline proclaimed that the Reds were on the advance, the Yellows had suffered a series of calamitous setbacks.

A large, new Unioncarb Preferred Paste stone on Mary Lu's third finger caught a random beam from the sinking sun. The new ring glittered as she snuggled close behind Rooke, eagerly waiting for him to open the cover page of the Master Warscript which had been flown out to them Saturday by the assigned producer.

"Who is it, darling?" Mary Lu said before the opening cover had quite revealed it.

Seated on the right, Rooke had the advantage: "Wow! Pan-Eastern against the Harold Hughes, Junior, Airfleet." Rooke glanced into his new, yet comfortingly familiar, wife's face. "Sonic dogfights! This looks like a dandy."

"I've never flown a plane," Mary Lu said.

"Neither have I. The stunters'll do the actual flying. We'll just appear on the cut-in cameras. Think of the great process effects. There we'll be, in the studio cockpit, and it'll look just like—"

"Two dollars for a cuppa java for a vet, mister?"

The bum's whine interrupted their excited talk. Against the dim twilight radiance in the sky, the bum was a sorry, decrepit figure in a filthy cape, with unclipped hair and untrimmed fingernails. He extended a palsied hand. Rooke goggled.

"Pierre!"

The bum blinked. "You know me?"

"Of course! You're Pierre Pell, former GBC correspondent. Nobody's seen you for months! Where have you been?"

"I don' know you," the bum said, with suspicion. "How about two dollars for a cuppa java, mac?"

Mary Lu shivered. "Oh, the poor creature."

Rooke leaped up. "Pierre, let us find a doctor for you."

"G'wan!" The derelict flailed loose, almost savagely." 'M okay. Gotta mission. Gotta tell people—wars 'r phony. Being tricked. Been wandering streets days 'n days. Nobody'll listen. They laugh. Throw rocks. Beat me up. Won' listen. They won' listen 'r believe." Large crocodile tears began to trickle down his cheeks, glistening in the fall sunset.

"Help him, darling," Mary Lu whispered, warm against Rooke's side.

"Yes, he needs—" Rooke stiffened. Pierre licked his lips. He seemed to peer right through them at nowhere. *Sotto voce*, Rooke said, "His collar."

Mary Lu looked, stifled a gasp. Pierre seemed oblivious. A telltale saffron ring was briefly visible. Rooke pressed his lips against her ear so the bum would not hear:

"Probably realizes he's failed his mission and it's driven him mad."

"Casualties," the false Pierre was saying with a sweeping gesture at the skyline. "Three hunner million casualties of th' wars of d'ception. Gotta tell the truth. Tell 'm they're all casualties."

"God," Rooke breathed with a shudder, "war is Hell. Even our kind."

"War's a lozzy phony deal," Pierre exclaimed.

With only the briefest twinge of conscience, Rooke said, "War is also, unfortunately, necessary. That's where you people made your mistake. You still expend your energies in real killing. We've learned." He indicated the skyline. "They've learned, too, even though they don't suspect a thing. That's why nobody would listen. That's why the government gave up looking for you a long time ago. Now get out of here."

"No money for a cuppa java for a vet?"

"No."

Pseudo-Pierre shrugged, blinked, burped. "Well, tha's showbiz," he said vaguely, as he turned and tottered away into the failing light.

*Philip José Farmer has always been known as one of the truly startling innovators in science fiction, ever since his first novel,*The Lovers *(1952), introduced sex into science fiction. His most famous work is the "Riverworld" sequence, beginning with* To Your Scattered Bodies Go, *a Hugo winner for 1971. A lifetime pulp-fiction enthusiast, Farmer has produced many amusing pastiches and pseudo-fact works in this area, including* Tarzan Alive, Doc Savage: His Apocalyptic Life, *and* The Adventure of the Peerless Peer. *The present story, published in September 1970, is related to his 1967 Hugo-winning story "Riders of the Purple Wage".*

THE OOGENESIS OF BIRD CITY
by Philip José Farmer

The President of the U.S.A. sat at the desk of the mayor of Upper Metropolitan Los Angeles, Level 1. There was no question of where the mayor was to sit. Before the office of mayor could be filled, the electorate had to move into the city.

The huge room was filled with U.S. cabinet heads and bureau chiefs, senators, state governors, industrial and educational magnates, union presidents, and several state GIP presidents. Most of them were watching the TV screens covering one part of the curving wall.

Nobody looked through the big window behind the President, even though this gave a view of half of the city. Outside the municipal building, the sky was blue with a few fleecy clouds. The midsummer sun was just past its zenith, yet the breeze was cool; it was 73° F everywhere in the city. Of the 200,000 visitors, at least one-third were collected around tourguides. Most of the hand-carried football-sized cameras of the reporters were focused at that moment on one man.

Government spieler: "Ladies 'n gentlemen, you've been personally conducted through most of this city and you now know almost as much as if you'd stayed home and watched it on TV. You've seen everything but the interior of the houses, the inside of your future homes. You've been amazed at what Uncle Sam, and the State of California, built here, a Utopia, an Emerald City of Oz, with you as the Wizard . . ."

Heckler (a large Negro woman with an M.A. in Elementary School Electronic Transference): "The houses look more like the eggs that Dorothy used to frighten the Nome King with!"

Spieler (managing to glare and smile at the same time): "Lady, you've been shooting your mouth off so much, you must be an agent for the Anti-Bodies! You didn't take the pauper's oath; you took the peeper's oath!"

Heckler (bridling): "I'll sue you for defamation of character and public ridicule!"

Spieler (running his gaze up and down her whale-like figure): "Sue, sue, sooie!

No wonder you're so sensitive about eggs, lady. There's something ovoid about you!"

The crowd laughed. The President snorted disgustedly and spoke into a disc strapped to his wrist. A man in the crowd, the message relayed through his ear plug, spoke into his wrist transmitter, but the spieler gestured as if to say, "This is my show! Jump in the lake if you don't like it!"

Spieler: "You've seen the artificial lake in the center of the city with the municipal and other buildings around it. The Folk Art Center, the Folk Recreation Center, the hospital, university, research center, and the PANDORA, the people's all-necessities depot of regulated abundance. You've been delighted and amazed with the fairy-land of goodies that Uncle Sam, and the State of California, offers you free. Necessities and luxuries, too, since *Luxury Is A Necessity*, to quote the FBC. You want anything—anything!—you go to the PANDORA, press some buttons, and presto! you're rich beyond your dreams!"

Heckler: "When the lid to Pandora's box was opened, all the evils in the world flew out, and . . ."

Spieler: "No interruptions, lady! We're on a strict time schedule. . . ."

Heckler: "Why? We're not going any place!"

Spieler: "I'll tell you where you can go, lady."

Heckler: "But . . ."

Spieler: "But me no buts, lady! You know, you ought to go on a diet!"

Heckler (struggling to control her temper): "Don't get personal, big mouth! I'm big, all right, and I got a wallop, too, remember that. Now, Pandora's box. . . ."

The spieler made a vulgar remark, at which the crowd laughed. The heckler shouted but could not be heard above the noise.

The President shifted uneasily. Kingbrook, the 82-year-old senator from New York, harumphed and said, "The things they permit nowadays in public media. Really, it's disgusting . . ."

Some of the screens on the wall of the mayor's office showed various parts of the interior of the city. One displayed a view from a helicopter flying on the oceanside exterior of Upper Metropolitan LA. It was far enough away to get the entire structure in its camera, including the hundred self-adjusting cylinders that supported the Brobdingnagian plastic cube and the telescoping elevator shafts dangling from the central underbase. Beneath the shadow of the box and legs was the central section of the old city and the jagged sprawl of the rest of Los Angeles and surrounding cities.

The President stabbed towards the screen with a cigarette and said, "Screen 24, gentlemen. The dark past below. The misery of a disrupted ant colony. Above it, the bright complex of the future. The chance for every man to realize his full potentiality as a human being."

Spieler: "Before I conduct you into this house, which is internally just like every other private residence . . ."

Heckler: "Infernally, you mean. They all look just alike on the outside, too."

Spieler: "Lady, you're arousing my righteous wrath. Now, folks, you noticed that all the buildings, municipal and private, are constructed like eggs. This futuristic design was adopted because the egg shape, according to the latest theory, is that of the universe. No corners, all curving, infinity within a confined space, if you follow me."

Heckler: "I don't!"

Spieler: "Take off a little weight, lady, and you'll be in shape to keep up with the rest of us. The ovoid form gives you a feeling of unbounded space yet of security-closeness. When you get inside . . .".

Every house was a great smooth white plastic egg lifted 18.28 meters above the floor of the city by a thick truncated-cone support. (Offscreen commentators explained that 18.28 meters was 60 feet, for the benefit of old viewers who could not adjust to the new system of measurement.) On two sides of the cone were stairs ending at a horizontal door on the lower side of the ovoid. These opened automatically to permit entrance. Also, a door opened in the cone base, and an elevator inside lifted the sick or crippled or, as the spieler put it, "the just plain lazy, everybody's got a guaranteed right to be lazy." The hollow base also housed several electrical carts for transportation around the city.

The President saw Kierson, the Detroit automobile magnate, frown at the carts. The auto industry had shifted entirely from internal combustion motors to electrical and nuclear power ten years ago, and now Kierson saw the doom of these. The President made a mental note to pacify and reassure him on this point later.

Spieler: ". . . *Variety Within Unity*, folks. You've heard a lot about that on FBC, and these houses are an example. In reply to the lady's anxiety about the houses all looking alike, every home owner can paint the outside of his house to express his individuality. Anything goes. From reproductions of Rembrandt to psychedelic dreams to dirty words, if you got the guts. Everything's free, including speech. . . ."

Heckler: "They'll look like a bunch of Easter eggs!"

Spieler: "Lady, Uncle Sam *is* The Big Easter Bunny!"

The spieler took the group into the house, and the cameramen went into the atrium, kitchen, and the ten rooms to show the viewers just what the citizens-to-be were getting for nothing.

"For nothing!" Senator Kingbrook growled. "The taxpayers are paying through the nose, through every orifice, with their sweat and blood for this!"

The President said, mildly, "They won't have to in the future, as I'll explain."

"You don't have to explain anything to any of us," Kingbrook said. "We all know all about the economy of abundance versus the economy of scarcity. And about your plans for the transitional stage, which you call ORE, *obverse-reverse* economy, but which I call *schizophrenic horrors in tremens!*"

The President smiled and said, "You'll have your say, Senator."

The men and women in the room were silent for a while as they watched the spieler extol the splendors and virtues of the house with its soundproof walls, the atrium with its pool, the workshop with machinery for crafts, the storeroom, the bedroom-studios, TV in every room, *retractable* and inflatable furniture, air conditioning, microfilm library, and so on.

Government shill: "This is fabulous! A hell of a lot better than any noisy rat-ridden dump on the ground!"

Spieler (quoting an FBC slogan): "*Happy and free as the birds in the air!* That's why everbody calls this Bird City and why the citizens are known as freebirds! Everything first class! Everything free!"

Heckler: "Except freedom to live where you want to in the type of house you want!"

Spieler: "Lady, unless you're a millionaire, you won't be able to get a house on the ground that isn't just like every other house. And then you'd have to worry about it being burned down. Lady, you'd gripe if you was hung with a new rope!"

The group went outside where the spieler pointed out that, though they were three hectometers above ground, they had trees and grass in small parks. If they wanted to fish or boat, they could use the lake in the municipal-building area.

Shill: "Man, this is living!"

Spieler: "The dome above the city looks just like the sky outside. The sun is an electronic reproduction; its progress exactly coincides with that of the real sun. Only, you don't have to worry about it getting too cold or too hot in here or about it raining. We even got birds in here!"

Heckler: "What about the robins? Come springtime, how're they going to get inside without a pass?"

Spieler: "Lady, you got a big mouth! Whyn't you . . ."

The President rose from his chair. Kingbrook's face was wrinkled, fissured, and folded with old age. The red of his anger made his features look like hot lava on a volcano slope just after an eruption. His rich rumble pushed against the eardrums of those in the room as if they were in a pressure chamber.

"A brave new concentration camp, gentlemen! Fifty billion dollars worth to house 50,000 people! The great bankruptopolis of the future! I estimate it'll cost one trillion dollars just to enclose this state's population in these glorified chicken runs!"

"Not if ORE is put into effect," the President said. He held up his hand to indicate silence and said, "I'd like to hear Guildman, gentlemen. Then we can have our conferences."

Senator Beaucamp of Mississippi muttered, "One trillion dollars! That would house, feed, and educate the entire population of my state for twenty years!"

The President signalled to cut off all screens except the FBC channel. The private network commentators were also speaking, but the federal commentator was the important one. His pitch was being imitated—if reluctantly—by the private networks. Enough pressure and threats had been applied to make them wary of going all-out against the President. Although the mass media had been restrained, the speech of private persons had not been repressed. For one thing, the public needed a safety valve. Occasionally, a private speaker was given a chance to express himself on TV and radio. And so, a cavalry charge of invectives had been and was being hurled at the President. He had been denounced as a Communist, a Fascist, a vulture, a pig, a Puritan, a pervert, a Hitler, etc., and had been hung *in absentia* so many times that an enterprising manufacturer of effigies had made a small fortune—though taxes made it even smaller.

From cavalry to Calvary, he thought. All charges admitted. All charges denied. I am human, and that takes in everything. Even the accusation of fanaticism. I know that what I'm doing is right, or, at least, the only known way. When the Four Horsemen ride, the countercharge cannot be led by a self-doubter.

The voice of the Great Guildman, as he was pleased to be called, throbbed through the room. Chief FBC commentator, bureau executive, Ph.D. in Mass Communications, G-90 rating, one who spoke with authority, whose personal voltage was turned full-on, who could, some said, have talked God into keeping Adam and Eve in the garden.

". . . cries out! The people, the suffering earth itself, cry out! The air is poisoned! The water is poisoned! The soil is poisoned! Mankind is poisoned with the excess of his genius for survival! The wide walls of the Earth have become narrowed! Man, swelling like a tumor with uncontrolled growth, kills the body that gave him birth!

He is squeezing himself into an insane mold which crushes his life out, crushes all hope for an abundant life, security, peace, quiet, fulfillment, dignity . . ."

The audience, tuning in on forty channels, was well aware of this: he was painting a picture the oils of which had been squeezed from their own pain. And so Guildman did not tarry overlong at these points. He spoke briefly of the dying economy of scarcity, obsolete in the middle 1900s but seeming vigorous, like a sick man with a fatal disease who keeps on going on larger and larger shots of drugs and on placebos. Then he splashed bright colors over the canvas of the future.

Guildman went on about the population expansion, automation, the ever-growing permanently depressed class and its riots and insurrections, the ever-decreasing and ever-overburdened taxpayers with their strikes and riots, the Beverly Hills Massacre, the misery, crime, anger, etc.

The President repressed an impulse to squirm. There would be plenty of blacks and grays in The Golden World (the President's own catch-phrase). Utopia could never exist. The structure of human society, in every respect, had a built-in instability, which meant that there would always be a certain amount of suffering and maladjustment. There were always victims of change.

But that could not be helped. And it was a good thing that change was the unchanging characteristic of society. Otherwise, stagnation, rigidity, and loss of hope for improvement would result.

Beauchamp leaned close to the President and said softly, "Plenty of people have pointed out that the economy of abundance eventually means the death of capitalism. You've never commented on this, but you can't keep silent much longer."

"When I do speak," the President said, "I'll point out that EOA also means the death of socialism and communism. Besides, there's nothing sacred in an economic system, except to those who confuse money with religion. Systems are made for man, not vice versa."

Kingbrook rose from his sofa, his bones cracking, and walked stiffly towards the President.

"You've rammed through this project despite the opposition of the majority of taxpayers! You used methods that were not only unconstitutional, sir! I know for a fact that criminal tactics were used, blackmail and intimidation, sir! But you will go no more on your Caesar's road! This project has beggared our once wealthy nation, and we are not going to build any more of your follies! Your grandiose—and wicked—Golden World will be as tarnished as brass, as green as fool's gold, by the time that I am through with you! Don't underestimate me and my colleagues, sir!"

"I know of your plans to impeach me," the President said with a slight smile. "Now, Senators Beaucamp and Kingbrook, and you, Governor Corrigan, would you step into the mayor's apartment? I'd like to have a few words—I hope they're few—with you."

Kingbrook, breathing heavily, said, "My mind is made up, Mr. President. I know what's wrong and what's right for our country. If you have any veiled threats or insidious proposals, make them in public, sir! In this room, before these gentlemen!"

The President looked at the embarrassed faces, the stony, the hostile, the gleeful, and then glanced at his wristwatch. He said, "I only ask five minutes."

He continued, "I'm not slighting any of you. I intend to talk to all of you in groups selected because of relevant subjects. Three to five minutes apiece will let us complete our business before the post-dedication speeches. Gentlemen!" And he

The Oogenesis of Bird City 219

turned and strode through the door.

A few seconds passed, and then the three, stiff-faced, stiff-backed, walked in.

"Sit down or stand as you please," the President said.

There was a silence. Kingbrook lit a cigar and took a chair. Corrigan hesitated and then sat near Kingbrook. Beaucamp remained standing. The President stood before them.

He said, "You've seen the people who toured this city. They're the prospective citizens. What is their outstanding common characteristic?"

Kingbrook snorted and said something under his breath. Beaucamp glared at him and said, "I didn't hear your words, but I know what you said! Mr. President, I intend to speak loudly and clearly about this arrogant discrimination! I had one of my men run the list of accepted citizens through a computer, and he reports that the citizens will be 100 percent Negro! And seven-eighths are welfares!"

"The other eighth are doctors, technicians, teachers, and other professionals," the President said. "All volunteers. There, by the way, goes the argument that no one will work if he doesn't have to. These people will be living in this city and getting no money for their labor. We had to turn down many volunteers because there was no need for them."

"Especially since the government has been using public funds to brainwash us with the Great-Love-and-Service-for-Humanity campaign for twenty years," Kingbrook said.

"I never heard you making any speeches knocking love or service," the President said. "However, there is another motive which caused so many to offer their services. Money may die out, but the desire for prestige won't. The wish for prestige is at least as old as mankind itself and maybe older."

"I can't believe that no whites asked to live there," Beaucamp said.

"The rule was, First apply, first accepted," the President said. "The whole procedure was computer-run, and the application blanks contained no reference to race."

Corrigan said, "You know that computers have been gimmicked or their operators bribed."

The President said, "I am sure that an investigation would uncover nothing crooked."

"The gyps," Corrigan said, then stopped at Beaucamp's glare. "I mean, the guaranteed income people, or welfares as we called them when I was a kid, well, the GIP whites will be screaming discrimination."

"The whites could have volunteered."

Beaucamp's lip was curled. "Somebody spread the word. Of course, that would have nothing to do with lack of Caucasian applications."

Kingbrook rumbled like a volcano preparing to erupt. He said, "What're we arguing about this for? This . . . Bird City . . . was built over an all-colored section. So why shouldn't its citizens be colored? Let's stick to the point. You want to build more cities just like this, Mr. President, extend them outwards from this until you have one solid megalopolis on stilts extending from Santa Barbara to Long Beach. But you can't build here or in other states without absolutely bankrupting the country. So you want to get us to back your legislative proposals for your so-called ORE. That is, split the economy of the nation in half. One half will continue operating just as before; that half will be made up of private-enterprise industries and of the taxpayers who own or work for these industries. This half will continue to buy and sell and use money as it has always done.

"But the other half will be composed of GIP's, living in cities like this, and the government will take care of their every need. The government will do this by automating the mines, farms, and industries it now owns or plans on obtaining. It will not use money anywhere in its operations, and the entire process of input-output will be a closed circuit. Everbody in ORE will be GIP personnel, even the federal and state government service, except, of course, that the federal legislative and executive branches will maintain their proper jurisdiction."

"That *sounds* great," Corrigan said. "The ultimate result, or so you've *said*, Mr. President, is to relieve the taxpayer of his crushing burden and to give the GIP a position in society in which he will no longer be considered by others as a parasite. It sounds appealing. But there are many of us who aren't fooled by your fine talk."

"I'm not trying to fool anybody," the President said.

Corrigan said, angrily, "It's obvious what the end result will be! When the taxpayer sees the GIP living like a king without turning a hand while he has to work his tail off, he's going to want the same deal. And those who refuse to give up won't have enough money to back their stand because the GIP won't be spending any money. The small businessmen who live off their sales to the GIP will go under. And the larger businesses will, too. Eventually, the businessman and his employees will fold their fiscal and pecuniary tents and go to live in your everything-free cornucopias!

"So, if we're seduced by your beautiful scheme for a half-and-half economy, we'll take the first step into the quicksand. After that, it'll be too late to back out. Down we go!"

"I'd say, *Up we go*," the President said. "So! It's All-or-None, as far as you're concerned? And you vote for None! Well, gentlemen, over one-half of the nation is saying All because that's the only way to go and they've nothing to lose and everything to gain. If you kill the switchover legislation in Congress, I'll see that the issues are submitted to the people for their yea or nay. But that would take too much time, and time is vital. Time is what I'm buying. Or should I say, trading."

Beaucamp said, "Mister President, you didn't point out the racial composition of this city just to pass the time."

The President began pacing back and forth before them. He said, "The civil rights revolution was born about the same time that you and I, Mr. Beaucamp, were born. Yet, it's still far from achieving its goals. In some aspects, it's regressed. It was tragic that the Negroes began to get the education and political power they needed for advancement just as automation began to bloom. The Negro found that there were only jobs for the professionals and the skilled. The unskilled were shut out. This happened to the untrained white, too, and competition for work between the unskilled white and black became bitter. Bloodily bitter, as the past few years have shown us."

"We know what's been going on, Mr. President," Beaucamp said.

"Yes. Well, it's true, isn't it, that the Negro, as a rule, doesn't particularly care to associate or live with the whites? He just wants the same things the whites have. But at the present rate of progress, it'll take a hundred years or more before he gets them. In fact, he may never do so if the present economy continues."

Kingbrook rumbled, "The point, Mr. President!"

The President stopped pacing. He looked hard at them and said, "But in an economy of abundance, in this type of city, he—the Negro—will have everything the whites have. He will have a high standard of living, a true democracy, color-free justice. He'll have his own judges, police, legislators. If he doesn't care to, he doesn't ever have to have any personal contact with whites."

Kingbrook's cigar sagged. Beaucamp sucked in his breath. Corrigan jumped from his chair.

Beaucamp said, "That's ghettoism!"

"Not in the original sense," the President said. "The truth now, Mr. Beaucamp. Don't your people prefer to live with their own kind? Where they'll be free of that shadow, that wall, always between white and colored in this country?"

Beaucamp said, "Not to have to put up with honkeys! Excuse the expression, sir. It slipped out. You know we would. But . . ."

"No one will be forbidden to live in any community he chooses. There won't be any discrimination on the federal level. Those in the government, military, or Nature rehabilitation service will have equal opportunity. But, given the choice . . ."

The President turned to Kingbrook and Corrigan. "Publicly, you two have always stood for integration. You would have committed political suicide, otherwise. But I know your private opinions. You have also been strong states-righters. No secret about that. So, when the economy of abundance is in full swing, the states will become self-sufficient. They won't depend on federal funds."

"Because there'll be no dependence on money?" Corrigan said. "Because there'll be no money? Because money will be as extinct as the dodo?"

The ridges on Kingbrook's face shifted as if they were the gray backs of an elephant herd milling around to catch a strange scent. He said, "I'm not blasphemous. But now I think I know how Christ felt when tempted by Satan."

He stopped, realizing that he had made a Freudian slip.

"And you're not Christ and I'm not Satan," he said hurriedly. "We're just human beings trying to find a mutually agreeable way out of this mess."

Beaucamp said, "We're horse traders. And the horse is the future. A dream. Or a nightmare."

The President looked at his watch and said, "What about it, Mr. Beaucamp?"

"What can I trade? A dream of an end to contempt, dislike, hatred, treachery, oppression. A dream of the shadow gone, the wall down. Now you offer me abundance, dignity, and joy—if my people stay within the plastic walls."

"I don't know what will develop after the walls of the cities have been built," the President said. "But there is nothing evil about self-segregation, if it's not compulsive. It's done all the time by human beings of every color. If it weren't, you wouldn't have social classes, clubs, etc. And if, after our citizens are given the best in housing and food, luxuries, a free lifelong education, a wide spectrum of recreations, everything within reason, if they still go to hell, then we might as well give up on the species."

"A man needs incentive; he needs to work. By the sweat of his brow . . ." Kingbrook said.

Kingbrook was too old, the President thought. He was half-stone, and the stone thought stone thoughts and spoke stone words. The President looked out the big window. Perhaps it had been a mistake to build such a "futuristic" city. It would be difficult enough for the new citizens to adjust. Perhaps the dome of Bird City should have contained buildings resembling those they now lived in. Later, more radical structures could have been introduced.

As it was, the ovoid shape was supposed to give a sense of security, a feeling of return-to-the-womb and also to suggest a rebirth. Just now, they looked like so many space capsules ready to take off into the blue the moment the button was pressed.

But this city, and those that would be added to it, meant a sharp break with the past, and any break always caused some pain.

He turned when someone coughed behind him. Senator Kingbrook was standing, his hand on his chest. The senator was going to make a speech.

The President looked at his watch and shook his head. Kingbrook smiled as if the smile hurt him, and he dropped his hand.

"It's yes, Mr. President. I'll back you all the way. And the impeachment proceedings will be dropped, of course. But . . ."

"I don't want to be rude," the President said. "But you can save your justifications for your constituents."

Beaucamp said, "I say yes. Only . . ."

"No ifs, ands, or buts."

"No. Only . . ."

"And you, Governor Corrigan?" the President said.

Corrigan said, "All of us are going along with you for reasons that shouldn't be considered—from the viewpoint of ideals. But then, who really ever has? I say yes. But . . ."

"No speeches, please," the President said. He smiled slightly. "Unless I make them. Your motives don't really matter, gentlemen, as long as your decisions are for the good of the American public. Which they are. And for the good of the world, too, because all other nations are going to follow our example. As I said, this means the death of capitalism, but it also means the death of socialism and communism, too."

He looked at his watch again. "I thank you, gentlemen."

They looked as if they would like to continue talking, but they left. There was a delay of a few seconds before the next group entered.

He felt weary, even though he knew that he would win out. The years ahead would be times of trouble, of crises, of pain and agony, of successes and failures. At least mankind would no longer be drifting towards anarchy. Man would be deliberately shaping—reshaping—his society, turning topsy-turvy an ancient and obsolete economy, good enough in its time but no longer applicable. At the same time, he would be tearing down the old cities and restoring Nature to something of its pristine condition, healing savage wounds inflicted by senseless selfish men in the past, cleansing the air, the poisoned rivers and lakes, growing new forests, permitting the wild creatures to flourish in their redeemed land. Man, the greedy savage child, had stripped the earth, killed the wild, fouled his own nest.

His anger, he suddenly realized, had been diverted from that other feeling. Somehow, he had betrayed an ideal. He could not define the betrayal, because he knew that he was doing what had to be done and that that way was the only way. But he, and Kingbrook, Corrigan, and Beaucamp, had also felt this. He had seen it on their faces, like ectoplasm escaping the grasp of their minds.

A man had to be realistic. To gain one thing, you had to give up another. Life—the universe—was give and take, input and output, energy surrendered to conquer energy.

In short, politics. Compromises.

The door slid into the recess in the walls. Five men single-filed in. The President weighed each in the balance, anticipating his arguments and visualizing the bait which he would grab even if he saw the hook.

He said, "Gentlemen, be seated, if you wish."

He looked at his watch and began to talk.

*James Tiptree, Jr., whose identity was the cause of much specula-
tion in the early '70s, has since been revealed to be Alice Sheldon,
a psychologist who worked for the U.S. Government for many
years. One of her three simultaneously-accepted first sales was to*
Amazing® Stories *in 1968. She is a Hugo and Nebula winner and is
the author of numerous short stories and two novels,* Up the Walls
of the World *and the recent* Brightness Falls from the Air. *This
story was published in May 1972.*

THE MAN WHO WALKED HOME
by James Tiptree, Jr.

—*Transgression! Terror! And he thrust and
lost there—punched into impossibility abandoned never to be known how, the
wrong man in the most wrong of all wrong places in that unimaginable collapse of
never-to-be-reimagined mechanism—he stranded, undone, his lifeline severed, he
in that nanosecond knowing his only tether parting, going away, the longest line to
life withdrawing, winking out, disappearing forever beyond his grasp—telescoping
away from him into the closing vortex beyond which lay his home, his life, his only
possibility of being; seeing it sucked back into the deepest maw, melting, leaving
him orphaned on what never-to-be-known shore of total wrongness—of beauty beyond joy, perhaps? Of horror? Of nothingness? Of profound otherness only,
certainly—whatever it was, that place into which he transgressed, it could not support his life there, his violent and violating aberrance, and he, fierce, brave, crazy—
clenched into total protest, one body-fist of utter repudiation of himself there in that
place, forsaken there—what did he do? Rejected, exiled, hungering homewards
more desperate than any lost beast driving for its unreachable home, his home, his
HOME—and no way, no transport, no vehicle, means, machinery, no force but his
intolerable resolve aimed homeward along that vanishing vector, that last and only
lifeline—he did, what?*

He walked.

Home.

Precisely what hashed up in the work of the major industrial lessee of the Bonneville Particle Acceleration Facility in Idaho was never known. Or rather, all those
who might have been able to diagnose the original malfunction were themselves ob-
literated almost at once in the greater catastrophe which followed.

The nature of this second cataclysm was not at first understood either. All that was
ever certain was that at 1153.6 of May 2, 1989 Old Style, the Bonneville laboratories
and all their personnel were transformed into an intimately disrupted form of matter

resembling a high-energy plasma, which became rapidly airborne to the accompaniment of radiating seismic and atmospheric events.

The disturbed area unfortunately included an operational MIRV Watchdog bomb.

In the confusion of the next hours the Earth's population was substantially reduced, the biosphere was altered, and the Earth itself was marked with numbers of more conventional craters. For some years thereafter the survivors were existentially preoccupied and the peculiar dustbowl at Bonneville was left to weather by itself in the changing climatic cycles.

It was not a large crater; just over a kilometer in width and lacking the usual displacement lip. Its surface was covered with a finely divided substance which dried into dust. Before the rains began it was almost perfectly flat. Only in certain lights, had anyone been there to inspect it, a small surface marking or abraded place could be detected almost exactly at the center.

Two decades after the disaster a party of short brown people appeared from the south, together with a flock of somewhat atypical sheep. The crater at this time appeared as a wide shallow basin in which the grass did not grow well, doubtless from the almost complete lack of soil micro-organisms. Neither this nor the surrounding vigorous grass were found to harm the sheep. A few crude hogans went up at the southern edge and a faint path began to be traced across the crater itself, passing by the central bare spot.

One spring morning two children who had been driving sheep across the crater came screaming back to camp. A monster had burst out of the ground before them, a huge flat animal making a dreadful roar. It vanished in a flash and a shaking of the earth, leaving an evil smell. The sheep had run away.

Since this last was visibly true, some elders investigated. Finding no sign of the monster and no place in which it could hide, they settled for beating the children, who settled for making a detour around the monster-spot, and nothing more occurred for a while.

The following spring the episode was repeated. This time an older girl was present, but she could add only that the monster seemed to be rushing flat out along the ground without moving at all. And there was a scraped place in the dirt. Again nothing was found; an evil-ward in a cleft stick was placed at the spot.

When the same thing happened for the third time a year later, the detour was extended and other charmwands were added. But since no harm seemed to come of it and the brown people had seen far worse, sheep-tending resumed as before. A few more instantaneous apparitions of the monster were noted, each time in the spring.

At the end of the third decade of the new era a tall old man limped down the hills from the south, pushing his pack upon a bicycle wheel. He camped on the far side of the crater, and soon found the monster-site. He attempted to question people about it, but no one understood him, so he traded a knife for some meat. Although he was obviously feeble, something about him dissuaded them from killing him, and this proved wise because he later assisted the women in treating several sick children.

He spent much time around the place of the apparition and was nearby when it made its next appearance. This excited him very much and he did several inexplicable but apparently harmless things, including moving his camp into the crater by the trail. He stayed on for a full year watching the site and was close by for its next manifestation. After this he spent a few days making a charmstone for the spot and left northwards, hobbling as he had come.

More decades passed. The crater eroded and a rain-gully became an intermittent streamlet across the edge of the basin. The brown people and their sheep were attacked by a band of grizzled men, after which the survivors went away eastward. The winters of what had been Idaho were now frost-free; aspen and eucalyptus sprouted in the moist plain. Still the crater remained treeless, visible as a flat bowl of grass; and the bare place at the center remained. The skies cleared somewhat.

After another three decades a larger band of black people with ox-drawn carts appeared and stayed for a time, but left again when they too saw the thunder-clap monster. A few other vagrants straggled by.

Five decades later a small permanent settlement had grown up on the nearest range of hills, from which men riding on small ponies with dark stripes down their spines herded humped cattle near the crater. A herdsman's hut was built by the streamlet, which in time became the habitation of an olive-skinned, red-haired family. In due course one of this clan again observed the monster-flash, but these people did not depart. The stone the tall man had placed was noted and left undisturbed.

The homestead at the crater's edge grew into a group of three and was joined by others, and the trail across it became a cartroad with a log bridge over the stream. At the center of the still faintly discernible crater the cartroad made a bend, leaving a grassy place which bore on its center about a square meter of curiously impacted bare earth and a deeply etched sandstone rock.

The apparition of the monster was now known to occur regularly each spring on a certain morning in this place, and the children of the community dared each other to approach the spot. It was referred to in a phrase that could be translated as "the Old Dragon." The Old Dragon's appearance was always the same: a brief violent thunder-burst which began and cut off abruptly, in the midst of which a dragon-like creature was seen apparently in furious motion on the earth although it never actually moved. Afterwards there was a bad smell and the earth smoked. People who saw it from close by spoke of a shivering sensation.

Early in the second century two young men rode into town from the north. Their ponies were shaggier than the local breed and the equipment they carried included two boxlike objects which the young men set up at the monster site. They stayed in the area a full year, observing two materializations of the Old Dragon, and they provided much news and maps of roads and trading towns in the cooler regions to the north. They built a windmill which was accepted by the community and offered to build a lighting machine, which was refused. Then they departed with their boxes after unsuccessfully attempting to persuade a local boy to learn to operate one.

In the course of the next decades other travelers stopped by and marveled at the monster, and there was sporadic fighting over the mountains to the south. One of the armed bands made a cattle raid into the crater hamlet. It was repulsed, but the raiders left a spotted sickness which killed many. For all this time the bare place at the crater's center remained, and the monster made his regular appearances, observed or not.

The hill-town grew and changed and the crater hamlet grew to be a town. Roads widened and linked into networks. There were gray-green conifers in the hills now, spreading down into the plain, and chirruping lizards lived in their branches.

At century's end a shabby band of skin-clad squatters with stunted milk-beasts erupted out of the west and were eventually killed or driven away, but not before the local herds had contracted a vicious parasite. Veterinaries were fetched from the market city up north, but little could be done. The families near the crater left and for some decades the area was empty. Finally cattle of a new strain reappeared in the plain and the crater hamlet was reoccupied. Still the bare center continued annually to manifest the monster and he became an accepted phenomenon of the area. On several occasions parties came from the distant Northwest Authority to observe it.

The crater hamlet flourished and grew into the fields where cattle had grazed, and part of the old crater became the town park. A small seasonal tourist industry based on the monster-site developed. The townspeople rented rooms for the appearances and many more-or-less authentic monster-relics were on display in the local taverns.

Several cults now grew up around the monster. One persistent belief held that it was a devil or damned soul forced to appear on Earth in torment to expiate the catastrophe of three centuries back. Others believed that it, or he, was some kind of messenger whose roar portended either doom or hope according to the believer. One very vocal sect taught that the apparition registered the moral conduct of the townspeople over the past year, and scrutinized the annual apparition for changes which could be interpreted for good or ill. It was considered lucky, or dangerous, to be touched by some of the dust raised by the monster. In every generation at least one small boy would try to hit the monster with a stick, usually acquiring a broken arm and a lifelong tavern tale. Pelting the monster with stones or other objects was a popular sport, and for some years people systematically flung prayers and flowers at it. Once a party tried to net it and were left with strings and vapor. The area itself had long been fenced off at the center of the park.

Through all this the monster made his violently enigmatic annual appearance, sprawling furiously motionless, unreachably roaring.

Only as the fourth century of the new era went by was it apparent that the monster had been changing slightly. He was now no longer on the earth but had an arm and a leg thrust upward in a kicking or flailing gesture. As the years passed he began to change more quickly until at the end of the century he had risen to a contorted crouching pose, arms outflung as if frozen in gyration. His roar, too, seemed somewhat differently pitched and the earth after him smoked more and more.

It was then widely felt that the man-monster was about to do something, to make some definitive manifestation, and a series of natural disasters and marvels gave support to a vigorous cult teaching this doctrine. Several religious leaders journeyed to the town to observe the apparitions.

However, the decades passed and the man-monster did nothing more than turn slowly in place, so that he now appeared to be in the act of sliding or staggering while pushing himself backwards like a creature blown before a gale. No wind, of course, could be felt, and presently the general climate quieted and nothing came of it at all.

Early in the fifth century New Calendar three survey parties from the North Central Authority came through the area and stopped to observe the monster. A permanent recording device was set up at the site, after assurances to the townsfolk that no hardscience was involved. A local boy was trained to operate it; he quit when his girl left him but another volunteered. At this time nearly everyone believed that the apparition was a man, or the ghost of one. The record-machine boy and a few others including the school mechanics teacher referred to him as The Man John. In the next decades the roads were generally improved; all forms of travel increased and there was talk of building a canal to what had been the Snake River.

One May morning at the end of Century Five a young couple in a smart green mule-trap came jogging up the highroad from the Sandreas Rift Range to the southwest. The girl was golden-skinned and chatted with her young husband in a language unlike that ever heard by The Man John either at the end or the beginning of his life. What she said to him has, however, been heard in every age and tongue.

"Oh, Serli, I'm so glad we're taking this trip now! Next summer I'll be busy with baby."

To which Serli replied as young husbands often have, and so they trotted up to the town's inn. Here they left trap and bags and went in search of her uncle who was expecting them there. The morrow was the day of The Man John's annual appearance, and her Uncle Laban had come from the MacKenzie History Museum to observe it and to make certain arrangements.

They found him with the town school instructor of mechanics, who was also the recorder at the monster-site. Presently Uncle Laban took them all with him to the town mayor's office to meet with various religious personages. The mayor was not unaware of tourist values, but he took Uncle Laban's part in securing the cultists' grudging assent to the MacKenzie authorities' secular interpretation of the monster, which was made easier by the fact that the cults disagreed among themselves. Then, seeing how pretty the niece was, the mayor took them all home to dinner.

When they returned to the inn for the night it was abrawl with holiday-makers.

"Whew," said Uncle Laban. "I've talked myself dry, sister's daughter. What a weight of holy nonsense is that Moksha female! Serli, my lad, I know you have questions. Let me hand you this to read, it's the guide book we're giving them to sell. Tomorrow I'll answer for it all." And he disappeared into the crowded tavern.

So Serli and his bride took the pamphlet upstairs with them, but it was not until the next morning at breakfast that they found time to read it.

" 'All that is known of John Delgano,' " read Serli with his mouth full, " 'comes from two documents left by his brother Carl Delgano in the archives of the MacKenzie Group in the early years after the holocaust.' Put some honey on this cake, Mira my dove. Verbatim transcript follows, this is Carl Delgano speaking:

" 'I'm not an engineer or an astronaut like John, I ran an electronics repair shop in Salt Lake City. John was only trained as a spaceman, he never got to space; the slump wiped all that out. So he tied up with this commercial group who were leasing part of Bonneville. They wanted a man for some kind of hard-vacuum tests, that's all I knew about it. John and his wife moved to Bonneville, but we all got together several times a year, our wives were like sisters. John had two kids, Clara and Paul.

" 'The tests were supposed to be secret, but John told me confidentially they were trying for an anti-gravity chamber. I don't know if it ever worked. That was the year before.

" 'Then that winter they came down for Christmas and John said they had something far out. He was excited. A temporal displacement, he called it; some kind of time effect. He said their chief honcho was like a real mad scientist. Big ideas. He kept adding more angles every time some other project would quit and leave equipment he could lease. No, I don't know who the top company was—maybe an insurance conglomerate, they had all the cash, didn't they? I guess they'd pay to catch a look at the future, that figures. Anyway, John was go, go, go. Katharine was scared, that's natural. She pictured him like, you know, H.G. Wells—walking around in some future world. John told her it wasn't like that at all. All they'd get would be this flicker, like a second or two. All kinds of complications'—yes, yes my greedy piglet, some brew for me too. This is thirsty work!

"So. 'I remember I asked him, what about Earth moving? I mean, you could come back in a different place, right? He said they had that all figured. A spatial trajectory. Katharine was so scared we dropped it. John told her, don't worry. I'll come home. But he didn't. Not that it makes any difference, of course, everything was wiped out. Salt Lake too. The only reason I'm here is that I went up by Calgary to see Mom, April twenty-ninth. May second it all blew. I didn't find you folks at MacKenzie until July. I guess I may as well stay. That's all I know about John, except that he was a solid guy. If that accident started all this it wasn't his fault.

" 'The second document'—In the name of love, little mother, do I have to read all of this? Oh very well, but you will kiss me first, madam. Must you look so delicious? 'The second document. Dated in the year eighteen, New Style, written by Carl'—see the old handwriting, my plump plump pigeon? Oh, very well, *very* well.

" 'Written at Bonneville Crater: I have seen my brother John Delgano. When I knew I had the rad sickness I came down here to look around. Salt Lake's still hot. So I hiked up here by Bonneville. You can see the crater where the labs were, it's grassed over. It's different, not radioactive; my film's o.k. There's a bare place in the middle. Some Indios here told me a monster shows up here every year in the spring. I saw it myself a couple of days after I got here but I was too far away to see much, except that I was sure it's a man. In a vacuum suit. There was a lot of noise and dust, took me by surprise. It was all over in a second. I figured it's pretty close to the day, I mean, May second, old.

" 'So I hung around a year and he showed up again yesterday. I was on the face side and I could see his face through the visor. It's John all right. He's hurt. I saw blood on his mouth and his suit is frayed some. He's lying on the ground. He didn't move while I could see him but the dust boiled up, like a man sliding onto base without moving. His eyes are open like he was looking. I don't understand it anyway, but I know it's John, not a ghost. He was in exactly the same position each time and there's a loud crack like thunder and another sound like a siren, very fast. And an ozone smell, and smoke. I felt a kind of shudder.

" 'I know it's John there and I think he's alive. I have to leave here now to take this back while I can still walk. I think somebody should come here and see. Maybe you can help John. Signed, Carl Delgano.

" 'These records were kept by the MacKenzie Group but it was not for several years'—Etcetera, first light-print, etcetera, archives, analysts, etcetera—very good! Now it is time to meet your uncle, my edible one, after we go upstairs for just a moment."

"No, Serli, I will wait for you downstairs," said Mira prudently.

When they came into the town park Uncle Laban was directing the installation of a large durite slab in front of the enclosure around The Man John's appearance-spot. The slab was wrapped in a curtain to await the official unveiling. Townspeople and tourists and children thronged the walks and a Ride-for-God choir was singing in the bandshell. The morning was warming up fast. Vendors hawked ices and straw toys of the monster and flowers and good-luck confetti to throw at him. Another religious group stood by in dark robes; they belonged to the Repentance church beyond the park. Their pastor was directing somber glares at the crowd in general and Mira's uncle in particular.

Three official-looking strangers who had been at the inn came up and introduced themselves to Uncle Laban as observers from Alberta Central. They went on into the tent which had been erected over the closure, carrying with them several pieces of equipment which the townsfolk eyed suspiciously.

The mechanics teacher finished organizing a squad of students to protect the slab's curtain, and Mira and Serli and Laban went on into the tent. It was much hotter inside. Benches were set in rings around a railed enclosure about twenty feet in diameter. Inside the railing the earth was bare and scuffed. Several bunches of flowers and blooming poinciana branches leaned against the rail. The only thing inside the rail was a rough sandstone rock with markings etched on it.

Just as they came in a small girl raced across the open center and was yelled at by everybody. The officials from Alberta were busy at one side of the rail, where the lightprint box was mounted.

"Oh no," muttered Mira's uncle, as one of the officials leaned over to set up a tripod stand inside the rails. He adjusted it and a huge horse-tail of fine feathery filaments blossomed out and eddied through the center of the space.

"Oh no," Laban said again. "Why can't they let it be?"

"They're trying to pick up dust from his suit, is that right?" Serli asked.

"Yes, insane. Did you get time to read?"

"Oh yes," said Serli.

"Sort of," added Mira.

"Then you know. He's falling. Trying to check his—well, call it velocity. Trying to slow down. He must have slipped or stumbled. We're getting pretty close to when he lost his footing and started to fall. What did it? Did somebody trip him?" Laban looked from Mira to Serli, dead serious now. "How would you like to be the one who made John Delgano fall?"

"Ooh," said Mira in quick sympathy. Then she said, "Oh."

"You mean," asked Serli, "whoever made him fall caused all the, caused—"

"Possible," said Laban.

"Wait a minute." Serli frowned. "He did fall. So somebody had to do it—I mean, he has to trip or whatever. If he doesn't fall, the past would all be changed, wouldn't it? No war, no—"

"Possible," Laban repeated. "God knows. All *I* know is that John Delgano and the space around him is the most unstable, improbable, highly charged area ever known on Earth and I'm damned if I think anybody should go poking sticks in it."

"Oh, come now, Laban!" One of the Alberta men joined them, smiling. "Our dust-mop couldn't trip a gnat. It's just vitreous monofilaments."

"Dust from the future," grumbled Laban. "What's it going to tell you? That the future has dust in it?"

"If we could only get a trace from that thing in his hand."

"In his hand?" asked Mira. Serli started leafing hurriedly through the pamphlet.

"We've had a recording analyzer aimed at it," the Albertan lowered his voice, glancing around. "A spectroscope. We know there's something there, or was. Can't get a decent reading. It's severely deteriorated."

"People poking at him, grabbing at him," Laban muttered. "You—"

"TEN MINUTES!" shouted a man with a megaphone. "Take your places, friends and strangers."

The Repentance people were filing in at one side, intoning an ancient incantation, "Mi-seri-cordia, Ora pro nobis!"

The atmosphere suddenly became tense. It was now very close and hot in the big tent. A boy from the mayor's office wiggled through the crowd, beckoning Laban's party to come and sit in the guest chairs on the second level on the "face" side. In front of them at the rail one of the Repentance ministers was arguing with an Albertan official over his right to occupy the space taken by a recorder, it being his special duty to look into The Man John's eyes.

"Can he really see us?" Mira asked her uncle.

"Blink your eyes," Laban told her. "A new scene every blink, that's what he sees. Phantasmagoria. Blink-blink-blink—for God knows how long."

"Mi-sere-re, pec-cavi," chanted the penitentials. A soprano neighed. "May the red of sin pa-aa-ass from us!"

"They believe his oxygen tab went red because of the state of their souls," Laban chuckled. "Their souls are going to have to stay damned awhile; John Delgano has been on oxygen reserve for five centuries—or rather, he *will* be low for five centuries more. At a half-second per year his time, that's fifteen minutes. We know from the audio trace he's still breathing more or less normally and the reserve was good for twenty minutes. So they should have their salvation about the year seven hundred, if they last that long."

"FIVE MINUTES! Take your seats, folks. Please sit down so everybody can see. Sit down, folks."

"It says we'll hear his voice through his suit speaker," Serli whispered. "Do you know what he's saying?"

"You get mostly a twenty-cycle howl," Laban whispered back. "The recorders have spliced up something like 'ayt,' part of an old word. Take centuries to get enough to translate."

"Is it a message?"

"Who knows? Could be his word for 'date' or 'hate'. 'Too late,' maybe. Anything."

The tent was quieting. A fat child by the railing started to cry and was pulled back onto a lap. There was a subdued mumble of praying. The Holy Joy faction on the far side rustled their flowers.

"Why don't we set our clocks by him?"

"It's changing. He's on sidereal time."

"ONE MINUTE."

In the hush the praying voices rose slightly. From outside a chicken cackled. The bare center space looked absolutely ordinary. Over it the recorder's silvery filaments eddied gently in the breath from a hundred lungs. Another recorder could be heard ticking faintly.

For long seconds nothing happened.

The air developed a tiny hum. At the same moment Mira caught a movement at the railing on her left.

The hum developed a beat and vanished into a peculiar silence and suddenly everything happened at once.

Sound burst on them, raced shockingly up the audible scale. The air cracked as something rolled and tumbled in the space. There was a grinding, wailing roar

He was there.

Solid, huge—a huge man in a monster suit, his head was a dull bronze transparent globe, holding a human face, a dark smear of open mouth. His position was impossible, legs strained forward thrusting himself back, his arms frozen in a whirlwind swing. Although he seemed to be in frantic forward motion, nothing moved, only one of his legs buckled or sagged slightly—

—And then he was gone, utterly and completely gone in a thunderclap, leaving only the incredible after-image in a hundred pairs of staring eyes. Air boomed, shuddering; dust rolled out mixed with smoke.

"Oh! Oh my God," gasped Mira, unheard, clinging to Serli. Voices were crying out, choking. "He saw me, he saw me!" a woman shrieked. A few people dazedly threw their confetti into the empty dust-cloud, most had failed to throw at all. Children began to howl. "He *saw* me!" the woman screamed hysterically. "Red, oh Lord have mercy!" a deep male voice intoned.

Mira heard Laban swearing furiously and looked again into the space. As the dust settled she could see that the recorder's tripod had tipped over into the center. There was a dusty mound lying against it—flowers. Most of the end of the stand seemed to have disappeared or been melted. Of the filaments nothing could be seen.

"Some damn fool pitched flowers into it. Come on, let's get out."

"Was it under, did it trip him?" asked Mira, squeezed in the crowd.

"It was still red, his oxygen thing," Serli said over her head. "No mercy this trip, eh, Laban?"

"Shhh!" Mira caught the Repentance pastor's dark glance. They jostled through the enclosure gate and were out in the sunlit park, voices exclaiming, chattering loudly in excitement and relief.

"It was terrible," Mira cried softly. "Oh, I never thought it was a real live man. There he is, he's *there*. Why can't we help him? Did we trip him?"

"I don't know, I don't think so," her uncle grunted. They sat down near the new monument, fanning themselves. The curtain was still in place.

"Did we change the past?" Serli laughed, looking lovingly at his little wife. For a moment he wondered why she was wearing such odd earrings; then he remembered he had given them to her at that Indian pueblo they'd passed.

"But it wasn't just those Alberta people," said Mira. She seemed obsessed with the idea. "It was the flowers really." She wiped at her forehead.

"Mechanics or superstition," chuckled Serli. "Which is the culprit, love or science?"

"Shhh." Mira looked about nervously. "The flowers were love, I guess . . . I feel so strange. It's hot. Oh, thank you." Uncle Laban had succeeded in attracting the attention of the iced-drink vendor.

People were chatting normally now and the choir had struck into a cheerful song. At one side of the park a line of people were waiting to sign their names in the visitors' book. The mayor appeared at the park gate, leading a party up the bougainvillea alley for the unveiling of the monument.

"What did it say on that stone by his foot?" Mira asked. Serli showed her the guidebook picture of Carl's rock with the inscription translated below: WELCOME HOME JOHN.

"I wonder if he can see it."

The mayor was about to begin his speech.

Much later when the crowd had gone away the monument stood alone in the park in the dark, displaying to the moon the inscription in the language of that time and place:

ON THIS SPOT THERE APPEARS ANNUALLY THE FORM OF MAJOR JOHN DELGANO, THE FIRST AND ONLY MAN TO TRAVEL IN TIME.

MAJOR DELGANO WAS SENT INTO THE FUTURE SOME HOURS BEFORE THE HOLO-CAUST OF DAY ZERO. ALL KNOWLEDGE OF THE MEANS BY WHICH HE WAS SENT IS LOST, PERHAPS FOREVER. IT IS BELIEVED THAT AN ACCIDENT OCCURRED WHICH SENT HIM MUCH FARTHER THAN WAS INTENDED. SOME ANALYSTS SPECULATE THAT HE MAY HAVE GONE AS FAR AS FIFTY THOUSAND YEARS AHEAD. HAVING REACHED THIS UNKNOWN POINT MAJOR DELGANO APPARENTLY WAS RECALLED, OR ATTEMPTED TO RETURN, ALONG THE COURSE IN SPACE AND TIME THROUGH WHICH HE WAS SENT. HIS TRAJECTORY IS THOUGHT TO START AT THE POINT WHICH OUR SOLAR SYSTEM WILL OCCUPY AT A FUTURE TIME AND IS TANGENT TO THE COMPLEX HELIX WHICH OUR EARTH DESCRIBES AROUND THE SUN.

HE APPEARS ON THIS SPOT IN THE ANNUAL INSTANTS IN WHICH HIS COURSE INTER-SECTS OUR PLANET'S ORBIT AND HE IS APPARENTLY ABLE TO TOUCH THE GROUND IN THOSE INSTANTS. SINCE NO TRACE OF HIS PASSAGE INTO THE FUTURE HAS BEEN MAN-IFESTED, IT IS BELIEVED THAT HE IS RETURNING BY A DIFFERENT MEANS THAN HE WENT FORWARD. HE IS ALIVE IN OUR PRESENT. OUR PAST IS HIS FUTURE AND OUR FU-TURE IS HIS PAST. THE TIME OF HIS APPEARANCE IS SHIFTING GRADUALLY IN SOLAR TIME TO CONVERGE ON THE MOMENT OF 1153.6, ON MAY 2, 1989 OLD STYLE, OR DAY ZERO.

THE EXPLOSION WHICH ACCOMPANIED HIS RETURN TO HIS OWN TIME AND PLACE MAY HAVE OCCURRED WHEN SOME ELEMENTS OF THE PAST INSTANTS OF HIS COURSE WERE CARRIED WITH HIM INTO THEIR OWN PRIOR EXISTENCE. IT IS CERTAIN THAT THIS EXPLOSION PRECIPITATED THE WORLDWIDE HOLOCAUST WHICH ENDED FOR-EVER THE AGE OF HARDSCIENCE.

—He was falling, losing control, failing in his fight against the terrible momen-tum he had gained, fighting with his human legs shaking in the inhuman stiffness of his armor, his soles charred, not gripping well now, not enough traction to break, battling, thrusting as the flashes came, the punishing alteration of light, dark, light, dark, which he had borne so long, the claps of air thickening and thinning against his armor as he skidded through space which was time, desperately braking as the flick-ers of Earth hammered against his feet—only his feet mattered now, only to slow and stay on course—and the pull, the beacon was getting slacker; as he came near home it was fanning out, hard to stay centered; he was becoming, he supposed, more proba-ble; the wound he had punched in time was healing itself. In the beginning it had been so tight—a single ray of light in a closing tunnel—he had hurled himself after it like an electron flying to the anode, aimed surely along that exquisitely complex sin-gle vector of possibility of life, shot and been shot like a squeezed pip into the last chink in that rejecting and rejected nowhere through which he, John Delgano, could conceivably continue to exist, the hole leading to home—had pounded down it across time, across space, pumping with desperate legs as the real Earth of that unreal time came under him, his course as certain as the twisting dash of an animal down its

burrow, he a cosmic mouse on an interstellar, intertemporal race for his nest with the wrongness of everything closing round the rightness of that one course, the atoms of his heart, his blood, his every cell crying Home—HOME!—as he drove himself after that fading breath-hole, each step faster, surer, stronger, until he raced with invincible momentum upon the rolling flickers of Earth as a man might race a rolling log in a torrent. Only the stars stayed constant around him from flash to flash, he looking down past his feet at a million strobes of Crux, of Triangulum; once at the height of his stride he had risked a century's glance upward and seen the Bears weirdly strung out from Polaris—but a Polaris not the Pole Star now, he realized, jerking his eyes back to his racing feet, thinking, I am walking home to Polaris, home! to the strobing beat. He had ceased to remember where he had been, the beings, people or aliens or things he had glimpsed in the impossible moments of being where he could not be; had ceased to see the flashes of worlds around him, each flash different, the jumble of bodies, shapes, walls, colors, landscapes—some lasting a breath, some changing pell-mell—the faces, limbs, things poking at him; the nights he had pounded through, dark or lit by strange lamps, roofed or unroofed; the days flashing sunlight, gales, dust, snow, interiors innumerable, strobe after strobe into night again; he was in daylight now, a hall of some kind; I am getting closer at last, he thought, the feel is changing—but he had to slow down, to check; and that stone near his feet, it had stayed there some time now, he wanted to risk a look but he did not dare, he was so tired, and he was sliding, was going out of control, fighting to kill the merciless velocity that would not let him slow down; he was hurt, too, something had hit him back there, they had done something, he didn't know what, back somewhere in the kaleidoscope of faces, arms, hooks, beams, centuries of creatures grabbing at him—and his oxygen was going, never mind, it would last—it had to last, he was going home, home! And he had forgotten now the message he had tried to shout, hoping it could be picked up somehow, the important thing he had repeated; and the thing he had carried, it was gone now, his camera was gone too, something had torn it away—but he was coming home! Home! If only he could kill this momentum, could stay on the failing course, could slip, scramble, slide, somehow ride this avalanche down to home, to home—and his throat said Home!—called Kate, Kate! And his heart shouted, his lungs almost gone now, as his legs fought and failed, as his feet gripped and skidded and held and slid, as he pitched, flailed, pushed, strove in the gale of timerush across space, across time, at the end of the longest path ever: the path of John Delgano, coming home.

John Varley's boldly inventive stories made a major impact on the field in the middle 1970s. He is particularly noted for his exuberant speculations in the area of the biological sciences. Many of his best stories are collected in The Persistence of Vision and The Barbie Murders. He has also written several novels, The Ophiuchi Hotline, Titan, Demon, Wizard, and Millennium, the last named soon to be a motion picture. One of his short stories, "Overdrawn at the Memory Bank," was recently dramatized on PBS. This story was published in January 1976.

MANIKINS
by John Varley

"You're sure she's not dangerous?"

"Not at all. Not to you, anyway."

Evelyn closed the sliding window in the door and made an effort to control the misgivings that tugged at her. It was a little late to discover in herself a queasiness about crazy people.

She looked around and discovered with relief that it wasn't the patients she feared. It was the fortress atmosphere of the Bedford Institution. The place was a nightmare of barred windows, padded rooms, canvas sheets and straitjackets and hypodermics and burly attendants. It was a prison. With all the precautions it was only natural that she should feel nervous about the people it was built to contain.

She peeked into the room again. The woman inside was so small, so quiet and composed to be the cause of all this fuss.

Doctor Burroughs closed the thick file he had been scanning. *Barbara Endicott. Age: 28. Height: 5'3". Weight: 101. Diagnosis: Paranoid Schizophrenic. Remarks: Subject is to be considered dangerous. Remanded for observation from criminal court, Commonwealth of Massachusetts, murder. Intense hostility to men.* There was more, much more. Evelyn had read some of it.

"She's got a massively defended psychosis. As usual, granting the illogical assumptions, the delusional system is carefully worked out and internally consistent."

"I know," Evelyn said.

"Do you? Yes, I suppose you do, from books and films." He closed the file and handed it to her. "You'll find it's a little different actually talking to one of them. They're sure of the things they say in a way that no sane person is ever likely to be. We all live with our little doubts, you know. They don't. They've seen the truth, and nothing will convince them otherwise. It takes a strong grip on reality to deal with them. You're likely to be a bit shaken when you're through with her."

Evelyn wished he'd finish and open the door. She had no worries about her sense of reality. Did he really worry that the woman would unsettle her with the kind of rubbish that was down in that file?

"We've had her on electroshock treatments for the last week," he said. He shrugged, helplessly. "I know what your teachers have said about that. It wasn't my decision. There's just no way to reach these people. When we run out of reason and persuasion, we try the shocks. It's not doing her any good. Her psychosis is as defended as it ever was." He rocked back on his heels, frowning.

"I guess you might as well go on in. You're perfectly safe. Her hostility is directed only at men." He gestured to the white-suited attendant, who looked like an NFL lineman, and the man turned a key in the lock. He opened the door, standing back to let her pass.

Barbara Endicott sat in a chair by the window. The sunlight streamed through and the bars made a cross-hatched pattern over her face. She turned, but did not get up.

"Hello, I'm . . . I'm Evelyn Winters." The woman had turned away as soon as she started talking. Evelyn's confidence, feeble enough in this forbidding place, threatened to leave her entirely.

"I'd like to talk to you, if you don't mind. I'm not a doctor, Barbara."

The woman turned back and looked at her.

"Then what are you doing in that white coat?"

Evelyn looked down at the lab smock. She felt silly in the damn thing.

"They told me I had to wear it."

"Who is 'they?' " Barbara asked, with the hint of a chuckle. "You sound paranoid, my dear."

Evelyn relaxed a little. "Now that should have been *my* question. 'They' are the staff of this . . . place." *Damn it, relax!* The woman seemed friendly enough now that she saw Evelyn wasn't a doctor. "I guess they want to know if I'm a patient."

"Right. They'd give you one of these blue outfits if you were."

"I'm a student. They said I could interview you."

"Shoot." Then she smiled, and it was such a friendly, sane smile that Evelyn smiled back and extended her hand. But Barbara was shaking her head.

"That's a man thing," she said, indicating the hand. " 'See? I have no weapons. I'm not going to kill you.' We don't need that, Evelyn. We're women."

"Oh, of course." She awkwardly stuffed the hand into the pocket of the lab coat, clenched. "May I sit down?"

"Sure. There's just the bed, but it's hard enough to sit on."

Evelyn sat on the edge of the bed, the file and notebook in her lap. She poised there, and found that her weight was still on the balls of her feet, ready to leap away. The bleakness of the room assaulted her. She saw flaking gray paint, yellow window glass set in a well behind a mesh screen, gun-metal bolts securing it to the wall. The floor was concrete, damp and unfriendly. The room echoed faintly. The only furniture was the chair and the bed with gray sheets and blanket   Barbara Endicott was small, dark-haired, with the smooth perfection of features that reminded Evelyn of an oriental. She looked pale, probably from two months in the cell. Under it, she had robust health. She sat in a checkerboard of sunlight, soaking up what rays passed through the glass. She wore a blue bathrobe with nothing underneath, belted at the waist, and cloth slippers.

"So I'm your assignment for the day. Did you pick me, or someone else?"

"They told me you'd only speak to women."

"That's true, but you didn't answer my question, did you? I'm sorry. I didn't mean to make you nervous, really. I won't be like that again. I'm acting like a crazy woman."

"What do you mean?"

"Being bold, aggressive. Saying whatever I want to. That's how all the crazy people around here act. I'm not crazy, of course." Her eyes were twinkling.

"I can't tell if you're putting me on," Evelyn admitted, and suddenly felt much closer to the woman. It was an easy trap to fall into, thinking of deranged people as mentally defective, lacking in reasoning powers. There was nothing wrong with Barbara Endicott in that direction. She could be subtle.

"Of *course* I'm crazy," she said. "Would they have me locked up here if I wasn't?" She grinned, and Evelyn relaxed. Her back loosened up; the bedsprings creaked as she settled on them.

"All right. Do you want to talk about it?"

"I'm not sure if you want to hear. You know I killed a man, don't you?"

"Did you? I know the hearing thought you did, but they found you incapable of standing trial."

"I killed him, all right. I had to find out."

"Find out what?"

"If he could still walk with his head cut off."

And there it was; she was an alien again. Evelyn suppressed a shudder. The woman had said it in such a reasonable tone of voice, without any obvious try for shock value. And indeed, it had not affected her as strongly as it might have a few minutes ago. She was revolted, but not scared.

"And what made you think he might be able to?"

"That's not the important question," she chided. "Maybe it's not important to you, but it is to me. I wouldn't have done a thing like that unless it was important to know."

"To know . . . oh. Well, *did* he?"

"He sure did. For two or three minutes, he blundered around that room. I saw it, and I knew I was right."

"Will you tell me what led you to think he could?"

Barbara looked her over.

"And why should I? Look at you. You're a woman, but you've swallowed all the lies. You're working for them."

"What do you mean?"

"You've painted yourself up. You've scraped the hair off your legs and covered them with nylon, and you're walking inefficiently with a skirt to hobble your legs and heels designed to make you stumble if you run from them when they try to rape you. You're here doing their work for them. Why should I tell you? You wouldn't believe me."

Evelyn was not alarmed by this turn in the conversation. There was no hostility in what Barbara was saying. If anything, there was pity. Barbara would not harm her, simply because she was a woman. Now that she understood that, she could go on with more assurance.

"That may be true. But don't you owe it to me, as a woman, to tell me about this threat if it's really so important?"

Barbara slapped her knees in delight.

"You got me, doc. You're right. But that was sure tricky, turning my own delusions against me."

Evelyn wrote in her notebooks: *Can be glib when discussing her delusional-complex. She is assured enough of her rightness to make jokes about it.*

"What are you writing?"

"Huh? Oh . . ." *Be honest, she'll know if you lie. Be straight with her and match her irreverence.* ". . . just notes on your condition. I have to make a diagnosis to my instructor. He wants to know what kind of crazy you are."

"That's easy. I'm paranoid schizophrenic. You don't need a degree to see that."

"No, I guess not. All right, tell me about it."

"Basically, what I believe is that the Earth was invaded by some kind of parasite at some point back in pre-history. Probably in cave-dwelling days. It's hard to tell for sure, since history is such a pack of lies. They rewrite it all the time, you know."

Again, Evelyn didn't know if she was being played with, and the thought amused her. This was a complex, tricky woman. She'd have to stay on her toes. That speech had been such an obvious paranoid construction, and Barbara was well aware of it.

"I'll play your game. Who is 'they' ?"

" 'They' is the all-purpose paranoid pronoun. Any group that is involved in a conspiracy, conscious or not, to 'get' you. I know that's crazy, but there are such groups."

"Are there?"

"Sure. I didn't say they had to be holding meetings to plot ways to bedevil you. They don't. You can admit the existence of groups whose interests are not your own, can't you?"

"Certainly."

"The more important thing is it doesn't matter if they're really an explicit conspiracy, or just have the same effect because that's the way they function. It doesn't have to be personal, either. Each year, the IRS conspires to rob you of money that you earned, don't they? They're in a plot with the President and Congress to steal your money and give it to other people, but they don't know you by name. They steal from everybody. That's the kind of thing I'm talking about."

Justifies her fear of external, inimical forces by pointing to real antagonistic groups.

"Yes, I can see that. But we all know the IRS is out there. You're talking about a secret that only you see. Why should I believe you?"

Her face got more serious. Perhaps she was realizing the strengths of her opponent. Her opponent always had the stronger arguments, it was the nature of things. *Why are you right and everyone else wrong?*

"That's the tough part. You can offer me reams of 'proof' that I'm wrong, and I can't show you anything. If you'd been there when I'd killed that fellow, you'd know. But I can't do it again." She drew a deep breath, and seemed to settle in for a long debate.

"Let's get back to these parasites," Evelyn said. "They're men? Is that what you're saying?"

"No, no." She laughed, without humor. "There's no such thing as a man, the way you're thinking about it. Only women who've been taken over at birth by these, these . . . " she groped in the air for a word hideous enough to express her distaste. She couldn't find it. "Things. Organisms. I said they invaded the Earth, but I'm not sure. They might be from here. There's no way to know, they've taken over too completely."

Leaves flexibility in her rationale. Yes, that would fit with what the books said. It would be hard to stump her, to ask her a question she couldn't answer in terms of her delusion. She admitted not knowing everything about the subject, and she was free to reject whole categories of argument as having been tampered with, like history.

"So how is it . . . no, wait. Maybe you'd better tell me more about these parasites. Where do they hide? How is it that no one but you is aware of them?"

She nodded. She now seemed totally serious. She could not joke about this subject when they got this specific.

"They're not strictly parasites. They're sort of symbiotic. They don't kill their hosts, not quickly. They even help the host in the short run, making them stronger and larger and more capable of domination. But in the long run, they sap the strength of the host. They make her more susceptible to disease, weaken her heart. As to what they look like, you've seen them. They're blind, helpless, immobile worms. They attach themselves to a woman's urinary tract, filling and covering the vagina and extending nerves into the ovaries and uterus. They inject hormones into her body and cause her to grow up with deformities, like facial hair, enlarged muscles, reduced thinking capacity, and wildly defective emotions. The host becomes aggressive and murderous. Her breasts never develop. She is permanently sterile."

Evelyn scribbled in her notebook to cover her emotions. She wanted to laugh; she felt like crying. Who could figure the human mind? She shuddered to think of the pressure that must have driven this outwardly normal woman to such a bizarre way of looking at the universe. Father? Lover? Was she raped? Barbara had been unhelpful in talking about these things, maintaining that they were no one's business but her own. Besides, they had no bearing on what she saw as the facts of the case.

"I hardly know where to begin," Evelyn said.

"Yes, I know. It's not the sort of thing they'd allow you to seriously consider, is it? It's too alien to what you've been led to believe. I'm sorry. I hope I can help you."

Damn! she wrote, then scratched it out. *Puts questioners on the defensive. Shows sympathy with their inability to see things as she sees them.*

"Call it the new biology," Barbara said, getting up and slowly walking back and forth in the confined space. Her loose slippers slipped off her heels with each step. "I began to suspect it several years ago. The world just didn't make sense any other way. You've got to begin to doubt what you've been told. You've got to trust the evidence of your intellect. You've got to allow yourself to look through your woman's eyes as a *woman* would, not as an imperfect man would. They've trained you to believe in their values, their system. What you begin to realize is that they are imperfect women, not the other way around. *They can't reproduce themselves*, shouldn't that tell you something? 'Males' live on our bodies as parasites, they use our fertility to perpetuate their species." She turned to Evelyn, and her eyes were burning. "Can you try to look at it that way? Just try? Don't try to be a man; redefine! You don't know what you are. All your life you've struggled to be a man. They've defined the role you should play. And you're not made for it. You don't have the parasite eating at your brain. Can you accept that?"

"I can, for the sake of argument."

"That's good enough."

Evelyn was treading cautiously. "Uh, just what do I have to do to . . . 'see things as a woman'? I feel like a woman right now."

"*Feel!* That's it, just feel. You know what 'woman's intuition' is? It's the human way to think. They've laughed at it to the point where we automatically distrust it. They *had* to; they've lost the capacity to see a truth intuitively. I can see you don't like that phrase. You wouldn't. It's been laughed at so much that an 'enlightened woman' like yourself doesn't believe it exists. That's what they want you to think. All right, don't use the word 'intuition.' Use something else. What I'm talking about is the innate capacity of a human being to feel the truth of a matter. We all know we have it, but we've been trained to distrust it. And it's gotten screwed up. Haven't you ever felt you're right for no reason you could name except that you knew you were *right?*"

"Yes, I guess I have. Most people do." *Rejects logical argument as being part of her oppression.* She decided to test that.

"What I've been . . . trained to do, is to apply the rules of logic to analyze a question. Right? And say it's no good, despite thousands of years of human experience?"

"That's right. It's not human experience, though. It's a trick. It's a game, a very complicated game."

"What about science? Biology, in particular."

"Science is the biggest game of all. Have you ever thought about it? Do you seriously feel that the big questions of the universe, the important truths that should be easily in our grasp, will be solved by scientists haggling over how many neutrinos can dance on the head of a pin? It's a tail-eating snake, relevant only to itself. But once you accept the basic ground rules, you're trapped. You think that counting and sorting and numbering will teach you things. You have to reject it all and see the world with new eyes. You'll be astounded at what is there, ready for you to pick up."

"Genetics?"

"Hogwash. The whole structure of genetics has been put there to explain an untenable position: that there are two sexes, neither of them worthwhile alone, but together they're able to reproduce. It doesn't hold up when you think about it. Genes and chromosomes, half from each parent: no, no, *no!* Tell me, have you ever seen a gene?"

"I've seen pictures."

"Hah!" That seemed enough for the moment. She paced the floor, overwhelmed by the scope of it. She turned again and faced Evelyn.

"I know, I know. I've thought about it enough. There's this . . . this basic set of assumptions we all live by. We can't get along without accepting almost all of it, right? I mean, I could tell you that I don't believe in . . . Tokyo, for instance, that Tokyo doesn't exist simply because I haven't been there to see it for myself. The news films I've seen were all clever hoaxes, right? Travelogues, books, Japanese; they're all in a conspiracy to make me think there's such a place as Tokyo."

"You could make a case for it, I guess."

"Sure I could. We all exist, *all* of us, Society isn't possible unless we can believe in second-hand reports of certain things. So we've all conspired together to accept what other people tell us unless we can think of a reason why we're being lied to. Society can be seen as a conspiracy of unquestioning acceptance of unprovable things. We all work together at it, we all define a set of things as needing no proof."

She started to say more, but shut her mouth. She seemed to be considering if she should go on. She looked speculatively at Evelyn.

Evelyn shifted on her cot. Outside, the sun was setting in a haze of red and yellow. Where had the day gone? What time had she come into this room, anyway? She was unsure. Her stomach grumbled at her, but she wasn't too uncomfortable. She was fascinated. She felt a sort of lassitude, a weakness that made her want to lie down on the bed.

"Where was I? Oh, the untested assumptions. Okay. If we can't accept anything that's told us, we can't function in society. You can get away with not accepting a lot. You can believe the world is flat, or that there are no such things as photons or black holes or genes. Or that Christ didn't rise from the grave. You can go a long way from the majority opinion. But if you evolve an entirely new world picture, you start to get in trouble."

"What's most dangerous of all," Evelyn pointed out, "is starting to live by these new assumptions."

"Yes, yes. I should have been more careful, shouldn't I? I could have kept this discovery to myself. Or I could have gone on wondering. I was *sure*, you see, but in my foolishness I had to have proof. I had to see if a man could live with his head cut off, against what all the medical books had told me. I had to know if it was the brain that controlled him, or if it was that parasite."

Evelyn wondered what to ask as Barbara quieted for a moment. She knew it wasn't necessary to ask anything. The woman was off now; she would not wind down for hours. But she felt she ought to try and guide her.

"I was wondering," she finally ventured, "why you didn't need a second case. A . . . check from the other side. Why didn't you kill a woman, too, to see if . . . " The hair stood up on the back of her neck. Of all the things she should have kept her mouth shut about, and to a homicidal paranoid! She was painfully aware of her throat. She controlled her hand, which wanted to go to her neck in feeble protection. *She has no weapons, but she could be very strong. . .*

But Barbara didn't pick up the thought. She didn't appear to notice Evelyn's discomfort.

"Foolish!" she exploded. "I was foolish. Of *course* I should have taken it on faith. I felt I was right; I *knew* I was right. But the old scientific orientation finally drove me to the experiment. *Experiment.*" She spat the word out. She paused again, calming down, and seemed to think back.

"Kill a woman?" She shook her head and gave Evelyn a wry smile. "Dear, that would be murder. I'm not a killer. These 'men' are already dead from my viewpoint; killing them is a mercy, and a defensive act. Anyhow, after I'd done the first experiment I realized I had really proved nothing. I had only disproved the assumption that a man cannot live with his head cut off. That left a whole range of possibilities, you see? Maybe the brain is not in the head. Maybe the brain isn't *good* for anything. How do you know what's inside you? Have you ever seen your brain? How do you know that you're not really a wired-up midget, two inches tall, sitting in a control room in your head? Doesn't it feel like that sometimes?"

"Ah . . . " Barbara had hit on a common nerve. Not the midget, which was only a fanciful way of putting it, but the concept of living in one's head with eye-sockets as windows on the universe.

"Right. But you reject the gut feelings. I listen to them."

The light in the room was rapidly failing. Evelyn looked at the bare bulb in the ceiling, wondering when it would come on. She was getting sleepy, so tired. But she wanted to hear more. She leaned back farther on the cot and let her legs and arms relax.

"Maybe you should . . ." She yawned, wider and wider, unable to control it. "Excuse me. Maybe you should tell me more about the parasites."

"Ah. All right." She went back to her chair and sat in it. Evelyn could barely see her in the shadows. She heard a faint creaking, as of wooden slats on a rocking chair. But the chair wasn't a rocker. It wasn't even made of wood. Nevertheless, Barbara's shadow was moving slowly and rhythmically, and the creaking went on.

"The parasites, I've already told you what they do. Let me tell you what I've managed to deduce about their life-cycle."

Evelyn grinned in the dark. *Life-cycle. Of course they'd have one.* She leaned on one elbow and rested her head on the wall behind her. It would be interesting.

"They reproduce asexually, like everything else. They grow by budding, since the new ones are so much smaller than the mature ones. Then doctors implant them into women's wombs when they know they're pregnant, and they grow up with the embryo."

"Wait a minute," Evelyn sat up a little straighter. "Why don't they implant them on all children? Why are girls allowed to . . . oh, I see."

"Yes. They need us. They can't reproduce by themselves. They need the warmth of the womb to grow in, and we have the wombs. So they've systematically oppressed the women they've allowed to remain uninfested so they'll have a docile, ready supply of breeders. They've convinced us that we can't have children until we've been impregnated, which is the biggest lie of all."

"It is?"

"Yes. Take a look."

Evelyn peered through the gloom and saw Barbara, standing in profile. She was illuminated by a sort of flickering candlelight. Evelyn did not wonder about it, but was bothered by a strange feeling. It was rather like wondering why she was not curious.

But before even that ephemeral feeling could concern her, Barbara loosened the cloth belt on her wrap and let it fall open. There was a gentle swell in her belly, unmistakably an early pregnancy. Her hand traced out the curve.

"See? I'm pregnant. I'm about four or five months along. I can't say for sure, you see, because I haven't had intercourse for over five years."

Hysterical pregnancy, Evelyn thought, and groped for her notebook. Why couldn't she find it? Her hand touched it in the dark, then the pencil. She tried to write, but the pencil broke. Did it break, she wondered, or was it bending?

She heard the creaking of the floorboards again, and knew Barbara had sat down in her rocker. She looked sleepily for the source of light, but could not find it.

"What about other mammals?" Evelyn asked, with another yawn.

"Uh-huh. The same. I don't know if it's only one sort of parasite which is adaptable to any species of mammal, or if there's one breed for each. But there are no males. Nowhere. Only females, and infested females."

"Birds?"

"I don't know yet," she said, simply. "I suspect that the whole concept of the sexes is part of the game. It's such an unlikely thing. Why should we need two? One is enough."

Leaves flexibility, she wrote. But no, she hadn't written, had she? The notebook was lost again. She burrowed down into the pile of blankets or furs on the cot, feeling warm and secure. She heard a sliding sound.

There in the peephole, ghostly in the candlelight, was a man's face. It was the attendant, looking in on them. She gasped, and started to sit up as the light got brighter around her. There was the sound of a key grating in a lock.

Barbara was kneeling at the side of the bed. Her robe was still open, and her belly was huge. She took Evelyn's hands and held them tight.

"The biggest giveaway of all is childbirth," she whispered. The light wavered for a moment and the metallic scraping and jiggling of the doorknob lost pitch, growled and guttered like a turntable losing speed. Barbara took Evelyn's head in her arms and pulled her down to her breasts. Evelyn closed her eyes and felt the taut skin and the movement of something inside the woman. It got darker.

"Pain. Why should giving birth involve pain? Why should we so often *die* reproducing ourselves? It doesn't feel right. I won't say it's illogical; it doesn't feel right. My intuition tells me that it isn't so. It's not the way it was meant to be. Do you want to know why we die in childbirth?"

"Yes, Barbara, tell me that." She closed her eyes and nuzzled easily into the warmth.

"It's the poison they inject into us." She gently rubbed Evelyn's hair as she spoke. "The white stuff, the waste product. They tell us it's the stuff that makes us pregnant, but that's a lie. It warps us, even those of us they do not inhabit. It pollutes the womb, causes us to grow too large for the birth canal. When it comes time for us to be born, girl and half-girl, we must come through a passage that has been savaged by this poison. The result is pain, and sometimes death."

"Ummmm." It was very quiet in the room. Outside, the crickets were starting to chirp. She opened her eyes once more, looked for the door and the man. She couldn't find them. She saw a candle sitting on a wooden table. Was that a fireplace in the other room?

"But it doesn't have to be that way. It doesn't. Virgin birth is quite painless. I know. I'll know again very soon. Do you remember now, Eve? Do you remember?"

"What? I . . . " She sat up a little, still holding to the comforting warmth of the other woman. Where was the cell? Where was the concrete floor and barred window? She felt her heart beating faster and began to struggle, but Barbara was strong. She held her tight to her belly.

"Listen, Eve. Listen, it's happening."

Eve put her hand on the swollen belly and felt it move. Barbara shifted slightly, reached down and cradled something wet and warm, something that moved in her hand. She brought it up to the light. Virgin birth. A little girl, tiny, only a pound or two, who didn't cry but looked around her in curiosity.

"Can I hold her?" she sniffed, and then the tears flowed over the little human. There were other people crowding around, but she couldn't see them. She didn't care. She was home.

"Are you feeling any better now?" Barbara asked. "Can you remember what happened?"

"Only a little," Eve whispered. "I was . . . I remember it now. I thought I was . . . it was awful. Oh, Barbara, it was terrible. I thought . . ."

"I know. But you're back. There's no need to be ashamed. It still happens to all of us. We go crazy. We're programmed to go crazy, all of us in the infected generation. But not our children. You relax and hold the baby, darling. You'll forget it. It was a bad dream."

"But it was so *real!*"

"It was what you used to be. Now you're back with your friends, and we're winning the struggle. We have to win; we've got the wombs. There's more of our children every day."

Our children. Her own, and Barbara's and . . . and Karen's, yes, Karen. She looked up and saw her old friend, smiling down at her. And Clara, and there was June, and Laura. And over there with her children was Sacha. And . . . who was that? It's . . .

"Hello, Mother. Do you feel better now?"

"Much better, dear. I'm all right. Barbara helped me through it. I hope it won't happen again." She sniffed and wiped her eyes. She sat up, still cradling the tiny baby. "What are you naming her, Barb?"

Barbara grinned, and for the last time Eve could see the ghostly outline of that cell, the blue robe, Doctor Burroughs. It faded out forever.

"Let's call her Evelyn."

Pat Murphy is a new writer, who has published widely in the past few years. She is a graduate of the famed Clarion Writers' Workshop. This was her first story for Amazing® Stories, *although not her first sale. This story was published in March 1983.*

IN THE ISLANDS
by Pat Murphy

Though the sun was nearly set, Morris wore dark glasses when he met Nick at the tiny dirt runway that served as the Bay Islands' only airport. Nick was flying in from Los Angeles by way of San Pedro Sula in Honduras. He peered through the cracked window of the old DC-3 as the plane bumped to a stop.

Morris stood with adolescent awkwardness by the one-room wooden building that houses Customs for the Islands. Morris: dark, curly hair, red baseball cap pulled low over mirrored sunglasses, long-sleeved shirt with torn-out elbows, jeans with ragged cuffs.

A laughing horde of young boys ran out to the plane and grabbed dive bags and suitcases to carry to Customs. With the exception of Nick, the passengers were scuba divers, bound for Anthony's Cay resort on the far side of Roatan, the main island in the group.

Nick met Morris halfway to the Customs building, handing him a magazine, and said only, "Take a look at page fifty."

The article was titled "The Physiology and Ecology of a New Species of Flashlight Fish," by Nicholas G. Rand and Morris Morgan.

Morris studied the article for a moment, flipping through the pages and ignoring the young boys who swarmed past, carrying suitcases almost too large for them to handle. Morris looked up at Nick and grinned—a flash of white teeth in a thin, tanned face. "Looks good," he said. His voice was a little hoarser than Nick had remembered.

"For your first publication, it's remarkable." Nick patted Morris's shoulder awkwardly. Nick looked and acted older than his thirty-five years. At the University, he treated his colleagues with distant courtesy and had no real friends. He was more comfortable with Morris than with anyone else he knew.

"Come on," Morris said. "We got to get your gear and go." He tried to sound matter-of-fact, but he betrayed his excitement by slipping into the dialect of the

Islands—an archaic English spoken with a strange lilt and governed by rules all its own.

Nick tipped the youngster who had hauled his bags to Customs and waited behind the crowd of divers. The inspector looked at Nick, stamped his passport, and said, "Go on. Have a good stay." Customs inspections on the Islands tended to be perfunctory. Though the Bay Islands were governed by Honduras, the Islanders tended to follow their own rules. The Bay Islands lay off the coast of Honduras in the area of the Caribbean that had once been called the Spanish Main. The population was an odd mix: native Indians, relocated slaves called Caribs, and descendants of the English pirates who had used the Islands as home base.

The airport's runway stretched along the shore and the narrow, sandy beach formed one of its edges. Morris had beached his skiff at one end of the landing strip.

"I got a new skiff, a better one," Morris said. "If the currents be with us, we'll be in East Harbor in two hours, I bet."

They loaded Nick's gear and pushed off. Morris piloted the small boat. He pulled his cap low over his eyes to keep the wind from catching it and leaned a little into the wind. Nick noticed Morris's hand on the tiller; webbing stretched between the fingers. It seemed to Nick that the webbing extended further up each finger than it had when Nick had left the Islands four months before.

Dolphins came from nowhere to follow the boat, riding the bow wave and leaping and splashing alongside. Nick sat in the bow and watched Morris. The boy was intent on piloting the skiff. Behind him, dolphins played and the wake traced a white line through the silvery water. The dolphins darted away, back to the open sea, as the skiff approached East Harbor.

The town stretched along the shore for about a mile: a collection of brightly painted houses on stilts, a grocery store, a few shops. The house that Nick had rented was on the edge of town.

Morris docked neatly at the pier near the house, and helped Nick carry his dive bag and luggage to the house. "There's beer in the icebox," Morris said. "Cold."

Nick got two beers. He returned to the front porch. Morris was sitting on the railing, staring out into the street. Though the sun was down and twilight was fading fast, Morris wore his sunglasses still. Nick sat on the rail beside the teenager. "So what have you been doing since I left?"

Morris grinned. He took off his sunglasses and tipped back his cap. Nick could see his eyes—wide and dark and filled with repressed excitement. "I'm going," Morris said. "I'm going to sea."

Nick took a long drink from his beer and wiped his mouth. He had known this was coming, known it for a long time.

"My dad, he came to the harbor; and we swam together. I'll be going with him soon. Look." Morris held up one hand. The webbing between his fingers stretched from the base almost to the tip of each finger. The light from the overhead bulb shone through the thin skin. "I'm changing, Nick. It's almost time."

"What does your mother say of this?"

"My mum? Nothing." His excitement was spilling over. He laid a hand on Nick's arm, and his touch was cold. "I'm going, Nick."

Ten years ago, Nick had been diving at night off Middle Cay, a small coral island not far from East Harbor. He had been diving alone at night to study the nighttime ecology of the reef. Even at age twenty-five, Nick had possessed a curiosity stronger than his sense of self-preservation.

The reef changed with the dying of the light. Different fishes came out of hiding; different invertebrates prowled the surface of the coral. Nick was particularly interested in the flashlight fish, a small fish that glowed in the dark. Beneath each eye, the flashlight fish had an organ filled with bioluminescent bacteria, which gave off a cold green light. They were elusive fish, living in deep waters and rising up to the reef only when the moon was new and the night was dark.

At night, sharks came in from the open sea to prowl the reef. Nick did not care to study them, but sometimes they came to study him. He carried a flashlight in one hand, a shark billy in the other. Usually, the sharks were only curious. Usually, they circled once, then swam away.

On that night ten years before, the gray reef shark that circled him twice did not seem to understand this. Nick could see the flat black eye, dispassionately watching him. The shark turned to circle again, turning with a grace that made its movement seem leisurely. It came closer; and Nick thought, even as he swam for the surface, about what an elegant machine it was. He had dissected sharks and admired the way their muscles worked so tirelessly and their teeth were arranged so efficiently.

He met the shark with a blow of the billy, a solid blow, but the explosive charge in the tip of the club failed. The charges did fail, as often as not. But worse: the shark twisted back. As he struck at it again, the billy slipped from his hand, caught in an eddy of water. He snatched at it and watched it tumble away, with the maddening slowness of objects underwater.

The shark circled wide, then came in again: elegant, efficient, deadly.

The shadow that intercepted the shark was neither elegant nor efficient. In the beam of the flashlight, Nick could see him clearly: a small boy dressed in ragged shorts and armed with a shark billy. This one exploded when he struck the shark, and the animal turned with grace and speed to cruise away, heading for the far side of the reef. The boy grinned at Nick and glided away into the darkness. Nick saw five lines on each side of the boy's body—five gill slits that opened and closed and opened and closed.

Nick hauled himself into the boat. He lay on his back and looked at the stars. At night, the world underwater often seemed unreal. He looked at the stars and told himself that over and over.

When Nick was in the Islands, Morris usually slept on the porch of whatever house Nick had rented. Nick slept on a bed inside.

Nick was tired from a long day of travel. He slept and he came upon the forbidden dreams with startling urgency and a kind of relief. It was only a dream, he told himself. Darkness covered his sins.

He dreamed that Morris lay on a dissecting table, asleep, his webbed hands quiet at his sides. Morris's eyes had no lashes; his nose was flat and broad; his face was thin and triangular—too small for his eyes. He's not human, Nick thought, not human at all.

Nick took the scalpel in his hand and drew it through the top layers of skin and muscle alongside the five gill slits on Morris's right side. There was little blood. Later, he would use the bone shears to cut through the ribs to examine the internal organs. Now, he just laid back the skin and muscle to expose the intricate structure

In The Islands 249

of the gills.

Morris did not move. Nick looked at the teenager's face and realized suddenly that Morris was not asleep. He was dead. For a moment, Nick felt a tremendous sense of loss; but he pushed the feeling away. He felt hollow, but he fingered the feathery tissue of the gills and planned the rest of the dissection.

He woke to the palm fronds rattling outside his window and the warm morning breeze drying the sweat on his face. The light of dawn—already bright and strong—shone in the window.

Morris was not on the porch. His baseball cap hung from a nail beside the hammock.

Nick made breakfast from the provisions that Morris had left him: fried eggs, bread, milk. In midmorning, he strolled to town.

Morris's mother, Margarite, ran a small shop in the living room of her home, selling black-coral jewelry to tourists. The black coral came from deep waters; Morris brought it to her.

Two women—off one of the sailing yachts anchored in the harbor—were bargaining with Margarite for black-coral earrings. Nick waited for them to settle on a price and leave. They paid for the jewelry and stepped back out into the street, glancing curiously at Nick.

"Where's Morris?" he said to Margarite. He leaned on the counter and looked into her dark eyes. She was a stocky woman with skin the color of coffee with a little cream. She wore a flowered dress, hemmed modestly just below her knees.

He had wondered at times what this dark-eyed woman thought of her son. She did not speak much, and he had sometimes suspected that she was slow-witted. He wondered how it had happened that this stocky woman had found an alien lover on a beach, had made love with such a stranger, had given birth to a son who fit nowhere at all.

"Morris—he has gone to sea," she said. "He goes to sea these days." She began rearranging the jewelry that had been jumbled by the tourists.

"When will he be back?" Nick asked.

She shrugged. "Maybe never."

"Why do you say that?" His voice was sharp, sharper than he intended. She did not look up from the tray. He reached across the counter and took her hand in a savage grip. "Look at me. Why do you say that?"

"He will be going to sea," she said softly. "He must. He belongs there."

"He will come to say good-bye," Nick said.

She twisted her hand in his grip, but he held her tightly. "His dad never said good-bye," she said softly.

Nick let her hand go. He rarely lost his temper and he knew he was not really angry with this woman, but with himself. He turned away without saying good-bye.

He strolled down the dirt lane that served as East Harbor's main street. He nodded to an old man who sat on his front porch, greeted a woman who was hanging clothes on a line. The day was hot and still.

He was a stranger here; he would always be a stranger here. He did not know what the Islanders thought of him, what they thought of Morris and Margarite. Morris had told him that they knew of the water-dwellers and kept their secret. "They live by the sea," Morris had said. "If they talk too much, their nets will rip and their boats sink. They don't tell."

Nick stopped by the grocery store on the far edge of town. A ramshackle pier jutted into the sea right there beside the store.

Ten years before, the pier had been in better repair. Nick had been in town to pick up supplies. For a month, he was renting a skiff and a house on Middle Cay and studying the reef.

The sun had reached the horizon, and its light made a silver path on the water. Somewhere, far off, he could hear the laughter and shouting of small boys. At the far end of the pier, a kid in a red baseball cap was staring out to sea.

Nick bought two Cokes from the grocery—cold from the icebox behind the counter. He carried them out to the pier. The old boards creaked beneath his feet, but the boy did not look up.

"Have a Coke," Nick said.

The boy's face was dirty. His dark eyes were too large for his face. He wore a red kerchief around his neck, ragged shorts, and a shirt that gaped open where the second button should have been. He accepted the Coke and took his first swig without saying anything.

Nick studied his face for a moment, comparing this face to the one that he remembered. A strange kind of calmness took hold of him. "You shouldn't go diving at night," he said. "You're too young to risk your life with sharks."

The boy grinned and took another swig of Coke.

"That was you, wasn't it?" Nick asked. He sat beside the kid on the dock, his legs dangling over the water. "That was you." His voice was steady.

"Aye." The boy looked at Nick with dark, grave eyes. "That was me."

The part of Nick's mind that examined information and accepted or rejected it took this in and accepted it. That part of him had never believed that the kid was a dream, never believed that the shark was imaginary.

"What's your name?"

"Morris."

"I'm Nick." They shook hands and Nick noticed the webbing between the boy's fingers—from the base of the finger to the first joint.

"You're a marine biologist?" asked the kid. His voice was a little too deep for him, a little rough, as if he found speaking difficult.

"Yes."

"What was you doing, diving out there at night?"

"I was watching the fish. I want to know what happens on the reef at night." He shrugged. "Sometimes I am too curious for my own good."

The boy watched him with dark, brooding eyes. "My dad, he says I should have let the shark have you. He says you will tell others."

"I haven't said anything to anyone," Nick protested.

The boy took another swig of Coke, draining the bottle. He set the bottle carefully on the dock, one hand still gripping it. He studied Nick's face. "You must promise you will never tell." He tilted back his baseball cap and continued to study Nick's face. "I will show you things you has got no chance of finding without me." The boy spoke with quiet confidence and Nick found himself nodding. "You know those little fish you want to find—the ones that glow?" He grinned when Nick looked surprised and said, "The Customs man said you were looking for them. I has been to a place where you can find them every new moon. And I has found a kind that aren't in the books."

"What do you know about what's in the books?"

Morris shrugged, a smooth, fluid motion. "I read the books. I has got to know about these things." He held out his hand for Nick to shake. "You promise?"

Nick hesitated, then put his hand in the kid's hand. "I promise." He would have promised more than that to learn about this kid.

"I has a skiff much better than that," Morris said, jerking his head contemptuously toward the skiff that Nick had been using. "I'll be at Middle Cay tomorrow."

Morris showed up at Middle Cay and took Nick to places that he never would have found. Morris read all Nick's reference books with great interest.

And the webbing between his fingers kept growing.

Nick bought a cold Coke in the grocery store and strolled back to his house. Morris was waiting on the porch, sitting on the rail and reading their article in the magazine.

"I brought lobsters for dinner," he said. Small scratching noises came from the covered wooden crate at his feet. He thumped on it with his heel, and the noises stopped for a moment, then began again.

"Where have you been?"

"Out to the Hog Islands. Fishing mostly. I spend most of the days underwater now." He looked at Nick but his eyes were concealed by the mirrored glasses. "When you left, I could only stay under for a few hours. Now, there doesn't seem to be a limit. And the sun burns me if I'm out too much."

Nick caught himself studying the way Morris was holding the magazine. The webbing between his fingers tucked neatly out of the way. It should not work, he thought. This being that is shaped like a man and swims like a fish. But bumblebees can't fly, by logical reasoning.

"What do you think of the article?" Nick asked.

"Good, as far as it goes. Could say more. I've been watching them and they seem to signal to each other. There's different patterns for the males and females. I've got notes on it all. I'll show you. The water temperature seems to affect them too."

Nick was thinking how painful this curiosity of his was. It had always been so. He wanted to know; he wanted to understand. He had taken Morris's temperature; he had listened to Morris's heartbeat and monitored its brachycardia when Morris submerged. He had monitored the oxygen levels in the blood, observed Morris's development. But there was so much more to learn. He had been hampered by his own lack of background—he was a biologist, not a doctor. There were tests he could not perform without harming Morris. And he had not wanted to hurt Morris. No, he did not want to hurt Morris.

"I'll leave all my notes on your desk," Morris was saying. "You should take a look before I go."

Nick frowned. "You'll be able to come back," he said. "Your father comes in to see you. You'll come back and tell me what you've seen, won't you?"

Morris set the magazine on the rail beside him and pushed his cap back. The glasses hid his eyes. "The ocean will change me," he said. "I may not remember the right things to tell you. My father thinks deep, wet thoughts; and I don't always understand him." Morris shrugged. "I will change."

"I thought you wanted to be a biologist. I thought you wanted to learn. And here you are, saying that you'll change and forget all this." Nick's voice was bitter.

"I has got no choice. It's time to go." Nick could not see his eyes or interpret his tone. "I don't belong on the land anymore. I don't belong here."

Nick found that he was gripping the rail as he leaned against it. He could learn so much from Morris. So much. "Why do you think you'll belong there? You won't fit there, with your memories of the islands. You won't belong."

Morris took off his glasses and looked at Nick with dark, wet eyes. "I'll belong. I has got to belong. I'm going."

The lobsters scratched inside their box. Morris replaced his sunglasses and thumped lightly on the lid again. "We should make dinner," he said. "They're getting restless."

During the summer on Middle Cay, Nick and Morris had become friends. Nick came to rely on Morris's knowledge of the reef. Morris lived on the island and seemed to find there a security he needed. His curiosity about the sea matched Nick's.

Early each evening, just after sunset, they would sit on the beach and talk—about the reef, about life at the University, about marine biology, and—more rarely—about Morris and his father.

Morris could say very little about his father. "My dad told me legends," Morris said to Nick, "but that's all. The legends say that the water people came down from the stars. They came a long time ago." Nick was watching Morris and the boy was digging his fingers in the sand, as if searching for something to grasp.

"What do you think?" Nick asked him.

Morris shrugged. "Doesn't really matter. I think they must be native to this world or they couldn't breed with humans." He sifted the beach sand with his webbed hands. "But it doesn't much matter. I'm here. And I'm not human." He looked at Nick with dark, lonely eyes.

Nick had wanted to reach across the sand and grasp the cold hand that kept sifting the sand, digging and sifting the sand. He wanted to say something comforting. But he had remained silent, giving the boy only the comfort of his company.

Nick lay on his cot, listening to the sounds of the evening. He could hear his neighbor's chickens, settling down to rest. He could hear the evening wind in the palms. He wanted to sleep, but he did not want to dream.

Once Morris was gone, he would not come back, Nick thought. If only Nick could keep him here.

Nick started to sleep and caught himself on the brink of a dream. His hands had been closing on Morris's throat. Somehow, in that moment, his hands were not his own. They were his father's hands: cool, clean, brutally competent. His father, a high school biology teacher with a desire to be more, had taught him how to pith a frog, how to hold it tight and insert the long pin at the base of the skull. "It's just a frog," his father had said. His father's hands were closing on Morris's throat and Nick was thinking, I could break his neck—quickly and painlessly. After all, he's not human.

Nick snapped awake and clasped his hands as if that might stop them from doing harm. He was shivering in the warm night. He sat up on the edge of the bed, keeping his hands locked together. He stepped out onto the porch where Morris was sleeping.

Morris was gone; the hammock was empty. Nick looked out over the empty street and let his hands relax. He returned to his bed and dozed off, but his sleep was disturbed by voices that blended with the evening wind. He could hear his former wife's bitter voice speaking over the sound of the wind. She said, "I'm going. You don't love me, you just want to analyze me. I'm going." He could hear his father, droning on about how the animal felt no pain, how it was all in the interest of science. At last he sank into a deeper sleep, but in the morning he did not want to remember his dreams.

Morris was still gone when Nick finished breakfast. He read over Morris's notes. They were thorough and carefully taken. Nick made notes for another paper on the flashlight fish, a paper on which Morris would be senior author.

Morris returned late in the afternoon. Nick looked up from his notes, looked into Morris's mirrored eyes, and thought of death. And tried not to think of death.

"I thought we could go to Middle Cay for dinner," Morris said. "I has got conch and shrimp. We can take the camp stove and fix them there."

Nick tapped his pencil against the pad nervously. "Yes. Let's do that."

Morris piloted the skiff to Middle Cay. Through the water, Nick could see the reef that ringed the island—shades of blue and green beneath the water. The reef was broken by channels here and there; Morris followed the main channel nearly to the beach, then cut the engine and let the skiff drift in.

They set up the camp stove in a level spot, sheltered by the trunk of a fallen palm tree. Morris cracked the conch and pounded it and threw it in the pan with shrimp. They drank beer while the combination cooked. They ate from tin cups, leaning side by side against the fallen palm.

"You can keep the skiff for yourself," Morris said suddenly. "I think that you can use it."

Nick looked at him, startled.

"I left my notes on your desk," Morris said. "They be as clear as I can make them."

Nick was studying his face. "I will go tonight," Morris said. "My dad will come here to meet me." The sun had set and the evening breeze was kicking up waves in the smooth water. He drained his beer and set the bottle down beside the stove.

Morris stood and took off his shirt, slipped out of his pants. The gill slits made stripes that began just below his rib cage and ended near his hips. He was more muscular than Nick remembered. He stepped toward the water.

"Wait," Nick said. "Not yet."

"Got to." Morris turned to look at Nick. "There's a mask and fins in the skiff. Come with me for a ways."

Morris swam ahead, following the channel out. Nick followed in mask and fins. The twilight had faded. The water was dark and its surface shone silver. The night did not seem real. The darkness made it dreamlike. The sound of Nick's feet breaking the water's surface was too loud. The touch of the water against his skin was too warm. Morris swam just ahead, just out of reach.

Nick wore his dive knife at his belt. He always wore his dive knife at his belt. As he swam, he noticed that he was taking his knife out and holding it ready. It was a heavy knife, designed for prying rocks apart and cracking conch. It would work best as a club, he was thinking. A club to be used for a sudden sharp blow from behind. That might be enough. If he called to Morris, then Morris would stop and Nick could catch him.

But his voice was not cooperating. Not yet. His hands held the knife ready, but he could not call out. Not yet.

He felt the change in water temperature as they passed into deeper water. He felt something—a swirl of water against his legs—as if something large were swimming past.

Morris disappeared from the water ahead of him. The water was smooth, with no sign of Morris's bobbing head. "Morris," Nick called. "Morris."

He saw them then. Dim shapes beneath the water. Morris: slim, almost human. His father: man-shaped, but different. His arms were the wrong shape; his legs were too thick and muscular.

Morris was close enough to touch, but Nick did not strike. When Morris reached out and touched Nick's hand with a cold, gentle touch, Nick released the knife and let it fall, watched it tumble toward the bottom.

Morris's father turned in the water to look up at Nick and Nick read nothing in those inhuman eyes: cold, dark, dispassionate. Black and uncaring as the eyes of a shark. Nick saw Morris swim down and touch his father's shoulder, urging him away into the darkness.

"Morris!" Nick called, knowing Morris could not hear him. He kicked with frantic energy, not caring that his knife was gone. He did not want to stop Morris. He wanted to go with Morris and swim with the dolphins and explore the sea.

There was darkness below him—cool, deep water. He could feel the tug of the currents. He swam, not conserving his energy, not caring. His kicks grew weaker. He looked down into the world of darkness and mystery and he sank below the surface almost gladly.

He felt a cold arm around his shoulders. He coughed up water when the arm dragged him to the surface. He coughed, took a breath that was half water, half air, coughed again. Dark water surged against his mask each time the arm dragged him forward. He choked and struggled, but the arm dragged him on.

One flailing leg bumped against coral, then against sand. Sand scraped against his back as he was dragged up the beach. His mask was ripped away and he turned on his side to retch and cough up seawater.

Morris squatted beside him with one cold webbed hand still on his shoulder. Nick focused on Morris's face and on the black eyes that seemed as remote as mirrored lenses. "Good-bye, Nick," Morris said. His voice was a hoarse whisper. "Good-bye."

Morris's hand lingered on Nick's shoulder for an instant. Then the young man stood and walked back to the sea.

Nick lay on his back and looked up at the stars. After a time, he breathed more easily. He picked up Morris's cap from where it lay on the beach and turned it in his hands, in a senseless repetitive motion.

He crawled further from the water and lay his head against the fallen log. He gazed at the stars and the sea, and thought about how he could write down his observations of Morris's departure and Morris's father. No. He could not write it down, could not pin it down with words. He did not need to write it down.

He put on the red baseball cap and pulled it low over his eyes. When he slept, with his head propped against the log, he dreamed only of the deep night that lay beneath the silver surface of the sea.